MALAFRENA

Also by Ursula K. Le Guin

MALAFRENA

by

Ursula K. Le Guin

G. P. Putnam's Sons
New York

Library of Congress Cataloging in Publication Data

Le Guin, Ursula K, date.
  Malafrena.

  I. Title.
PZ4.L518Mal 1979   [PS3562.E42]   813'.5'4
ISBN 0-399-12410-1   79-11042
Printed in the United States of America

CONTENTS

Except the Lord build the house: their labor is but lost who build it.

Except the Lord keep the city: the watchman waketh but in vain.

It is but lost labor that ye haste to rise up early, and so late take rest, and eat the bread of carefulness: for so he giveth his beloved sleep.

Psalm 127

PART ONE

In the Provinces

I

In a starless May night the town slept and the river flowed quietly through shadow. Over the empty courts of the university loomed the chapel tower, full of silent bells. A young man was climbing over the ten-foot iron gates of the chapel quadrangle. Clinging to the ironwork he dropped down inside, and crossed the courtyard to the doors of the chapel. He took out of his coat pocket a large sheet of paper, and unfolded it; fished around and brought out a nail; stooped and took off one of his shoes. Having got the paper and nail positioned high on the iron-barred oak door he raised the shoe, paused, struck. The sound of the blow crashed around the dark stone courts, and he paused again as if startled by the noise. A voice not far off shouted something, iron grated on stone. He struck three more blows until the head of the nail was driven home to the wood, then, holding one shoe and wearing the other, he ran hopping back to the gates, threw his shoe over, climbed up and over, caught his coattails on a spike, jumped down outside with a tearing noise, and vanished into the shadows just before two policemen arrived. They peered into the chapel yard, argued in German about the height of the gate,

11

shook its lock, and went off, boots ringing on the cobbles. Cautiously the young man reappeared, feeling about in the shadows for his shoe. He was laughing wildly but silently. He could not find the shoe. The guards were returning. He went off in his stocking feet through the dark streets as the bells of Solariy cathedral struck midnight.

As the bells were striking noon next day a lecture on the apostasy of Julian ended, and the young man was leaving the hall with other young men when his name was spoken: "Herr Sorde. Herr Itale Sorde."

The students, deaf mutes, walked past the uniformed officer of the university guard without a glance; only the one called stopped.

"Yes, the Herr Rector will see you, this way please, Herr Sorde."

A handsome red Persian carpet, badly worn, covered the floor of the rector's office. There was a purplish growth on the left side of the rector's nose: a wart, a birthmark? Another man stood near the windows.

"Please answer our question, Mr Sorde."

He looked at the paper which the other man was holding out: a sheet about a yard square, half of a poster announcing the sale of draft-oxen in Solariy Market, June 5th, 1825. On the blank side was written in large, clear letters:

> O come, put your neck in the collar
> Of Müller, Von Gentz, and Von Haller!
> All the best Governments
> Have replaced Common Sense
> With Von Haller, and Müller, and Gentz.

"I wrote it," the young man said.

"And . . ." The rector glanced at the other man, out the windows, and asked in a mild deprecating tone, "And you nailed it on the door of the chapel?"

"Yes. Alone. No one was with me. It was entirely my idea."

"My dear boy," the rector said, paused, frowned, and said, "My boy, if nothing else the sanctity of the place—"

"I was following an historical precedent. I'm a student of history." From white he turned red.

"Until now, an exemplary student," the rector said. "This is really most regrettable. Even understood as a mere prank—"

"Excuse me, sir, it was not a prank!"

The rector winced and shut his eyes.

"It's obvious that the intent was serious; why else have you called me in?"

"Young man," said the other man, the man with no wart, no title, no name, "you talk about seriousness; you can find serious trouble, you know, if you insist upon it."

The young man went dead white this time. He stared at the man, and finally managed a very short, stiff bow. He faced the rector again and said in an unnatural voice, "I do not intend to apologise, sir. I will withdraw from my college. You have no right to ask more of me."

"I haven't asked that, Mr Sorde. Please control yourself and listen. This is your last term at the university. We should wish you to finish your studies without hindrance or disturbance." He smiled, and the purplish wart on his nose moved up and down. "I ask you therefore to promise me that you will attend no student meetings during the remainder of the term, and to stay home, in your rooms, after sunset until morning. That is the long and the short of it, Mr Sorde. Will you give me your word?"

After a short pause the young man said, "Yes."

When he had gone the provincial inspector folded up the paper and laid it on the rector's desk, smiling. "A young man of spirit," he observed.

"Yes, mere boyish folly, this sort of thing."

"Luther had ninety-five theses," the provincial inspector said, "he has only one, it seems."

They were speaking in German.

"Ha, ha, ha," the rector laughed, appreciatively.

"He plans a civil career? Law?"

"No, he'll go back to the family estate. An only son. I taught his father, my first year of teaching. Val Malafrena, up there in the mountains, depths of the country, you know, a hundred miles from anything."

13

The provincial inspector smiled.

When he had gone, the rector sighed. He sat down behind his desk and looked up at the portrait on the facing wall; his look, absent at first, gradually sharpened. The portrait was of a well-dressed, well-fleshed woman with a thick lower lip, Grand Duchess Mariya, first cousin once removed of Emperor Francis of Austria. On the scroll she held, the red and blue colors of the nation of Orsinia were quartered with the black two-headed eagle of the Empire. Fifteen years ago the portrait on the wall had been of Napoleon Bonaparte. Thirty years ago it had been of King Stefan IV in his coronation regalia. Thirty years ago when the rector had first become a dean he had called boys onto the carpet for their follies, he had tonguelashed and excoriated them, they had been sheepish and they had grinned. They had not turned grey in the face. He had not felt this painful wish to apologise, to say to young Sorde, "I'm sorry— You see how it is!" He sighed again and looked at the documents he must approve, governmental revision of curriculum, all in German. He put on his spectacles and opened the sheaf, his hands reluctant, his face weary in the radiance of May noon pouring in the windows.

Sorde meanwhile had gone down to the park along the Molsen and was sitting there on a bench. Behind scrubby willows the river stretched smoky blue in sunlight. Everything was quiet, the river, the sky, the willow-leaves against the sky, the sunshine, a pigeon sunning and strutting on the gravel. At first he sat with his hands on his knees, frowning, his face vivid with emotions; then gradually he relaxed, stretched out his long legs, then stretched out his arms along the back of the bench. His face, distinguished by a big nose, heavy eyebrows and blue eyes, got to looking more and more dreamy, even sleepy. He watched the river run.

A voice went off like a gunshot. "There he is!" He looked round slowly. His friends had found him.

Blond, stocky, scowling, Frenin said, "You haven't proved your point at all, I disallow the proof."

"That words are acts? Those were *words* I nailed up—"

"But the act was nailing them up—"

14

"But once they were there it was them, the words, that would act and bring about results—"

"What results did they bring about in your case?" inquired Brelavay, a long, thin, dark young man with an ironical look.

"No meetings. House arrest nights."

"Austria will keep you pure, by God." Brelavay laughed delightedly. "Did you see the crowd in front of the chapel this morning? The whole college saw it before the Ostriches found it. Almighty Christ! I thought they'd arrest the lot of us!"

"How did they know it was me?"

"Go to the head of the class, Herr Sorde," said Frenin. *"Das würde ich auch gerne wissen!"*

"The rector didn't say anything about Amiktiya. There was an Ostrich there. Do you think it'll make trouble for the society?"

"Another good question."

"Look here, Frenin!" Brelavay burst out—both had spent the last hour in anxious search for Itale, and were upset and hungry— "You're the one who keeps telling us that we talk and do nothing. Now Itale's done something and you start complaining about it! Personally I don't care if the society gets into trouble, it's a stupid lot of fellows, I'm not surprised there's a spy amongst them." He sat down by Itale on the bench.

"If you'd let me finish, Tomas," said Frenin, joining them on the bench, "what I was going to say was this. There are about five of us in Amiktiya who are serious about the ideas, right? Well, after this, with Itale under observation and the whole society suspect, we're getting to the time when we have to decide how serious we are. Are we in it for the wine and the songs, or is there more to it than that? Do you nail up your verse, and take your scolding, and finish the term and go home to your farm, or are there in fact further consequences? *Are* our words acts?"

"What are you thinking of, Givan?"

"I'm thinking of Krasnoy."

"What would we do there?" Brelavay asked, skeptical, startled.

"There's nothing here in Solariy. There's nothing in the provinces—these damned burghers, your peasants. We can't

15

fight the Middle Ages. The capital is the only place for us, if we're serious. My God, is it so far away, Krasnoy?"

"I suppose the Molsen was running through it a day or two ago," said Itale, looking at the blue river beyond the trees. "Listen, this is an idea, this is a real idea, Givan. I've got to think. I've got to eat something. Come on. Krasnoy, Krasnoy!" He looked at his friends joyously. "We can't go to Krasnoy!" he said. They went off together laughing.

When they parted late in the afternoon and Itale set off home his mood was still one of joyful and wondering anticipation. Was it possible that a new life was going to begin? Would he in fact go to the city, live there, work with other men in the cause of freedom? It was inconceivable, fantastic, splendid, how did one go about it? There must be men in the city who would welcome them and put them to work. There were said to be secret societies there, which corresponded with similar groups in Piedmont and Lombardy, Naples, Bohemia, Poland, German states; for throughout the territories and satellites of the Austrian Empire and even beyond, throughout Europe, stretched the silent network of liberalism, like the nervous system of a sleeping man. A restless sleep, feverish, full of dreams. Even in this sleepy town people referred to Matiyas Sovenskar, in exile on his estate since 1815, as "the king." Which he was, by right and by the will of his people, hereditary and constitutional king of a free country, and emperor and Empire be damned! Itale went striding down the shady street like a summer whirlwind, his face hot, his coat open.

He lived with the family of his uncle Angele Dru; before supper he explained to his uncle that he was under nightly house arrest. His uncle laughed. He and his wife, parents of a large brood, had given their nephew a small room, large meals, and unlimited trust; their own elder sons were none too steady, and sometimes they seemed as surprised as they were pleased by Itale's justification of their trust. "What's the scrape, what did you pups do now?" his uncle asked.

"Posted up a silly poem on the chapel."

"Is that all? Have I told you about the night we brought the Gypsy girls right into the college? They didn't use to lock it up at night," and Angele retold the story. "So what's your poem, eh?"

16

"Oh, politics."

Angele continued smiling but a line of dismay or disappointment appeared in his forehead. "What sort of politics?" To appease him Itale repeated his verse, and then had to explain it.

"I see," Angele said vaguely. "Well, now, I don't know. Things have changed since I was your age. All these Prussians and Swiss, Haller, Müller, Jesus Mary, what's that to us? Now I know who Von Gentz is, he's the head of the Imperial Police, that's a very important position. What such men do is none of our affair."

"None of our affair! when everything we do is theirs? when we're arrested if we open our mouths?" Itale always meant to avoid discussing politics with his uncle, but his ideas were so clear and the facts so patent that, each time, he was sure he could convince him. Angele got more and more alarmed and obstinate, till he was refusing to admit even that he disliked the foreign militia who policed the city and the university, and that he, too, thought of Matiyas Sovenskar as the king. "It's just that we got on the wrong side in '13. Should have joined the Alliance and let Bonaparte hang himself on his own rope. You don't remember what it's like when all Europe's at war, all you hear is war, the Prussians lose, the Russians win, an army's here, an army's there, the food gets short, nobody's safe in bed. Plenty of money to be made but no security in it—no stability. Peace is a great thing, lad! If you were a few years older you'd have learnt that."

"If the price of peace is liberty—"

"Oh, well, liberty, rights—don't be fooled by words, Itale my lad. Words go down the wind, but peace is a God-given thing, that's the truth." Angele was sure he had convinced Itale: the ideas were so clear, the facts so patent. Itale, at least, gave up arguing. At table, Angele went off into a tirade against the new tax laws imposed by the grand ducal government which an hour ago he had been defending. He ended on a plaintive note; when he smiled and glanced around apologetically at his family he looked very like his sister, Itale's mother. The young man looked at him with affection, forgiving him. He could not be blamed for his obtuseness; after all, he was nearly fifty.

At midnight Itale was sitting at his table in his little attic bedroom. His legs were stretched out again, his chin was on his

17

hands, he gazed over stacks of books and papers out the open window into the dark. There was the rustle and storm and hush of trees in the May night; the house was near the edge of town, and no other light was to be seen. Itale was thinking of the window of his room at home over Lake Malafrena, and of going to Krasnoy, and of the death of Stilicho, and of the blue smoky river beyond the willows, and of man's life, all in one long unarticulable thought. The clap of two pair of military boots, Austrian issue, came down the street, stopped before the house, went on.

"If it must be so, it must; it's necessary," he thought with apprehensive joy, as if these words summed up the rest, and listened to the soft storming of the leaves. His climb over the gate into the silent courts of the university and his interview with the rector now seemed to have occurred long ago, when he was a boy, before his acts had significance. It now seemed to him that when Frenin had said, "I'm thinking of Krasnoy," he had expected the words: they had to be said; they were inevitable. He would not go back and live out his life on the farm in the mountains. That was no longer possible. It was so completely impossible that he was free to look back on that existence, which until today he had considered his unquestionable destiny, with longing and regret. He knew every foot of the earth there, every act of the day's work, every soul, knew them as he knew his own body and soul. Of the city he knew nothing.

"It must be, it must be," he repeated with conviction, joy, and fear. The night wind, fresh with the smell of damp earth, touched his face and swayed the white curtains; the town slept on under the stars of spring.

II

His memories of childhood were fathomless, dateless, all place and no time, the rooms of the house, the floorboards of the stair-landing, the blue-ringed plates, the fetlocks of a great horse

18

standing at the smithy, his mother's hand, sunlight on gravel, rain on water, the outlines of the mountains against dark winter sky. Among these one time was distinct: that time when he stood in a room lit by four candles and saw a head on a pillow, the eye-sockets pits of black, the large nose shining like metal; and a hand lay on the quilt, but did not move, as if it were not a hand but a thing. A voice kept murmuring. It was his grandfather's room but his grandfather was not there. His uncle Emanuel cast a huge shadow that moved behind him on the wall. There were huge shadows behind all the people, the servants, the priest, his mother, he was afraid to look at them. The murmur of the priest's voice was like water lapping up the walls of the room, higher and higher, singing in his ears, closing over his head. He began to gasp for breath. In suffocating terror and shadow he had felt a big hand touch his back, and his father had said quietly, "You're here too, Itale?" And his father had taken him out of the room, and told him to play in the garden a while. He had run out gladly, discovering that outside the room with the candles it was not even dark yet; the bronze of sunset still glowed on the lake, the humped back of the mountain called the Hunter over Evalde Gulf, the peak of San Larenz in the high west. His little sister Laura had been put to bed. He stayed out alone, and did not know what to do; he tried the door of the tool-house but it was locked; he picked up a reddish stone from the path, and whispered to himself, "I am Itale. I am seven years old," but he was not sure of that, a child wandering in a garden in the broad, dark wind of night, lost, lost, until at last his aunt Perneta came scolding and reassuring and hurried him off to bed.

Itale Sorde the grandfather had lived in France in the 1770's and had travelled in Germany and Italy. His neighbors of Val Malafrena slowly forgave him, though some of them never trusted him again. At forty he had returned for good to the mountain province and to his wife, a cousin of his neighbor Count Guide Valtorskar; had improved his estate, rebuilt his house, and settled down. He sent his sons down to Solariy to college, but both returned without further divagation to the Montayna, the elder to run the estate and the younger to practice law, moderately, in Portacheyka. Their father never left the

19

province after 1790. Over the years his correspondence with friends abroad had slowly decreased, then stopped; they were dead, or had forgotten him, or knew he had chosen to be forgotten. After his death in 1810 he was remembered for his good management of the estate, his stately kindness, his skill as a gardener.

The family was of the *domey*, the commoner-landowner class, which had in 1740 been granted by royal charter equal privilege with the nobles of the kingdom. In the eastern provinces the *domey* still stood outside the old social hierarchy, insulated off; in the center and west they had, with the burghers of the capital and the major cities, become more closely engrafted with the nobility by intermarriage and custom than convention permitted most people to admit, more numerous and potentially more influential than most of them realised themselves. The magic of names still held minds enchanted. The *domey* did not have names; they had property.

Dom Itale's property was small, but excellent. The house he built there looked out on three sides on the lake; it stood on a blunt peninsula, the end of a ridge running down from the shoulder of San Givan Mountain. The steep ridge was crowned with native oak and pine, so that approached from the east the house seemed to stand alone in a somber sweep of lake and mountain. But coming from Portacheyka, the town in the pass, one saw the fields and orchards and vineyards, the peasants' and leaseholders' houses, the roofs of other manors. The estate raised wine-grapes, pears, apples, rye, oats, barley; it was a dramatic but not a harsh climate. In a hard winter snow lay deep on the forested peaks, but not for a century had the ice frozen across Malafrena or the other lakes that stretched in a chain among the mountains to the southwest border of the land. Summers were long and hot, and thunderstorms roamed growling among the mountains. The years there were marked by drought or great rain, vintage, weather, harvest, rather than by the events of history; whether King Stefan ruled, or Napoleon and Grand Duke Matiyas, or Francis and Grand Duchess Mariya, it did not much affect the weather and the earth, the flavor of the wine, the aspects of the hills. Landowners and their tenants lived wholly

20

within the mountain barrier. Taxation they grumbled at; so had their great-grandfathers.

Guide Sorde, the inheritor, was a tall man, spare, dark, with acute grey eyes, a good type of the taciturn peasants of his province, from whom his ancestors had risen to be landowners in the seventeenth century. His wife Eleonora, born in Solariy on the southern plain, was the only thing he had found outside the mountains that he prized; and he brought her back with him, for good.

In 1803 their son was born, their daughter three years later. Eleonora taught both children until Itale was eleven and Laura eight; then, since education had got to be a tradition in the family and Guide upheld all traditions, a tutor began to come in thrice a week for Laura, and Itale went off to school with the Benedictines on Sinviya Mountain. He came home most weekends; it was only seven miles. On the Thursday half-holiday he would go down to Portacheyka, whose peaked slate roofs and climbing streets lay under the windows of the monastery school, and have dinner with his uncle Emanuel and aunt Perneta in their high wooden house with its garden full of marigolds, pansies, phlox, and its view over the dark streets and roofs out through the pass. The town was set in a deep gap between Sinviya and San Givan Mountains; framed by the towering slopes, Portacheyka's northward view had a quality of vision. It seemed as if the shadowed pass could not lead out to those remote and sunlit, azure hills, but only look down on them as if on fabled kingdoms across the barrier of possibility. When clouds gathered full of thunder on the peaks and hung low over the town sometimes the view of the lower hills shone out in a clear, golden light, an enchanted realm, free of the storm and darkness of the heights. Idling by the Golden Lion Inn, Itale saw the coaches of the Southwestern Post set off for distant cities or come in, high, swaying, dusty, from their journeys; and Portacheyka, the gateway of his province, had for him the glamor of voyage and the unknown that a seaport has for one whose country's border is the sea.

Saturdays at noon he walked down through town, through the oak-wooded rolling foothills, past the slopes of vine and orchard, to the house by the lake. On the way he might meet and stop

21

with his friends among the boys of the estate, or stop to talk with Bron, the master vintner, a long-legged, high-shouldered, grim old man. He would ask and tell Bron all the events of the week; if they were mishaps Bron would say, "So things go," and if triumphs, "Aye, but work's certain and reward's seldom, Dom Itaal!"

When he was seventeen the monks of Sinviya sent him home with blessings and a first prize in Latin, and he took up the life of a young landowner, learning how to prune grape stocks and drain fields and keep accounts, hunting, riding, sailing his boat Falkone on the lake. The work filled his time but not his mind. He got restless. An important person to his family, he felt he ought to do something important. Status was obligation: that he had learned from his father, who never talked about duty but, autocrat as he was, served it unquestioning. Seeking a worthy duty, the boy studied the lives of great men. Aeneas had been his first hero; his grandfather had told him the story, then he had read it in school in his father's battered school copy; but he found others in the meager lot of books he could get: Pericles, Socrates, Hector, Hannibal. And there was Napoleon. His childhood passed under the Empire, his boyhood during the exile. Powerless on his island jail, defeated, humiliated, Napoleon loomed there like Prometheus in chains, while over the broad lands of Europe and Russia ruled little, apprehensive kings. . . . In his grandfather's library the seventeen-year-old found so many French books that—enlisting his sister's willing aid, for she was being tutored in French—he taught himself enough of the language to be able to read Voltaire. Laura tried to read with him, but found it boring and returned to her mother's favorite, the *New Heloise*, at which Itale was relieved, since at the monastery school Voltaire had been mentioned only in the same breath with the devil, and he was not quite sure what he was getting into. There were some odd volumes of the *Moniteur*, the French government newspaper. He looked at one from 1809 and found it like all newspapers he had ever seen, the mouthpiece of authority. But later he chanced on a volume from the early 1790's. He did not at first recall what had been going on in Paris then—the monks had not been strong on recent history. He came

22

on speeches made by M. Danton, M. Mirabeau, M. Vergniaud; they were strangers to him. M. Robespierre he had heard mentioned, along with Voltaire and the devil. He turned back to the year 1790 and began reading steadily. He held the French Revolution in his hands. He read the speech in which the orator called down the wrath of the people on the house of privilege, the speech that ended, *"Vivre libre, ou mourir!"*—Live free, or die. The yellowed newsprint crumbled under the boy's touch; his head was bowed over dry columns of words spoken to a lost Assembly by men thirty years dead. His hands felt cold as if a wind blew on him, his mouth was dry. He did not understand half what he read, knowing almost nothing of the events of the Revolution. It did not matter. He understood that there had been a Revolution.

The speeches were full of rant, cant, and vanity; he saw that clearly enough. But they discussed freedom as a human need, like bread, like water. Itale got up and walked up and down the quiet little library, rubbing his head and staring blankly at the bookcases and the windows. Freedom was not a necessity, it was a danger, all the lawmakers of Europe had been saying that for a decade. Men were children, to be governed for their own good by the few who understood the science of government. What did this Frenchman Vergniaud mean by stating a choice—live free or die? Such choices are not offered to children. The words were spoken to men. They rang bald and strange; they lacked the logic of statements made in support of alliances, counter-alliances, censorships, repressions, reprisals. They were not reasonable.

Itale came late to supper, looking feverish. He ate little, and soon escaped the house, going down to the lake-shore in the darkness. There he wrestled for some hours with the angel, the messenger, who had challenged him that afternoon. He put up the best fight he could, since, for a nineteen-year-old, he regarded clear thinking highly; but the angel won hands down. Itale could not refuse what he had wanted and sought: the ideal of human greatness, not embodied in a person, but to be won for all by the fellowship of mankind. So long as one soul is unjustly jailed I am not free, thought the new convert, and when he thought of these things his face took on a stern expression, and also a look of great happiness. His twentieth year was in fact the happiest of his life. When out of long silence he would reply to something his mother said, she would look at him wistfully and wonder where it was he had been, so far from her that his blue eyes looked at her with joyous recognition, as if he had been long away in distant lands.

She knew before he did that he wanted to leave home; he found it out for himself that summer. When his work was done he would take his boat and run the shining lake, returning at dusk from the farthest, eastern gulfs where the river Kiassa sprang from the lake and started down the forested mountainsides to the foothills and the plains, to join the Molsen and run on with it. The stream he watched chasing down amongst the rocks would, by summer's end, have reached the sea; while he stayed home by the still lake.

Guide Sorde was told that it was natural for a young man to want to leave home for a while, but he saw it as mere folly. The estate had to be run; Itale was the heir; if one had a job, one did it. Eleonora, following her brother-in-law's suggestion, had proposed sending Itale to college in Solariy. "After all, your father sent you and Emanuel there. . . ."

"There's nothing there he needs," said Guide in his quiet voice in which one could hear, like a wind blowing from the edge of distant storm, a muted resonance of passion. "Waste of time."

Eleonora had never combatted her husband's arrogant provincialism for herself, but for Itale she did. "He needs to meet people, to know the world a little. What good will he be to his peasants if he's no more than another peasant?"

Guide scowled. His wife was using his own weapons against him, more cleverly than he could use them; and he felt besides that he had not been able to express his real reason for not wanting to let the boy go. He was angry at his family for not understanding this motive which he did not understand himself, and offended because he knew he must give in. Everybody knew he would give in, even Itale. Only Eleonora had the tact to argue with him.

So in September of 1822 Itale set off on the Montayna Diligence, northward through the pass and down. Looking back he saw the mountains above long rising ranges of foothills, their familiar outlines changed and changing. San Givan had revealed a great falling eastern slope, Sinviya a second peak; the faint blue outline beyond them, the farthest away, must be the Hunter. As it sank out of sight Itale got out his watch, his grandfather's silver watch, and checked the hour: nine-twenty of the morning. Here on the descending road, now bending towards the southeast, it was sunny, crickets sang in the mown fields, harvesters were at work, the villages were deserted, tranquil in the sunlight. It was the golden land he had seen from beneath the stormclouds of Portacheyka. They passed through towns and villages whose names he knew from hearsay, Vermare, Chaga, Bara; with the last they left the Montayna Province, and at Erreme he changed to the Sudana Post. He looked intently at the people, the houses, the chickens and pigs, as the Sudana Post rolled along, to see what pigs, chickens, houses, people looked like, down here.

In Solariy all things were sleepy. Livestock was fat, houses drowsed in their overgrown gardens full of roses, even the Molsen slept as it flowed through Solariy under the old bridge, sending its wide flood slow and shining to the south. The students of the university did not work hard, they did not duel, they drank a lot of wine and fell in love continually, and the girls of Solariy fell in love with them. In his second year Itale, abandoned by a faithless baker's daughter, renounced love violently and turned to politics. He became a leader in the student society, Amiktiya. The government was barely tolerant of Amiktiya; all such student groups had been outlawed in the Germanies; a society at the University of Wilno so aggravated the Tsar of All the Russias that in 1824 he disbanded it, exiled the boys that led it, and put the entire student body and faculty under permanent surveillance. It was this sort of thing that gave Amiktiya its spice. They drank a lot of wine and sang the society's forbidden anthem, "Beyond this darkness is the light, O Liberty, of thine eternal day." They passed contraband books around, discussed the revolutions of France, Naples, Piedmont, Spain, Greece, talked of constitutional monarchy, equality before the law, popular education, a free press, all without any clear idea of what they were getting at, where it all led. They were not

25

supposed to talk, so they talked. So the third year passed and Itale thought himself ready to go home for good, until he found himself half-shod and laughing in the dark court of the chapel, until he heard Frenin saying in the sunlight over the river, "I'm thinking of Krasnoy."

III

Emanuel Sorde cleared his throat and remarked with the carelessness suitable to an explosive topic, "The newspaper's quite a puzzle this week. I wonder if the Estates aren't going to be convened after all."

"The National Assembly? Why, dear me, they haven't met, have they, since King Stefan died."

"Thirty years ago, that's right."

"How extraordinary."

"It's only my guess, count. The *Courier-Mercury* says nothing; therefore one suspects something."

"Yes." Count Orlant Valtorskar sighed. "My wife used to have me subscribe to the Aisnar *Mercury*. It seemed to have more facts in it. Whatever became of it?"

"It was banned so long that its owners went bankrupt," Itale answered, with heat. "Since then we've had no free press at all."

"What if the Estates do meet?" said Guide in his slow, hard, quiet voice. "They'll talk and do nothing, as in '96."

"Talk!" said his son, setting down a wine glass, which continued to ring for a moment. "It's not unimportant that—" But Emanuel interrupted him: "They might be able to do something about taxation, at least. The Hungarian Diet's won back control over their taxes from Vienna."

"What if they did? Taxes won't be decreased. Taxes are never decreased."

"The money wouldn't go to support a foreign police force, at any rate," said Itale.

"What's that to us up here?"

Count Orlant's long face, smooth and rosy for his years, wore a look of increasingly bewildered compunction as the discussion went on. He felt sorry for them all, emperors, policemen, tax-collectors, poor fellows caught in the webs and pressures of material affairs, but he knew something more than sympathy was expected of him, and he was never able to meet their expectations. There was Guide looking black, Emanuel watchful, Itale getting hotter and hotter and finally bursting out as usual, "A time will come—!" But to Count Orlant's relief Guide spoke setting the challenge aside: "Let's go out to the terrace."

They joined the women on the railed and paved garden old Itale had built out over the lake under the south windows of the house. It was a warm evening, the last of July. The water reflected the pale blue sky evenly except where, in the large shadows of the mountains, it lay translucent brown. Far off east where the lake was hidden by slopes descending sheer into it a little haze veiled the water. In the west sunset still colored the sky behind San Larenz Mountain and lighted the air so that the white flagstones of the terrace, the white nicotiana flowering in pots, the white dress Laura wore, the blue surface of the lake all were faintly flushed with rose, fading now as the sky paled and Vega overhead sent its first broken radiance down through the quiet air. The cypress at the outer corner of the terrace stood black against luminous water and sky, and the air bore a scent of dusk, dampness, flowers, and the murmur of women's voices.

"Oh, Lord, Lord, what a wonder of an evening!" sighed Count Orlant, in a strong provincial accent, submissively, as if asking what he had ever done to merit so fine an evening. He stood looking out over the lake, his long face serene. Eleonora and her sister-in-law were going through the week's gossip, which they exchanged weekly, Eleonora reporting on Val Malafrena and Perneta covering events in Portacheyka; the two girls, Piera Valtorskar and Laura, were talking together, and lowered their voices when the men came out. "He can't dance at all," Laura was saying.

"The hair on the back of his neck looks like moss on a stump," said Piera, dreamily, with complete lack of feeling. She was sixteen years old. Her face, like her father's, was long and

27

naturally serene. She was small, and her figure and hands were still childishly plump.

"If only there was somebody new. . . . For a real ball. . . ."

Piera asked with sudden interest, "Do you think they'll have vanilla ices?"

Perneta meantime had interrupted a complex narration to ask her husband, "Emanuel, isn't Alitsia Verachoy Alexander Sorentay's second cousin?"

"No doubt. She's related to everybody in the Montayna."

"Then it was his mother who married a man from Val Altesma named Berchoy in 1816, wasn't it?"

"Whose mother?"

"Alitsia's husband's."

"But Perneta dear," said Eleonora, "Givan Verachoy died in 1820, so how could his wife have remarried in 1816?"

"Su, su, su," Emanuel went, and escaped, while Perneta said, "But Rosa Berchoy is Alitsia's mother-in-law, don't you see," and Eleonora cried, "Oh, it's Edmund Sorentay you mean, not Alexander, and it was her *father* that died in 1820!"

Guide's brother, though six years younger than he, was greyer; his face was more mobile, less strongly marked. Unambitious and sociable, he had chosen to live in town and practice the law, in which he had taken his degree at Solariy. He had twice refused a judgeship, never explaining his refusal, which most people ascribed to indolence. He was in fact indolent and inclined to irony, describing himself both as a superfluous man and a supremely fortunate one. He deferred to his brother; he would counsel him, but unwillingly. A lawyer's experience of humanity had rubbed him down, worn the corners off him, while Guide, like a flint never dislodged from its cliff above the torrent, had kept every angle and salience of his character intact. Emanuel and Perneta had had one child, stillborn. She, an active woman of a temperament dryer and more sardonic than his own, made no comment when he described himself as supremely fortunate; nor did she ever meddle in the upbringing of her niece and nephew; but they were her sunlight, her pride, her fortune.

Itale joined his uncle at the balustrade under the cypress. The young man's face was still flushed, his hair and cravat were rather wild. "You saw in the *Courier-Mercury* that the Provincial Diet of the Polana is meeting? That's the man I was talking about, Stefan Oragon."

"I remember. So he'll be a deputy, if the Assembly meets."

"Yes; he's what we need; a Danton, a man who can speak for the people."

"Do the people want to be spoken for?"

This was not the kind of question the members of Amiktiya had asked one another.

"And which people?" Emanuel pursued his advantage. "Our class is scarcely 'the people'— The merchants? The peasants here? The city rabble? Don't the different classes have rather different demands?—"

"Not ultimately," Itale said, thinking as he spoke. "The ignorance of the uneducated limits the usefulness of education in those who receive it; you can't limit the light. You can't build equity on any foundation but equality—for four thousand years that has been proved over and over again—"

"Proved?" Emanuel demanded, and they were off, full gallop. Their discussions always started thus with Emanuel in control, pressing Itale to defend his opinions, and always ended with Itale out of control, prevailing through sheer goodnatured eloquent conviction. Then Emanuel would reorganise, provoke another defense, all the while persuaded that he did so to keep his nephew from second-hand thinking, and not because he, too, craved to hear and speak the words, our country, our rights, our freedom.

Itale's mother called to him to fetch Perneta's shawl which she had left in the gig. When he returned sunset was over, the breeze smelled of night. Sky, mountains, lake lay drowned in a deep obscurity of blue, shot through with luminous mists. Laura's white gown showed against the shrubbery with the same misty gleam. "You look like Lot's wife," her brother said.

"The stickpin's coming out of your tie," she retorted.

"You can't see it in the dark."

"I don't need to. Your tie has never been the same since you read Byron."

Laura was tall like her brother, thin, with strong, delicate

29

wrists and hands. She loved her brother passionately, but was ruled by an imperative honesty of heart. When Itale's mother brought him down out of the clouds she scarcely knew it and never intended it; his sister, admiring and intolerant, always did. She wanted him to be himself, considering him, in himself, superior to all fashions, opinions, authorities. A very gentle, unassuming girl of nineteen, she was in this as intransigent as her father. Itale valued her opinion of him above any other, but at this point he was merely mortified, because Piera Valtorskar was listening; having rapidly adjusted his necktie, he said with pedantry, "I have no idea why you think I should want to imitate Lord Byron in any way, except perhaps his death. He died a hero, no doubt of that. But the poetry is trivial."

"But last summer you made me read that whole book about Manfred! And you were quoting him today—Thy something or other wings are something—"

"'Thy wings of storm are held at rest,' that's not Byron, that's Estenskar! You mean you haven't read the *Odes*?"

"No," said Laura, meekly.

"I have," said Piera.

"Then you know the difference, at least!"

"But I haven't read the translation of Lord Byron. I think papa hid it." Piera spoke very softly.

"That's all right, at least you've read Estenskar. You liked it, didn't you? That was 'The Eagle'—and it ends,

> But, caged, thou seest the centuries
> Open before thee, like the open sky.—

Ah, really, that's magnificent!"

"But who is it about?" Laura inquired in honest confusion. "Napoleon!" her brother thundered, outraged. "Oh, dear, Napoleon again," said their mother. "Itale, dear, will you fetch my shawl, too? it's in the hall, or call Kass, but I expect he's having his dinner now."

Itale brought her shawl and then hesitated, standing by her chair, as to where to go next. He ought to return to his uncle at the balustrade and have a sensible, manly conversation, thus proving to Piera and himself that it was only because she was so childish that he appeared to be childish when he was with her. But he wanted to stay and talk with the two girls.

His mother looked up at him. "When ever did you grow so tall?" she asked in a puzzled, musing tone. Light from the house windows shone on her upturned face. When she smiled her under lip hid beneath the top one, and this gave her a demure, sly look that was perfectly charming. Itale laughed for no reason, looking down at her, and she laughed at him because he looked so tall and because he was laughing.

Count Orlant had wandered over and asked, touching his daughter's hair, "You're not cold, contesina?"

"No, papa. It's lovely out here."

"I suppose we should be going in," Eleonora said comfortably, not moving.

"What's become of the picnic in the pine forest?" asked Perneta. "We've been promised it all summer."

"Oh, I forgot to say, if we want we can go tomorrow, the weather will hold, won't it, dear?"

"Likely," said Guide, who sat near her, sunk in his own thoughts. He did not like the discussions his son and his brother carried on at his table. He treated all political discussions with contempt. Some of his fellow landowners, who had no interest in events outside the province but were engrossed in local politics, returned the contempt: "Sorde never looks up from his plough." Others said with envy, "Sorde's one of the old breed, the independent gentry," comparing him to their fathers and grandfathers for whom, as usual, life had been so much simpler. But Guide knew well enough that his father had not been one of the "old breed." He remembered the letters that had used to come from Paris, Prague, Vienna, the guests from Krasnoy and Aisnar, the discussions at table and in the library. Yet old Itale had taken no part in local politics and had never explained his own ideas except in direct answer to a question. There had been more to his silence and self-exile on the estate than natural tolerance and reserve; it had been a choice, scrupulously kept, made perhaps in self-knowledge, perhaps in the bitterness of defeat: Guide did not know. The child of that choice, he had never questioned it.

Now for the first time he was forced to, and to consider that what he had considered his destiny was also, perhaps, an unacknowledged, unexamined choice. So he sat somber in the mild summer dusk. His son's voice, the girl's voices flowed past him like water. Perneta sat silent; Count Orlant and Eleonora had joined Emanuel at the terrace edge; the three young people were talking softly.

"It's going to sound very silly, but you know, I have an idea about that," Laura was saying. "I don't believe you have to die, if you don't want to. I mean, I know you do, and still . . . I can't believe people would die if they really, absolutely wanted not to." She smiled; her smile was like her mother's. "I told you it was silly."

"No, I've thought the same thing," said Itale. He found it extraordinary, mysterious, that he and his sister had had the same thought. He admired Laura: she had had the courage to speak it, he had not. "I can't find the reason for dying, the need. People simply get tired, give in, isn't that it?"

"Yes. Death comes from outside, a disease, or a whack on the head, something from outside, not oneself."

"Exactly. And if one were really oneself, one would say, 'No, sorry, I'm busy, come back later when I've done everything I have to do!'" All three of them laughed, and Laura said, "And that would be never. How could you ever get everything done?"

"You certainly can't in seventy years. It's ridiculous. If I had seven hundred, I'd spend the first century thinking—finishing thoughts I never have time to finish. After that I could do things properly, instead of rushing in and making a mess every time."

"What would you do?" Piera asked.

"Well, one century for travelling. Europe—the Americas— China—"

"I'd go somewhere where no one knew me at all," said Laura. "It wouldn't have to be that far, Val Altesma would do. I'd like to live where no one knew me, and I didn't know anyone. And I think I'd like to travel too; I should like to see Paris; and the volcanoes in Iceland."

"I'd stay here," said Piera. "I'd buy up all the land around the lake, except yours, and make the disagreeable people move away. I shall have an enormous family. Fifteen at least. On July thirty-first every year they'll all come home from wherever they were and we'll have a great, enormous party on the lake, with boats."

"I'll bring fireworks from China for it."

"I'll bring volcanoes from Iceland," said Laura, and again they all laughed.

"What would you do with three wishes?" Piera asked.

"Three hundred more," Laura said.

"Not allowed. It's always three."

"Well, I don't know, what would you wish, Itale?"

"A decent-sized nose," he said gravely, after consideration. "One that people didn't take notice of. And I'd like to be at King Matiyas's coronation."

"That's two. What else?"

"Oh, nothing else, that's enough," Itale said with his quick, broad smile. "I'll give the third one to Piera, I expect she has a use for it."

"No, three's plenty," Piera said; but she would not tell what her three wishes were.

"All right," Laura said, "I'll use up Itale's spare wish. I'd wish we find out we were right, and all live seven hundred years."

"And come back summers for Piera's party on the lake," Itale added.

"Can you make any sense of it, Perneta?" Eleonora inquired.

"I never listen to them, Lele," Perneta answered in her dry contralto. "It's no use."

"It's just as sensible as all that about whose mother-in-law is somebody else's stepsister's uncle!" Laura retorted.

"And far more profound," said her brother.

"Oh, but the Sorentays' ball, we haven't even decided on Piera's dress, and when is it to be, the twentieth?"

"The twenty-second," both girls replied. The conversation turned with vigor to the subject of taffeta, organdie, swiss; empire, tuckered, à la grecque; "White swiss with tiny green dots, with a dropped tucker, I can show you the very thing in Perneta's book."

"But mama, that's ancient, that book's from 1820!"

33

"My dear, if we did dress in fashion up here, who would know it?" Eleonora inquired without asperity. She had been a beautiful and admired girl in Solariy, but had left all that behind her, "down there," without a backward glance, when she married Guide Sorde. "I think the dropped tucker is an uncommonly pretty style. Do you like the idea, Piera?"

Piera's mother had died, fourteen years ago, in an epidemic of the cholera that had also taken the Sordes' last-born, a baby girl. There were nurses and servants aplenty in Count Orlant's house, an ancient great-aunt, cousins, relatives of the mother; but Eleonora had taken charge of the two-year-old Piera at once, firmly, as if by right. Count Orlant, grieving, anxious, grateful, soon dared not decide anything concerning his daughter without consulting Eleonora: who in turn had never presumed on the privilege of affection. She and Piera loved each other more easily, more cheerfully, than any mother and daughter could do however good their disposition.

Piera, often slow to speak, was considering Eleonora's question. "Yes," she said, and thought a little longer. "I'd like a grey silk gown with panels," she said, "like that plate for the Court Ball dress. And a gold scarf. And silk shoes with gold roses."

"Oh dear," said Eleonora.

Count Orlant was listening. He had never got over a deep wonder at the fact that Piera, this young person who was so candid yet so secret, and in whom he glimpsed when he least expected it a whole, strange world of ideas, knowledge, and emotions which could not possibly have had time in sixteen years to grow so deep and strong, that this extraordinary child on the point of becoming a woman was, when you came right down to it, his daughter. Though he relied upon her love he was often afraid of her. Just now the wonder returned: he saw her vision, a royal maiden in silk and cloth of gold. "That sounds very charming," he said, timidly proffering his opinion to the wise ladies. They sighed, hedged. "Perhaps a gold scarf with a white organdie?" Eleonora went on trying to soften the veto. The Valtorskars, father and daughter, accepted the judgment without question, listened to further suggestions, and, listening, continued to entertain their tacit and contented vision of magnificence.

Guide and Emanuel were talking about hunting; it was Itale that now sat unheeding, tense with his thoughts. Down in Solariy he had planned to tell his family his decision on the night he came home: he must not deceive them by letting them think him home to stay. He had been home three weeks now and had said nothing. Coming in at the Golden Lion in Portacheyka, as he swung down off the coach, he had seen his father turn to look for him. On Guide's face had been the rare smile that made him look a different man, awkward, vulnerable. At the memory of it Itale clenched his hands in unavailing protest. It was unjust of his father to be so happy, to show his happiness, at his return! How could a man act like a man, say what he had to say and do what he had to do, when all these unspoken feelings clung and clustered round him holding him back, tying him down? And not only other people's feelings—he would admit—but his own; all the happiness of his boyhood around him once again, unchanged, all his own love and loyalty, all his old expectations of life. The earth itself held him here more strongly than any other bond, the red dirt of the vineyards, the long great lines of the mountains against the sky. How could he leave all that? The scythe he was honing or the boat tiller or the book in his hand would be forgotten for a moment and he would look unseeing out over Malafrena, with a heaviness in him. It was as if a spell was laid upon him here, which he could not break, though he might escape from it; a charm that grew strongest in certain hours, certain conversations—he did not want to think about it. That was the rankest injustice, the least tolerable. He could not fall in love here, with a mere child; there was no question of it, of childish flirtations and unspoken understandings: he had outgrown all that. It was love he wanted, adult love, and he would find it in Krasnoy; for he had to go to Krasnoy. Beneath all his hesitations the same voice said to him, resolutely and mournfully, "It's necessary, it must be."

"Did you track her, Itale?" Emanuel was talking of the she-wolf that had been seen up on San Larenz.

"No luck," he answered; and as he spoke he decided that he must speak to his father.

He prepared himself for the ordeal by speaking to his uncle, that night after the others had gone indoors. Emanuel seemed not unprepared for the revelation. After he had determined Itale's plans—which consisted of going to Krasnoy and finding how he could be useful to the patriotic cause, if in fact there was one—and after he had watched and listened to his nephew a while, he made his meditative noise: "Su, su, su . . . It all sounds vague, it all sounds dangerous, to me; but lawyers always see the wrong side of things. . . . I don't know how Guide will see it. I'm afraid it will make no sense whatever to him, in any terms."

"Surely he'll understand me, if he'll listen to me."

"He won't. He's counted on you these twenty years to work with him. Grudged you the three years in the south. Now this? . . . Besides, I don't know that you understand what you're doing yourself. You aren't following reason, as well as I can see. Like him, you act from passion, a passion for moral clarity, the will to be yourself. And now your will is different from his, radically different. You think you're going to discuss that difference reasonably and come to an agreement? I doubt it!"

"But father believes in duty, in serving principle. Of course in a way I'd rather stay here—I wish I could stay here—but this is more important than any private wish, and I know he could understand that. I can't stay here until I'm free to stay here."

"And you're to win that freedom by serving other men's needs?"

"I won't win it," the young man said. "Freedom consists in doing what you can do best, your work, what you have to do, doesn't it? It's nothing you have or keep. It is action, it is life itself. But how can you live in the prison of others' servitude? I can't live for myself until everyone is free to do so!"

"Until the Kingdom is come," Emanuel murmured ironically, with pain. The lake stretched away from them very dark, very still, barely a noise of water lapping the foundation of the terrace or the pilings of the boat house. Eastward, the bulks and slopes of the mountains stood outlined against a dim whiteness in the sky, moonrise; westward was only darkness and the stars.

IV

"Hoy-y!"

The cry re-echoed off the water that lay sparkling between the boats, but there was no answering call, and the sharp brown sail ahead of them skimmed on unheeding.

"Call again, Count Orlant."

"They're too far away," said Perneta.

"Oh dear, and we'll never catch Falkone. Itale! Dear!"

"They're turning," said Count Orlant, frowning into the dazzle. The brown sail, sharp as a hawk's wing, was coming round. Count Orlant brought Mazeppa into the wind, heading her home; soon the smaller boat had come up even with her and they heard the boatsman's hail, "Hoy there!"

"Hoy!" Eleonora hailed gallantly, sounding like a quail. "Clouds— It's going to storm— We ought to start home!"

"What's up?"

"Home!" Perneta contributed, waving at the passing thunderclouds over San Larenz.

"Laura wants to hunt mushrooms at Evalde!"

"Oh dear, I can't shout any more—do tell them it'll take too long to hunt mushrooms, and I already have two barrels down in pickle— It's going to ra-ain! Oh dear." They heard laughter in Falkone, and presently Emanuel's voice: "Mushrooms?"

"No mushrooms!"

"Evalde?" called Itale, standing up in the prow.

"Home!" Count Orlant roared in an unexpected mountaineer's bellow. The figure in the prow of the other boat made a sweeping bow, executed a few dance steps, and vanished. "He fell in!" Eleonora cried, but Falkone sailed on past them, Itale and Laura now performing a minuet in the stern. By the time Mazeppa lumbered in, Emanuel and the three young people were already up on the terrace. Itale was expounding something; his blue eyes shone in his wind-flushed face. Eleonora and Perneta both looked at him with unqualified admiration, and Perneta said, "Itale, what on earth did you do with your hat?"

"It's all wet," Eleonora said, "you did fall overboard!"

Piera suddenly laughed, a loud irrepressible laugh. "He was fishing with it. . . ."

"With his hat?"

"With his hat," said Emanuel. "And two young ladies holding a leg apiece and shrieking 'Don't kick! Don't kick!'"

"But what for?"

"My ferns."

"Piera dropped her ferns overboard when the boom came round, so I tried to get them back, and what's become of the dipper I keep in Falkone?" He and the girls were red with laughter.

"I begged you to let me come in Mazeppa," Emanuel said.

"And Laura, you never once put up your parasol, now you'll be freckled till Michaelmas."

"Freckles," said Count Orlant, thoughtfully. "I remember when this contesina was small and running about all day, I once counted eighteen freckles on her nose alone. Rather becoming, I thought."

"And a fine thing if they go to the Sorentays' ball looking like a pair of old saddles," said Eleonora. "You needn't look so pleased with yourselves, you two!"

Itale looked at Piera as she stood half turned from him and saw on the slender nape of her neck, below the wind-loosened chignon, three freckles: a pleasant sight.

"And he never even got the ferns," said Laura.

"Because neither of you would hold on, and I couldn't keep my face out of the water!"

"He bubbled," Piera said, and they all began laughing again. "Oh, he lay there on the water waving his arms and b-bubbling, oh—" When they recovered, Eleonora said, wiping her eyes, "How can you all be so silly? Is Guide still out? he probably hasn't even looked up at the sky. . . ."

"Dear lady," said Emanuel, taking his sister-in-law by the waist. "Twenty-seven years in Val Malafrena and she still isn't used to thunderstorms!"

"Twenty-eight years, dear, but I do think it's a shame all the best days up here end in a lot of pouring and growling and Guide coming in dripping on the floor." She and Emanuel rocked back and forth on their heels, beaming at the others. There was a long roll of thunder from San Larenz, and one of them said, "Here it comes." The thunderheads had massed, grey and grey-black, boiling over the mountain and reaching across the lake. "In with us!" said Eleonora.

Guide was standing at the south windows of the living room. Itale stopped short in the hall, looking at that black figure against the stormy light.

"Tea. Eva!" cried Eleonora, vanishing kitchenward.

"A beautiful day," said Count Orlant, sitting down with relief in one of the heavy old oaken armchairs. "Wish you'd been with us, Sorde."

"I should be having some days free soon. I'd like you to try the hawk old Rika's trained."

Falconry was still a common sport in Montayna. Guide and his son were adepts, Emanuel took pleasure in it, and Count Orlant could appreciate the points of a hawk, though in his heart there was no great desire to go trotting about the countryside carrying on his wrist a big bird before whose cruel, straight stare he felt, somehow, inferior.

"I wish you'd take her out, Itale," Guide was saying. "She should fly. I haven't had the time, working with Starey."

"I will."

He answered the simple request with a bad conscience, and was relieved when his mother interrupted the falconers' talk, coming in with Eva the cook and tea. The pleasure of the day was gone; as soon as he had entered the house he could think of nothing but that he must speak to his father tonight. He sat, his damp hat between his knees, like an awkward guest who could neither talk nor take his leave. The women were aware of his attitude. His mother was profoundly uneasy, knowing there was some change in him. Laura thought he was up on his pedestal showing off again; she did not know why he would no longer talk to her about what preoccupied him, and felt cheated and resentful. Perneta thought him very funny and very handsome

39

as he sat there nursing his weed-looped hat; she never worried about him, convinced no harm could come to a boy like that. As for Piera, who sat next to him on the couch, she was aware of his silence, of the blue coat he wore, of the slight rough darkness of his cheek, of his presence, the weight and reality of his being there. She went no further. Had he spoken she would have listened to his voice as part of that inexplicable presence; he was silent; she listened to his silence. She thought she had never been so happy as she was right now, and most likely would never be so happy again, since things would not be exactly the same again. Her joy, undulled by age and habit, unfounded on any permanence of life, knew its own defenselessness. She dared not handle it, clear and fragile as glass. If she felt the trouble in him it was as part of her own trouble and joy, part of the strangeness of him and of their sitting side by side on the couch drinking tea.

Count Orlant returned from prowling in the library: "That must be an interesting botanical collection your father made, Sorde. I wish he'd gone in for astronomy. I suppose no one much reads those?"

"Itale's in there a good deal, but not for botany," said Laura, hoping for a rise out of her brother.

"I remember your grandfather teaching you the Latin names of the plants, out in the garden; I don't suppose you remember that."

"At least Itale can still tell me the name of that exotic under the east windows, that I always forget again immediately, what is it?" Eleonora said.

"Mandevilia suaveolens," said her son.

Brief hard rain whitened the windows. The thunder had passed over; low sun shone gold on the lake through rain.

"Oh, do you know, these summer storms are pleasant, they lighten the air. . . ."

"I get much the best results with my telescope after a thundershower," Count Orlant confirmed. As Emanuel asked him something about his astronomy, Itale said to Piera, without knowing he was going to say anything, "Have you read Estenskar's other books?"

"Just the *Odes*."

"May I lend you *The Torrents of Karesha*? It's very fine."

"If— If papa approves."

Itale frowned. "Estanskar is a great poet. And a noble mind. It's fear that bans his works, but mere sloth that accepts the ban. You should insist on a freedom which is your obligation."

The sixteen-year-old countess, with her round arms, her curly hair and slender, freckled neck, glanced at her father, who was saying, "But if a comet came very close to the earth there's no telling . . ." and looked at Itale, and said, "I will." After a moment she added, "Papa likes to know what I read, and I think he did hide Lord Byron, but I don't think he'd really stop me from reading anything. . . ."

"I didn't mean him exactly, that is, not personally. But let me lend you the book, Piera. I really think you'll find it very fine." He ended up pleading. The matter, like everything that came up that day, seemed of illimitable importance.

"I'd like to read it very much, Itale."

He started up to bring the book from his room.

"But you'll be over Tuesday night, and if you brought it then, papa wouldn't notice me carrying it home and ask."

He hesitated. "I'd better give it to you now."

She was puzzled, but took the book he brought her and did not ask what could keep him from coming to Valtorsa on Tuesday night.

Everyone went out together to leave or say goodbye; as they went down the path there was a gust of perfume about them in the rainwashed evening air. Piera asked, "Is that the mandevilia . . . ?"

"Suaveolens," said Itale, walking beside her, and smiled.

As Emanuel and Perneta were driving up to Portacheyka, fields and wooded hills flowing past them molasses-dark in the late evening, the clop of the horse's hooves dull on the dust-thick road, the wife broke a long silence between them. "Our nephew's come home moody."

"Mh," said the husband.

"Owl."

"What?"

"Owl flew over."

"Mh."

"He and Piera. . . ."

"Girl's sixteen."

"I was nine the first time I saw you."

"You're not saying they're in love."

"Certainly not. But you never think anyone's in love."

"Don't know what the word means."

"Mh," said Perneta in her turn.

"No, I suppose I do. I've seen it once. Guide, in '97. He was a new man in a new world, that year. So they married. How long did it last? Eight months, ten months? Most people never have that much. A few hours, if anything. Rubbish."

"Funny old man," said his wife, in one of her rare and always private impulses of tenderness. "But all the same, Piera and Itale. . . ."

"Of course. It's the most natural thing in the world. But Itale's leaving."

"Leaving?"

"Going to Krasnoy."

The horse snorted several times, starting the pull up towards the pass.

"Why?"

"He wants to work for a patriot group."

"Politics? But there are offices here to be had."

"Our provincial politics are a swindling game played by idle landowners and professional incompetents."

"Well, but—" Perneta meant that was what all politics meant to her, and Emanuel understood her.

"Itale's not looking for an office, but for a revolution."

"Do you mean," she asked after pondering, "the Sovenskarists—those people? Like that writer in Aisnar that was put in jail?"

"Yes. They're not common criminals, you know. They're mostly gentlemen and parish priests, I believe. Decent men all over Europe are involved in this sort of thing. I don't know. I don't know anything about it," Emanuel said violently, and shook the patient horse's reins.

42

"Does Guide know?"

"Do you remember when Giulian's flourmill blew up?"

She stared; then nodded. "When did Itale tell you?"

"Last night."

"Did you encourage him?"

"I? I, at fifty, encourage a boy of twenty-two to go remake the world? Su!"

"This will break Eleonora's heart."

"No, it won't. I know you women. The more risks he runs, the more follies he commits, the prouder you'll be of him. But Guide! The boy is Guide's future— To see that at risk, astray—"

"The boy is his own future," Perneta said very gravely. "But how much risk is there in this?"

"I don't know. I don't want to think about it. I think too much about risks, about people's feelings, all that— That's why I'm a provincial lawyer and have never done anything that took courage. And never will, because I'm too old now to upset the housekeeping. I wish that once, only once, when I was twenty-two, I'd said to someone as Itale said to me, 'This is important.' Even if it wasn't important, even if it wasn't true!"

Perneta put her large, hard hand over his, lightly. She said nothing. They drove on through the warm night to Portacheyka that lay, a few scattered lights, below them in the pass.

At about the same time Itale, standing at the foot of the stairs, was saying, "This is rather important, father."

"Very well. Come into the library."

In the high-windowed room starlight defined the shadows of leaves against the glass. Guide lit a lamp and sat down at the table in his carved, age-black chair, a relic of the furniture of the house built by his great-grandfather in 1682 and rebuilt by his father a century later. The table was piled with documents, some written in the fine cursive of law clerks dead two hundred years: the deeds and titles, contracts and records, of the Sorde estate. Most of them concerned rents and settlements with the tenant farmers or deeds and rights to new properties acquired over the generations. That stack of Latin documents, Itale had thought when he saw Guide and Emanuel at work on them, was the Middle Ages: obscure, intricate, muddled, arid, beneath the aridity pungent with life and overwhelming in its concreteness, its multifarious humanity, its absorption in the land, the land worked, owned, rented, leased, the land that made a peasant bound and a landowner free, the land source, root, subject and end of life. Over against all that was a sheaf of printed papers to which Emanuel would refer, scowling: The Tax Laws of 1825, concise, precise, impersonal, modern, and when applied to the Middle Ages in the form of those piled-up records, meaningless. Here was the Family and the Land; here was the State and Uniformity; and nothing existed to bridge the gulf between, no revolution, no representation, no reforms, nothing.

At Itale's end of the long table, not yet swamped by documents, lay only a copy of Rousseau's *Social Contract*, which he had been rereading. He picked it up and turned it round absently in his hands as he spoke.

"Since Austria wants us to use Napoleonic tax methods, it would help if she'd let us carry out the reorganisation the French began here, wouldn't it?"

"It would. If they must have money why don't they come to me for it, do they think the peasants can raise cash? City men. . . ."

Guide's face stood out heavily shadowed against the obscurity of the book-lined walls. It was a hard, strong face, but what impressed Itale in it as a quality he had never consciously seen in it before was its repose. That was not temperament, for Guide's temper was not reposeful; it was character, the gift of time, and not only the years of Guide's own life but the time he had accepted and made his own, the seasons and the generations past. Itale could see in his father's face that he was tired tonight, that he wished Itale would say what he had to say and at the same time dreaded what he might say; all that was plain enough. But beneath it was the passive, unmoved repose, the will underlying all personal emotion; his inheritance.

"I want to try to explain some—a change in my thinking, father."

"I'm aware that we disagree on certain matters. Times change. We needn't think alike on everything. Time spent discussing opinions is time wasted."

"Some ideas are more than opinions. To hold them is to serve them."

"That may be. But I have no wish to argue, Itale."

"Nor have I." The *Social Contract* came down on the table with a light thump, raising dust from the old papers and parchments. "None at all. But I wish to act by my principles, as you do by yours."

"Your mind is your own. Your time is your own. So long as you do your work here, and you do; you always have done."

"My work's not here."

Guide raised his head at that. He said nothing.

"I have to go to Krasnoy."

"You have to do nothing of the sort."

"I'm trying to explain—"

"I don't want explanations."

"If you won't listen there's no use my trying to speak." Itale stood up. So did Guide: "Stay here," he said. He walked down the room and back, down it and back a second time. He sat down again in the carved chair. Itale remained standing by the table. Behind the house in the valley a sleepy cock crowed; old Eva was singing in the kitchen, rooms away.

"You want to go to Krasnoy."

Itale nodded.

"Do you expect to take money from the estate to support yourself there?"

"Not if you are unwilling to let me have it."

"I am."

Itale tried to repress his resentment and defiance, making so harsh an effort over himself that it weakened him physically. For a moment the reaction was so strong that he wanted to go to his father like a child and ask his pardon: anything to spare this anger. He sat down as before across the table from Guide, picked up the book as before, watched the lamplight flicker on its worn gold edging, and finally said, "I will find work. My friends and I hope to write—perhaps to start some kind of journal."

"For what purpose?"

Itale did not lift his head. "Freedom," he said.

"For whom?"

45

"All of us."

"You think freedom's yours to hand out?"

"What I have I can give."

"Words, Itale."

"These are words, too. This book. It brought the Bastille down. Those are words, those documents about our land. You've given your life to what they stand for."

"You're very eloquent."

There was a long pause.

Guide spoke with careful restraint. "Let me tell you how I see this. You want to go down there, mix yourself up with other people's business; you say you see that as a matter of principle. Of duty. What I see much more clearly is your duty here, to your family and your property and the people on it. Who is to run this estate when I die? A Krasnoy journalist?"

"That is unjust!"

"It is not. It is the difference between duty and self-indulgence."

"You cannot speak to me as if I were a child. I'm not a child. I am what you made me, and I know what duty is; and I respect your principles; therefore I ask you to respect mine."

Guide was speechless a moment before Itale's self-confidence. "Respect? Respect for what? Your theories, your opinions, your secondhand words that you want to throw away all this for? You are of age, you needn't obey me, but you can't touch your inheritance until you're twenty-five, and thank God for that."

"I would never touch it against your will—"

"But you're throwing it away, you're turning your back on it, everything I've worked for. It's not yours to throw away!" That was a cry from the heart. The young man answered desperately, "I'm not—I'll come back when you need me—"

"I need you now. If you go, you go."

"I'll go," Itale answered, on his feet. "You can keep all that, but you can't take my loyalty to it, to this house, to you— A time will come when you'll see that—"

"A time will come, will it!" The *Social Contract* landed on the floor, pages down, a loose endpaper skittering across the room like a scared bird. "Not in my time, or in yours!"

Both were suffocated with self-righteous anger, both knew there was no more to say, nothing.

Guide turned away at last. "If you think better of this," he said in a stifled voice, "no more needs to be said. If not, the sooner you go the better."

"I'll go on the Diligence, Friday."

Guide said nothing.

Itale bowed and left the library.

His silver watch said eight-twenty. They had gone into the library only a few minutes before. He felt that hours had passed.

"Itale?"

His mother came into the hall, looking puzzled. "Is your father in the library, dear?"

"Yes." He went quickly upstairs, to his room, and shut the door. The room was full of the blue of late evening reflected upward from the lake beneath the windows, a warm unreal atmosphere in which objects seemed to hang suspended like the dim plants seen underwater just off shore. The serenity of light, vague, weightless, picked up and opened out the anguish that bore him down; he felt he could draw breath again. But never in his life had he felt so lonely and so deathly tired.

V

It was the fifth of August, a day hot with the dull intensity that ends in storm. Since dawn the fields had baked in sunlight; the lake lay glassy; the sun was warped and reddish in the sky pale with heat. Crickets sang in the mown and the yellow fields, in the orchards, under the oaks. Shadows now touched the lake from the western peaks and there was a softer color low in the sky, a vague blue-violet, but still no wind rose, and Malafrena lay like a bowl of heat and light. Piera Valtorskar was coming downstairs, an action that to her, in this huge timeless afternoon of August, seemed to last a long while, an interval full of intangible thoughts and manifold sensations. The house, built of limestone and marble, was cool; one knew it was a hot day only by the dryness of the air, the cricket-chant, the molten glare of a sun-streak finding its way through a shuttered window. Piera was wearing the women's dress of her province, a full dark-red skirt, black vest, linen blouse embroidered at the neck. The sleeves of the blouse were stitched at the shoulder into twelve pleats: it had been made in Val Malafrena. A blouse made in Val Altesma would have gathered sleeves, and certain motifs and stitches of the embroidery would be different, a flower design instead of a pattern of birds and branches. All these things were as they should be, as they had always been; so Piera preferred this dress to any other. As she descended the stairs she was smoothing out the skirt, aware of the garnet color, feeling the cool grainy texture of the homespun cloth. Her right hand was on the marble stair-railing, soap-slick and cold. Step by step she descended, feeling herself descend, feeling the heavy skirt sway, feeling the railing under her hand, thinking of a great deal though she could not have said what. On the fourth step from the bottom she began to hum the song, "Red are the berries on the autumn bough"; on the last step she stopped humming and ran her finger down the backbone of the Cupid on the newel post. He was a crude, squat, provincial Cupid carved of grey Montayna marble. He looked anxious and dyspeptic. Piera poked his belly to see if he would belch; then all at once she wheeled round and darted up the stairs in a fifth the time it had taken her to come down them.

The upstairs hall was dark and smelled of dusty velvet. She listened at her father's door. Silence. Count Orlant was still asleep. On hot days he generally slept away the afternoon on his old leather couch, though he never meant to. Piera went back down the stairs smartly, trip-trip-trip, swung round the newel post using Cupid as a fulcrum, and went off to her great-aunt's room.

Auntie—so she was always called, and the servants called her Countess Aunt—was very old. She had been very old during all Piera's life. She had birthdays, like other people; but she could not possibly remember them, as Piera remembered all her birthdays since the eleventh one; and what difference could a ninety-fifth birthday make? Whether she was ninety-three or ninety-four or ninety-five, Auntie sat in her straight-backed chair, wearing a black dress and grey shawl, and sometimes dozed and sometimes did not. Her face was netted with countless dry lines radiating from her mouth and the corners of her eyes. Her features, nose, cheekbones, cheek-hollows, were as if obliterated by that network of tiny lines. Most of her teeth were gone, her lips sunken. Her eyes were like her grandniece's eyes, grey, translucent. Auntie was not dozing this afternoon. She looked at Piera with clear grey eyes across the gulf of eighty years.

"Auntie, did you ever dream you could fly?"

"No, my dear."

Auntie usually answered No.

"This afternoon when I was lying down, I dreamed I could float. All it takes is knowing you can. You just push off from the wall, so, with one finger, holding your breath, and then take long steps, you see? and to change direction you just push off the wall again. I'm sure I was doing it. I came clear downstairs without touching. . . . Shall I hold wool for you?"

Auntie's hands had got too stiff years ago for knitting or embroidery, but she liked to hold needles and wool, or a panel and silk, and doze with them; and she particularly liked to wind the hanks of wool and silk into balls. Piera also enjoyed this. She could hold hanks for Auntie for an hour, watching the red or blue or green yarn slip off her parallel hands and gleam in Auntie's stiff, deliberate fingers winding it round and round and round.

"Not now, my dear."

"Is it time for your tea?"

Auntie said nothing; it was not time for her tea. She dozed, and her grandniece slipped away. She looked into the kitchen, an enormous low room darkened by the oaks outside. The house of Valtorsa, built in 1710, was screened from the lake by trees and faced the valley and the foothills: old Itale Sorde's notion of building his house right on the water had been one of his foreign fancies. No one was in the kitchen now but Mariya the cook, gutting a hen. Piera came and looked.

"What's that, Mariya?"

"The crop, contesina."

"All full of seeds, yes . . . What's that?"

"An egg, contesina, didn't you ever see an egg?"

"Not inside a hen. Look, there's more of them!"

"It's that old fool Maati, I told him the brown hen with white specks and he brought the Kiassafonte hen instead, and her head off already, the old fool. She's old but she was a fine layer. Look there, the bitty eggs, like beads on a necklace. . . ." The stout woman and the girl peered into the blood-scented innards, Mariya roused to momentary interest by Piera's interest.

"But how do they get there?"

"Why, the he-bird. . . ." Mariya shrugged.

"Yes, I know, the he-bird," Piera murmured. She sighed, wrinkling her nose at that dry smell of blood. "Are you going to bake this afternoon, Mariya?"

"Thursday afternoon?"

"Oh, I knew you weren't, I just asked. . . . Where's Stasio?"

"In the fields."

"Everybody's in the fields all day, they might as well have died and gone to heaven. I wish winter would come!" Piera spun round to make her skirt balloon out, investigated a huge iron soup-kettle hanging in a corner of the hearth, then wandered out. Her domain was desolate. All the farm people were getting the late hay in, Mariya had nothing to say, Auntie was asleep, the count was asleep, the governess was off on her holiday, it was too dull to stay indoors and too hot to go outdoors, and she could not go to see Laura because Itale was leaving tomorrow, leaving all at once for the city, forever. She wandered to the front room with its drawn blinds, marble fireplace with more marble Cupids, its long, shiny, empty floor and sparse, stiff furniture. The floor looked cool; she knew it was cool, and was tempted to lie down on it flat on her stomach as she had used to do on hot afternoons. But she was too old, in her garnet skirt and linen blouse, to go crawling on the floor. She curled up on the windowseat and peered out between the shutter and the frame at the empty, shady side yard. The whole trouble was that there was nobody to talk to, nobody to understand what she did not understand, nothing to do with the life that filled her, nothing to do. . . . Piera sat still, her feet tucked under her, her hand holding aside the corner of the linen blind so that she could see the same dull bit of the yard and the foothills building up towards Sinviya Mountain, and she was sad, sad, sad, with the dull, deep, immense sadness of August, of a hot eternal afternoon of August.

The Sorde house was also silent, but under the summer trance there was some coming and going, now and then the sound of voices. Itale's bedroom was hot; he had opened the window to get air, indifferent to the bar of fiery sunshine that lay across the floor. He was in shirtsleeves and his hair, wet with sweat, stuck up in tangles above his forehead. He was sorting through papers, putting most of them back in a tin box, leaving out a few to take with him. Soon done with the task, he shoved the box back under the table and stood up. The first breath of wind broke the day's great stillness: a catspaw streaked the lake near shore, taking long to disappear, and the topmost paper of the little pile on the desk stirred. He put his hand on it mechanically, then looked down. *Not this time a dream, O Liberty.* . . . It was a poem on the revolution of Naples he had written last winter; his friends in Amiktiya had thought it very fine. He began to stuff the papers into the valise open on the bed. Metastasio's words to his mistress, sung in the streets of Naples by a people briefly free, went on in his head, *I am not dreaming this time.* . . . *Non sogno questa volta, non sogno libertà!*—over and over, like the cricket-chant, till he stopped listening. The breath of wind had passed. The bar of sunlight lay across the bare floor, intolerably bright.

A knock; Laura came in at his word. "Here's the linens. Mother's finishing a shirt for you to wear tomorrow."

"All right. Thanks."

"Can I help?"

"All done except for these." He began stuffing the clean shirts into the valise, needing something to occupy him in Laura's presence; each felt oppressed, unnatural, and aware of the other's feeling so.

"Let me. You're folding them all wrong."

"Oh, well." He let Laura pack the shirts.

"Piera said she had a book of yours."

"The Estenskar—get it from her when she's done with it. You ought to read it. Don't post it to me, it's a contraband edition." He stood looking out the window again. "It's going to be a real storm tonight."

"I hope so." Laura straightened up and watched with him the slow faint massing of clouds in the southwest, behind the Hunter.

"Ten to one Count Orlant hasn't got his hay in from Arly's Field. Every year I can remember he's raced a storm for that hay."

"I hope it's a huge storm. . . ."

"Why?"

There was no one but Itale who could ask her "Why?" and smile because he knew the answer. There was no other man to whom she could talk as an equal, whom she could trust absolutely. There were beloved parents, relatives, friends, but one brother only.

"I wish I could go too."

He went on looking at her and finally asked, "Why?" in a different tone, a voice full not of unconscious but conscious, regretful love.

"Why are you going?"

"I'm obliged to, Laura."

"I'm obliged not to."

Neither was able to put that fact in question.

Among women, all of whom he desired, all of whom baffled and frightened him, among them all there was one sister only.

"Will you go to Evalde, Laura?"

Until he went to college he and she had gone every year at dawn of the spring equinox across the lake to the gulf of Evalde, where a river broke from caverns in a high cascade to the lake. On the shore there was a high rock curiously marked, called the Hermit's Rock; Count Orlant ascribed the markings to druids, others, dubious of druids, said it marked the place where St Italus the Missionary had preached to the heathen tribes of Val Malafrena. The spirit it roused in the brother and sister was heathen enough; to them in adolescence the true year began with that silent course before dawn across the lake and arrival on that shore, a solitary celebration of rock and mist and light above the waters.

"Yes, I will."

"In Falkone."

She nodded.

"And you'll write."

"Of course. But will you? Real letters? You wrote such stupid letters before you came home!"

"I couldn't explain about being under house arrest. Everything got so complicated. . . ." Laura was at last getting the whole story of Müller, Von Haller, and Gentz, when her mother came in; she and Itale had been laughing, they felt ashamed of laughing on the day before Itale left, knowing that their mother had wept for his going. Laura escaped, and Eleonora showed him the shirt she had ironed herself. "To wear tomorrow," she said. She was used to the inadequacies of life, to the shirt ironed because the words cannot be said, or will do no good. He was not.

"Mother, you do understand—" He stopped.

"I think so, dear. I only wish you were happier about it yourself." She looked into his valise. "Will you wear your blue coat?"

"How can I be happy if father—"

"You mustn't hold anger against him, dear."

"I don't. Only if he—" Itale stammered slightly when he was keyed up. "If he'd try to understand that I'm trying to do right!"

Eleonora was silent; then she said, mild and tenacious, "You mustn't hold anger against him, Itale."

"Believe me, I try not to!" he said with his passionate candor and seriousness, so that she turned to him smiling. "But if we could only talk to each other, if I could explain to him—"

"I don't know if people can ever really explain," she said. "Not in words, anyway." She saw he did not believe her. That was all right. She too had once believed that people could be entirely honest with one another; she did not consider herself better for having lost that faith. If she were to be entirely honest with her son right now she would beg him to stay home, not to go, for if

53

he went he would never come home again; so she repeated, "Will you wear your blue coat? It'll be cold on the coach in the morning."

He nodded unhappily.

"I want to put up a lunch for you; Eva saved some roast beef," she said, and at that, the reality of the roast beef, the coach wheels turning, the dust of the road that led away from home, the silence of the dining room where she and Guide and Laura would sit down tomorrow without him, all this threatened her all over again, and she left him hastily so that she could struggle with it alone.

He went on down to the boat house, having time to reset Falkone's tiller, a job he had promised himself to do before he left. The long light was intense on the road and the green, hollow lawn above the boat house. Behind the Hunter now clouds banked heavy; there was a greenish cast to the air over the lake. When the steering was mended he set to waxing the seats and rail of the boat, wanting to be busy. It was hot and dim in the boat house, smelling of wax, soaked wood, water-weeds. The raw pine roof trembled with webbed, moving reflections of the sunlit water. Men were coming back from haying, he heard their voices on the road above. One went by after the others singing a song that rose and fell on a few notes in the minor.

Red are the berries on the autumn bough,
Sleep, my love, and sleep thee well,
The grey dove sings in the forest now,
Sleep till thou wilt waken.

He finished his job, went up the grassy slope and through the line of poplars to the road. The men from haying in the north field had all gone by, done in good time, for Guide was seldom caught racing a storm for his hay; no one was on the road but old Bron and David Angele returning from the vineyards, and with them Marta, Astolfe's wife. The men wore somber, shapeless work-clothes; only on feastdays would there be any color about their dress, and the vivid white of the heavy embroidered shirt. Bron strode along long-legged, unhurried, self-contained, like an

54

old animal, taciturn: his strength was that of old age, economical, a wisdom of movement. David Angele, a young man, looked entirely insignificant beside him. On his left Marta, in garnet-red skirt and embroidered blouse, took two steps to his one. She had been a beauty ten years ago, when she was twenty. The smile that creased her cheeks and showed her bad teeth was still radiant, as she said to her landlord's son, "And you're off again, Dom Itaal!"

"Tomorrow, Marta."

They all knew, of course, that Dom Guiid and Dom Itaal had quarreled. David Angele glanced slyly at Itale; Bron was silent; only Marta knew how to continue the dangerous subject with tact. "And it's the king's city you're going to this time, so David Aangel says?"

"So Dom Guiid told young Kass," David Angele put in hastily, exculpating himself.

"What a grand place it must be," Marta went on, evidently without the least desire to see it. "People thick as flies on sugar, they say."

"But you're not to call it the king's city now, Marta," said the young vintner, again with a sly glance. "You know there's no king in these days."

"There's the foreign duchess lady, you needn't teach me, lad. But I like the sound of the old name, it's how my mother always called it, ain't I right, uncle?"

"Aye," said old Bron, striding along. Itale asked Marta about her three little daughters, which made her laugh. She laughed about them since, as she explained, they couldn't yet give her cause to cry. With Bron he discussed the state of the grapes and the new planting of Oriya vines; he had been Bron's student and disciple in the vineyards all his life. But they were already at the Dowerhouse Road, and Marta said, "You must turn off here, then I wish you a safe journey and Godspeed, Dom Itaal." Worn and solid, gap-toothed, she gave him her radiant smile. Itale shook hands with David Angele with a warmth that rose from bad conscience at disliking him, and turned last to Bron: "When I come back, Bron—"

"Aye, you will." Their eyes met. It seemed to Itale, because he so much desired it to be so, that the old man understood all he meant, knew more than he himself knew, and found no need to say it. So they parted, and he went to the house for supper.

They ate early because they must be up early. They did not linger over the meal. When Eva came in from the kitchen to change the blue-ringed plates, her slippers creaking, they looked up at her with relief. But her old face was as gloomy as any of theirs.

Guide went out to the stables after supper, the women sat with their sewing in the front room. Itale stood at the windows that looked over the terrace to the lake. The light was strange: the water nearly black, but above Evalde the long forested ridge unearthly bright against a somber sky. A strong wind blew from the southwest now, breaking the water into netted streaks. Air and lake darkened fast with the night and storm coming on together. Itale turned round and looked at his mother and sister. So they would sit together here, their faces bent to their work, when he was gone; those who kept the house. His mother glanced up at him as she always did from sewing with a grave, peaceable look, then said, "It's going to be very pretty, I think; see?" —shaking out the goods she was working on, a drift of white stuff. "It's her first real evening dress."

"Aye," he said, staring at it. "I'll go see the Valtorskars, I think. The count should be in by now."

"It's going to storm any minute, isn't it?"

"I won't stay. Any messages for them?"

He went up to his room three steps at a time—he had been twelve when he got tall enough to take the stairs three at a time, he recalled for a moment as he went—and looked over his bookcase hastily, and took out a small book bound in whitish leather, well worn; a translation of Dante's *Vita Nova* which he had bought in Solariy. He sat down with it at his desk and there in the dusk wrote on the flyleaf a few words, his name, the date; then slipped it in his pocket and went out.

No one was about. The sound of his steps on the path was the only sound. Crickets were silent, birds had left the air. The wind was down and the sky dark except for a green streak over San Givan, the last of daylight. As he brought his boat out and set off

56

westward, skirting the shore, it was so quiet that he heard across the breadth of the lake the remote music of the waterfall at Evalde. Then a mutter of thunder; then the first, huge whisper of rain on the slopes across the lake. The sail went slack. The twilight seemed all at once to give place to black night: the noise grew and grew, he felt rain on his hands, on his face, and then the storm was on him, dark and stiff as all the trees of the forests, a roar of rain, a wall of wind, lightning, thunder echoing redoubled off the water. The boom swept right across as Falkone jibbed like mad and ran in towards shore. It took all his strength to hold the wet sail, on which the wind pushed with demented violence; he could not bring the boat back against the wind, and now she bucked and heeled till the sail touched the water. In a half-lull he got the sail down and got out the oars. His clothes clung to him like silk, his hands were so cold with rain and so stiff from fighting the sail that he could hardly feel their grip on the oars. He rowed into the storm, getting through it if he could not harness it, defeated, immensely happy.

On the marble steps of Valtorsa he took off his hat, poured the water off the brim, got his breath for a minute, and knocked. The Valtorskars' old servant opened the door and stared in wonder. "Are you drooned, Dom Itaal?" he said at last. "Come in! Come in!"

Count Orlant was shouting from the front room in his unexpectedly strong voice, "Hoy, who's there? That you, Rodenne? What the devil sent you out in this storm?" He came into the hall. Itale would not come in, saying he was too wet and had to get back home, so Count Orlant wished him good luck and goodbye there beside the coatracks, earnestly shaking his wet hand while Itale clutched the *Vita Nova* in the other. He had turned to take his leave when Piera appeared. "You're going, Itale?" she said. Her face was bright and startled. The old servant drew back, and she came to the doorway where Itale stood with the rain and wind behind him.

"I wanted to give you this." He held out the book. "I wanted to give you something."

She took the book, did not look at it, but at him. "Did you come in Falkone?"

"Aye, nearly turned her over." He smiled self-deriding, exulting. The wind blew in past him, making Piera hug her arms to her sides.

"I must say goodbye, Piera."

"Will you never come back?"

"I'll come back."

She put out her hand, he took it; their eyes met; she smiled.

"Goodbye, Itale."

"Goodbye."

She did not move to close the door but stood within the doorway looking at the rain and flashing darkness where he had gone, till old Givan bumbled up and shut the door. "Look there, that rain, not stopped yet, crazy to take a boat out in such a storm."

Piera went down the hall, looked in the living room; her father and Auntie were ensconced there, with yarn-skein and astronomical chart. She slipped upstairs to her own room. Curtains hid the darkness, the candlelight was golden and serene; but she heard the sound of the rain, the sound of Itale's voice. He had been wet with rain, wet through, his hand strong and cold. Had he actually come? She shivered. The little book in her hand was cold and slightly damp.

She looked down at it and read the title, *The New Life*. She turned a few pages and saw prose, full of thereasmuches and wherefores, and verse: "Of Love so sweetly speaking that all my will is his. . . ." The book opened of itself to the flyleaf and she held it closer to the candle to read what was written there.

"Here begins the new life."
Piera Valtorskar from Itale Sorde, August 5th, 1825.

She sat looking at the words, written clear and black, the capital S blurred from hasty blotting or the rain; she smiled at last as she had smiled at him, and bent her head, and kissed his name.

PART TWO

Exiles

I

The mountains lay far behind, lost long since beyond the hills and rivers and plains of the southwest, the clouds and weathers of the journey. The Southwestern Post was climbing into the hills of the Molsen Province, uncultivated, dull gold under a blue-grey August sky. "Five more miles to Fontanasfaray," said the handsome, swagbellied driver. "The grand duchess comes to Fontanasfaray every August to take the waters."

"How far is it from the city?" asked the young provincial gentleman on the box.

"Sixteen miles, eight with the brakes on. We won't see West Gate much before nightfall."

The horses, heavy, gleaming greys, pulled effortlessly; a slow mile went by. Itale pulled his hat over his eyes against the warm morning sun and dozed. The horses pulled, the high coach creaked and swayed.

"Village of Kolpera," the coachman pointed out. Kolpera was a humble cluster of huts off the road on a high slope.

"Looks like sheep country," Itale said.

"I wouldn't know," the coachman replied with disdain; I am

61

from the city, I know nothing and care nothing about sheep, said his manner; and Itale, rebuked, stretched out his legs and gazed at the great lonely hills where, sure enough, far away and like a cloud-shadow on the tawny slope, he made out a flock of sheep.

Fontanasfaray was a cool, rich town high up in the hills. The inside passengers took lunch in the Park-Restaurant; Itale, who had refused to borrow money from his uncle or to take more than twenty kruner from the estate cashbox, and that as a loan, bought a roll at a bakery and ate it by himself in the park in the shade of the elms, watching the fancy rigs go by on Gulhelm Street. He finished his roll and was hungry. Through summery leaf-dappled light he saw a low foreign chaise coming, drawn by matched bays. In the chaise was a parasol and in the warm white shadow of the parasol a face was turned towards him, a long bored face with heavy lips and tired eyes, so familiar that Itale expected her to speak to him, which cousin was she?— The chaise passed, the parasol became a white blot down the dappled street. Itale brushed crumbs off his waistcoat. "Well, so that's the grand duchess," he said to himself, and felt unspeakably mournful and insignificant.

The coach set off with new horses and several new passengers. One of these Itale had seen on Gulhelm Street, bowing to the grand duchess' chaise, a young man elegantly dressed, with a pale, handsome, heavy face. He sat up outside with Itale and made conversation, chattering along so amiably that Itale soon forgot to act sophisticated, and began to enjoy himself. A little cautious, for he was not used to talking with strangers, he listened more than he spoke; this pleased his companion, who was not much in demand as a talker among his own associates. In their mutual appreciation they introduced themselves: Sorde, Paludeskar. As soon as the names were spoken each must perform a little silent guesswork and assessment, Itale wondering which rank of the nobility his new friend might belong to, Paludeskar deciding that although the young provincial was a commoner and had a hat which looked as though he had gone fishing with it, he was quite safely a gentleman. And it was very pleasant to talk to someone who knew so little about everything, and never set him straight. He talked on, and Itale listened, and each was grateful to the other.

The coach came at five o'clock to the summit of the hills, and Itale saw for the first time the broad sweep of the river valley to the distant eastern range, the shining curve of the Molsen through it, and, hazy and glimmering in the low warm light, the city on the river's bend. They were some miles from its outskirts. The pale hills behind them were silent, a pale sky arched overhead. The city slept in its wide valley in the afternoon sunlight, indistinct, beautiful, unutterably calm. Paludeskar smiled with proprietary pleasure, glancing at Itale's intent gazing face.

"Is that the Roukh?"

He pointed to a building that bulked large in bluish shadow over the vague surrounding streets, in the southwest quarter of the city.

"Right. There's the Sinalya, at the edge of that green bit, that must be the park, the Eleynaprade."

The Sinalya Palace was the residence of the reigning grand-ducal family; the kings of Orsinia had lived in the Roukh Palace.

"That must be the cathedral," Itale said, and his voice caught, for the spires rising above the golden mass and shadow of the city were its center both in place and in the passage of centuries. "Right," said Paludeskar, "and south of it there, that's River Quarter, nobody lives there; north of it the Old Quarter, that's where everybody lives. Is that my house? Can't be sure. There's the opera house, see the dome by the river?" But the coach, descending, entered a pass between high hills, and the view was lost.

It reappeared at intervals, each time nearer and more complex, as the road wound down. Their last sight of the city as a whole was when the valley was vague, the eastern hills had dimmed away, and lights were beginning to glimmer through the grey haze. They changed horses at Kolonnarmana, supped there, and in the warm dusk set off again, rolling easily on a smooth road, the glow of the city under its haze brightening always in the sky before them. Exalted by the darkness and warmth, the wind and movement of the ride, the great presence of the city awaiting them, the two young men talked from their souls.

"The important thing," Itale said, "is a force inside you, that belongs to you alone. It is yourself, actually, all that makes you a self, a man. Once you've found it, that force or will or need, whatever it is, then all you have to do is obey it—stay on the road it takes you."

"But if you can't find the road. . . ."

"You can if you want to."

"How many people really want to?"

"To find their destiny? To be themselves? Surely everyone does?"

"Takes work," said Paludeskar.

"Well, it does. And it's true most people don't even seem to try. They do what comes next, or what's expected of them, and get lost in a meaningless tangle of—of desires, frivolities, contingencies," said Itale with an abolishing wave of his hand. "Why don't they simply do what's necessary?"

"Easier not to."

"But how stupid it is. Even if you sit in a chair for ten years still the years go by. So why not get up and walk, make it a journey? I used to envy adults when I was a boy, I thought they were all going somewhere, but now I see most of them not really going anywhere, never getting home, lost in eating and sleeping and talking and visiting and meaningless work—not the poor of course, I mean people free to do as they please—they do nothing, they lose their souls out of sheer carelessness!"

"Civilisation's wasted on humanity," said Paludeskar. "If I had it to hand out I'd give it to the bees. Industrious little bastards."

"I don't know if it's wasted on us, but most of us seem to waste it."

"I used to think I'd like to add my bit. But I don't know. I suppose I really haven't anything to add."

"You do," Itale said, and Paludeskar replied with equal simplicity, "I know. But it's getting away from me. I'm not religious, you know, and all that, but I'm going to be twenty-five in November— I'd like to— You know, to think that I was going to do something worth doing— Before the end."

"That's it, that's it," Itale said.

"Come and stay the night, I want to talk more about this," Paludeskar said earnestly, and Itale agreed. The coach was among the suburbs of Krasnoy, and in ten minutes more it came to a halt inside the West Gate. Stiff, bemused, disjointed, its passengers descended into the coachyard of Tiypontiy Street under the dark looming inn buildings. Glare and shadow, neighing of horses and clatter of ironshod hoofs on stone, clatter of voices, moths swarming at smoking lamps, smells of leather, horsedung, sweat, hot stone, the streets of stone.

In the cab both regretted the invitation which had seemed so natural on the coach. They said no more about destiny and civilisation; each looked out his window. The cab stopped before a handsome house on a wide, quiet street. As Paludeskar took him up the steps Itale heard a great bell striking the hour across the dark roofs and streets, a deep, quiet voice in the restless air of the city night.

He was handed over to a servant, taken up imposing stairs and down a long passage to a room with a curtained bed, marble fireplace, Turkish carpet, red-draped windows, and a very large painting of a racehorse with a fat round body and tiny head and feet. As the one servant departed a second one arrived, carrying his valise. "Thank you," Itale said, relieved to see the familiar object, an anchor in a sea of strangeness. His effort to get the valise away from the man was foiled with skill, courtesy, and ease; after that defeat there was no hope of making the man go away. He was French and middle-aged; as he unpacked Itale's valise he intimated that his name was Robert, that he was M le baron's man, that Itale must change into his other coat, that a clean shirt was also desirable, that a gentleman did not put on his own shirt, that Robert was perfectly aware that Itale was young, poor, provincial, and possessed no articles of toilet besides a hairbrush, but did not hold it against him—some of this in words, some by other means. "If monsieur will permit," he said, circling behind Itale at the looking glass, and in five hypnotic motions transformed Itale's cravat into a model of austere symmetry. "It is the best knot, but not every man can wear it so, it requires the long face," he said, admiring his handiwork so honestly that Itale warmed to him at last and let him help him into his coat without a struggle.

Then he had to go downstairs alone.

The long, bright drawing-room was a confusion of people, light-coated men, light-gowned women. He did not see Paludeskar anywhere. A tall, fair woman glanced at him frowning. He dared not move farther forward, he dared not go back. There he stood, like a rock. Near him a group broke out laughing at the end of a story, and he smiled too, until he found he was smiling. Another tall, fair woman in violet was approaching him, or was it the same one? She was coming straight at him. He looked away. He began to edge backwards towards the hall.

"Mr Sorde?"

He bowed.

"I am Luisa Paludeskar."

He bowed.

She looked at him coolly; made up her mind; and took him to present him to her mother.

The young baroness was robust and handsome like her brother; the old baroness, sitting near a gold-encrusted Erard piano with two other ladies, looked pinched, sick, and sour. She said how do you do to Itale and had no more to say to him. Baroness Luisa took him on to a side room, where to his relief he found Paludeskar devouring cold chicken and champagne, and was invited to do the same. While he ate he managed to shake off the paralysis of total self-consciousness and make some observation of other people. He found that nobody was wearing trousers at all like his, and that conversation with these people was very difficult, as they all spoke quickly and bounced on from one subject to the next like rabbits. "Will you be long in Krasnoy, Mr Sorde?" asked a man to whom he had just been introduced and whose name he had instantly mislaid, and before he had decided how to answer the other bounced on, "Absolutely dead just now, few remaining fragments of civilisation are gathered in this room. And the opera's not opening until November."

"I hope to see the opera," said Itale, and was able to take a deep breath, having produced a comprehensible if not dazzling sentence.

"You're musical?" asked the other man—was his name Hacheskar? Harreskar? — "It's not precisely Paris, as you can imagine, and old Montini lost his high A last season, but it does very well."

"Paolina," Itale brought out, the name of a local diva whom he had heard praised at Solariy. "Aha," said Helleskar—that was it, Helleskar, but baron? count? prince?— "have you heard Paolina? is it she that brings you here?"

Itale stared at him. What was he to say— "No, I am here to subvert the government"? He said, flatly, "No."

Helleskar smiled. He was pale, like Paludeskar, but his figure was slight and his face fine-drawn. "I'm sorry, I'm always boring people with music," he said, and though Itale appreciated that goodnatured courtesy he was unable to respond to it.

"Luisa," said Helleskar, a little later in the other room, "who is your brother's new friend?"

"I have no idea, George."

"Literary," Helleskar proposed.

Luisa Paludeskar shrugged.

"Epic poems . . . Or, no; I know. He is planning to found a clandestine journal, full of long quotations from Schiller."

"No idea at all."

"He was simply found on the coach, like someone else's hat? He might be a spy for Gentz, he might steal the silver. I had no idea Enrike was so rash. But then, no spy could possibly tie his cravat that well; at least not a spy for Austria. It must be Schiller after all."

"Introduce him to Amadey, then."

"Is he here? How is he?"

"Wretched, of course. I don't know why he doesn't leave that woman. There's your friend, take him over to Amadey. Mr Sorde!"

Itale, startled, looked round. His eyes met Luisa Paludeskar's, and for an instant she too looked startled, taken off guard; then her face closed and looked bored, even rancorous.

"Count Helleskar has been speculating that your propensities are literary," she said, drawling, and Helleskar broke in: "I leave speculation to bankers, baronina, I never go further than entertaining fancies. I have a bad habit of deciding what people ought to do without consulting them; I had rather decided you ought to publish."

Defend yourself, Mr Sorde."

"Is it an accusation?" Itale asked naively.

Helleskar laughed. "We'll have to consult Estenskar. Is literature a crime, a fault, or merely a misfortune? The—"

"Estenskar? Amadey Estenskar?"

"You stand self-accused, Mr Sorde," Helleskar said. "He's here tonight; may I introduce you?"

"He has no—that is, there's no— I don't—"

"Come along," the count said, and Itale meekly came, obeying Helleskar's flawless self-assurance. But halfway across the room his protest became audible again. "Count," he said earnestly, "I can't intrude on Mr Estenskar—"

"You set him higher than the rest of us," Helleskar said, with his ironic smile. "Quite right. Come on." He led on. "He'll be in here no doubt, the mausoleum, library I mean. Refurbished catacomb. There he is." And bringing Itale to a wiry, red-haired, white-faced man who stood reading in a corner of the bookcases, he introduced them. "A fellow exile, Amadey," he said.

Estenskar had gained his fame with the publication of *The Torrents of Karesha*, when he was nineteen. His *Odes* and a novel had confirmed his reputation; at the age of twenty-four he was the best-known writer in his country, passionately reviled and praised, a stormbringer, one of those after whose passing things are not the same. "Very glad," he said in a dry voice. There was a pause. "You're from my part of the country?"

"From the Montayna."

"I see."

"What are you reading, Amadey? Herder. *Weh 'st mir!* Literature is a vast slough of German poets."

Estenskar shrugged. Itale observed the shrug with awe, and burned to go reread Herder as soon as possible; but as Helleskar continued to make conversation and Estenskar to cut it short, the talk did not grow more interesting. Of course there was no reason why a genius should converse with a flippant worldling like Count Helleskar. The genius' manners were disagreeable, but that was because he was so far above his company. All these

68

people did was gossip; Itale had listened now to a dozen conversations of gossip—as a matter of fact Estenskar was now embarked on some gossip, and apparently enjoying it. "A year in Paris couldn't civilise that ass," he was ending his tale, with an artificial, unpleasant tenor laugh, "nothing could." And Helleskar laughed and said, "Civilisation is wasted on humanity," and Itale struggled desperately to swallow a yawn. He looked up from the struggle to find Estenskar's cold gaze on him.

"Did you know about Adanskar's new literary magazine, Amadey? To which only noblemen may contribute?"

Estenskar laughed his high, loud ha-ha-ha. "What next?"

"The name—that's the beauty of it. He discussed it with me at length. Pegasus, Aurora, all nine muses, couldn't use them; Greek, low connotations. Tried French: *Revue du Haut monde*. Aha, I say, that'll put that new *Revue des deux mondes* in its place. No, no, can't have that, low connotations again. Then the divine afflatus swept into him before my very eyes, and he said, 'I shall call it *The Journal of Nobility and Genius!*'"

"My God, what a fool the man is."

"He'll do it, too, you know. You must contribute."

"I'd do it in order to lose him his Censor's permit."

"It's not that bad, surely," Helleskar said, with a very slight change of tone. Estenskar shrugged and was silent. "You still haven't got the printing permit for the new book?" Helleskar said, and again Estenskar shrugged; he stuck Herder back on the bookshelf, looked at his fingernails, turned away, then swung back and burst out shrilly, "I've been trying to get it for six weeks now. They want changes. One of the poems cannot to be published at all. Why? Why not? It's about listening to music, what in the name of God is political about that, because it's music does it have to be the Marseillaise? Oh, no, Mr Estenskar, you don't understand—I don't understand my own work, but they do—it's not the subject of the poem that is undesirable, but the meter. The meter! The meter! By the bowels of Christ what is radical about iambic tetrameter? Do you know? Can you imagine what he said? It's a *national* meter—common in songs, popular— dangerous—and then my ode, the bad one, you know, 'To the Youth of My Country,' you know—it was, by God, it's in iambic

69

tetrameter, and I can't go around reminding people of it. So this poem can't be published, the book can't have the Censor's permit so long as it's there. And my friend at the Bureau, my good friend Censor Goyne, who can't spell 'recommend,' Goyne takes the trouble to recommend improvements. All I have to do is add an extra foot to each line, just a word or two, he showed me how to do it, really very simple, he said. They banned what I've written, now they rewrite what I write!"

The eyes in the white face were round, yellowish, glaring. Itale thought of the half-grown hawks he had tamed, their rage and resistance that only exhaustion could control; and even in defeat they would cry out in their shrill terrible voices, defeated, not tamed.

"You have endured six years of this," Helleskar said. "How do you have the courage to go through it all again!"

"I don't. When I get this book in press, I'm done. Going home. I can't fight to try to get it distributed. It won't be. I will stay just long enough to be sure the text isn't changed, to keep Goyne's improvements out of it. I don't know why I bother even with that. What difference will it make?"

"A great deal, Mr Estenskar," Itale said, stammering. "Because the book will be printed by the clandestine press—I've never seen your books but in the clandestine editions—"

"Victory without profit," the poet said drily.

"No man, not even a genius, can win this kind of battle unsupported. If there were a group, a real group, with a publication, a journal, ready to come up against the Bureau of Censorship every day, for every word, a steady united pressure— And if the Estates are convened, censorship will be an issue—"

"I see it's true you've only been here two hours," Estenskar said, turning back to the bookcase. He scanned it as if seeking a title while he spoke. "A group? . . . Literary men are afraid of jail, as a rule. . . . As for getting help from the politicians, I suppose you're joking."

Itale was paralysed; Helleskar said, as easily as ever, "Why so, Amadey? If the Estates meet, there will be some new men in town."

70

"You're in an optimistic fit tonight?"

"I am an optimistic man. I merely keep it to myself so that I won't get laughed at. As 'To the Youth of My Country' got laughed at, for example."

"And rightly. It's the stupidest thing I ever wrote. I suppose Mr Sorde disagrees."

Perhaps it was invitation, but Itale took it as reproof, understanding only that his enthusiasm had been gall to Estenskar. "How can I argue with you?" he said almost inaudibly.

Helleskar frowned. "You wrote it; let us read it, Amadey. Allow us our little privileges. They don't encroach on yours. I believe we need a change of muse. Luisa's in a vile mood tonight, she always plays well in a vile mood, shall we go demand some Mozart?"

Though enmeshed in self-castigation, Itale was vaguely aware that Helleskar had come to his defense, and in an equally vague persuasion of obligation followed the two back into the salon, though what he wanted was to get away from Estenskar before he antagonised his hero any further. Luisa Paludeskar agreed to play; he stood with the group around the piano. It was past midnight. He was worn out. The radiant music passed him by as so much noise. Helleskar and Baron Paludeskar talked beside him; he did not listen, and he would not open his mouth again, not if he were damned for it. Why am I here, he thought, what am I doing here? Why did I leave home?

When she had played what was asked of her Luisa Paludeskar sat on at the piano listening to the others talk. Every now and then she glanced up at the tall, stiff, speechless young man. There he stood with his chin stuck into his collar; the epitome of boorish, provincial, male complacency. She would have liked to kick him.

"Who is that fellow, baronina?"

"Enrike found it on the coach. I don't plan to keep it around long."

Estenskar smiled disagreeably. "He hardly seemed to partake of the *ton*," he said. He was on the attack again. Luisa, who loved battles, rose to the challenge, and performed a rapid outflanking manoeuvre: she smiled straight at him, and said, "You're not really going off east, are you, Amadey?"

"I haven't decided."

"What is there to decide? Is there anything in the Polana besides the east wind and sheep? Will the sheep listen to you? I know we're sheep, to you, but we are attentive sheep—adoring sheep—your own woolly flock—"

"Sheep's clothing."

"That's you, the wolf. The Polana wolf. Don't run away, Amadey; not now."

"I'm not running away. I'm going home."

"'Home!'" She played a light derisive arpeggio. "We have a 'home' too, you know, up in the Sovena. I know all about rain and wind and mud and sheep and the neighbors' visits. They tell you hunting stories. How they shot the wolf. How they bagged three poets in the marsh last winter. . . ."

"I'll come back for your wedding."

"Oh indeed! My wedding with whom?"

"George, of course."

"How silly you are. I can't marry an old shoe."

"If the shoe fits. . . ."

"Always twist the knife a little before you remove it. No, I think I shall marry a total stranger, someone found on a coach."

"Why?"

"Because there would be a few weeks before he knew how to hurt me very much—before he learned where the nerves are. Unless he was a poet, of course. But you mustn't leave Krasnoy, Amadey. What shall I do without you? without my daily anti-opium?"

"I wish I had fallen in love with you, Luisa."

"Yes; but you didn't."

She looked up into the man's unhappy face, and smiled again.

When he got to bed at two-thirty, Itale could not sleep. The Mozart sonata to which he had not listened rang note for note in his head, the red-curtained bed swayed like a coach at the trot, his ears were full of voices and his eyes of faces; he lay and twitched and turned. The deep, soft bell told the quarters and the hours, three o'clock, four o'clock, over the dark roofs, the dark streets, the endless houses where two hundred thousand people slept and he among them awake, a prisoner.

II

Robert the man-servant waked him, late in the morning; he could not elude assistance in getting dressed. He found his way through the huge, cold house to the breakfast room. The baron was already there, and the sister soon arrived. The two young men were stiff and shy with each other. Itale remarked that it was hot, Enrike that it was damned foggy, and they got no further. Luisa, dressed very plainly in brown, seemed to have set aside her arrogant manner with her evening dress. She was pleasant and gracious, without affectations, and within a few minutes Itale found himself almost at ease talking with her. But she was beautiful, more beautiful than he had realised last night, more beautiful than any woman he had ever spoken to; and he realised as they talked that she was younger than he, twenty at most, which by adding youth to her opulence of beauty, wealth, and wit cowed him, making him feel a hopeless clod. And the brother glowered across the table. It was a relief when the meal was done at last.

Frenin had been living in the city for a month, and had sent Itale his address. Itale asked Enrike where the street was. "What? Never heard of it," the baron growled. "Going off, are you? Can't stay? No? Well. Glad, very glad."

When Itale had escaped, the baron followed his sister up to the music room. "You hear that, Lulu? He's going to some damned street in the River, Somebody's Tears Street, now what the devil, coming all the way from the damned mountains. I thought he was a gentleman, yesterday."

"He is, don't be stupid, Harry."

"But nobody lives in a place like that!"

"Students—"

73

"Students! Exactly!"

She knew what was upsetting her brother. Through boredom and a dim sense of shame at his uselessness, Enrike was trying to secure a minor diplomatic post. He had decided that his new acquaintance was politically suspect, therefore not to be cultivated; but he was ashamed of his own motives, and preferred to act the snob. All this was clear to Luisa. Her boredom was far more drastic than her brother's, her ambitions clearer, and she set herself up as a conscious enemy of hypocrisy in all its forms.

"You're afraid you've entertained Robespierre unawares," she said, "poor Harry!"

"But you can see that I can't afford to associate with these patriot fellows. I made a mistake. I own up to it. So all I'm asking is that you don't . . . take him up—make a pet of him out of curiosity the way you do—"

"Make a pet of him! a bit like making a pet of a cart-horse."

"Yes, well, exactly, he's just not quite our sort. It seemed all right on the coach. But he doesn't belong here. So that's all right, we just won't see him again."

"But of course I asked him to dinner tonight."

Enrike breathed heavily, defeated once again.

"He hasn't anywhere to stay; and if he stays here of course we have to feed him; but I'm sure it will do no harm. No one is coming except Raskayneskar."

"Oh my God!" Enrike cried. "You can't—you can't have him here with Raskayneskar! Luisa!" But he knew as he spoke that she would do just as she pleased, just as she always did, and that whether he fretted or shouted, it would make no difference at all.

Meanwhile Itale had set off at random into the warm morning. Sunlight breaking through the mist of the river valley gilded the housefronts, the roofs, the double spire of the Cathedral of St Theodora, only a few streets away. He made for the cathedral. It was not as easy to get to as it looked. Though rarely losing sight of the spires he involved himself in the crisscross of broad, similar avenues of the Old Quarter, took a wrong turning into Sorden Street and wandered down it between palaces of the seventeenth and sixteenth centuries rearing their elegant arrogant façades one against the other. From that sunless, silent grandeur he emerged into the glare and bustle of the Great

Market. Men bent double, hauling carts, yelled at him to make way, heavy-shouldered horses pulled their wagons across his path, women selling leeks and cabbages shouted at him to buy leeks and cabbages, young women lugging sacks of gleaming vegetables jostled him with the sacks, old women lunged past him to make a bargain, fishmongers waved eels in his face and to avoid the eels he backed into beef carcases hung round the butchers' stalls amidst shrilling swarms of flies. Portacheyka's weekly market would not have filled a corner of it, it went on for blocks sprawling, displaying, hauling, carrying, bargaining, arguing, selling, buying, stinking, shining, shouting in the young heat of the August sun, and over it all, against the large, quiet morning sky, rose the dun spires of the cathedral.

He made it safe to Cathedral Square at last. A few old people sat on benches on the west side under plane trees thick with summer dust. He stopped in the middle of the square, letting desultory cabs and purposeful walkers pass round him, and gawped at the cathedral of Krasnoy, the heavy, complex towers, the leap of the spires, the triple portal of carven saints and kings, the great bulk buoyant and serene as a ship under sail. He stood and looked, and the old men on the benches looked at him; they had seen the cathedral before. At last he went forward and entered the church under the north portal, under St Roch, auxiliary patron of the city of Krasnoy, smiling in the ogived shadow his stiff, kind, four-hundred-year-old smile.

As soon as he came inside the cathedral he felt himself at home. It was home. His family, his people, had lived there for eight or nine centuries. Like the churches of the Montayna the cathedral was dark, bare, its high barrel vaults leaving a great deal of room for God. It was as simple and purposeful as a fort. Low mass was in progress. Lost in the airy darkness of the nave a few people, faceless, separate, similar, knelt on the bare patterned pavement. Itale joined them. The priest droned, like the old priest of St Anthony of Malafrena, "Credo in unoom Deoom," and the little old women in black shawls whispered, "Omni-potentem," and like an unheeding angel or thunder among mountains the organ whispered on above them, rehearsing the high mass to be sung on St Roch's Day.

Itale did not stay long. Reassured, yet restless, he went back out into the sun's heat and brightness as the great bell struck ten, vibrating in the stone and in the blood. There was the city, the traffic, the faces of strangers, the streets of stone. He put on his hat and set off striding into River Quarter, without the least idea where he was going.

Few cities in 1825 had much of a sewer system; this oldest quarter of Krasnoy had none at all, beyond paved or unpaved trenches in the middle of the narrow streets that wound down towards the river. The stench of River Quarter was a mighty presence in itself, more impressive even than the steep darkness of the streets between houses toppling their upper storeys across the way as if in conspiracy against the sky, and the noise of voices and the constant press and passage of people around the tenements. Out of these choked alleys shot up the fragile towers of old churches; from the noisy crowding at a ragged street-market one came suddenly into a silent square, to a covered fountain brimming with cool water and typhoid fever, and looked up to see on one hand the cathedral spires, on the other the pointed windows of the university on its hill, another world. In such a square Itale stopped. He was frightened. He was lost, had lost himself in the streets, the crowding houses, the dank archways leading to brawling courtyards, the voices, the smells, the swarms of children, women, men all nameless, so that he was nameless, knowing none of them, lost. He stood there holding onto his left wrist with his right hand, combatting panic. He sat down on the stone seat by the wellhead and gazed persistently at the pavement at his feet. On one stone was a smear and curl of human excrement. He gazed at it; at the stones beneath and around it, square bluish cobbles grained and glazed with dirt; at the thread of water gleaming in the jointure between two of them. That is all here, he thought; I am here; I cannot be lost. At last he looked up, looking slowly round him, and discovered that he shared the bench with another man.

This one wore broken shoes without stockings and some kind of coat or cape, shapeless and colorless, wrapped carefully around him despite the warmth. He was old, the skull showing in his face. Out of webbed sockets his eyes stared straight at Itale, a terrible stare, until Itale realised he was blind.

76

"Hello, granddad," he said huskily.

The old man munched and stared. Abruptly he spoke; Itale did not understand the wheezing voice and the strong dialect. "A long way from home," he seemed to have said.

"That's true. Do you know of a street called Magdalen's Tears, granddad?"

The old man went on staring, muttering, "Eya, eya, eya, eya. . . ." He stood up, gathering the decrepit coat around him. "Come on!" he said.

"Is it nearby?"

"Mallenastrada, how can I tell you, come on!" Wheezing and muttering but moving fairly quickly he set off down an alley, and Itale followed. Children screamed playing or fighting in a courtyard as they passed. The old man cursed at them and waved his hand muttering, "Had a stick, had a stick . . . Eya, eya, eya . . ." Evidently he had some sight, for he picked his way without hesitation, and kept closer to Itale's side than was agreeable to Itale, for he stank. He talked as they went, and Itale understood about half of it: he had been a tailor, till his eyes went bad and they turned him out of the shop, there was a brother-in-law who had done him wrong, a story about costs rising and shop rents; his voice cracked and grated, he chopped his rigid hands in the air and screamed, "Dirty Jews! Dirty Jews!" He felt or saw Itale sheering off from him and hurried his gait pathetically. "Almost there, young sir, almost there. That big church that's Sankestefan, the basilisk, now this way, young sir." They were at the base of the Hill of the University; streets shot up the hill in crazy angles and flights of steps. "Thought I was blind, eh, thought I was blind, eh!" The hobbling guide stopped. "This is it, Mallenastrada, this is it." The street name Frenin had sent was the Street of the Tears of St Magdalen; Itale could see no sign or token along the narrow way or at the corner, but he was ready to get free of the old man. He gave him a quarter-krune, putting it into the rigid hand; trying to get it into some pocket or hidingplace in his ragged coat the old man dropped it, and Itale picked it up for him, for he stood blind and groping, unable to bend down to the pavement, and his hand was too arthritic to close on the little coin.

Number 9, opposite the pawnshop, Frenin had written. There were no numbers, but there were two pawnshops. He tried across the way from the first one. A fat woman met him in the dark hall, which had a rich, sharp, feral stink of its own. She sent him up the stairs, which were alive with thin, scabby cats, all of them more or less white. He knocked on the door of the first landing, and Frenin opened it.

The square, hard face, the familiar voice saying his name, were a tremendous relief and pleasure. They embraced like brothers. "It's good to see you, it's good to see you, Givan!"

"Come on in." Frenin began to repress his own pleasure. "Don't let those damn cats in. Why didn't you write you were coming?"

"I came on the same coach the letter would have come on. Last night."

"Where are you staying?"

"Fellow I met on the coach. Paludeskar."

"In Roches Street? The rutabaga baron?"

"I don't know—"

"Well, you're certainly coming in at the top."

"I don't really know who they are. On the coach—"

"They're in Brelavay's scandal-sheet every issue."

"Brelavay's what?" Frenin's manner irritated Itale a little; like everybody here, he seemed to know everything.

"He's working for a weekly society tattler, the *Krasnoy Scurrility* he calls it. Money, mistress, our Tomas is doing well."

Frenin's tone was unpleasant.

"Big place you have here," Itale said. The room was low but long, and the almost complete lack of furniture made it seem vast.

"Four of these rooms. Dirt cheap, even for the River. It's too big, I'm getting out end of the month. Try this chair. The back falls off that one."

"What are you doing?"

"Odd jobs for a Catholic monthly, and reading proof for Rochoy, the publishers. I get by. What are your plans?"

"Find work, first."

"Work? What for?"

78

It seemed to Itale, perhaps unfairly, that Frenin's question was disingenuous.

"What does one generally work for?"

"Depends who one is."

"I have twenty-two kruner. That's who I am."

He felt himself to be disingenuous. But it was not easy to talk about not having money. He got up and wandered around the shabby room, looking out the windows. "Your windows could use a wash."

"No help from home, eh?"

"No."

Frenin, the son of a wealthy Solariy merchant, was as used to having cash in his pocket as Itale was, but he was also used to talking about money, both the having and the wanting, and that gave him now the advantage he always sought over his friend, and seldom gained.

"Your father doesn't approve of your coming here, I take it."

"Right."

"Is he an Austrianiser?"

"Not in the least."

"Family quarrel, eh?"

"It's immaterial, Givan."

"Twenty-two kruner, eh. About two weeks' worth. Well, what can you do?"

"What anybody else can do—how do I know?" Itale said. His anger satisfied Frenin, who dropped his cool superiority of manner and said with a grin, "All right, all right. Are you looking for a place to live, or have you settled down with the rutabaga queen?"

"I don't know—my bag's there— I don't want to stay there."

"Why not? It's free."

"I can't . . ." Itale waved his hands. "Footmen at breakfast."

"How's the young baroness at breakfast?"

"I don't know. Very polite. It's—" He waved his hands again. "I shouldn't be there."

Frenin grinned again. "Well, come here, if you like. It's not Roches Street, or an estate on Lake Malafrena; but then it only costs fifteen kruner a quarter. We can share for a bit."

"That is very good of you, Givan," Itale said with warmth and gratitude. His deafness to Frenin's gibes exasperated the latter and at the same time disarmed him. He had never succeeded in establishing between Itale and himself the social barrier that his jealousy asserted to be there. At the same time a barrier did exist between them, despite all Frenin's efforts to break through it: that of Itale's careless, impervious personal reserve. Itale would not allow him to humiliate either of them; his flashes of anger were not followed by any grudge or punishment; he offered a simple, steady friendship. Frenin wanted more of him, though he did not know what more. What good was friendship? He wanted to get at this defenseless man, understand him, change him, and could not do it. It was perhaps for Itale's sake, to keep in touch with Itale, that Frenin had conceived the plan of coming to Krasnoy.

"We'll settle it with the Catwoman. She was downstairs, wasn't she? Mrs Rosa she calls herself. Listen, Itale. I've been here two months and nothing has happened—nothing is happening. There is no radical movement here."

Itale sat down at the table which, with three decrepit chairs, constituted the furniture of the room. "There has to be," he said. "I haven't found it."

"But the Cafe Illyrica—"

"Old men and fifth-rate poets. And Austrian agents."

"There are secret societies—"

"There were; they're dead. Years dead. The Friends of the Constitution, yes, that's still going, a lot of retired army men in the east, in the Kesena and Sovena, but not here. Nothing here. Unless you count Amiktiya."

"Well, then it's up to us! A publication—what we talked about in Solariy."

"What's the good? A literary monthly—"

"Who won our bet concerning the power of the written word?"

"Who got put under house arrest?"

"Look here, 1789 didn't rise unpremeditated from the breast of the people, it was the *writers*—"

"All right, but we haven't got any Rousseaus here."

80

"How do we know? Besides, we do have Rousseau, and Desmoulins, and all the French and English and American writing of the last hundred years to draw on. Why else is the government so afraid of print? Listen, I found something Gentz said recently, I've taken it for my guide, my inspiration—he said, 'As a preventive measure against the abuses of the press, absolutely nothing should be printed for years. With this maxim as a rule we should soon get back to God and the Truth.'"

"God and the Truth," Frenin repeated softly in awed disgust, and they were both silent a minute. The opinion of the Chief of the Austrian Imperial Police was undeniably impressive.

"All right," said Frenin. "Assume a journal is the thing. How do we finance it, first, and who'll dare print it, second?"

"That's what we're here to find out."

"All right. Let's go meet some people. . . ."

Itale got back to the Paludeskar house at six, having spent the afternoon with Frenin at the Cafe Illyrica, which despite Frenin's strictures was still, and would be for twenty-five years more, a meetingplace for radicals of all degrees. There they had met their friend Veyeskar from Solariy, a dark young man named Karantay who wrote stories, a pair of Greek refugees, a ranting alcoholic old poet who talked of his mistress Liberty, a group of students; the talk had been of Greece. As Itale walked up Roches Street he was telling himself that if nothing could be done here he would go to Greece, as Lord Byron had gone, to the plains of Marathon where they still laid down their lives for freedom. He was drunk with Greece and strong coffee and strong ideas, and was not sobered even by entering the large, rich, cold house. He strode up the marble staircase as if he owned the place, and hearing music in the room at the top of the stairs stopped a moment to listen, as if the music was for him.

"Mr Sorde," said Luisa Paludeskar at the piano, another splendid piece of gold and rosewood like the one downstairs, the evening sunlight striking gold through the long windows across her hair, music rippling under her long hands.

"Baronina," he said with untroubled resolution, "I must be leaving. May I thank you for your kindness, and hope that I will have the privilege of making some return for it." The formal provincial turns of speech came ready to his tongue and he never wondered what conceivable return of hospitality he could make from a cat-haunted tenement in the River Quarter; he still spoke with his feet planted on the shores of Malafrena.

"But you're not leaving, Mr Sorde? We thought you would make our house yours for a few days at least!"

She seemed dismayed, disappointed; he grew embarrassed. "It's very good of you, baronina. An old friend of mine is here, he wants to put me up—"

"But you can't always desert new friends for old ones, and Enrike will be very disappointed."

"It's very good of you—"

"We know people, quantities of people, I had thought we really might be of some use to you."

"It's very—" He had said it was very good of her twice already. "You're very kind, baronina, but I—" He did not know what to say; his resolution dissolved like wet sugar.

"At least you will dine with us tonight? I do claim that much!"

"Of course, with great pleasure." Damn the woman! As he went down the hall the house resounded to the abrupt brilliant harmonies, played very deftly, of a Mozart presto.

After her talk of quantities of people, he had expected another large party, and was surprised when he went down to dinner (in his black coat well brushed by Robert) to find a *partie carrée*: himself, Luisa and Enrike Paludeskar, and a Count Raskayneskar. Baroness Paludeskar, a lady in waiting to the grand duchess, was dining at the palace. This dinner was, presumably, in Luisa's style: intimate, elegant. The four French doors of the dining room stood open to the August night. Stars hung thick in the black sky, an intermittent wind moved in the shrubbery of the walled garden; the murmur of a fountain, the stir of leaves, the smell of damp earth and roses, the unease and subtle darkness of a summer night all entered and mixed strangely with the conversation at the candle-lit table. Luisa, at the head of the table, was so beautiful, so much more beautiful even than she had appeared last night or in the morning, that Itale was afraid of her; he vaguely felt himself to be in the presence of a dangerous force of nature, a forest fire or a maelstrom; it occurred to him that when poets called a woman a goddess sometimes they meant exactly what they said. Enrike wore an anxious, surly look and said very little, and Luisa and Raskayneskar ignored him.

Raskayna was one of the great holdings in Val Altesma, thirty miles southwest from Malafrena. Itale knew the name well. He knew nothing about the landholder, and it was evident that if Raskayneskar had ever visited his estate it had been as no more than a visitor. He was entirely urbane. He was a well-kept man of forty or so, with long, liver-colored lips, a high forehead, and fine dark eyes.

"So!" he said, leaning back a little, when they had come to the sweet wines. "It's quite certain the Estates will meet."

"Lot of talk," Enrike growled.

"Not at all—unless you're referring to the meetings themselves, in which case I agree with you! But they will be convened. Cornelius will announce it next month, I fancy, and the great event will come off in the autumn of '27. Ha, ha, ha! do you know what the emperor said about these diets and assemblies? It rather puts them into perspective. He said, 'I have my Estates, and if they go too far I snap my fingers at them and send them home. . . .'"

"Just as Louis XVI did," said Itale to his plate.

"Oh, come," the count said, genial, "the Estates General of France are one thing, our little Assembly is quite another. Its convention is merely an act of courtesy on the emperor's part."

"If the Assembly is rude to him, will he snap his fingers?" Luisa asked.

"Yes, of course; that is, Cornelius will do it for him, he needn't be bothered himself."

"Has Cornelius that authority?" asked Itale.

"As the prime minister of the head of the state, the grand duchess, I should think so. Possibly she'd have to do it herself."

"Under the Charter of 1412 the Assembly is subject only to the king. There's nothing that subjects them to the orders of a duchess or her minister."

83

"Nothing but the Austrian army," Raskayneskar said mildly.

"If the grand duchess called in the Austrian army to close the National Assembly, that would constitute invasion. We are an ally and protectorate of the Empire, we are not an Austrian province."

"Paper truths, Mr Sorde. The Austrian army is here, now, controlling our provincial militias; no Assembly is going to try to lead us into a revolt, or a war if you prefer, against the most powerful state in Europe. The idea is laughable."

"That depends on one's sense of humor," Luisa observed.

"True, very true," said Raskayneskar, who never contradicted directly, but went at it round about. "When the balance of peace is so delicate, when there is the possibility of intervention by one of the great states, Russia perhaps—it's not so much laughable as terrifying. The war years all over again. One can only respect Metternich for having, in these past ten years, made such a chance remote, a fantasy, rather than an imminent threat. An incredible man, Metternich! He bears the weight of Europe on his shoulders."

"If he put it down it might turn out to be able to walk by itself," Itale said, with a slight tremor in his voice, but clearly. Enrike, whose sense of humor was simple, gave a snort of laughter, and then shut his eyes and turned red.

"To walk straight into war, I fear," Raskayneskar said.

"I'd prefer to walk into war than to be carried into slavery."

"My dear young man," said Raskayneskar, who had no desire to quarrel at Luisa Paludeskar's table, "I don't think you know much about war; and I fear slavery has become a fashionable word and so lost its significance. I suppose a black African on a plantation in the Carolinas is a slave, poor brute, but his situation has very little in common with yours or mine."

"I don't know," Itale said innocently; "the American slave can't vote, has no representative in the government, and must get his owner's permission to learn to read or write, or publish, or speak in public, doesn't he? If he does any of that without permission he can be locked up for life without trial. I'm not sure how far our situations differ in those respects; of course we are allowed to wear frock coats."

There was only the slightest pause before Count Raskayneskar added, "And to read Jean-Jacques Rousseau."

"If we can find a clandestine edition."

The count laughed, indulgently, the laugh of a statesman addressing enthusiastic youth. Enrike shut his eyes again. Luisa laughed very softly, watching Itale. Then she turned to Raskayneskar and said, with all the manner of a hostess easing over a difficult moment, "Which reminds me, count, I am relying upon you for the Paris journals, you must not let me down!" —to which Raskayneskar replied courteously as ever, with a somewhat pinched smile. He cared nothing at all for Itale's opinions, but he cared a good deal for Luisa's opinion; and he knew now that he had lost a battle that he had not thought worth fighting.

The next day he told a fellow bureaucrat in the Ministry of Finance that the convocation of the Estates was not entirely an empty gesture, since certain fashionable salons were openly cultivating patriotic sentiments. "Silly fads," the colleague said, but Raskayneskar, pinching his long lips together significantly, murmured, "National pride. . . ." as if it were the name of a horse he thought of backing.

Itale left the Paludeskars as early as he could decently do so, and found his way past the cathedral, around the Hill of the University, behind the basilica of St Stephen, through the frightening crowds and more frightening emptinesses of the River Quarter, to the narrow street where he was to live. He went to bed, and lay there on the pallet they had fixed up, his eyes on a crack of light under the door; Frenin was up, writing, in the front room. The night was warm and filled with voices and inexplicable sounds, the swarming city atmosphere. There was no silence. Itale thought of the garden of the Paludeskar house, roses in the dark, the fountain, the golden light on Luisa's throat, and these images changed to yet more tormenting ones: vivid, unbearable: the roofs of Portacheyka, the neat, mountain-shadowed yard of Emanuel's house, the lake, the window of his room above the lake. Never had he felt such anguish of homesickness. And among those glimpses of the lost beloved there were faces, all the faces he had seen in the streets, the sweating carriers, old women praying, the endless faces of the city, of the poor, and a

85

rednosed, greyhaired man crying, "My mistress, Liberty!" and the bony, swollen, bare legs of the old blind man who had guided him.

III

"By the assistance of the Dog, man was ennerbled—"

"Enabled."

"Enabled to hunt such animals as were neces-sary to preserve his own extents—"

"Existence."

"Existence and to destroy those which were no-shows and the greatest enemies of his race."

"Noxious. Very good. Vasten, go on please."

Itale stood leaning his arms on the lectern, watching the three copies of Buffon pass from hand to hand, the fifteen serious faces. The youngest pupil was twelve; the eldest, Isaber the pupil-teacher, was sixteen. As each boy read, Isaber looked at him with fierce and pleading eyes. The bell of a nearby church struck noon, little Parroy gabbled through his reading, and Itale dismissed them. As the others left, Isaber came up to him.

"Don't look so worried, Agostin. They're doing very well."

"It's Vasten, sir, he won't apply himself. . . ."

Itale watched the boy with patient affection, his long thin throat in which the adams-apple bobbed up and down as he spoke, his big, red hands and clear eyes. Isaber never laughed, and smiled only when he thought Itale wanted him to smile.

Another teacher looked in. "Hold on, Brunoy, I'm coming," Itale said, and soon joined them. "Poor Isaber, what a conscience the boy has! Come on, I'm hungry. Oh God, how I am coming to hate the noble Buffon as translated by the noble Prudeven as executed by aspiring youth. . . ." They left the gloomy halls of the derelict grain storehouse, now occupied by the Ereynin School, where Itale had been employed as a teacher for six weeks. Someone at the Cafe Illyrica had mentioned the place, he had investigated, and found himself hired to teach Reading, Composition, and History five mornings a week before he had ever heard of the Lancaster system or Pestalozzi's works on education. Ereynin, a philanthropical grain-speculator, had founded the school; fifty boys, sons of day laborers and artisans, were enrolled in it, some paying a low tuition, some none. It was the only lay school in the city where a poor man's son might learn to read and write. In hiring Itale, Ereynin had given him a three-hour lecture on education, but that was the last anyone had seen of him: the rumor was that he had found a new hobbyhorse to ride. So far, by nagging Ereynin's secretary, the three teachers had managed to draw their salary, but there was no money for books, chalk, coal, and so forth. Brunoy, who taught the younger boys, was philosophical. "It's lasted over a year," he said, "I never thought it would last so long."

As they came out into the sweet air of the October noon Brunoy coughed and laughed. "You like Isaber, do you?"

"Of course."

"He worships you."

"That's his age. You have to make a hero out of somebody, at sixteen. If there's any purpose in this education business, it's enlarging their world enough so that they can find proper heroes, real ones, instead of makeshift and tinsel."

"Why shouldn't you be his hero?"

"Because my heroism consists, first, in my educated accent— he thinks it's educated, you think it's provincial—and second, in the fact that I stand six feet tall. Discrimination," Itale said, waving his arm, "discrimination is the purpose of education!"

Brunoy smiled; they walked on a little way, and Itale broke out afresh, "I admire your patience so much, Egen,—I get cross with them— How do you stay patient?"

"I have nothing but patience to fill the gap between my old ideals and my actual achievement."

"That gap—that gap between what we want to do and what we do—you call it patience, I call it waiting for God. It's in that gap, that gulf, that creation occurs. But I haven't the strength to wait, I leap in and try to play God. And spoil everything."

"Eleven," Brunoy said to a short, dark, spectacled man walking briskly past them.

"Thirteen," Itale added.

The man nodded, said, "Seventeen," and went on past. When he was around the corner Itale released a stifled snort and said, "This life is crazy!"

The short man in spectacles was the third teacher in the Ereynin School, a mathematician who believed that the secret of human destiny was written, codelike, in the sequence of the prime numbers. An atheist, he was offended by Brunoy's and Itale's inert Catholicism, and did his best to convert them to the mystery of the primes. The salutation they had just exchanged gave him a good deal of pleasure.

"You don't belong in it," Brunoy said gently.

He was a thin, brown-haired man in his early thirties, with a look of ill health and a mild manner. At first Itale had seen in him the signs of disillusion, enthusiasm soured, which he had learnt to expect from men of the generation before his who had given themselves to hopeless efforts of reform or innovation in education, economics, or politics in the century's first two decades: old liberals, old radicals, still haunting the Illyrica, still breaking out with gusts of defeated passion, honest ineffectual ghosts. Very soon he realised that Brunoy was not this sort at all. A watchmaker's son who had gone through the university on scholarship, unmarried, solitary, poor, Brunoy had not turned sour or cynical; he had merely accepted silence as his lot, silence until the end. Yet he had let Itale break that silence.

"Nor do you," Itale said as they went into the workmen's tavern where they took their midday dinner.

"All I ever wanted was to teach."

Itale brought their mugs of beer to the table. "Listen, you said you'd written something once, a theory of education."

Brunoy nodded.

"Can I see it?"

"I burned it."

"Burned it?" Itale said, shocked.

"Years ago. It was unpublishable; the censors would never

88

have let it pass. And the ideas are mostly current now in other men's works."

"You shouldn't—you shouldn't burn your ideas— Could you rewrite it?"

"No. The ideas are common now. And anyhow, why? There's nowhere to publish anything of that kind."

"Yes, there is. Will be."

Brunoy cocked his head.

"I am asking you for a contribution to the first issue of *Novesma Verba*."

Still Brunoy said nothing.

"How do you like the name?"

"'The newest word'—I like it very much. But whose word?"

"Ours. Me, Brelavay, Frenin, you—the country—Europe—mankind . . . I'll tell you,—the name is my idea, the others like it, it sounds right, but I'll tell you what it means to me. We have something to say, and we haven't said it yet. We stammer. We try to learn to speak, like infants. We don't know how. We say a little of what we have to say sometimes, in different languages, in a painting, in a prayer, in an act of knowledge. Every so often we learn a new bit of it, a new word. The newest word is the word Freedom. Maybe it's no more than a new way of saying one of the old words. I don't think so. It's new. Still we're a long way from being able to say the whole thing yet. But we must learn the new words, all of us, we must all be able to speak them. They're no good if you don't say them aloud. . . ."

"O Prometheus," Brunoy said very softly.

"All right, that's all my notions. The point is, it is now possible that we may actually publish this journal. And I am asking you to contribute to the first number. Since the first number will very likely be the last, my request gains urgency. . . ."

Brunoy raised his beer-mug, gestured to Itale to do the same, and touched mugs in salute. "To *Novesma Verba*, long life!" They drained their mugs.

"So?" said Itale, triumphant, setting down his mug.

Brunoy shook his head.

"Why not, Egen?"

The older man looked down, was silent for a minute. Their food was served. Itale began to eat, shoveling it in, though he continued to watch Brunoy in puzzlement and hope. Brunoy looked at his plate, did not eat, and said finally, "Fear."

"I don't believe you."

"Not fear of the Censor, fear of the police. If that was all I had to fear. . . ."

He made some pretense of eating, set his fork down again.

"In order to do what you're doing, Itale, one must believe in it entirely, passionately. One must believe in the importance, the necessity of it. That belief is wealth, strength . . . health. . . ."

"I don't know that we're doing the right thing, Egen, or doing it the right way. I am doing all I know how to do—all I can find to do— It may all be useless, worse than useless."

"You know it is not."

"I hope it is not. And you, too."

"I do not hope. I do not have time for hope. I am a poorer man than you know, than you're able to know. You have no idea what poverty is, Itale." He spoke with open affection, tenderly, so that Itale, confused between what he had said and how he said it, did not know what to reply.

"I gave up all I had," he said at last, painfully.

"You gave up all you could. It's not your fault you're rich!"

"What I care about— What I care about most in the world, it's no use talking about it here, I didn't know it myself, until I gave it up. That's what's so stupid, I keep going ahead, working for the time to come, that's what I care about, you say. But what I know is that my home is behind me, that I've lost it—let it go."

"Your home?"

"My home, no metaphor, I mean the land, the place, the house I was born in—the dirt, the stupid dirt! I am tied to that land like an ox tied to a stake. . . ."

"If you don't know where your home is, how shall you be a pilgrim? —You're a hypocrite, Itale, you wouldn't trade your homesickness for all the freedom in the world."

"But I am ashamed of it."

"Shame is the conscience of the rich."

"Oh, come on, Egen, write for us!"

Brunoy coughed, smiled, shook his head.

"You're not afraid."

But his friend only smiled, luminous, elusive.

When he left Brunoy Itale set off to see Brelavay, going some blocks out of his way to walk through the Eleynaprade. It was a sunny, hazy autumn day, the city grey and golden; leaves drifted underfoot in the walks of the great park. Itale liked the chestnut alleys and long lawns of old Queen Helen's Fields, but the new "English" addition, with ruins, grotto, and so-called waterfall, struck him as contemptible. He thought of the caverns of Evalde over Malafrena, caves where sensation was drowned in the enormous, ceaseless thunder of an emprisoned stream plunging through darkness till it broke out torrential into sunlight and leaped to the lake a hundred feet below; what price plaster grottoes? He crossed the river on Old Bridge and headed out towards the Boulevard Prussia. All this section of the Trasfiuve had been built up in the last twenty years: long, straight streets of row houses, row after row after row. Because they were all alike there seemed no reason for any one of them to be there, and there also seemed no reason why they should ever cease, they might run on forever house after house, row after row: but if one walked on far enough, they ceased, stopped being, and with them the city ceased to exist, giving place to a field of burdock and mullein and shards, a dirt road going nowhere, perhaps a decaying shack or warehouse, and the hazy eastern hills. Walking those long dreary streets gave Itale the feeling of being caught in a stupid dream, and, as befitted the dream, when he got where he was going Brelavay was out. He left a note and started back. Crossing Old Bridge he leaned a while on the parapet to watch the silky bluish water running quietly to the south, reflecting the lindens of the Molsen Boulevard on the west bank. At the end of the parapet stood a stone figure of St Christopher, his large, stiff hand with fingers all the same length raised in benediction over all pilgrims and traffic of the bridge.

River Quarter stank, shrieked, loomed, swarmed as ever, and in the doorway of 9 Mallenastrada sat the landlady Mrs Rosa, her seamed, dark face glowering over the cat, one or another of all her mangy cats, that sat in her lap. But she smiled tightly at Itale.

91

She liked having a gentleman in her first-floor back, though he paid no more rent than the weaver's family in the first-floor front. When Frenin moved out, she had divided the four rooms into two flats, which meant Itale had to go through his neighbor's rooms to reach his own—a small inconvenience for a ten-krune rent. The weaver, Kounney, was at his loom when Itale came through; he was at his loom fourteen or fifteen hours a day. He worked on the putting-out system: the factory issued him thread, he worked at home, and returned the cloth to the factory for finishing and cutting: a system very popular among owners, since the workmen competed in isolation instead of cooperating in union. The smell of dye, the rhythmic thump and rattle of the loom, were ground-texture to all Itale's hours in his rooms; the loom filled half that bare room where he had first talked with Frenin. The family were thin, fair, white-faced people, cautious and wary in their ways, subdued; Itale could not get much response even from the five-year-old, and almost none from Kounney; they were, he thought, afraid of him, afraid of everyone except one another. He slipped past the great complex loom on which the white band of cloth grew relentlessly slow, faultlessly even, like some inhuman process of the world, the movement of the shadow on a dial, the progress of a glacier. Kounney nodded. The baby was crying thinly in the other room. Itale sat down at his table to write, but his conversation with Brunoy and his fruitless errand into the Trasfiuve had left him depressed, and he lay down on the cot in the closet that served him as a bedroom, intending to read Montesquieu and forget his troubles. Within ten minutes he had forgotten them and Montesquieu as well, the book on his chest, his hands on the book, fast asleep. He was waked by a knock and staggered into the other room, which was full of hot red sunset light, expecting Brelavay. He did not recognise the red-haired man in the doorway.

"Estenskar. We met at the Paludeskars' in August."

It was Estenskar all right, the poet, the great poet. Itale stood staring, utterly floored.

"Sorry to disturb you," Estenskar said in his high, hard voice.

"Not at, not at all— Please sit down— Not that chair, the back falls off—"

Estenskar tested the back of Frenin's chair, found that it did indeed come off the seat, removed it, laid it aside, and sat down on the seat as on a stool. "I came to make an apology, Mr Sorde."

"An apol, an apology—"

"I had no right to be rude to you, that night."

"Every right," Itale said, waving his hands.

"I'm sorry about it."

"It's absolutely unnecessary, Mr Est," Itale's throat dried up in the middle of the name.

"No; it was necessary, if I wanted to talk with you again." And Estenskar smiled, a brief, unjoyful, youthful smile. "There are a lot of stupid people at the Paludeskars' and I have got into a habit of being rude to them, since they expect it of me. But to be rude to you was a mistake, and I knew it at the time. Are you really trying to found a review, a journal?"

"Yes. Please, this chair's all right—"

"I like this one. How far have you got?"

"Enough money for a couple of issues, and enough promised for several more. A printer who knows what he's in for. A letter from Stefan Oragon, in Rakava—"

"That could be more a liability than an asset."

"If the Estates meet it could be a real asset."

"What about the Censor?"

"My friend Brelavay thinks he's getting somewhere. With the—the man you mentioned. Goyne."

Estenskar gave his short, artificial-sounding laugh. "How many of you are there?"

"Four of us from Solariy. Six or seven from Krasnoy now. Givan Karantay is one of them, perhaps you know him."

"Yes. A splendid talent and a good man. Virtuous; Givan Karantay is a virtuous man. You are lucky to have him. Is it to be a literary journal, then?"

"At first. The Bureau seems more approachable if we keep to literature."

"Yes!" Estenskar said harshly but with real amusement. "You can always get around them in the long run, because they don't really believe words can do anything, they don't really listen to Metternich. He knows better! If Metternich could have his heart's desire every poet in the Empire would be locked up in the Spielberg prison for the rest of his life. I admire Metternich, he is an enemy, an equal. He has the wits and the enlightenment to fear the power of ideas, the power of the word. He's of the breed of '89—not one of these nouveaux, these Gentzes with their turncoat opportunism and illiterate mysticism, these worthy servants of the Habsburg-Bourbon-Romanov-Cretins, who wouldn't recognise an idea if it was pointing a gun at their empty heads. Thank God Metternich is off in Vienna and all we have to fight here is nineteenth-century stupidity, not eighteenth-century intelligence!"

All barriers fell under that onslaught. "We're calling it *Novesma Verba*," Itale said, and they were off, interrupting each other, excited, ardent, gesticulating, pacing, while the red light flared and sank in the room, and the loom rattled next door, and the bells of St Stephen's, the university chapel, and the cathedral struck six and all the quarters and then seven, and the roofs and chimneypots across the courtyard dimmed in brown autumnal dusk and grew dark and hard against the sky. Itale thought to light a candle at last. As he stood by the table, tinderbox in hand, making sure the wick had caught, he looked up and in the smoky light his eyes and Estenskar's met.

"You see why I had to come," the poet said.

"I am glad you did," Itale said in his quiet voice.

"I recognised you, that night." Estenskar continued to watch Itale with his peculiar, yellowish, immobile gaze. "I don't know if you know what I mean by that. One comes to certain places, certain persons, to which one must come. To fail to recognise them, to turn aside from them, is to fail one's destiny. Do you know what I mean?"

"I think so."

"But one's destiny isn't always good, you know—I think you haven't considered that yet— Are you Catholic?"

"Yes. As I eat with a knife and fork, and wear a hat instead of feathers."

"So was I. I took off the hat."

"Forms are unimportant," Itale said broadly.

"Not to a poet. But never mind. I'd like—I want to tell you about myself, Sorde." He spoke with intensity, turning away from the light of the candle; then his voice hardened as he said, "I suppose you know all about it from the Paludeskars."

94

"I've never been back there."

"You haven't? Luisa has spoken of you several times; I thought you went there often. But I'm surprised they said nothing that evening. Discretion's not their virtue. They love gossip, the more sordid the better, the stupider the better—love affairs, they're called. The old word for it is adultery. If you know me, you'll know this, I'd rather tell you myself. Two years ago I performed the action known as falling in love; I became a lover. The object of my love is a married woman who is rather stupid, very greedy, very cruel, not particularly beautiful. As soon as I saw her she slipped her hands under my skin and took hold of me on the raw flesh and nerve and I've been her puppet ever since, I dance when she raises a finger. I am her possession. If she called for me now I would crawl to her house on all fours. I have stood on the doorstep and begged the footman to let me in, I have gone to her husband and asked him in t-tears— Excuse me, Sorde. I'm going. Not fit." He had stood up, neat and abrupt in his well-cut coat and fine linen, his voice still clear, and was blundering towards the door. Itale, with no consideration of his act, blocked his way: "You can't go now!" he said fiercely.

Estenskar felt for the backless chair, sat down, sat hunched up for a minute, crying. He got out his pocket handkerchief and wiped his eyes and nose. "No good," he said in a soft, boyish voice, and then, shoving back his red hair and speaking in his usual tone or very near it, "What's your name?"

"Itale."

"Amadey. What . . . What sort of cheese is that?"

"Portacheyka."

"Did you bring it with you?" It was about a yard across.

"My aunt sent it. God knows how she bribed the carrier; he brought it to the door here. Are you hungry?"

They were soon sitting at the table; the huge cheese, looking more prosperous in its blue coat than its owner did in his, sat between them, with a knife, a half-loaf, and a jug of rather stale water. There was one plate. "I don't do much entertaining," Itale observed, "I like to keep to the old country ways, you know, nothing ostentatious, no plates, no forks, no manners."

"An aunt sent this, you said? What other family have you got up there?"

"Aunt and uncle, sister, parents. Hardly counts as a family in the Montayna."

"More than I have. One brother, never leaves the estate. You're the heir, then. You left something, to come here."

"It seemed the thing to do."

"The thing to do. . . ." Estenskar looked at Itale, at the cheese, at the candle-flame. "How easily you say that. And I can guess pretty well at how much you had to give to earn the right to say it. . . . To do the thing one has to do, that's the way, the right road, of course. And I've lost it."

"But your writing—"

"I haven't written a word for months. Of course that's my road, but when it leads to a wall? or a hole in the ground? . . . The End. You can't start a book with 'The End,' can you?" He spoke without excitement, and went on munching his bread and cheese contentedly. "This is first-rate cheese," he said. There was a knocking on the hall-door, the sound of voices in the weaver's room, a rap on Itale's door, and in burst Brelavay. He now sported a brocade vest and silk hat, but looked just as he had looked in college, thin, buoyant, and, ironic. "Victory! Triumph!" he proclaimed, and then noticed the stranger. "Sorry! Am I in the way?"

"No, of course not— Tomas Brelavay, Amadey Estenskar. What's up? Do you want some cheese?"

"Very honored indeed, Mr Estenskar," said Brelavay, taken aback and so looking ironic to the point of being diabolical. "I— This is a real privilege— No, I don't want any cheese, for God's sake, this is no time for cheese!"

"What is it for?"

"Go on with your cheese, please don't let me disturb you. Will this chair hold together if I sit down carefully?"

"I've got the trick one," Estenskar said, still munching.

"Did you talk with Goyne?"

"I did. Late this afternoon. And I don't want to hear any more talk about old Brelavay, he's a jolly sort but he never does anything, I know the kind of talk that goes on among these damned seditious radical groups, especially since you haven't got the manners to wait until my back's turned. Do you want to hear what I said to Goyne and then what Goyne said to me and then what I said to Goyne with infinite tact and diplomacy *und so weiter, und so weiter*, or shall I—"

"Come on, Tomas!"

"Entire sanction and license for the publication of—"

"No! By God! you got it!" Itale shouted, jumping up, and Brelavay, only less excited because he was so pleased with himself, said, "Let me tell you about it, will you?" They continued to talk more or less simultaneously for some while. Amadey Estenskar watched them. He was envious of their old friendship, envious of their jubilation, and dubious of it. What did it amount to, this little crack in the immense wall of indifference, this glimmer in the dead endless night of intellect? And yet this was what he had come here for, driven, exactly this, hope; and it caught at him as he watched them, so that exultation began to grow in him and brought him too to his feet. "Come on," he said, "where do you fellows meet? The Illyrica? This calls for the open air."

"Exactly, come on, Itale!"

"All right, I'm coming, just let me get my hat!" They ran down the black stairs, out of the house into the streets full of early night and a gusty, dry, autumnal wind blowing from the east. "Come on!" Itale urged when the others slowed their pace in the pressure of talk, and he went ahead, full of that same exultation and certainty, letting the dark wind of October blow by him and singing out loud the banned hymn, "Beyond this darkness is the light, O Liberty, of thine eternal day!" so that passing whores and locked-out children turned and laughed or looked at him.

IV

The same dry east wind was singing next day in the pines of the mountainsides and lashing up whitecaps on Malafrena, bright and wild in the morning sun. Piera Valtorskar came wandering down the lane that led through the valley from the

97

pass. To her right lay the stubble fields and orchards of Valtorsa, to her left, the orchards and stubble fields of the Sorde estate. All things, trees, apples on the trees, clods, mountains, were distinct in the acute autumn light. Piera's hair blew loose and her red skirt flashed in gusts of wind. In her left hand she carried an apple with a bite out of it, in her right a bunch of wild grass and flowers.

Down from a side path along the Sorde apple orchard came a mounted horse with a neat quick gait. Recognising the fat mare and thin rider, Piera waved her wildflowers in the sunshine. Guide raised his hand in salute and came riding up to her. "I thought, whose lass is that in her Sunday dress? But it's no one but thee in common clothes. . . ." Sometimes he called her by her title, sometimes he still used thou to her as to a child. She called him you and Mr Sorde, but that was the extent of her formality with him. At times she pondered the questions: did she love Mr Sorde as much as she loved her father? ought she to? and why did she? She found no answers, no scales for weighing love, no reasons. She loved him because he loved her. That she knew, better perhaps than he did. Not being responsible for her, he was free to show his feelings to her, as he was not free with his own daughter and son. He could play with Piera long years after he had ceased to tease and praise and play with Laura. He looked down at her now smiling, seeing the flash of her red skirt, her blown hair, her clear, bright eyes, seeing her a frail, wild bit of the bright day of wind; his look was praise.

"I stole one of your apples, see? Should I put it back?"

"Eat it, eat it," said he.

"It's got a worm right through it."

"That's the serpent that tempted thee, Eve."

She looked up at him and laughed. "May I feed it to Bruna? Are you in a hurry, Mr Sorde?"

She stood at the mare's head, offering the apple. Bruna tossed her head and mouthed her bit, and Guide had to slap the bit out so she could eat Piera's apple. He did not mind humoring the girl and the wilful old mare. The beauty of the morning put him in a patient mood, a mood that fit the season; he liked the autumn above all seasons, because it brought him that quietness.

"You're going in to Portacheyka, Mr Sorde?" Piera asked in a ladylike tone. She was always changing that way from country Eve to proper miss, in a breath, for no reason.

"Aye." Guide shifted in the saddle and added the explanation: "The Post comes in today."

"Oh, of course." Piera scrubbed her horse-slobbered hand with Bruna's long mane quite as a child would do, while remarking with womanly tact, "And it's a lovely morning for a ride."

"And for escaping lessons, eh?" he teased her a little heavily.

"Oh, Miss Elisabeth never gets up till eight. I have hours and hours before lessons." She was twining the one bright flower of her October nosegay, a last cornflower, into the mare's mane. When Guide had left her and was riding on towards town his gaze fell on the blue nodding flower, and he felt a curious tenderness, an ache, as he looked at it. They passed on the road, she at sixteen and he at fifty-six, and she left him a blue cornflower twined in his horse's mane. It was queer, he thought, how you met and passed souls thus, and a few of them left sweetness with you. You passed one another and parted, it might as well be forever, and yet there remained the touch of sweetness, and of pain.

Piera wandered on towards Valtorsa, murmuring a French irregular verb. As she murmured, her mind, also, wandered. The Post came in today. It would stop, high, dusty, swaying, at the Golden Lion. On it, in one of the two or three mail sacks containing the fortnight's correspondence to all the people of the Lakes, would be a letter to the Sordes, a square envelope of heavy, cheap paper addressed in black ink, the corners bent and dirty from the long trip. These letters were thoroughly familiar to Piera. Eleonora and Laura read them alone, read them together, read them with Piera, read them to each other, quoted them, misquoted them (especially Eleonora), interpreted them, dreamed about them, and twice a month awaited them with a longing that made the post coach's delay a disaster, its arrival a festivity. Till now one or both of the women had driven in to meet the Post, and Piera wondered why this time Guide had gone. They were expecting something unusual, perhaps. That afternoon, when her lessons were over for the day, she told Miss Elisabeth that she was going to visit with Laura, and came straight along the lakeside path to the Sordes' without any wanderings off to the side. By now she was certain that Itale was coming home—in fact he had probably been on the coach.

Laura was seeing out the old tutor, Mr Kiovay of Portacheyka, who came once a week to read French with her, as he came to Valtorsa to improve Piera's spoken French. He had improved the French of every young lady in Val Malafrena for forty years; and the French spoken there did not resemble that spoken anywhere else on earth, being, to a considerable extent, Mr Kiovay's own invention. He had taught Eleonora, now he taught her daughter, whom he liked, because she was quiet; but he dreaded Piera. He quailed as she came up the path beside the mandevilia. *"Que je vinsse!"* she cried aloud at them. *"Que tu vinsses! Qu'il vînt!"* She had mastered the Past Subjunctive of Venir.

"Mais viens donc!" said Laura.

"Vient-il?" said Piera. Mr Kiovay escaped, while the girls went into the house. "There was a letter, wasn't there?"

"Mama has it, I'll get it. They're going to have a journal, Itale's going to be an editor."

"But he's not . . ." Piera did not finish. He was not coming home, of course. Whatever had possessed her to think he was?

Laura prised the letter away from her mother, promising not to damage it or lose it, and went with Piera down to their favorite haunt on sunny afternoons, the lawn by the boat house, now a sweep of golden green in the mellow light. Sitting there Piera read and Laura reread Itale's letter. It was, as always, rather stiff, bookish, impersonal. He talked about plans for the journal. He attempted to describe Amadey Estenskar, but on this subject his language became stuffier than ever, probably because he was self-conscious or over-conscious of his readers as he wrote. There was a good deal of detail about the complexities of dealing with the bureaucrats at the Censor's office, which was hard to follow. But the dry, stiff letter was permeated, penetrated, shot through and through with joy. A great work to do, the friendship of great spirits, the road open before him, the world to be renewed and the strength to renew it.

"What became of that baron . . . and baroness . . . that he wrote about at first?" Piera inquired, gazing out over the dark, bright lake.

"He hasn't mentioned them again," said Laura, folding the letter carefully. "Oh dear, I wish . . ."

"What?"

"That I weren't envious of him."

Piera brooded over this for a while. It did not make much sense to her at first. Laura was Laura, and was here; Itale was Itale, and was there. Piera's mind did not easily mix the absent with the present. Her imagination did not move lightly in and out of possibilities; so she was seldom envious, and seldom discontented. She was cautious about entering the realm of the possible, for when she did her will came with her.

"It really isn't fair," she said at last, "him getting all the excitement, and you none."

"It isn't the excitement. It's just that he's . . . doing something, being someone. I don't get bored, it isn't that."

"I am so dreadfully bo-aaard," Piera said nasally, imitating the eldest Sorentay daughter, and she and Laura both giggled.

"I never get bored. I just feel unnecessary. It's what Itale says here about Mr Estenskar, that's what I mean—" She already knew the sentence by heart: "'He seeks with all his strength to find the way that he and only he can, and hence must, follow.' So is Itale trying to do that. And he will do it. But anybody in the world could do everything I do."

"Nobody else could be Laura Sorde, though."

"What's the use *being* me if I don't *do* anything?"

"If you weren't you what would I do? Who would I talk to? How could I even be me? Anybody can run around doing things, but nobody can be you except you. And I hope you never change."

"I won't change in what I love," Laura said. Her face was turned to the western sunlight and the dark reflecting bulk of San Larenz Mountain above the lake. "But you see, you're already in love, you've started on your way. . . . I haven't. I have no way. I just wait and time goes by and by and by and life goes by. . . . Surely I was made for more?"

Piera did not answer for a while. She felt more than the three years' age difference between herself and Laura, the very great difference between sixteen and nineteen years old; she felt an inferiority of character that had nothing to do with age. She was in love, Laura said. And indeed six weeks ago she and Alexander Sorentay had become secretly engaged, and she had rushed to tell Laura the secret and show her Alexander's carnelian ring on a chain around her neck. That was so, that was true. But as Laura spoke Piera blushed as if she had been caught stealing jam. She was engaged to be married, but she did not, in her deep heart, take it seriously. Laura did. It would never occur to Laura that one might experiment with betrothal, or play at love—that one could even speak of being in love without having given one's whole heart. The little girl felt Alexander's carnelian ring a cold lump against her breastbone, and thought, "I'm a pig, I'm a pig, I'm a pig."

"When you fall in love," she said, "it'll be with a tremendous man, a king. Nobody around here! A man from far away, a man like a lion, and you'll go away with him and see, oh, I don't know, Vienna and all the cities, and do wonderful things, and write letters home and I'll be envious. . . ."

"Silly," said Laura. "What would I leave Malafrena for? Let's go to vespers at St Anthony's, Peri."

"Oh, Miss Elisabeth wanted to, I forgot. Come on!" Piera jumped up like a branch suddenly released; Laura uncurled and followed her. They left the letter with Eleonora, went by Valtorsa for the pony cart and the governess, and got to St Anthony's barely in time for the service. There at the base of San Larenz the sunlight was long gone. The granite chapel looked like a toy set down between the forested ridge and the deep curve of the lake. Inside the chapel smelled of stone, whitewash, balsam, pine. The two girls, the fat, quiet governess, a young peasant couple, and three old women were all that evening's congregation. They heard vespers in the silence of the lonely place, in the growing cold of the mountain evening. When they came out the far reaches of the lake were grey with dusk and the water in the shadow of San Larenz was streaked with a cold, strong, silent wind rising.

Laura and the priest, Father Klement of Sinviya, old friends, fell to talking, and there was a matter of arranging to have some firewood brought to the cottage of one of the old women, and then the priest came back with them in the pony cart for supper at the Sordes', so that Piera and Miss Elisabeth got home rather late, delaying supper at Valtorsa by a few minutes. After supper Count Orlant, Miss Elisabeth, neighbor Rodenne, and the count's new overseer played whist. Vist, it was called in the Montayna, and many autumn and winter evenings were given up to vist. Auntie sat in her straight-backed chair, a ball of red yarn on her lap. Piera sat by the marble fireplace with her lesson book. She was supposed to write a composition on the Duties of the Young Female. She hated to write compositions, or letters, or notes, or anything. They were always very dull, and then Miss Elisabeth made red circles around the misspellings. She had composed one sentence so far: "Young girls should be obeidient."

"Auntie, would you like me to read to you?"

"No, my dear," said Auntie, slowly, slowly rewinding the red yarn.

"Young girls should be obeidient." Piera thought and thought. "They should not argue or talk very much loudly. Their are numierous things young girls should not do. But these are not duties." Her pen made a row of dots on the paper, then of its own accord drew three profiles of young men with large eyes and noses, facing left, and a lion with a curly mane, facing right. "Young girls should get M and have B" she wrote very small and then crossed it out very black. "It is important for them to learn there lessons but less important than for young gentlemen to learn there's as they will find them more useful in life. They should be neat and orderly." The pen drew three maidens with Grecian noses all facing left. Piera gave it up and began to watch the card-players.

Her father had his cards up under his nose, not because he was suspicious, but because he was nearsighted. Neighbor Rodenne had a good hand and looked smug. He was a small landowner; vist and hunting were his passions, and he had never married, stating that a wife would keep him from vist and hunting. Miss

Elisabeth looked, as usual, contented. She was a placid soul; nothing stirred her; she praised God with a mild heart. Next to her the new overseer, Gavrey, looked thin and sharp as a knifeblade. He was a Val Altesma man, and had been with Count Orlant only a month. Piera had not paid much attention to him, as he was always busy with papers and account books, speaking to her father but not to her, and missing dinner more often than not because he was working in the office or the orchards or the fields. He was sitting quiet now, alert, studying the other players' faces; so Piera studied his. He was a good-looking man, thin-lipped, dark-eyed, with a ruddy brown complexion. The best thing about being engaged to Alexander, Piera thought, was that it gave her a safe refuge, a look-out tower, from which to look at other men.

Since she was twelve she had been trying to fall in love. It was hard work, falling in love with pictures, strangers glimpsed in Portacheyka, heroes of romantic novels, and the few boys she met who were not put out of the running by warts or stupidity. It was hard work and unrewarding. But she kept at it. She practiced: as a musician practices on his violin, not coldblood-edly, yet methodically, not for present profit or enjoyment, not because he longs to play each scale ten times over, but because to play the violin well is his gift, his need, his job. So Piera practiced at the art of love. She had known Alexander Sorentay all her life. No social event took place along the northern lake-shore without representatives from the Sorentay, Sorde, and Valtorskar families. In the last generation the latter two had got few in numbers, even to the point where the Valtorskar name would die with Piera; but the Sorentays abounded. There were never less than fifteen of them under the dynastic roof, northwest of Valtorsa in a flank valley of Sinviya Mountain. The senior family of the estate had six children, three girls and three boys, all tall and boisterous except the eldest, Alexander, who was short and quiet. He was Laura's age, and when they were both sixteen he had written her a long love-letter embellished with quotations from *The New Heloise* (which his mother had borrowed from Eleonora the year before and forgotten to return). Laura had shown the letter almost at once to her mother, who counselled inaction. Nothing had come of it except a lasting embarrassment for both Laura and Alexander; at every party the memory of the letter lay like a tombstone between them. For three years they danced together at every dancing-party in stony and tormented silence. It was a great relief to Laura when she could hand Piera over to Alexander and do her dancing with Papa Sorentay, the uncles, the cousins, the brother-in-law, and the rest of the inexhaustible fund of Sorentays. This handing-over took place at the August ball, the ball they had discussed one July evening by the lake, the ball to which Piera wore a white gown with gold flowers embroidered down the bodice, her first evening gown. Alexander gawped at her as if he had never seen her. Indeed he never had. In her first evening gown Piera was new as the newborn, her childhood left behind, her womanhood fresh from the hands of God and the seamstress. By midnight Alexander had decided that if she would not marry him life was meaningless. Three weeks later, in the evening of a long, loud picnic day in the pine forest across the lake, he climaxed a spasmodic but earnest wooing with the offer of marriage. Piera accepted at once. "Yes," she said. She was sitting on a fallen log near a stream. Alexander hovered about her, not daring either to kneel or sit down.

"May I speak to your father?" he said.

"Perhaps we should wait a while," she said.

She gave no reason why, and he asked none. They agreed without discussion that the engagement should be kept secret; neither thought to ask why. They were in perfectly good faith. Alexander, experiencing real desire, never questioned that he was in love. Piera was more aware that they were playing a game, yet it was not a game to her; what she was playing was the moto perpetuo or the tarantella that follows the well-practiced scales; a beginner's piece, but music. She did not know why he said he would marry her. She said she would marry him because she needed to practice her art. She scarcely thought about their getting married. They were engaged to be married: betrothed. That was enough, for the present. They deceived each other— Piera deceived him more than he did her—and they deceived themselves—he deceived himself more than Piera did herself. But they were quite happy. Piera looked up into Alexander's blocky, callow face, and he looked down at her sitting on the log and said, "My bride!"

Later on he said, "Our properties touch, you know, at Galia's Hill."

He was the principal heir to the Sorentay property; Piera was the only heir to Valtorsa. The joined estates would be an excellent holding. Piera found it very interesting that he had seen this and thought about it; she admired him for doing so. Her father was an impractical man, inept at the management of his property and miserable when he had to deal with money matters. Guide Sorde was always trying to set him straight. But Guide, though a good farmer and manager, was not a practical man either; he loved the work, not the profit from it. Alexander saw the work neither as a punishment nor an end in itself, but as a means to an end. He preferred work in the estate office to the fields, and had been his father's accountant for two years. All his talk of loss and profit, income and outlay, was quite new to Piera, and she listened with deep interest to all he told her. That intelligent interest, and her honest and unqualified admiration of his talents, soon won Alexander to her with a bond stronger, perhaps, than his desire.

The sweetest moment of it all for Piera was when she told Laura that she was betrothed. She felt triumph; Laura felt envy; but those were mere emotions, twinges, straw on the current of their friendship. Piera's love-affair brightened Laura's life, a life that ran too quiet and too solitary; while, without Laura, Piera would not have enjoyed her betrothal very much at all. Indeed she preferred talking about Alexander with Laura, to being with Alexander himself.

She did not see him often, as he could not call on her openly. She had requested secrecy, and a call from a young man on a young woman, in that small watchful society, was as good as a proposal. They met in secret, and Laura's connivance was needed to arrange the meetings. She was as drunk with the romance of it all as Piera and Alexander; she waited on guard on the lawn beneath the stars, tense and ecstatic, while they whispered in the shadow of the boat house. She was perhaps happier than they.

They had kissed once: the first evening. Given abruptly and received awkwardly, the kiss had landed near Piera's ear. After it neither had dared move. They had held still so long their necks began to ache. Piera had tried with all her heart to feel delighted, but not even when she was alone could she manage it; and she did not mention the kiss to Laura. Alexander did not offer to repeat it. At most he held her hand: and when he did, his was wet. She did not much like that soft, nervous touch, and as they talked would contrive to withdraw her own hand, and he would not notice.

Once, in one of the endless conversations that were their chief pleasure, Laura had said, "You know, Peri, I can tell you something now."

"What, what, what?"

"Nothing really. I used to wonder what it would be like if you and Itale fell in love. You know how you think things like that, just arranging the world to suit yourself. . . ."

Piera nodded.

"It wouldn't have done at all, really."

"Why not?"

"Oh—his politics. And both your tempers. And anyhow, he isn't Alexander!"

As she sat by the fire, her composition on the Duties of the Young Female on her knee, Piera thought again of that brief conversation, of Laura's wistful, teasing, loving look, and the same chill of fear ran through her. Fall in love with Itale, marry him? No! That was something altogether different from Alexander Sorentay and being engaged and holding hands. That was no game she could play, nothing she could manage, it was not to be thought of; nor was he to be thought of, the scent of mandevilia, and the roar of summer rain, and the door open and he standing there. She had not read the book he had given her, the *New Life*. It stood in her bookshelf in her room, and she never took it out. And she had believed, this morning, that he was coming back! That was nonsense. He was not coming back. He was gone.

Auntie's eyes had closed, her fingers lay motionless on the red yarn. "Young girls should be obeidient. . . . They should be neat

107

and orderly. . . ." Piera yawned, and neighbor Rodenne said grinning from the card table, "Don't swallow the fireplace, contesina!"

Voices and steps outside. Piera bounced up; visitors, thank God! It was Father Klement wanting a word with Count Orlant about the next meeting of the Catholic Men's Sodality of Val Malafrena, and the Sordes come along with him for the walk. Eleonora had brought some new silks for Auntie. "Is your rheumatism any better, Auntie dear?" she asked, and the old lady, raising her clear grey eyes from sleep without the least surprise, said, "No." Guide and neighbor Rodenne fell to talking hounds. Piera went off to the kitchen to stir up the cook, for Count Orlant never let a guest leave unfed. The new overseer rose from the interrupted vist game to stretch his legs and warm his back at the fire. Laura, who had seen him only a few times before, asked politely, "Are you liking it here at Malafrena, Mr Gavrey?"

"Aye, miss," he answered. She blushed as she always did when talking to a stranger. That was all their conversation.

As the Sordes went home by the lake-shore path Laura asked, "What sort of man is Count Orlant's new overseer, father?"

"A considerable improvement. He may get the estate run something like properly, if he keeps at it."

"I can't find out much about him," said Eleonora. "Of course he's not one of the Gavres from Kulme, it's Gavrey; his father's a farmer, freeholder, near Mor Altesma, he's the second son. He's very closemouthed, none of the women at Valtorsa know a thing about him. I hope he's honest. How can you trust a close-mouthed man?"

"You can trust him not to blabber," Guide said with dry good humor. He was still in the good mood of the early morning. He breathed the night air of autumn as they walked, felt his body as straight and lithe as ever, and held his wife's arm in his own. Fifty-six wasn't the worst time of life. It was pleasant to walk home in the darkness of October, under pines and stars, between two well-beloved women.

When Laura bade him good night before going upstairs he

kissed her and sketched the cross on her hair, as he did rarely since she was grown.

Eleonora watched, and thought, "You have your daughter, but I do not have my son." But the flicker of bitterness was lost as she looked at Laura's face: all evening long, as always when she was tense or troubled, Laura's likeness to her brother had been very strong, Itale had been in the turn of her head, in the tone of her voice. On whose head had Guide set his blessing? His eyes, his hands, were kinder than his head, and wiser.

She followed Laura upstairs after a little. As she passed the empty bedroom something moved, a figure between the doorway and the grey starlit window.

"I thought you were in bed."

"I wanted to look at the lake."

In her white nightgown Laura was very tall and thin, a white crane startled from the reeds at night.

"You're barefoot! Come to bed before you catch a pleurisy." She followed Laura to her bedroom, which looked out onto the valley, the orchards, San Givan dark against stars. The window was half open, letting in the sweet, dry odors of an autumn night in farmlands. Laura curled up in bed, her mother sat down by her. Her long, thin hand lay on the coverlet, and the girl looked at it and at the wedding ring, of soft gold, worn thin.

"Mama, when you fell in love first. . . ."

"With your father."

"Not the Cavalry Lieutenant?"

Eleonora laughed, and her underlip drew in, demure and sly. "Oh, no; that was just moustaches . . . and the boots. . . ."

"Can people fall in love intentionally?"

Eleonora considered. "I really don't know. It sounds very odd. But I believe . . . Well, so much of love comes after marriage. At least for us." She meant, for women. "I don't believe one can force an inclination; but if it is there, one can certainly improve upon it."

They sat in peaceable silence for a minute, the girl thinking forward, the woman thinking back.

"Wasn't Father Klement funny about the soup?"

109

They both laughed. "I never see him," said Eleonora, "but I think of the grey hen Eva was so fond of, do you remember it? it had such a peculiar way of clucking when it laid an egg, he sounds very like it." They both laughed again. Guide's step was on the stairs, coming up; Eleonora rose. She looked at her daughter with her head a little to one side. "You're sad," she said.

"Oh, no."

The mother said nothing, but continued to gaze.

"I miss Itale. On letter nights."

"It's high time we answered Matilda's letter."

Eleonora's brother Angele Dru and his wife Matilda, in Solariy, had invited Laura to stay with them over the winter.

"I'd rather go in spring," Laura said imploringly.

"The winter down there would be good for your chest. And some new faces at Christmas. . . . Well, we really must think about it, dear. Put your feet under the covers, do you breathe through your toes? Good night, my darling." Eleonora blew out the candle on the chest of drawers and went out, a little round figure in the darkness. Laura did not lie down, but put her feet obediently under the covers; with her arms round her knees she sat for a long time looking out at the mountain and the hazy stars beside and above it, flaring in the gulfs of night and autumn and the wind.

PART THREE

Choices

I

In the autumn of 1826 Piera set off for Aisnar, some forty miles north of her home, to complete her education. Her father went with her, and Miss Elisabeth, who was a native of Aisnar, and Cousin Betta Berachoy of Portacheyka who wanted to visit friends there and was of course invited to share the Valtorskar carriage, and Count Orlant's man, and old Godin who had been the Valtorskar coachman for fifty years. They set off from Valtorsa on a morning of late September in the immense, creaking, luggage-laden family carriage, older even than the coachman. Piera's face, pressed to the window to bid farewell to her friends and Malafrena, looked small and pale. Laura burst into tears, and Alexander Sorentay trotted his horse beside the carriage all the way to Portacheyka, though he could not talk to Piera since the window was stuck shut.

There had been some coolness between him and Piera that summer. As the secret engagement wore on into its second year, he had begun to question the necessity of its secrecy; and Piera had at once begun a quarrel with him. It did not get very far, because he would not quarrel: he went into a flat panic at the

113

thought of losing her. He promptly revived the *New Heloise* and the meetings at the boathouse after dark. But Piera had played all those scales a hundred times, and was getting bored. She would have much preferred a good quarrel and either a reconciliation with tears or no reconciliation and a broken heart; but Alexander would not quarrel. He was staunch, he was tender, he was patient, he was faithful. He said, "Every hour you're gone I'll think of you. I will never change, Piera!" She had wept at their last parting. Now as the carriage came to the wide gates of Portacheyka, Alexander reined in his horse and raised his hand in farewell. She looked back at him as long as she could through the yellowish isinglass of the rear window of the carriage. She pressed her hand against the carnelian ring beneath her bodice. She saw the young figure on the motionless horse dwindle away, dwindle away down the street, as if she saw her own childhood, the years spent amongst dreams and mountains in the stillness of Malafrena valley, dwindle away behind her and be lost to sight. Yet her eyes were dry, now. "Discreet young fellow, that Sandre Sorentay," Count Orlant said with a chuckle that was, for him, sly. "I wondered if he'd have the face to escort us straight through town. . . ."

Through Portacheyka and out through its northern gate, past the ruined Tower Keep of Vermare, down into the golden lands. Towards evening a fine rain fell, veiling the hills. Concerted efforts had got the window unstuck, and Piera leaned out head and shoulders into the grey, wet freshness. Count Orlant was not one for long stages, and old Godin was protective of the fat horses: they spent the night a little less than halfway, at the inn of Bovira village. Next day they came down out of the hills, onto the long, faintly rolling plain of the Western Marches, a quiet sea of earth. In the evening they came to Aisnar and drove up Fontarmana Street beneath plane-trees already touched with gold, beside fountains, between grave, high houses to left and right. Piera had visited Aisnar when she was eight. All she remembered of it was Fontarmana Street, the fountains, the over-arching trees. Now she saw the houses row after row, the elegant equipages at the Round Fountain, well-dressed women walking in a way no woman in the Montayna knew how to walk;

she was wild with silent excitement. The city, she thought, the city, the city!

It was a very quiet city. The loudest voice in Aisnar was the voice of water: the fountains. There were no still covered wells; the water leapt up into light and air and fell back with a silver rush at every corner and courtyard. From the dormitory of the convent school two fountains could be heard, the bright, thin jet down in the court and the Ring Fountain on the triangular place in front of the school, a dialogue without pauses, sweet and serene, like a colloquy of blessed souls who have been so long together in heaven that they can talk and listen at the same time. That was Piera's fancy, her first nights in the dormitory. Her mind ran more than usual on images of the blessed, since she had not before lived among nuns, and worn a nun-grey uniform, and walked by twos on the street—nun, little girls, middle-sized girls, big girls, nun—and knelt with fifty other girls and women at dawn on bare stone in a bare chapel for hour-long devotions. None of the customs of this new life fretted her, even after her father had gone and silent excitement had turned into silent and miserable homesickness. She liked the city, the school, the new friends, and willingly changed her garnet-red skirt for the grey uniform, not pining for the long liberty of her childhood. She did not pine for her father, Laura, the familiar beloved faces of home. It was her home itself she missed, Valtorsa, the high cool rooms, the orchards and vineyards and fields, the line of the mountains on the sky, the lake, the stones of the lake-shore. Piera was one to whom the thing, not its use nor its meaning, but the thing itself mattered; she knew the thing only, as a lark knows the sun or a wolf the rain. What was given her she accepted, willingly. But what was taken from her she missed, and did not cease to miss.

All round Aisnar stretched calm, soft-colored fields. On clear days Piera looked southwards from the windows of the convent school, to see the bluish drift or massing of clouds, the clouds behind which lay the mountains and the lake.

She was seventeen. She had grown an inch since April. The conventual fashion of her hair revealed a broad forehead, gentle and stubborn, like the forehead of a little bull. In the grey school

115

dress she looked cleanly and novicelike, and she moved and spoke more quietly than she had used to do; for she was in love now with the French teacher, Sister Andrea Teresa, a frail woman of infinite restraint, and all that was restrained, delicate, modest, gracious was now holy to Piera. All her thoughts that autumn were devotional. At the height of her love for Sister Andrea Teresa and in the spirit of Christian sacrifice, she wrote Alexander Sorentay, returning him his carnelian ring. The letter was sincere and tender, written in an ecstasy of renunciation. But for the rest of her life she never thought of it and of the grubby little packet containing his ring without a deep, hard stab of shame.

Came Christmas; she did not go home for the holidays, for the Montayna roads were deep in snow and rain and mud. She would have liked to stay on at the school, with the nuns, as did a few other girls; but obedient to her father's wish she went to stay with the relatives they had stopped with in September, cousins on her mother's side, the Belleynins.

The house was on the New Side, in Prince Gulhelm Square, four blocks from the Roman Fountain. It was about a hundred years old, built of the yellow Aisnar sandstone; in its walled garden was a little fountain. Inside and out the house was plain and elegant, more shabby than shiny. The aristocrats of Aisnar did not polish. Silver needs polishing, gold does best left alone; that was their attitude. Emerging from their walled gardens and high-ceilinged privacies they could be formidable, but they were not arrogant; they were too peaceable. Their manners were reserved and gentle. They had been civilised for a long time, here in the west of the country. Piera, who unlike Laura and Itale was seldom at the mercy of overpowering emotions, felt at ease amongst these people. Her feelings were slow-moving, obscure, and mute, beneath a surface play of vivacity. In the convent and with the gentlefolk of Aisnar the vivacity was subdued, the reserve refined; she behaved with the pleasant sedateness of seventeen. The Belleynins had already become very fond of her. He was a handsome, short man of sixty with a slight stammer, she, born Countess Rochaneskar, was a delicate grey-gold lady of fifty. Their two daughters, long since married, lived one in

Brailava, the other around the corner. Life in the house in Gulhelm Square was ordered, serene, a little desolate. Since it was Christmas time and they had a young guest the Belleynins did more entertaining than usual, yet the days passed very quietly. Piera fitted in so well that she might always have lived there, might have been their late daughter and have played away a solitary childhood in the golden-walled garden on the lawn between the pear tree and the fountain.

Very much the same people were at all the holiday dinner parties and evenings of the Belleynins' circle. Most of them, to Piera's eyes, were old. She did not mind. She was used to being the youngest, and knew how to enjoy the position. And among the elderly she did not feel threatened. Young men were frightened and frightening; things always went awkwardly with them. It was much easier to talk to men of forty, there was nothing serious about it, it was like meeting an interesting foreigner.

The New Year's Eve party was at the house of a close friend of the Belleynins' son-in-law, a widower named Koste. His sister was hostess, and his young son was allowed to stay with the guests for an hour before being taken off to bed. Piera and four-year-old Battiste had met before and had taken a fancy to each other. She had not been with little children very much, and she found the little boy's conversation wonderfully funny and touching. He was as handsome and well-bred as his father and his maiden aunt, but had not yet achieved their deep reserve: he prattled to Piera, admired her artlessly, and pleased her by giving her a trust and affection she had done very little to win. It was a pleasant task to attempt to deserve them. When the father, a shy, grave man, reproved Battiste for bothering her, she defended the child warmly. That earned her Battiste's gratitude; also, perhaps, the father's. When Battiste's hour was up she went with his nurse to see him to bed, and got warmly kissed, and returned to the salon thinking what an extraordinary thing a child was and how pleasant it would be to have children around. Just as it was pleasant to have men around, to hear the bass notes of the human voice, not always the tweedle-tweedle-tweedle of the convent. She sat down near the fireplace. The party was

117

cheerful and quiet. Talk flowed as clear and unhurried as the water of the fountains of Aisnar. There were some faces Piera had not seen before, but their owners behaved like all the rest. The quarter-hours slipped by quickly, marked by the tiny ping! of the French clock on the mantel. Piera sat mostly in silence, enjoying her silence, her decorum, the knowledge that by it she pleased the others. At ten a few last guests entered, Baron Arrioskar and his wife and sister and brother-in-law and their visitor from Krasnoy.

The visitor was a young woman. Perhaps in deference to provincial sobriety she wore no jewels at all, but her violet dress was magnificent, and her bearing was superb. A woman who could walk like that did not even need to be beautiful. Piera sat and gaped at her. She could not keep her eyes off her. All her standards of the admirable shook to their foundation. What was Sister Teresa beside this? mild, tenuous, sterile. This was not the brittle beauty of restraint, but the splendor of a woman's strength and freedom. "She is wonderful," Piera thought, "that's what people ought to look like, she is wonderful." They were introduced: Countess Valtorskar, Baroness Paludeskar.

The lady from the capital acknowledged the introduction in a cool, distinct contralto and prepared to be led on to the next introduction, but Piera spoke, utterly without premeditation. "I believe we both know a mutual friend, baroness," she said, terrified at what she was saying and how stupidly she said it. The beautiful baroness smiled inquiringly.

"Mr Sorde, of Malafrena—"

"Sorde!" Baroness Paludeskar's onward movement definitely ceased, and her eyes for the first time definitely looked, for an instant, at Piera. "Really, do you know him?" she asked indulgently.

"We're neighbors of the Sordes', my family. In Val Malafrena."

"Then you've known Itale a long time."

"All my life," Piera said; and blushed. No becoming rosy flush but a hot, red blush; her cheeks stung, her ears sang; she stood rigid and could think nothing but "O please stop, stop, stop!" If the beautiful baroness would just go away, go on, then this

118

stupid embarrassment would pass off, she would never say anything to a stranger again.

The baroness smiled at her escort, relinquishing further introductions, and sat down in the gilt chair by the hassock on which Piera had been sitting.

In despair, Piera sat down, and folded her hands in her lap.

"My dear cousins have walked me clear around Aisnar twice today, I think," the baroness said, and smiled a mischievous, friendly smile. "I have been longing to sit down. But what a pleasure to meet someone that knows Itale! I'm very fond of him, you know. We've known him since he first came, what is it, over a year now. How he's changed!"

"Yes, he—has he— How?"

"Oh, well, when he first came he was funny, you know—very stiff, disapproving, altogether suspicious of everyone. It was inexperience; he cuts a quite impressive figure now—without intending to, I should add." Her voice was beautifully modulated. Piera listened to it with fascination, and smiled stiffly in response to the lingering, mocking, friendly smile, which deepened now. "Tell me, tell me," the baroness said, leaning forward ready for confidences, "tell me what the father's like, the ogre!"

"Itale's father?"

"Yes. I want to know, I really want to know what sort of creature disinherits his son because the son wants to live like a civilised human being in the city for a while! What does the man want? What are they like, up there among the mountains? I've never met a woman from the Montayna, you see, that's the trouble; men never can explain things. You explain it to me. Are you all very passionate souls?"

The beautiful woman was not teasing her; she was friendly and kindly; she did not mean to tease. It was just that Piera was a stupid provincial schoolgirl who didn't know anything and couldn't talk. "I don't know," she whispered.

"I think Itale is the most passionate man I have ever known," Baroness Paludeskar said, her voice now soft and thoughtful. "It's the secret of his success, of course. If he had been a saint in the old days, he would have converted whole nations of the

119

heathen! —You know that he is becoming very well known in Krasnoy, these days?"

"No, I didn't— I don't—"

"One can never believe it of someone one played with as a child. I know! You're thinking, 'What, him? but he used to have warts and pull his sister's hair, *he* can't be famous!' I've known little boys who I'm now asked to believe are councillors and judges and radicals and I don't know what all. . . . And one must take them seriously, you know, countess. It is up to women to take men seriously. If we didn't, society might quite crumble away; the men would be left taking each other seriously while the rest of us laughed. . . . Well, that's all nonsense, but it is true that our friend is taken almost too seriously by some important people. But you don't believe me. . . ."

"Oh, yes, yes, I do," Piera mumbled wretchedly. If only she didn't have to say anything, but could just watch the baroness and listen to her and try to understand the things she said. If only she didn't keep talking about Itale: that confused Piera. When she looked down she saw the baroness' slim foot in a silver sandal. She tucked her own feet under her dress. She had to say something. "I suppose it's the—the paper—"

"What? The paper?" the baroness said brusquely. "Oh, his journal, yes. It's quite popular, I believe. It isn't that sort of thing that matters, you know. The fact is, Itale is in fashion—his ideas, I should say, although I wonder— But now we're all patriots, you see!"

"Oh, yes, I see," said Piera, in despair. She was completely lost. The baroness went on, smiling so charmingly, and telling a story about Itale and somebody named Helleskar and some general and something about Austria, and it was funny at the end, so that she should have laughed, but she only smiled and nodded. Her throat was so contracted that she no longer trusted herself to say "Yes" to show she was listening. When their host came over to them she looked at him as if across a chasm, gazing wistfully at his quiet face. The baroness had not yet been introduced to the Belleynins, and he took her over to them. Presently he returned and sat down where the baroness had been sitting. "I am sorry to have interrupted your chat," he said

120

in his shy, grave way. Piera thought he knew she had been miserable and had saved her, and was now saving her pride; full of gratitude to him for his simple kindness, she said, "Oh, I couldn't say a word to her, she's too beautiful—"

"Oh yes," Mr Koste said. "Wonderfully fashionable," with the mild, deadly judgment of the provincial on his own ground. He looked at Piera, not smiling, but with unquestioning acceptance of her, a simple confidence in her, that went far to restore her self-respect. He brought up some indifferent subject, and they talked; as they talked, Piera saw that somehow her ill-matched conversation with the baroness had been a battle, and that she had lost it. But why a battle? Over what? And why could not one just talk easily and trustfully, as she and Mr Koste were talking now?

"Are there any patriots in Aisnar, Mr Koste?" she asked him. He looked a little surprised; paused; and answered with seriousness: "Patriots? You mean, I imagine, in the sense of nationalists? Yes, certainly. The liberal tradition here is very old, you know. It goes back to the struggle of the western provinces against the authority of the Krasnoy monarchy, I suppose. A habit of independence remained."

"But the patriots, the nationalists—they want to have the monarchy restored, don't they?"

"Yes. Duke Matiyas' accession would signify the end of Austrian domination."

"Then they don't like the Grand Duchess Mariya because she's an Austrian—is that all?"

"That's the essence of it."

"I thought perhaps they didn't want any more kings at all," Piera said, looking disappointed. "That hardly seems enough of a change to bother about."

"Oh, quite enough. If Duke Matiyas became king he would take his crown from the people, swearing obedience to a constitution drawn up by the Assembly of the Estates General. He would not be the source, but merely the vehicle or channel, of authority." He explained this without the least shade of condescension. "Are you interested in the nationalist movement, contesina?"

"I don't know. I never understood it before."

"It is a very complex matter. I doubt that anyone truly understands what 'nationalism' is—why those whose word is liberty seek the national, the particular destiny, while those who deny the old barriers of language and custom and kind often would sacrifice all liberty in the name of peace."

"Are you a radical, Mr Koste?"

"I? No, contesina."

"Shouldn't the country be independent again, though? I mean, why should the Austrians rule us? They can't even speak our language. Why can't they let us rule ourselves?"

"Well, because none of us is alone. This peace, since Napoleon, is a fragile one. Even a minor ally of the Empire, like us, or the North Italian duchies, might shatter it, if we were free to change allegiance."

"But is it worth while if it's so very fragile?"

"Perhaps not," Koste said, slowly, with an intense, inward look. "But is any war worth while?"

"Surely not," Piera said, as intense as he was. "But actually the radicals don't want a war, do they? They just want not to have the Austrians here, and free elections, and the king—don't they?"

Koste nodded. "Independence; free elections; representation; the reform of corrupt institutions—great matters. But even if they can be achieved without either revolution or war, they are like revolution and war in this, they're matters too great for any individual; they override the individual man and all that may be good in his life as it is. Where men are very poor, a movement of reform that might carry them upward with it is their only hope. So in Rakava, or in Foranoy, the radical movement grows every year in strength. But here in the west we have little real poverty; people here are mostly free to make of their lives what they choose to make of them. We have attained something, here in Aisnar; nothing very large; but it took many centuries in the making. It will be lost in half a decade if it's jumbled in with the needs and wants of other classes and kinds of people. I prize this life, and these people; they are dear to me. So I cannot give my sympathy to those who in reforming the face of the earth will destroy my little, harmless corner of it."

Piera listened carefully as he spoke, and understood him. To know what attainments he wanted preserved she had only to look at him, his child, his house, and his city, the quiet city full of the sound of fountains. To them, to him, all change was loss. And because she was talking with him and liked him very much, she agreed with him. Reform was all right elsewhere, where they needed it.

She was aware than in adopting this attitude she was turning against Itale's beliefs; and the consciousness of it gave her pleasure. Very well! Let him be a radical, and let everybody in Krasnoy talk about him, and let Baroness Paludeskar talk about him all she liked. She did not care what they did in Krasnoy. She lived in Aisnar, and was her own woman. Her decorum and schoolgirl self-consciousness dropped away, and gayety flashed out in her like the flash of a garnet. Other people joined them; she was at the center of the group. The orchestra of three was tuning up. It was customary in Aisnar to dance the New Year in. Piera danced. She had a new gown, grey silk, the skirt caught up on one side with a rose of cloth of gold. She was slender and held her head back proudly; her dark, rosy face looked ready to break out into a laugh at what her partner, himself smiling as he handed her up the row, was saying to her. Givan Koste watched her. She and Baroness Paludeskar advanced to meet, curtsied in a mingling shimmer of violet and grey, retreated to the facing rows. Koste watched the prompt and yielding grace with which she let her partner sweep her off for their figure. He watched her eat a vanilla ice, after the dance; she ate every drop of it. He crossed the room to where she sat and asked her for the dance about to begin. She looked up in surprise. A widower of barely two years, he did not dance. She met his eyes. "Yes," she said, rising to take his hands as she spoke, and the piano and fiddle and bass began the sweet insistent rhythm of a polonaise.

The music stopped before the dance was done, drying off in mid-chord: the little French clock was pinging out midnight. "It's the new year," Koste said. "We ended the old one together, shall we begin the new one?" He gave the musicians the signal, the music began, Piera took her position for the dance without replying.

"A charming girl, your little Montayna countess," said Luisa to Koste's sister.

"Yes, she's a sweet child," said Miss Koste. "Do you see her about? I wanted to say a word to her, but I haven't seen her the last few minutes. Since last year, I should say." She laughed softly at her little joke.

"She's spent the year so far dancing with your brother."

"With my brother," Miss Koste repeated without expression, and looked at the dancers for a long minute. "It is pleasant to see my brother dance again," she said. "After so long."

"He has been unwell?" Luisa asked, struggling with a yawn.

"He lost his dear wife two years ago next month. I am so glad to see him forget himself a moment in his kindness to the child."

Kindness indeed, child indeed! Luisa stared at Miss Koste. Her mouth was set, her fingers laced tight together. She might well spend the morning of the new year in tears, in her neat bedroom upstairs where no man but her father and her brother had ever been; but nothing would escape her downstairs, in company. She was too shy, too proud. There was nothing to be got from these Aisnar people, shut in their little world, inexorably and intolerably polite. Luisa gave up struggling, and yawned. "Yes, indeed," she said. She looked at Givan Koste's face, dark and bright as a live coal, and at the silken whirl of Piera Valtorskar's skirts, and yawned again, openly, vindictively.

She spoke to Piera again as the evening ended. "It was a pleasure to talk with you of our mutual friend, contesina. Perhaps we can all have a good chat together when he comes."

"When he comes?"

"Hasn't he mentioned it to you? He may come here with my brother, in March, for a week or two."

"Oh, I hope so," said Piera. "Good night, baroness, I'm so happy to know you!" Off she went, happy, yes, seventeen years old and drunk with dancing; Luisa, leaving, heard her long, sweet laugh.

Piera returned to her convent school, put on her uniform,

walked sedate behind a nun on Thursday afternoons, knelt an hour every morning in the cold chapel; but the piety she had striven for and enjoyed for three months had evaporated overnight, leaving scarcely an odor of sanctity behind, a faint perfume. She waited for weekends now not because of Sunday high mass but because of Saturday night, which from four to eleven, she was permitted to spend with the Belleynins. She knew all that would happen there: tea in the parlor, quiet talk, dress for dinner, dine with a guest or two from among old friends or kinfolk, then coffee, perhaps a little music, then Mr Belleynin would walk her back to the convent. That was all. But these tranquil evenings centered upon her, were-for her; they were lessons, the happiest kind of lessons in the subtlest of subjects. She was an apt pupil. After a few weeks any stranger would have taken her for an Aisnar girl born and bred, a bright and gentle daughter of that aristocracy. The reward of her docility was the appreciation of all around her, their kindness to her, their acceptance of her as one of themselves. The reward might not have been quite enough but for two added elements; one was that they asked only outward conformity of her, leaving her feelings her own, untouched. Reserve was the keystone of the delicate arch. They taught Piera a coherent system of behavior, but did not meddle with the spirit in her. And the other inducement to the Belleynins' Saturday evenings was Givan Koste, the man of sorrows, the widower twice her age, the faithful visitor.

"What a joy it is to see Givan himself again," said Mrs Belleynin over coffee, only the three of them present; and her husband assented with his slight stutter, "Well, th-there is balm in Gilead." They both smiled, and the smile somehow referred itself to Piera so that she too smiled, feeling herself important, valued, loved. How nice they all were to her! It was delightful, and it must go on and on, exactly the same, nothing must change.

On the first Saturday of March she walked through the rain to her cousins' house at four o'clock, and entering found Givan Koste there. He often came in the evening, but no one came Saturday afternoons. Mrs Belleynin was distrait. She talked more than usual, Koste less. She poured tea, then rose, saying, "I believe I must go look for Albrekt myself, he must be in his study," and left Piera and Koste together alone.

Instinct, training, two months' preparation, mere guess, any of them could tell Piera what was coming, and did so; but she turned away and shut her mind, she opened her mouth and said to Givan Koste, "Have you seen Baroness Paludeskar lately?"

"Not lately."

"I haven't seen her since New Year's Eve, at your party, except on the street, just to nod to. She is so beautiful, she's so completely elegant. Sometimes I feel like the animals in Noah's ark when I have to go by her with all the girls two by two. . . ."

He mustered up a smile, but no words.

"She and I both know, we have a mutual friend, isn't that strange, since we come from so far apart. He lives in Krasnoy now, of course. The baroness said he might visit Aisnar this spring. It's so odd to meet a person you don't know that knows a person you do know, isn't it?" It would not do, it would not do at all. Her teeth were chattering. She looked at him imploring him to speak and make her stop talking, to let the ax fall.

He proposed marriage to her. She accepted him.

She looked down at their clasped hands. He had taken off the gold wedding-ring. When, she wondered, today or earlier? She had never thought to look. His hand was dark, strong, well-kept; she liked the look of it, the warmth of it. She bent her head and kissed his hand. "Piera, O my God," he whispered, and she felt, between alarm and pleasure, the tremor that ran through his whole body. He drew away from her, and walked up and down the room a couple of times.

"I shall write your father," he said, as if threatening.

"Of course. So shall I."

"There is the child."

"I know the child!"

"I am nearly forty," he said, rounding on her.

"Thirty-eight," she said.

That threw him off. "It may not please Count Valtorskar," he said less fiercely. "You are only seventeen."

126

"My mother was seventeen when they married. He was thirty-three. Anyway, papa is usually pleased by what I do."

"He cannot be pleased to lose you, Piera."

"But—we'll go home sometimes, won't we? To Malafrena?" This time she was disconcerted.

"Certainly."

"Then that's all right," she said, her distress vanishing. The word "lose" had gone through her like a knife, for an instant: to lose her father, to lose the lake, the house, the fat Cupid newel-post— But they would go home often, she need not live down here forever. She thought no more about it.

Givan Koste had stopped his pacing and was working himself up to say something, to suggest, no doubt, a new obstacle to his heart's desire. She smiled at him. She felt so sorry for him, and he was such a handsome man, with his poised body and grave, dark face. He turned, saw her smiling at him, and swallowed without speaking, hit amidships.

"I thought—perhaps next Christmas time—" he brought out.

"Next Christmas time?"

"Your father will want you to complete your year at St Ursula's. And a year is . . . customary . . . something less than a year in fact—"

"Ten months," she said dreamily, looking down at her hands.

"Is it too soon?"

"Oh, no. Must we announce it directly?"

"Not until you choose to," he said with a gratitude she did not understand.

"I do want to tell the Belleynins, and papa of course. And Laura. Oh, you'll like Laura, Mr Koste!"

"My name is Givan," he said, politely; they both heard the politeness, and they both laughed. Their eyes met. He looked like a boy, embarrassed. It was a wonderful relief to laugh. "Who is Laura?" he asked.

"My friend, Laura Sorde." Saying the name she grew shy again suddenly. "She's very nice." She looked down, inept, a schoolgirl.

Koste was most at ease with her when she was shy, not

offering him unconstrained the fulfilment he could not yet believe in. He came to her and took her hand lightly; his face and voice were warm with feeling. "I want you to talk with your cousins, Piera. I want you to have time, to be certain, I feel that I— Loving you is privilege enough— I should go now. I'll come back when you say I should."

"Tonight?"

"Tonight," he said, with that smile that lit his face and left it unchanged; and he went out. She sat still. Four silver-mounted glasses full of cold tea reposed on the table beside her. She jumped up and went to find Mrs Belleynin. She did not want to be alone. They met on the stairs. "Has he gone?" the older woman asked anxiously. "Yes," Piera said, and burst into tears.

"Oh my dear, my dear," Mrs Belleynin murmured, hugging her there on the stair landing. "There, there, it's all past. I'm so sorry!"

"I didn't know I was going to cry," Piera sobbed, burying her face in the soft, sweet-smelling shoulder.

"Poor child, it's all our fault. How stupid I am! What a misery, what a misery!"

"But it isn't— I mean, we are to be married— Next Christmas. I didn't know I was going to cry!"

"Next Christmas? You are betrothed?" said Mrs Belleynin, who was in tears herself. "Oh dear me! I didn't understand—I thought we'd made a dreadful mistake— But you aren't happy, Piera? is something wrong?" She looked down at the broad, stubborn, childish brow which was all she could see of Piera's face, and repeated the question still more tenderly. For her conscience was alert and sensitive; and neither of her own daughters, tranquil and self-possessed women by the age of seventeen, had ever clung to her thus in confused and passionate need.

"No, I'm very happy," Piera sobbed, weeping so that Mrs Belleynin gave up all questions and led her upstairs to her room to comfort her. "There, there," she murmured, "there, Piera, don't cry any more, it's past. . . ."

II

Itale stood at a window of a house on Fontarmana Street, watching the moon rise over old gardens dim with evening and hearing the lilt of the fountain below the window as the west wind sprang up and moved in the leaves in the dusk. He was dressed in a plum-colored coat, his mother's Christmas gift; his linen was fine and well starched, his hair was orderly, his cravat and stickpin were controlled, his face was quiet and a little forlorn. He was wondering if looking south from here on a clear day you could see the mountains.

"Never saw a chap look out windows as much as you do," said Enrike Paludeskar, entering the room after a feeble rap. "What do you see out of 'em, Sorde? —Roofs, trees, moon, nothing going on. Same view I've got. Are you ready?"

"Yes," said Itale, turning his forlorn look to Enrike's heavy, well-shaven, goodnatured face.

"How d'ye like my rig? English fashion. Everything has to be English. I don't know why. Come on, Luisa's waiting. What's the time? These damn trousers are so tight I can't get my watch out without performing a sort of dance. We mustn't be late, the old lady's a dragon."

Itale looked at his watch, which said two-thirty. It had stopped running several weeks ago, and he kept meaning to have it fixed. "Must be near six."

"We'd better drive, then."

Luisa smiled up at them from the foot of the broad staircase. "Don't be silly, Harry, it's only around the corner."

"Town's all squeezed up together," Enrike grumbled. "Hate arriving on foot." But on foot they set off into the evening of early spring. The fountains sang, the budding branches of the plane-trees interlaced above the street, the wind was soft and cool, the moon poised bright above the roofs. All things were poised: in balance. All things here, Itale thought, were in harmony.

They were to dine with one of the inmost circle of Aisnar society, the marchioness Feldeskar-Torm. Itale was well received. They knew who he was: a landowner's son of Val Malafrena, one of the western *domey*; a house-guest of one of themselves; therefore, temporarily, one of themselves. Evidently they also knew what else he was, for after supper the marchioness, a small, plain, old woman, said pleasantly to him, "Well, Mr Sorde, are you bringing the revolution to Aisnar? I should have thought we were scarcely worth fomenting."

There seemed no point in hedging. "No, markesa," he said. "I'm only trying to lure some of your young men away to Krasnoy."

"You city people always want the revolutions all to yourselves," the old lady said with a ghostly laugh. "I've read many of your articles, Mr Sorde. They are interesting; eloquent."

He bowed in thanks.

"They remind me sometimes of what our Valtura used to write for the old Aisnar *Mercury*, and of Kostant Veloy in the Krasnoy *Review*. Then I think Veloy has been dead for twenty years, Valtura has been in prison in Austria for ten—I suppose he is dead too. Four generations of radicals I've seen, Mr Sorde, but I haven't seen the revolution."

The challenge was direct, and he answered it directly: "I believe you will see it, markesa."

"You keep trying. I grant you that. I see you've won over our handsome baroness." She looked at Luisa, who was talking politics with Mr Belleynin and a Feldeskar-Torm great-nephew. "I doubt Valtura could have done that."

"If he'd had the chance . . . ."

"But he wouldn't have had the chance," she said, looking at him with shrewd, cold eyes.

He left the pleasant dinner party somewhat depressed in spirit. The marchioness had placed several darts in him with exquisite accuracy. She had reminded him that his cause had been defeated time and time again; she had reminded him that the Paludeskars were very curious companions for a revolutionary; she had reminded him of the ambiguity of his own position. And yet she had done all this not, he admitted, in enmity to his cause,

130

but in support of it. She had as good as asked, Where is our revolution? What are you doing about it?

He walked restlessly about his room in the Arrioskar house, then went to the window that overlooked the garden, opened it, and leaned out. The fountain lilted in its stone basin, a thin silvery sound in the night. A fountain at the street crossing a few doors down interwove a faint counterpoint. The wind was down. It was profoundly still, the stillness of the long fields that stretched on from the city on every side. A few stars burned humidly bright in the sky washed blue with moonlight. Beauty, balance, harmony. . . . Sick of himself, Itale tried to lose himself in the moonlight, the quiet, but could not; in this germinant darkness, this moment between March and April, between sleep and wakening, he found only anger, uncertainty, and fear.

Turned back upon himself he tried to face himself, demanding the source of the trouble. When had his work become, not an end, but a mere distraction from—or means toward?—some different and obscurer end? What necessity was he shirking, with what angel must he wrestle? In asking the questions, it seemed to him that the trouble lay in his presence here, now, in this house. All his uncertainties of the last months might clarify themselves if he could simply answer the question, What am I doing here?

His mind veered at once from the question, replacing it with a different one, the question others might ask of him. Enrike, for instance; did he wonder occasionally why Itale was with him in Aisnar? If so he gave no sign of it. He had known Itale on and off for a year and a half now, at his own house and at the Helleskar house, and probably assumed that anyone he had known so long had to be a friend. Their brief warm flare of companionship on the coach was long forgotten, they had never had a conversation of any consequence whatever since; Enrike simply took Itale for granted. And his hosts here, the Arrioskars? . . . But this was no good. He came presented as the Paludeskars' friend and a gentleman, and naturally they accepted him as such. Why not admit that he felt at home with them, in this comfortable, quiet house, as he never felt at home in his two cold rooms in Krasnoy, eating bread and cheese by himself, and listening to the endless

131

thud of Kounney's loom? But that was no good either. The matter of comfort was irrelevant, the question of his right to be here no question. The point was, what was he doing here? Was this one of the places to which he had to come, as Krasnoy was? Again his mind sheered off from the matter, asking with self-pity if he might not have a little comfort and good company now and then while he did what he had to do: but what it was he had to do, he did not know. Leaning out the window he gazed southward over the rooftops, straining his eyes as if he looked for something real and present beyond the moonlit wash of air; his mind was quite empty; he said aloud, "Why am I wasting my time?"

He drew back thinking he had seen a movement, someone looking up, in the darkness under the trees.

The air inside the room was close. He loosened his high stock, began to take off his coat, then shrugged it back on and with a cautious, decisive step left the room, went down the hall, down the stairs, through the music room and out the side door of the house into the garden. There all was luminous and cool. The fountain sang, stars gleamed through budding branches, rows of narcissus by the paths gleamed in the moonlight and the warmer glow of the few lighted windows of the house. Itale walked to the fountain and stood watching the play of the water, then sat down on a bench near it, his hands in his pockets, his eyes still on the slender jet of water that seemed to hang suspended over the basin, catching the moonlight, falling and renewing in one motion, constant change in changelessness, alive.

"Itale?"

He got up quickly.

"It's hot in the house, I can't bear it. . . . I can never sleep in spring." Her voice was no louder than the sound of the fountain. She had thrown a shawl over her light dress, and in the broken light and shade of the garden nothing of her was clear but her face, simplified by that mixed light into simple beauty.

"I've wanted to talk to you ever since you came. There's never a moment. . . . Are you content, Itale? Are you content with what you're doing?"

"I wouldn't be doing anything else."

132

"But is your life what you want it to be?"

"No," he said, and moved restlessly, clasping his hands behind his back. Luisa sat down on the bench, drawing the shawl around her shoulders.

"If you were free, no responsibilities, no duties, entirely free, what would you do?"

"I can't imagine freedom without responsibility."

"Oh, bah," she said, "how stuffy you can be. And how it helps you evade answering. If you were free to do exactly what you wanted to do—what would you do?" In her voice was an impertinent tenderness, a note he had never heard before and that struck him as her true note, herself speaking without defense, nervous, mocking, intent.

"I don't know," he said. "I'd go home."

"Where is home?"

"Malafrena —But the fact is I am doing what I want to do. Your idea of freedom is a child's idea, baronina."

"Probably. Women are all childlike, aren't they? And spiritual, too, of course, Perhaps my idea of freedom is spiritual. A bit ghostly: choice without consequence. Well, I know what I would do if I were free, like a child, or a ghost. . . . I would do very nearly what I do now."

"Then you are happy."

"Very nearly happy."

He had turned to face her, wanting to see her face, which was in shadow now.

"I imagine that only moral people, like you, are very happy or unhappy," she said. "I am always both, and most of all on spring nights when I can't sleep, and have to walk in the garden wondering what on earth would ever make me happy without making me unhappy."

"There is no reason why you should be unhappy."

"None at all; I know. I am young, and rich, and very well dressed, and in any case I am a woman, and it takes very little to make a woman happy—a toy or two, a necklace or a fan."

"I did not mean that," Itale said stiffly.

"What did you mean?"

He did not reply for a while; when he did his tone was low and unwilling, without warmth. "I meant I don't want you to be unhappy."

"I know that. You want me to be happy; you want to think of me as happy, because it is so much pleasanter. And easier. If you think of me as unhappy then you have to do something about it, find a toy to amuse me . . . if you are my friend, of course."

"You know I am your friend, baronina."

"Don't call me baronina, please. It's a stupid title. I suppose you believe all titles are stupid. Ours certainly is. I wish my grandfather had had the courage to appear as what he was, the best of his class; I should be proud to be a *haute bourgeoise*, nothing more and nothing less. But he had to buy us into the nobility, and leave us clinging tooth and nail to the lowest rung of the rotten old ladder leading nowhere—pretending that it isn't money that made us, and makes us, and will take us wherever we do go. . . ." She looked up at Itale and laughed suddenly, a laugh of real amusement. "Oh, God, Itale, you are infectious! Lectures in the moonlight. . . ."

"Do I lecture?"

"Almost continually."

"I'm sorry," he said, chagrined.

"I don't mind. I like your lectures. At least they're serious, at least you talk seriously to me—though whether you're talking to me I often wonder; but at least you allow me to be present while you talk. Some day, perhaps, you will in fact talk to me."

"I don't . . ."

"No, I know you don't. You never have."

"I don't know what you mean."

"I mean that under all the theories, the politics, the lectures, there is silence, a granite silence, unbroken. No, I take that back. I think you said something to me, just a minute ago, and it took me so by surprise that I almost missed it. You said that you loved— But no, you didn't say it after all, now I think of it; I could simply hear in the way you said the name that you were finally talking about something to me, something real, not an idea, not a theory."

"What name?"

"Malafrena."

He half turned away again towards the fountain, his hands deep in his pockets, and shrugged.

"I miss it sometimes," he said.

She said nothing, watching him.

"It isn't far from here." He looked up as if he wanted to say more, but he did not say any more. She continued to watch him, the tall hunched figure in front of her, the profile, big nose, mouth firmly closed, a portrait in charcoal, plain and strong. A few streets away the half hour struck on the bells of Aisnar cathedral. A faint wind had come up, moving the leaves, making the air feel chill. In the house, behind them, a light went off silently, leaving the path they were on and the flowers beside it cold white.

"Though you don't talk to me, you talk to yourself sometimes."

"When?"

"At your window, a few minutes ago. You said, 'Why am I wasting my time?' That's why I asked you if you were happy. Knowing that you weren't." She spoke very low, in the silence after the bells.

"I don't know what I meant."

"It's almost frightening to hear someone say the very words you're thinking, but not say them to you."

"I wasn't talking about anything particular."

She stood up. "I hate to watch men lie," she said, her voice a little more distinct. "I hate anything done clumsily. But if you're not interested in the truth, why should I be?" She turned to go. Her shawl had slipped from her shoulders and lay in a pool of silken white on the path. He picked it up; she had stopped at his movement. He set the shawl on her shoulders; as he did so she turned towards him, and reached up taking his right hand, the delicate film of silk between their hands. They stood a moment motionless.

"Luisa—"

"Itale!" she mocked him, that discordant tenderness in her tone. He bent to kiss her mouth, the warm silk slipping beneath his hand, and she slipped away, broke from him, and turned to him again at a little distance. Her face was smooth as a bright

135

mask; her eyes were exultant and terrified. "Good night," she whispered, and slipped away into the shadow, into the open door, of the house.

Itale stood there a while and then walked under the trees, where he had seen her first. He came to the wall of the garden. He put his hands on it, then leaned against it, his forehead on his arm. For a minute he was intensely aware of himself, felt the rough brick against his palm, smelt the extreme sweetness of the narcissus blooming at his feet, saw the late, serene night around him; then it all slid away again, and again returned, as if he were swimming in an invisible sea, warm, tumultuous, silent, from which he broke free long enough to breathe, feel his heart pounding, see the stars, then he went under again. When the cathedral bell struck three he turned slowly round and made his way to the house; he lay down on his bed fully dressed, and immediately, as if knocked out, went to sleep.

Next day he went about the business that had brought him to Aisnar—if it was business that had brought him to Aisnar. He did not consider the question. He considered nothing that was not directly under his nose. As soon as one conference or conversation was over he forgot it and went on to the next. He was if anything more decisive and efficient than usual, but at any given hour he could not have said without an effort of thought what he had been doing an hour earlier, or, perhaps, what he was doing now. One person he met broke through his insulation: an Italian, exiled for his part in the Piedmont revolt of 1820, who had spent a year in Aisnar and was about to set off for England. Something in this man reached Itale, and afterwards he recalled vividly Sangiusto's long face, high forehead, curly hair, his cordial voice, as they sat at a cafe table in the leaf-dappled late sunlight on Fontarmana Street: "A liberal is a man who says the means justify the end," he said, and the words too stayed with Itale.

The light got lower, dustier, more golden down the tree-arched street, a few carriages rolled by slowly, the wind smelled of ploughed fields and the moon rose over the old houses. Itale went back to supper with his hosts. Luisa's cousin was a cold, shy woman, and Arrioskar had little conversation in him; Enrike was dining elsewhere; Luisa, whose manners were as good as she wanted them to be, kept up just enough talk that no one felt awkward, to the evident gratitude of the Arrioskars. Coffee was served upstairs at ten and at ten-fifteen the evening ended. It was now Holy Week, there would be no more parties until Easter was past.

Back in his room Itale did not open the window, or look out of it. He took off his coat, sat down at the escritoire, and began going through a pile of local and foreign pamphlets and manuscripts he had gathered in the course of the day. He read steadily, annotating occasionally, never raising his head. The room was bright with candles, but chilly, as he had let the little fire go out.

The bell of the cathedral, a soft deliberate baritone, struck midnight. Itale hunched his shoulders and went on reading.

"There must be no confusion," said the pamphlet, "of such manifestations of radicalism as the secret societies of France, Italy, and the Germanies, nor such excesses of radical opinion as the revolutionary leagues of the last decade in England, with the liberal faction in our own country, which the Government of Orsinia not only tolerates but will indubitably come to favor as a benign and harmless indication of peaceful popular enlightenment. To forbid the publication of . . ." Itale went back and crossed out the word "faction," crossed out "indubitably," scowled and crossed out the entire sentence, then put the thing aside and put his head in his hands.

He got up, went about the room putting out the candles, took up his coat, went downstairs and out.

The air was colder tonight; the moon, a night past full, was veiled by a slight mist. The jet of the fountain blew astray now and again in the slight breeze. Itale stood by the stone bench, looking at the narcissus blooming at his feet. He heard the latch of the house door. Luisa came to him, a long dark scarf wrapped about her over her light dress. "I heard you," she whispered with a laugh in her voice. "I was listening for you. . . ."

"Baronina—"

"Dom Itaal!" she mocked.

"I cannot call you Luisa."

She sat down on the stone bench, drawing the dark, voluminous scarf up about her neck, smoothing the fall of it across her skirt.

"And what else can you not do?"

"You are—unjust," he said.

"Am I? But then I'm only a woman. No one expects justice from a woman. As you can't call me by my name, so I can't treat you with justice."

"You are unjust to yourself."

"Am I?" she said again, but without anger, thoughtfully. "I wonder. You may be right." She looked up at him, with so direct a gaze that he could not turn from it. "You have the power to hurt me. How strange that is."

"I have no wish to hurt you. Don't you understand—"

"No."

"I have no power to— You know what I am," he said desperately, "and how I live, and where I live—"

"What of it?"

He could not answer.

"I am not asking you for manners, I am not asking you for mercy, I am asking you for the truth. To speak to me. Just once, to speak to me!"

"What can I say?"

The fountain, blown aside by the wind, rustled and pattered.

"What good would it do if I said it?" he asked in anguish.

"None," Luisa whispered. "None." She rocked herself a little, holding her arms about her sides, drawn into herself.

"All we can do is hurt each other, it's no good—"

She rose suddenly, reaching out to him. His first response was startled and awkward, as her movement had been awkward. Then he held her to him more strongly, their inept embrace became searching, her tension melted into yielding, fused towards him till they clung together, pressed together in an insatiable kiss.

From it she broke at last, twisting away blindly, he reaching blindly after her. With control, a reaction of momentary shock and sickness came into him, and he sank down on the bench and sat bowed forward, his head down. She stood hearby; her body trembled slightly from time to time; she watched him.

When he looked up he did not meet her eyes, but spoke to her arms, in an angry, pleading whisper. "Don't you see?"

"Do *you* see now? At last?"

When he understood her his expression began to change from dazed to dazzled. He stood up, and putting out his hands towards her in an uncertain gesture, said, incredulous and gentle, "Luisa—"

"Ah," she said, "there!" She took his hands and held them, standing facing him, separate, smiling, her face raised. "I will be just," she whispered with that exulting smile. "I will be merciful."

He could say nothing coherent, but stammered praise and desire.

She took his arm and walked with him up and down the path, and across the lawn to the garden wall, and back to the fountain. Most of his consciousness was centered upon the warmth of her arm and her side and the warm faint fragrance of her hair. He agreed without hesitation when she said, "Now we can choose. . . . What I can't bear, what I can't bear is falseness, dishonesty, the stupid rules made for stupid people, the rules of lying. . . . What I want is the truth, and only the truth."

"I love you," he said.

"We are not children, and not fools, and not slaves. We can choose what we do. That is what I want, that's all I want, the freedom to choose! Do you understand, Itale?"

"Yes," he said, because she was so eager and intense, because she wanted freedom, happiness, as he did, because the pressure of her arm on his made his head swim with happiness.

"If you judged me now," she continued in her intense whisper, "I would despise you. But you won't. All you do, all your friends and their ideas, they're trivial, but you're above them, above all that. There's no freedom but what one makes oneself, for oneself."

He agreed.

"And that's why we must choose, Itale, this week— I go back

139

to Krasnoy Wednesday; you'll come a week later—that's enough time. We must each choose, both choose, what we wish to do, no one and nothing forbidding us or compelling us. I will use my life and my love as I see fit to use it. We will set each other free, Itale."

The tremor in her voice might be exaltation or terror. He drew her to him and kissed her mouth. But as her lips softened against his, she began to draw away. He let her go. She whispered, "Only a week!" Before he realised she was going she had gone, a glimmer between moonlight and darkness on the path. "Luisa," he said, "wait—" The house door opened and shut quietly. He stood there by the fountain, bereft and confused. Why had she gone? Had he misunderstood again? Were they not lovers, or to be lovers? He had understood her as she spoke, as she spoke of freedom, but now he did not know what she had said. A light glimmered faint behind curtains in a room upstairs: her candle; her bedroom. He sat down on the stone bench once more, shivering with cold and the aftershocks of frustrated desire, groping after the immense happiness he had felt only a minute before. "A week," he repeated, finding the words a talisman. "Only a week."

III

On Saturday afternoon Itale cut short a meeting with the author of what he thought of as the Indubitably Pamphlet, alleging another obligation. "I have to see someone out in the country," he said abruptly. The author of the pamphlet, in awe of conspiracies, asked no questions. Itale left the house and walked straight down the street; he had no objective at all. Town houses gave place to villas set back behind low walls, villas gave place to farmhouses and open fields, and the pavingblocks of the street to the red dirt of a country road. Overhead stretched a wide, changeable April sky, reflected underfoot in long puddles left from the morning's rain. Weeds bloomed coarse and timid by the fences; grain and grass were bright green on the plough-lands. The road, very long and straight, the Roman road that had crossed the Western Province to the garrison at Aquae Nervi, was empty; the fields were empty, except for a lone ploughman who silently answered Itale's silent salutation from the road. It was a gentle land, monotonous, noble in its coherent and unbroken vastness from horizon to horizon. Itale walked straight on, vaguely contented by the fresh wind and the rough road under his feet, noticing more clearly from time to time a wild iris, a cloud shadow fading across a field, a lark playing in the high air, a rain-washed stone.

In four days he would go back to Krasnoy. His mind revolved perpetually about the end of that trip: what would he do, what should he do? He was sick of thinking about it and never ceased to think about it. How had he let himself be involved in an unsuitable, an impossible affair like this? a marriageable heiress, a spectacular woman, who could not possibly manage to have a lover without her brother and probably half a dozen of her suitors finding out about it—and if they did not she might very well tell them; for she was nervous, capricious, insanely wilful; spoilt. A spoilt girl. A proud, sensitive, frightened girl, a woman risking herself, offering him everything and asking nothing in return—nothing but that his courage equal hers. . . . It was freedom she wanted; liberty. What did all his work for liberty amount to? Two rooms on Mallenastrada, an irregularly pub-lished journal of very uneven quality, a succession of jobs taken to keep the rent paid, a circle of feckless and unstable acquain-tances all professing devotion to the cause but quarreling about it continually—and was this to be his life? Was this what he had left Malafrena for?

For a liberal the means justify the end. To attain freedom one must live free. It was freedom she wanted, freedom she of-fered—and he was already so lost among contingencies, petty considerations, and conventional moralities that he could con-sider rejecting that offer! Was he a man or not? Not yet, maybe; he had been a boy, until now. He had come at last into his majority. He was and would be a man.

141

But which man? a hand-to-mouth radical journalist, or a baroness' lover?

Why could he not be both? Was he supposed to live celibate for the cause of liberty, was it a religion and he its holy hypocrite? — He strode through the bright fields of afternoon in a rage, sometimes waving his right arm as he argued fiercely with himself; and all the while he knew in the center of his heart that he might or might not go to Luisa Paludeskar when he returned to Krasnoy, but that it was not reason that would, or could, make the choice. Reasons abounded, but within him something single, whole, indifferent, waited for a sign.

The road led up and over one of the long, low rises of land that made up the immense level of the plain. So gradual was the ascent that slope and summit were all one. Itale stopped and looked back. Aisnar lay five or six miles away, made entire by distance, tile roofs red in the declining light, the calm towers of the cathedral rising above blue shadow. Near where he stood was the ruin of a hut, a few stones and rain-rotted planks. He sat down there on what had been a doorstep or a hearthstone, between the city and the sun. The blowing of the country wind had finally blown his thoughts away. For a long time he sat hearing only the wind in the new grass. He sought stillness of heart, the void, the gap, the silence that had been his kingdom in the sunlit afternoons of the years at Malafrena. That was liberty, but it was gone. He had lost it. He turned to look southward; the same long plains ran varied and changeless as the sea to a soft haze on the horizon.

"What would you do if you had seven hundred years to live?"

There they were, Laura in a glimmering white dress, Piera, and himself, on the terrace in late midsummer dusk, the Hunter standing dark across the blurred and shining lake. He said he would travel to China and America, Laura wanted volcanoes, and Piera, what was it she had wanted to do? But what the devil, Piera was in Aisnar. She was not there in a remembered dusk above the lake any more than he was. She was here, under one of those red-tiled roofs, in some convent school; the Belleynin he had met at the marchioness' house was her cousin.

Itale stood up, stretched, and started back to town. He could not stay in the same town with Piera Valtorskar for two weeks and leave without a sign to her; things weren't that bad with him yet.

At about five he was at the Belleynins' front door. "The countess is not here today, sir," said the old servant, polite, but mistrustful of the dusty stranger. Itale asked where he might find her. "The countess lives in the Ursuline school, sir. On the Old Side, facing the Ring Fountain." The countess, the countess. Young Piera, with freckles on her neck. Itale marched off across Fontarmana Street to the Ring Fountain. There was a big, tightlipped building with barred windows. A porter opened to his knock and said there were no visiting hours on Easter eve; come next Saturday. Itale pleaded the fact that he must leave on Wednesday, and his right hand put a small silver piece in the porter's without his left hand knowing a thing about it. He was shown into an icy parlor containing four straightbacked chairs and one nun. He pleaded with the nun. An older nun was called and he pleaded with her, eloquently tactful; he was, as he had been since he got to his feet in the ruined hut on the hill, determined. The second nun went away, the first retired to a chair in the hall just outside the open door, and Piera came in.

"Oh Itale," she said, and they put their arms round each other and kissed each other on the mouth. "Oh my dear Itale!" she said, tears in her eyes, laughing, in the first, great flash of joy that ran through them both; and then they dropped their arms, and did not know what to do with them.

"My God, how did I even know you?" he said, still dazzled by the flash, and she laughed again. "Don't swear here! I've grown two inches, nearly."

"It's like coming home to see you, Piera."

"I know—to see you too—and you still talk Maalafren! —Come and sit down, we don't have to stand." Her last words were conventionally gracious. Chill grew where the bright warmth had been. Itale sat down on one of the rigid chairs. "I can't sit down," he said, standing up again at once, and Piera giggled: the last flare. It went out.

"It's very strange to see you here," he said, looking about the room, his hands behind his back.

143

"I know."

Four walls, four chairs, two doors. He had to look back at her.

"How long have you been in Aisnar?"

"Ten days. I should have come before—I've been seeing a lot of people, time gets away. Sorry I caused all this regulation-breaking."

"Anything rather than not seeing you at all."

"Do you like it here?"

"Yes, it's very nice."

"When will you go home?"

"I'll leave here in June, and stay with the Belleynins for a while," she said. Her voice was hesitant; she stood hesitant, yet calm, in her sleek grey dress and white apron. "Will you not tell anyone, I mean write them, please, Itale? because there hasn't been time yet for papa's letter to come, my letter went on the last post—I wanted to tell you, I won't be going home exactly either, I'm going to live in Aisnar. I'm engaged to be married. This coming winter. Or perhaps after Easter next year."

"I see, I'm very glad for you," he said, with a prolonged stammer. "Who is—?"

"Givan Koste. He's a lawyer. Do you know the Belleynins? They've been so kind to me, I'm so fond of them— He is a friend of theirs. It's all going to be as quiet as can be, since he's a widower with a little boy." He did not remember her voice being so thin, or so sweetly modulated, a young-lady voice. "I'm very fond of him, of Battiste," she said. That was very nice, everything was nice, everyone was kind and fond, why was she telling him all this? Let her get on with it and marry her damned widower, what was it to him?

"I suppose that's the end of it," he said.

"Of what, Itale?"

He waved his arm. "Knowing each other. The part of life when we knew each other."

"It doesn't have to be," she said in that thin voice. "If you come to Aisnar I hope you'd come see me. And we might be at Malafrena again, summers—"

"But we've left Malafrena," he said. "It's taken me a while to learn that. Life's not a room, it's a road; what you leave you

144

leave, and it's lost. You can't turn back. That's how it is; we most likely won't meet again."

"Perhaps not," she said.

There was a considerable pause.

"Are you happy in Krasnoy?" she asked.

"Happy? No, not particularly, I suppose. I'm doing what I went to do there."

"I see your journal sometimes."

"They let you read seditious papers here?" He looked about with a hard grin at the walls and doors.

"Not here. Your articles are very interesting."

"Why the situation of linen-weavers in Krasnoy slums should be interesting to you I don't know, but thanks." He had heard the valor in her tone, he heard the hypocrisy in his own; he could endure no more. "I must go now, Piera," he said flatly. She turned towards him. "Goodbye," he said, and she took his hand and said, "Goodbye, Itale."

That was that. Outside by the double-tiered, silver-stranded Ring Fountain he looked at his watch; it said two-thirty, as usual, but the cathedral bell had just struck, it must be six. He was late for an appointment he had made with two likely contributors to *Novesma Verba*. He set off hastily to the cafe where they were to meet. "Life's a road," he heard his voice saying fatuously, fraudulently, "Life's not a room, it's a road"—yes, sure enough, a road going nowhere, on and on, meaningless. No turning back, no stopping, no end, no goal; best to go alone, allowing no claims. Let the dead bury their dead!

The two men he met at the cafe were young, one an ex-seminarian, the other an unsuccessful candidate for representative to the National Assembly, which was to be convened this September in Krasnoy. Itale's unmoved familiarity with their hopes and questions left them impressed and admiring. He saw that, and grew still more dry and hard in his replies, but they would not be discouraged. He left them as soon as he could and went to the hotel to which he had moved when the Paludeskars left; he had a chop sent up to his room, and went through the last few days' notes and papers. His fortnight in Aisnar was proving profitable. There was money here for the support of both

145

journals, there were contributors of talent, and the prosperous middle class of the city followed the liberal tradition established in the last century. It was all very encouraging. Drearily, he got his work in order, ate the dinner he had allowed to get cold, sat down again to work. One had to go alone; no use looking for anything one had left behind. Take what happiness might come, get the work done, and no complaining. It was the only way. Alone; to be free one had to be alone.

He was getting a headache, and to shake it off he went out around eleven to walk. As he went down Fontarmana Street, all black-dappled with shadows of branches cast by lighted windows, alive with the night wind and a quiet coming and going of people, someone hailed him from a cafe table: the Italian exile, Sangiusto.

"Have a coffee with me, Sorde!"

Itale stopped by the table, but did not sit down. "I was thinking of looking in the cathedral."

"Ha, it's Easter. I'll come, you don't mind? My bill, please, five coffees." They went on together. "Monday I leave to go to England," said Sangiusto. "Now I don't want to go. I speak the language better, but I like your country. I like Krasnoy, I like this Aisnar, I don't know why I go to England!" He laughed, showing his strong white teeth. "Only at times it's good to get out from the Empire, neh? But I shall come back, I think."

"I hope they'll let you in, after we've published your articles from England."

"Oh, here I'm even more insignificant than in my country. And your police are not so good as those in the Piedmont. But I shall not stop in Vienna to obtain permission. . . ."

"What if we use a false name on your articles?"

"Why not? I have been 'Carlo Franceschi' in Turin already. You look tired, Sorde."

"I am."

"And I'm full of coffee, like a ship that's sinking. Every night I drink coffee, what else to do. . . ." He laughed again. "What a life! —Look at the poor devils, they want to be home in their Bohemia or where they come from." They had passed a pair of militia-men, imposing in the Imperial uniform. "Like all of us.

146

Easter night! We would go to mass in the boat across the lake."

"What lake?"

"Lago d'Orta," Sangiusto said, lingering on the name with conscious love, saying it with pleasure, tenderness.

They approached the doors of the cathedral, which stood open showing a glimpse of dusk and gold within. A little procession was crossing the cathedral square coming from Old Side, nuns and girls, heavily shawled. Itale recognised the grey uniform Piera had worn. She was among the tall girls at the end of the line, no doubt, head bent submissively as she walked. She would not see him nor could he tell which of the slender, shawled figures she might be.

"Pretty ducklings," said Sangiusto. "I see them take their walk in the afternoons, so neat, with bright eyes seeing everything like telescopes. I like the girls of convent schools, they always know so much. Excuse me, you feel religious?"

It made Itale laugh. "No," he said.

"I should like to see your mountains where you came from, as you spoke of them yesterday I thought this sounds like my country."

"I wish I could take you there, Sangiusto."

"Oh, well, the time will come. If you wait the time comes, I find. To learn how to wait, that's the job for the exile, isn't it? I will remember your invitation, Sorde, thank you. Come on, the mass begins." They went into the church, into the grieving, the waiting, the fulfilment of Easter night. "Christ is risen" the choir sang, the music like sunrise in the heart of night. "Christ is risen in glory!" and the joy washed over Itale's heart like rain on a stone of the roads, like sunlight over stone.

IV

Country women starting home from the Great Market of Krasnoy, where they had arrived at dawn to sell stuff from their suburban gardens and dairies, leeks, apples, eggs, cream cheese,

147

were halted on this morning of early September as they straggled back towards Cathedral Square with their empty baskets to meet up with the farm wagons going home. Foreign militia and a squad of the palace guard in their crimson uniforms were blocking one street, clearing another, shouting orders; cockades nodded between horses' nervously working ears, gilt buttons flashed in the misty sunshine, already growing warm. Those people who had got nearly to the square before they were stopped in a crowd could see a whole battalion of guardsmen drawn up in rows before the doors of the cathedral. "Don't they all stand there like red tenpins," said a broad goodwife of Grasse to her neighbor. "Let 'em stand all they like, I'm sick of standing," said the tall and skinny neighbor, shifting her basket on her arm. "I'd just as soon not be standing next to your goat cheeses, mother," put in her neighbor on the other side, a man in a cobbler's apron, with a smiling mouth pursed and lopsided from holding ready all the shoenails of all the years. "Stick to your last, cobbler," the skinny woman said smartly. "Is it a parade?" shrilled the gaptoothed daughter of the woman from Grasse. "Oh dear little Jesus, remember the Holy Sacrament parade in Grasse, ma, and all the grand gold things? What's a Sembly, ma?"—"How would I know?" said ma. "Do ye know what all the crowding and the soldiers are about, cobbler?"— "City folk idling," the skinny wife snarled. "It's a great day, mother," said the cobbler, his mouth doing its best to stretch back to normal, "didn't you know? We've all turned out to see the Assembly go by."—"Who'd have turned out," said an irritated clerk squeezed up against the cobbler by the growing throng behind, "if the damned guards hadn't started pushing people around? I'd be in the office now if they'd just let me alone with their damned horses."

It was ten o'clock; the people at Cathedral Square heard the bell of St Stephen's under the Hill, the bell of St Roch's in Old Quarter, but not the great bell of the cathedral. It was silent until, at nearly quarter past the hour, the whole carillon gave a mighty, hair-raising, triumphant clash and then settled into pealing tremendously treble down to bass, treble down to bass. "What the devil's all that about?" the nervous clerk said, while the farm

148

women crossed themselves. "It means the bendiction of the Assembly's over," said the knowledgeable cobbler, "now watch, old woman, you'll see 'em coming out and heading up Tiypontiy Street to the park."—"What's the Benediction of the Sembly, ma?" the gaptoothed daughter squealed. "Oh look! Look! Oh dear little body of Jesus, look at 'em all!"

The Assembly of the Three Estates of the Kingdom came forth from the Cathedral of St Theodora in the order prescribed by the Revision of 1509: the Archbishop and his college of canons, and the deputies of the Clergy of the Ten Provinces, in order of rank, in robes befitting the season of the ecclesiastical year; following these, the deputies of the Nobility of the Ten Provinces, in armor or suitable attire, in order of rank, each attended by a squire bearing visibly the arms of the house; lastly the deputies of the Commons, in black gowns and hats of cloth or fur, though not of ermine or of sable; the whole to be attended and duly honored in their progress to the Palace by the Royal Guard, and to be met and greeted there by the King, the Rector of the Royal University of the City of Krasnoy, the Mayor of the City of Krasnoy, and the Masters of the eight Great Guilds. They went by, in their robes and top hats. Far off in the park a trumpet sounded sweetly. A few cheers went up for known faces among the Commoners, the city's own deputies and Oragon, the deputy from Rakava. As soon as the cordons were raised the people scattered, a few following the procession across the park, the farm women across the square to meet their wagons, the clerks to their offices, the cobblers to their lasts.

Inside the Sinalya Palace, in the large, cold Assembly Room, like a marble barn, the convocation proceeded in good order. The deputies sat, the officers of the guard stood armed at each door. Grand Duchess Mariya pronounced, in Latin, the sovereign's address of welcome.

Up in the gallery, a kind of pigeon-cote to the marble barn, twenty men stood gasping for air and jammed elbow to rib, trying to see out the four two-foot loopholes that gave on the Assembly Room below. The gallery had been built to accommodate a few court secretaries, not a score of eager reporters. "And I asked to get into this hellhole!" moaned Brelavay. "Pressed goose!" He was there with a pass, stamped by six officials of the Bureau of Censorship, the Militia, the Palace, etc., and issued to the scandal-sheet of Court confidences and city gossip that employed him. Frenin had got a similar pass for his Catholic monthly, which carried parish news and imspirational readings for priests. Itale had the pass for *Novesma Verba*. The rest were reporters for the government's organ, the *Courier-Mercury*, or lookers-on with connections in the ducal court who had wangled themselves passes out of curiosity or self-importance. Givan Karantay stood next to Itale and watched, fascinated, the chopping motions of the grand duchess's long chin as she read her Latin address. Karantay's novel *The Young Man Liyve*, published in the spring, had made an unprecedented hit; he had become something of a national figure. The government in Vienna did not like national figures, but knew when not to meddle with them. Karantay had got a pass, signed by Prime Minister Cornelius, simply by asking for it.

The grand duchess droned to a close. "It must be four-thirty," Brelavay groaned. The rector of the university, dark-jowled and tremendous in his gold-faced doctor's gown, strode to the rostrum. *O miserere, Domine!*" Brelavay moaned to him. The rector laid a roll of papers down on the rostrum, placed his hand upon it, and began to deliver his speech extempore. One thin, clerkish reporter for the *Courier-Mercury* was making notes; Itale tried to do the same, referring for help to Brelavay, who had been a Latin First Prize in Solariy. Brelavay moaned and recited Virgil. *"Mugitusque boum!"* he said. "Why are you scribbling, Itale? it's only *mugitus boum*. Moo! Moo!" he bellowed inaudibly at the rector. The clerkish reporter, scribbling, hissed malevolently for silence in the gallery. After the rector's orotund half hour the mayor of Krasnoy rose and made a short, Ciceronian address of which he evidently understood not a word, reading it in bursts of syllables like random gunfire. Then in place of the Masters of the Great Guilds, which had been disbanded as had all workingmen's associations, came the prime minister of the grand duchy, Johann Cornelius, who spoke pleasantly and fluently in good Germanic Latin for twenty minutes. The *Courier's* prize scholar took it down in shorthand. Itale desperately made notes. "Forget it," Brelavay whispered, "that's not shorthand, he's trying to scare us, it's just hen-tracks." —"What if somebody says something important?" Itale protested. "Nobody will," said Frenin.

The speeches of welcome were over; the Assembly was adjourned for lunch.

At the Cafe Illyrica everybody was gathered awaiting the four reporters, vociferous with questions about what had gone on in the Assembly's first session. "Mooing," Brelavay said. All the others shouted, argued, questioned, answered; the four who had been in the Sinalya were rather silent. They had known the Assembly would speak in Latin, they had known it would begin with formalities . . . but the day had been a very long time coming, and was half over already, and it had amounted to nothing: nothing at all. A pageant, a fraud. Itale got back in a corner of the turbulent restaurant with Karantay. The novelist's goodhumored equanimity was a refuge to him from the indisciminate and beery enthusiasm of the Illyrica crowd. Karantay combined passion and patience to an unusual degree; he was an ardent and reliable Constitutionalist and Republicanist, ready to risk his already brilliant career for the cause, but unwilling ever to close his intelligence to unwelcome fact. There was a toughness in him that was increasingly welcome to Itale; and it was an endearing quality, that toughness or pragmatism, because Karantay's novel was wildly, dramatically, whole-heartedly romantic, implausible, and magnanimous; and yet, like its author, in no way was it dishonest. In the complexity of the likeness and unlikeness of the author and his work Itale saw some adumbration of the complex relations of the real and the ideal; and he also saw a good deal that made him like Karantay better the better he knew him. They drank their beer now, and did not say very much, while the old Illyrican shouted as ever about his mistress Liberty.

Back in their chill airless gallery they watched the deputies resume their seats. A member of each Estate was to speak, thanking the Crown for convening the Assembly. The grand duchess' seat was now empty; sovereignty had made its gesture. Johann Cornelius, slender and greyhaired, with a benevolent

151

smile, took his place to the right of the empty chair, and the ornate Latin speeches were addressed to him since the grand duchess was absent— "And since Metternich is also absent," said Frenin. "We thank the puppet minister of a puppet duchess vassal to a puppet emperor controlled by a German chancellor for his kindness in letting us speak a dead language together for six hours a day according to the ancient custom of our people. My God! why are we standing here watching a puppet show?"

The senior prelate of Orsinia, the archbishop of Aisnar, opened the order of the day at last. Itale had seen him last in Aisnar cathedral on Easter night, a stiff golden figure in a glory of lights and singing. In Church Latin in a thin voice he opened the meeting and placed before the deputies the suggestion that they vote unanimous thanks to the grand duchess for the convocation.

A speaker rose from the seats at the left. The archbishop conferred with assistants and finally said cautiously, in Latin, "We recognise the deputy."

"My Lord Bishop, my lords and gentlemen, my fellow deputies," the speaker said sonorously not in Latin but in their own tongue, "I propose this emendation of the motion before us: the Assembly of the Nation will vote thanks to the sovereign, the vote to be taken and the resolution stated in the vernacular language of the nation." There was silence, then an outbreak of voices. "My Lord Bishop! Please call for order, I still have the floor. My name is Oragon, deputy to the Third Estate, elected by the Provincial Assembly of the Polana Province. I speak not for my province only, but for my country, to you who have met here in the name of that country: I speak of our rights and of our sacred duties—" The powerful, assured voice rose, letting the words fill the cold empty spaces of the Assembly Room: my country, my people, our rights, our responsibilities. Any word long unspoken, forbidden, gathers in it all the strength of silence. That strength, the strength of years, filled Oragon's speech, and he knew it, and spoke on unhesitating, knowing also that his might be the first and last such speech made in that room. Up in the gallery they were all trying to get his words down verbatim. As fast as he spoke, Itale wrote, for he knew the speech already, he had learned it years ago in the quiet dark library of the house at Malafrena, the speech that has used so many words in so many languages over the years, but can all be said in four: live free, or die. Oragon spoke for forty minutes, and when he finished his voice was hoarse, the audience was dazed, and Itale dropped the pencil he could not hold any more. Karantay retrieved it and the notebook, for the Assembly was in a noteworthy state. Speakers arose on every side; the poor archbishop's eyes rolled. Cornelius had sat quietly through Oragon's speech. Like Itale he had heard it before, and unlike Itale he believed its day was done. But as the debate went on in the vernacular, half out of control and increasingly tumultuous, the prime minister began to look grim. Enthusiasm and disorder were his enemies. During an incoherently martial and patriotic speech by a baron from the Sovena, Cornelius rose and consulted softly with the archbishop. Oragon stood up again. His big, coarse voice, used to addressing all kinds of meetings indoors and out, cut through the baron's speech: "My Lord Bishop, I request that we return to the Order of the Assembly of the Kingdom. Herr Cornelius, not being a deputy to any Estate, is a guest in this Assembly, without right to speak unless permission be granted by a majority of the deputies present."

Cornelius walked back to his seat through a cowed yet sardonic silence. "I waive my opportunity to request permission to speak," he said without raising his voice, heard only by the Clergy in the front rows. "Let discussion proceed, please." But the martial baron was now tonguetied. Somebody called out, "Take the vote on Mr Oragon's proposal!"—"My Lords and gentlemen," the archbishop said, "further debate and the vote must be adjourned; it is past five o'clock. With the—" A Krasnoy deputy was on his feet. "Excuse me! Excuse me! I think we vote on whether to adjourn session!" The archbishop rubbed his forehead, setting his archiepiscopal hat askew, and said, "I must implore your patience, I have not yet become entirely familiar with my duties as president of the Assembly. I will now propose that the members of the Assembly vote on closing this day's session." A clerk popped up next to him like a jack-in-the-box. "*Sic et non*," he shouted. "*Sic?*"—"Hold on!" somebody shouted from among the Nobility. "Finish the business on hand! I want to be recognised!" After a long stretch of amputated orations and confusion a vote on adjournment was taken, and had to be counted. One hundred and forty voted to remain in session, one hundred and thirty-one voted to adjourn, forty-seven abstained. The archbishop ruled that the session be suspended two hours for dinner, and this was accepted. "That does it," said Brelavay. "They'll go stuff, come back sleepy, and vote to carry on further debates in Sanskrit." But when the proposal was finally put to the vote, at eleven that night, there were less than a dozen voices in favor of Latin. A second proposal introduced by Oragon as connected to the first, which by changing certain rules of procedure in the provincial diets would give the Third Estate a majority in the Assembly, was shelved by the archbishop, who had evidently been crammed along with his dinner on how to spot subversive tactics and control them by using parliamentary procedures. On this note of obscure victory the session was adjourned.

Itale and Karantay left the others at the Illyrica and went to the Old Quarter, to the Helleskar house. They were greeted with champagne and cheers by George Helleskar, Luisa, Enrike, Estenskar, and others of "the liberal circle." "Well, did ye declare war on Austria?" demanded the old count, George Helleskar's father.

The old count, a colonel of the defunct national army, had held his last command at Leipzig, under the Grand Army of the French Empire. Itale had first met him two years before, when he had yielded to George Helleskar's repeated invitation and come to this house for supper. The place was very much grander and austerer than the Paludeskars' and the occasion had been a fairly formal one. Itale, at his most defiant, had played the didactic republican; George Helleskar had been too busy as host to rescue him from the morass of offended silence in which he had gradually and ineluctably foundered. As he sat in self-imposed exile in the farthest corner of the vast drawing-room, the old count had come over to him, walking slowly and heavily, and sat down. "I knew your grandfather," he said. "Itale Sorde of Malafrena."

Itale had stared at him, too involved at first with detesting himself and everyone else there to understand.

"George has spoken of you, but I didn't place the name till I saw you," the old man went on. "You look like him."

"Where— Where did you know him, sir?"

"Paris. I was a young fellow, he was near forty. We came home about the same time, he back to the estate, I to take my commission. We wrote for some years. I suppose he's been dead these many years."

"He died in 1810."

"I never knew a man like him." The old man spoke gravely, his eyes fixed on Itale.

"What was he doing in Paris, sir?"

"Living there as you're living here. There were a lot of us foreigners in Paris in the seventies. There always are. Polish exiles—best swordsmen I ever saw—Germans, us, and the French to keep us all talking. And we talked. . . . A deal of blood and water has run under the bridges since young fellows used to sit about in coffee-shops discussing the *Social Contract* in the shadow of the Bastille—eh, Mr Sorde? Everything has changed— everything."

"But we still have the *Social Contract*," said Itale, without defiance.

"Eh? Oh aye, we do, and much good it's done us. That was another age, Mr Sorde, a golden age. Milk and honey, before the milk went sour! I wasn't in Paris in '93 to see the butchers, but I was in Vienna in '15 and saw the vultures. . . . It was your grandfather that showed me that golden age, and told me about the new world that was coming, and a grand world it was, before it came! But what became of him? Back to his vineyards, and dies there like any farmer on his land. And I to take my four hundred to be cut to pieces for Napoleon at Leipzig, and come home to sit here and watch the vultures gobble. . . ."

"Well, time hasn't run out yet, sir," Itale said, blowing his nose; part of his ill temper at the beginning of the evening had been due to a severe cold; he was always getting colds since he lived in Mallenastrada.

"It has for us here. Go to America, you young fellows, and

find the new world there with the savages, but don't waste your time here!"

"If there's a new world it's here, here or nowhere, always," Itale said, and the old man said equally fiercely, "All right! it's your time and your right to say that. The good years of my life were those years in Paris before the Revolution. I don't forget that, Mr Sorde, though I don't believe what Itale Sorde and I believed then, that all it takes to bring the golden age is hard work and good will. It takes more than that. But let me never say to a young man that it can't be done at all!" He pounded his chair-arm with a big fist spotted brown with age, and glared around at Itale, his son George who had joined them, and the receding perspectives of the salon, dotted with beautifully dressed, amicably chattering guests.

Since that night he and Itale had been friends, linked always in Itale's thought and the old count's memory by that other Itale who lay beside the chapel of St Anthony under the pines of Malafrena; and Itale had first admitted a liking for George Helleskar when he saw the younger man's pride in and tenderness toward the irascible, frail old soldier.

This night Count Helleskar recalled the last meeting of the Estates, in 1796: "They were trying to choose a king then, and went all to pieces over it. Maybe they'll do better at getting rid of a grand duchess, eh?" He laughed, like a wolfhound barking. Among his son's radical friends he enjoyed stating the most extreme opinions, outdoing the young men in attacking Austria, the Metternich system, censorship, the Sinalya court, and so on. The emotion was real but the opinions, if he tried to defend them rationally, disintegrated; at their root was only esteem for courage, scorn for opportunists, and the bitter pessimism of a nobleman who saw his class becoming obsolete and an officer whose last battle had been lost.

Estenskar soon joined them. Old Helleskar did not like the poet, but was polite to him, as to all guests of the house, a forced, fine courtesy that reminded Itale painfully of his own father. Others came over; not Luisa, though she had signified with one glance as Itale entered that she wanted to see him

156

tonight. The old count had some records of the '96 convocation, and took the group to his study to look these up. Like everyone else he had, after the day's unlooked-for triumph, begun to hope great things of the Assembly. He and Estenskar talked vehemently. Itale listened. It had been a long day. George Helleskar looked in on them and had a bottle of brandy brought in with the message, "To restore the Deputy from the Fourth Estate." Itale drank a little and fell fast asleep, deep in a leather armchair. The others left without disturbing him. An hour went by very quietly in the oak-panelled study, no sound but the tick of the clock and the crackle of the fire. Luisa came in, moving softly. She wore black; her mother had died in July after cruel illness, through which Luisa had cared for her; it was a suspicion of that illness that had brought her back from Aisnar before Easter. She had said nothing of it to Itale then and as little as possible about it since; she spoke plainly of her mother's death as a release, and showed no grief. She had lost the robust, radiant quality of beauty she had had at twenty, when Itale first saw her. She was thin, and looked thinner still in black, and rather pale. Her bearing was tense and proud. She stood beside the armchair for some little while, watching the face of the sleeping man, his hands that still laxly cupped the empty brandy glass on his lap. Her face showed no expression but watchfulness. At last she took the glass from his hands, and as he woke she said, "Can you come tonight?"

He stared, shook his head, rubbed a hand over his face and hair, yawned, and said aloud, "What?"

She set the glass down on a table, went over to the bookcases, and repeated, half turned from him, "Can you come tonight?"

"What time is it?" He pulled out his watch. "Two-thirty?"

"About two."

"Did I fall asleep? Listen, has Karantay left? We have to get to the office tonight and write up the report—*Verba* goes to press Wednesday noon, that's tomorrow, today now— Listen, tomorrow night, Luisa." He struggled out of the deep chair and went towards her. She did not turn to him, but moved on along the shelves looking at the titles of books.

157

"I'll be at court tomorrow night," she said. "Here he is, George, the Sleeping Beauty wakened by my kiss. Don't you wish you'd gone to sleep too?"

"No," said young Helleskar. "You'd probably have bitten me. All the radical elements in the salon are looking for you, Sorde."

"We have to get this issue set up so the Censor can look it over, last week they took fifty-six hours to pass it— Come on with us, Helleskar, these all-night bouts are entertaining." Refreshed and wide awake, Itale's vitality was as bright and warm as the fire on the hearth, and George Helleskar said, "All right! if I won't be in the way?"

"We'll put you to work, don't worry. Good night, baronina," he said gaily, frankly, using her title as he always did before other people.

"Will you forgive the absconding host?" George Helleskar asked her with his kindly effrontery. She smiled and said, "I have been trying to make Enrike take me home this hour. Enjoy yourselves. Do you really think the Censor will let you print anything, now?"

But Itale had met up with Karantay at the doorway, and did not hear her, or pretended not to hear her.

V

From the first time she saw him, fresh off the Montayna coach, bewildered and out of place in her salon, Luisa had been afraid of him. Everything about him frightened her, his height, his blue eyes, his big nose, his strong hands, his awkwardness, his vulnerability, his ideas, his masculinity, the spirit that she saw play in him as bright and dangerous as lightning in a heavy sky. He was completely strange to her: completely different from her. She shared nothing with him. His reality was a denial of hers. To touch him would be to destroy him or to be destroyed. —So extreme a reaction displeased her; she sought control over herself, both mind and body; coolness, courage, self-possession

158

were her own ideals. Itale's presence was a severe test of these qualities, but to avoid him, which would have been the simplest and most natural thing in the world, to send him off and not see him again, would also be cowardice, admission of defeat. She had invited him back, against Enrike's feeble protest. Helleskar and Estenskar had both taken him up, and now the whole group of radical journalists were people of some note in the city; she would have had to meet him in society anyhow, unless to escape him she had gone over the widening gap and joined the "Viennese," the conservative and pro-Imperial salons. She kept in touch with that portion of society by accepting the very minor position at court which had been her mother's; she was called to the palace once a week or once a fortnight, while the grand duchess was in town. She enjoyed the contrast of the sad, stuffy, shabby court formalities with her own increasingly brilliant and animated circle. She enjoyed testing her own nerve and her power on these ambitious and argumentative men. For most of them she had a good deal of contempt, which she concealed most of the time. Towards Itale, no degree of self-control and self mockery could dispel the attraction she felt, or the fear of that attraction, and the resentment of it, and the terror and pleasure of his presence, which challenged all she was and all she thought she wanted.

She had grown up, not in Krasnoy for the most part, but on the immense family property in the Sovena province which her grandfather had accumulated. The parents most stayed in Krasnoy, for the court connection was the important thing in Baroness Paludeskar's life; the children were left in the country in the care of nursemaids and servants, until when he was eleven Enrike was sent off to a military school for noblemen's sons, where he was unspeakably unhappy, and Luisa at eight was left alone among the servants. She had done pretty much as she pleased in those years of her childhood in the big, bleak house, isolated on a knoll amidst the flat, fertile, windswept fields of her inheritance. Her playmates were the children of the estate overseer and of the tenant farmers: one step above the peasants, having had a year or two of schooling, shy, dark children, hard as nails, slaves to "the baronina's" whim until, goaded too far, one of them would turn on her and call her a papist, their worst insult, and spit in her face, fight her, and often beat her. She could not get on with any of the girls, it led always to a fight. Her companions were boys, whom she could lead in exploits that lack of imagination, or dour sense, would have forbidden them. But they did not like being dominated either, and when she was ten she crept home with a broken wrist; she had teased the smith's son Kass into a rage and he cracked her arm across his knee as he would crack a willow-stick. When her mother arrived for her annual visit a week later the story was that the baronina had had a fall from her horse. "She's very wild, ma'am," the nurse said, weakly sounding an alarm. The baroness gave orders that Luisa should stay in to study six hours a day with her tutor, the house priest, and should not be allowed to play with Protestant children, and these orders were more or less obeyed until the end of the month, when the baroness left, and Luisa was off to the barns to find Kass before the carriage was out of sight on the long road across the windy plains.

A year later she and Kass took to playing a game which they called the wild dancing. Father Andre's history lessons had included some confused accounts of heathen superstitions and rituals and Roman methods of divination. They could find out everything that was going to happen in the future, Luisa told Kass, if they danced the right way and killed a hen and read the messages inside her. They stole and killed a hen from the farmyard. Luisa was scared by the awful simplicity of the head-twist, she had never liked to watch that, but the boy was excited by her fear and disgust, by theft, waste, gratuitous killing: he tore the bird open with his hands, plunged his hands into the entrails, and pushed her face into the bloody mess jeering, "Read it! Read it!" She had fought down screams and vomit and said, "I see it—I see the future—I see fire, fire, a house on fire—" He danced for her, naked on the threshing-floor in a dark autumn evening of fog and fine rain. They were alone among the long, dreary fields. His thin, white, child's body flashed before her, dancing, strong, wet with mist and sweat. She had not danced for him. After that night they had scarcely spoken to each other again.

When she was thirteen she began the relationship that finally got her sent back to Krasnoy. She had always been savagely rude and arrogant to the overseer's eldest son, jeering at him and inciting the other boys to bedevil his life; now she suddenly made a friend of him, and very shortly the overgrown, over-mothered boy of sixteen had achieved great power over her, cowing and fascinating her with his causeless rages, caresses, intimate talk, fits of laughter, fits of tears and threats of suicide. He told her how he had seduced a peasant girl, describing every word and act vividly, and how they had met again, and again, and all they had done. Luisa listened and at last, envious, jealous, a little incredulous, tried to match his stories, using her imagination freely. She told him that Kass had slept with her "hundreds of times." The boy believed her, approached her and began a fumbling attempt to undress her. She took her clothes off and stood still. He made her lie down, and lay on her, but he was impotent: she began to hit at him, scratch at his face when he would not let her go, and she got away from him and scrambled into her shift and dress. The next day he talked her into trying again and the same thing happened. The boy went home and tried to shoot himself with his father's hunting-piece; his mother came into the room as he was in the act, and he shot her instead, and blew her right hand off at the wrist. Some connection with Luisa was made out from his blubberings and wild talk. It was all kept quiet. Baron Paludeskar, then dying of cancer, never heard of it, and Luisa came back to Krasnoy to a convent school. Now after ten years all her Sovena childhood seemed infinitely far away, another person than herself in another world; yet sometimes she remembered the overseer's son and his soft, struggling, impotent body; or, remote, the brief vision of a boy dancing naked in dusk and rain.

She did not like touching, the kisses women were expected to exchange, handshakes. She did not permit her maid to dress her or to brush her hair.

When Itale first came to her in April in the room she had taken in a hotel near West Gate she had been in unconcealable terror, trembling and stiff, silent, her eyes dry and wide. Yet she had been there waiting for him, like an animal that has walked into a

161

trap. Nothing could have set her free but the intensity and impersonality of his desire. His passion submerged her fear like a wave over a sandcastle, and all the fear turned to equal passion, all the sand to the water of life . . . for a night; sometimes, some nights, for a while, since then.

When her mother's illness became severe she was not able to come at all. During June and July she did not see Itale alone and only twice briefly in company. Her time was given entirely to the dying woman; she nursed her through a nine weeks' agony, patient and competent. Her mother died clinging to her hand. After the funeral she stayed home, seeing no one, for a week, and then had taken up her usual life in so far as the customs of mourning permitted; but she made no sign to Itale. He would not be turned away, now, and she gave in to him; for the first time he made love to her in her own house. With some caution regarding Enrike and the servants, that had become their usual arrangement, her maid letting him in very late at night. Often she put off a planned meeting or made obstacles to setting a night; often when he did come she was, at first, passive and cold in manner. Never until the night at Helleskars had he told her he could not come.

She waited for him, a night in mid-September. He was late. He was at the Illyrica, or at the office of his journal, or with Karantay or with Estenskar or some or any of the others, the other men, in their world, his world, the political world. She looked about at her world with an ironical eye: the high-ceilinged, blue and white painted bedroom. Yet she had been right, that night, about the journal. "Will the Censor let you print anything, now?" she had asked, and they had not listened, going off in high spirits and goodfellowship to write up the events of the great day. The Bureau of Censorship had returned the proofs to them three days later with all reports on the Assembly's first session deleted: it was the day the journal went to press: all they could do was take out the type and run the first three pages through entirely blank except for the heading *Novesma Verba* and the date.

On the same day, the third day of debate in the Assembly, the President announced that the decision to use the vernacular had not received the grand duchess' sanction and was thus invalidated. Oragon at once raised the question of the grand duchess' power of sanction and veto, since the articles of the Assembly declared it to be subject only to the king, and there was no king. Since then debate had struggled on, the left trying to put the question of sovereign authority and the right interrupting mainly with demands from the chair that the deputies speak in Latin. Itale and the others had written up a cautious report of these sessions. The Censor stamped it out and the journal appeared that week with one column on its news page, a hastily composed patriotic effusion by Karantay, and the rest of the sheet dead blank. The only news the public got of events in the Assembly Room was the brief summary of motions and votes on an inner page of the *Courier-Mercury*. Prime Minister Cornelius saw no need for violence, which was abhorrent to the system; it was merely a matter of laying one's trump card down quietly at the last moment, game after game.

And it was a game that he, as surely as his idealistic opponents, had staked his life on. Only he had the soldiers and the Empire on his side, which made the contest somewhat uneven. She saw that; she did not think Itale, or Estenskar, or even Helleskar saw it clearly. She did not say much about it, but she continued to fulfil her duties at court, and she entertained men who could help Enrike in his modest diplomatic ambitions whenever he asked her to or when she saw the opportunity herself. She saw no disloyalty in this. Why should she be loyal to a cause from which she was excluded? How could she be? She could not play the game, therefore she did not care who won it.

Still he did not come. It was past two. She had been sitting at her dressing table; she lay down with the magazine he had brought her, the *Bellerofon*, a monthly which took most of the literary stuffing out of *Novesma Verba*, which had become frankly political and philosophical. In this issue Itale had a long review of a *Dictionary and Historical Grammar of the Orsinian Language and its Dialects* by a professor at Solariy, the leading article. Apparently they were all excited by the dictionary and grammar. Patriotism. She tried to read it. Itale's written style was terse, logical, and didactic; effective but not seductive; not for reading lying down. Luisa yawned and began skipping. Estenskar had contributed the second part of a long review of Karantay's novel. There weren't even enough of them to quarrel healthily, they all had to praise one another. It was small, their world, it was shabby, as mediocre as the dreary court of the grand duchess, as futile. They were not free, though they talked forever about freedom. Nobody was free.

"There's a nice picture," said Itale's quiet voice. She had gone to sleep; she opened her eyes, struggling for consciousness, but did not move. She knew from his voice that he was smiling. "Fell asleep over my review, did you?" he said bending over her, so that she smelt the night air on him and felt the warmth of his mouth brush her cheek. "Novel-reader."

"You can read dictionaries if you like them," she said, opening her eyes and then shutting them again to stretch a long, supple stretch and yawn. "Don't ask me to. I don't trust words. You're very late."

"I know. I'm sorry." He took off his coat and stock and sat down on the bed in waistcoat and shirtsleeves. His face looked grave and shadowed in the light of the single candle. She watched him, studied his face, as she always did, as if by watching him she could find out what he was.

"At the Illyrica," she said. "Talk and talk and talk. Words and words and words. . . ."

"No, I was with a friend. From that school I taught at for a while. He's out of work."

"You're all out of work, always."

She knew he did not like to be teased about the erratic jobs he had taken to pay for his rent and bread, until *Novesma Verba*, thriving, could pay him a tiny salary. She knew the subject of his relative poverty was one of the most dangerous ones that lay between them. It was precisely because it was dangerous that she began to edge near the crater. But no temper stirred in him now; he merely nodded, and said, "Egen quit his job, he had a good one, tutoring a family, some grain-merchant in the Trasfiuve. He's consumptive and a doctor told him that living with the children he put them at risk. So he moved out. They tried to make him stay. I don't know what to do for him. If he could just have a year or so to get his health back—" Itale put his head in his hands. "I don't know, I don't see how he can get free at all, but it can't. . . ."

"Yes, it can; it probably will; it generally does. And there is nothing you can do about it! Why do you torment yourself?"

"I don't. He's my friend."

"You do. None of your friends is worthy of you. They are all doomed, defeated in advance."

"Estenskar?" he said with a kind of laugh.

"Estenskar most of all. He is in love with defeat."

"I don't want to talk about all that now," he said impatiently. "I'm tired." He turned to her, but she swung off the bed with a lazy, evasive motion, gathering her silk dressing-gown about her, went to the dressing-table, sat down before the glass and began to brush her hair. He lay back across the bed, his arms over his head.

"Don't forget to wind the clock and say your prayers," Luisa said.

"What have I done wrong now?" he asked in a dry tone, but goodhumoredly enough.

"Marriage is not what I want."

"I know that."

"Do you?"

There was a pause before he answered. "Luisa, there has to be a certain amount we take for granted, an area of trust between us, or we can't get on at all. We can't start over every time."

"Yes, we can. That is precisely what I want, what we should do. Nothing taken for granted. Nothing settled, expectable, cut-and-dried. Each night the first night. —But there's no use, so long as you come to it from . . . where you do come from."

"What do you mean, where I come from?"

"All the men you waste your breath on. All the second-rate people. The people you don't belong with. Let the weak lean on one another. You cannot share pain; that's the worst hypocrisy of all, the most degrading. Charity, humility, the vile Christian virtues—what are you doing in that cage?" Her voice was light and mild, she continued to brush her hair with a long rhythmic stroke. "You come to me from a cage and never know you've left it. And run back to it in the morning. . . ."

165

He sat up on the bed and sat for a while gazing off into the shadowed end of the room, where long white drapes hid the windows. "I come to you for . . . for what no one else ever gave me, ever offered me,—it is trust; the greatest trust. I don't know how to handle it. I'm no good at it, I know I hurt you. All I can do is offer you what you give me, that trust, that care."

"That cage. . . ." He had stood up as he spoke, and she rose, turning to him, meeting him in the center of the room, her hair loose and her body warm and fresh in the flowered robe; the sleeves dropped back from her arms as she put them up to embrace him. "I want to fly beside you, like falcons, like eagles over the mountains, never looking down, never looking back. . . ."

"I love you," he whispered, gathering her against him, a much more expert lover now than he had been in the garden in Aisnar but no less tender, responsive to her response, so that although she wanted to go on talking, wanted to tell him "I am your freedom, and what I see in you is freedom," she said nothing, feeling the words dissolve and the barriers go down and the joy she feared so deeply pick her up and sweep her off like foam on the torrents of the thaw.

He lay asleep beside her when she roused in early dawn. She lighted a candle; he did not stir. Again she studied his face, warm and heavy in sleep, undefended. To lie together all night naked, that was trust; yes; but she did not like the word; if there was only a way to get free of words altogether. . . . But the servants would be getting up. He liked to leave while it was still dark, he had been bitterly resentful of the humiliation he had felt once when he slept in her bed till ten and had to be spirited out by her and her maid in a comic opera scene that she would have found very funny if only he had found it funny. He was so naive and so provincial, still; the disapproving schoolboy, the humorless Robespierre, the bumpkin pedant; self-righteous. So the fear hastily reinstating its rights and boundaries within her, rebuilding the barriers, denied gratitude, denied the yearning, brooding warmth of her body against his, her face watching his, and made her wake him sharply, saying his name.

166

He started up, then lay back with some inarticulate word.

"Wake up, wake up."

"I am," he said, turning his face against her shoulder.

"What a nose you have," she murmured, sinking back for a moment into the warmth. "Like a ship's prow. Ever onward."

He was asleep again.

"It's getting light."

"I don't want to go," he groaned, and sleepily began kissing her throat and breast. She tensed, slipped away and out of the bed, and put the flowered gown about her, turning her back on him. "I'll tell Agata to watch the back stairs for you."

"Luisa. Wait."

She half turned, impatient.

He sat up, scratching his head. "I meant to talk about this last night. But it was late, and we . . ." He pushed back his hair and looked at her through the dim sphere of the candle light; his face still had the heavy, defenseless look in it, the innocence of sleep, the lips slightly swollen. "I may be out of town for a while."

"Where? How long?" she responded without emotion.

"Amadey has asked me to go home with him. I'd like to do that. And then go on to Rakava, and do a series of articles on the situation there, or find a correspondent there who can do it for us. A few weeks in all, I suppose."

She did not like the sensation of her long, heavy, fair hair loose and tangled on her head and over her shoulders; she had not braided it last night, because they had had to make love. She went to the dressing table and brushed her hair back from her face with harsh, practiced strokes. "When did Amadey finally make up his mind?"

"He asked me to come with him a couple of days ago."

"Well, he's been on the brink of going back to the Polana ever since I met him five years ago. He won't stay long. . . ." If Itale went there would be a month, two months, that she could sleep alone, that her mind would not have to go through all the miseries of jealousy, anxiety, resentment, and terror that her body, or her soul, or some blind stupid omnipotence, forced upon her. She would be free. "Don't stay too long," she said.

167

"I won't. No fear!" he said with naive gratitude. He got up and began dressing; in the mirror she watched him put on his shirt and button it, then his collar and stock, the stately mysteries of male clothes, the waistcoat, the tailed coat. "I'll be back by mid-November at the latest," he said. He had obviously been afraid she would object to his going, and was relieved that she did not.

"Perhaps I'll go to Vienna with Enrike while you're gone," she said. "He'll never get up the energy to go by himself, and he's got to meet the ambassador if he's ever going to get any sort of position. Though I suppose if I went I'd have to stay through Christmas. What a bore. I don't know. Why don't you come to Vienna? It would broaden your mind a good deal more than Estenskar's sheep-farm and dirty Rakava. . . . We'll stay at the König von Ungarn, just behind the Dom. . . . Do, Itale!"

Sitting on the bed to put on his shoes he looked up to meet her mocking, challenging glance over her shoulder. "Oh, God, you are so beautiful even at five in the morning," he said, muffled, bending down; then, standing up again. "I can't go to Vienna. . . . Some day," a little sheepishly, but also ready to take offense if she went too far, for it was a question of money, of course. It was always a question of money.

She nodded politely, dismissively, and went to put Agata on the alert. Most of the servants were reliable, she knew exactly whose servants they exchanged news with, and did not care what they said; but Enrike had hired a footman away from Count Raskayneskar recently, and she did not want to be discussed by that lot. Raskayneskar was exactly the sort of man who got his gossip from his servants, and then used it maliciously.

"Pier's still asleep, ma'am," Agata murmured.

She looked back into the room and said to Itale, "All clear." He came up to her in the doorway, dressed, armored in the wholecloth of this age of respectability, formidable, a stranger; she shivered, barefoot, in her thin silk gown. "I don't want to go," he said softly, not touching her. "I don't want to go now. I don't want to go to Rakava." He leaned down, kissed her very lightly on the lips, and went out. She could not even hear his step on the stairs.

168

She went back to bed and curled up in the place under the covers that was still warm. Now I can sleep, now I'm alone, she thought, but instead of sleeping she began to cry, hiding her face under the sheet, grinding her fists into her eyes like a child.

PART FOUR

The Way to Radiko

I

In the cool dawn of the equinox the statue of St Christopher of the Wayfarers stood distinct over Old Bridge, over the river and the light mist on the surface of the water. A purity of light, a stillness of air and sky effaced the boundaries between living and inanimate; the stone saint seemed to have paused there to look eastward, smiling and unseeing. There were no clouds. The sun rose over dark hills and sent its first rays straight in the eyes of two horsemen riding over Old Bridge, dazzling them, making them squint and smile. The bridge was crossed, the riders entered the shadow of a long street, eight hooves clattered with a clipped, brisk noise on the cobbles of the Trasfiuve between files of sleeping houses. One rider turned in the saddle to see the new light on the towers of the cathedral behind them, across the river. "Look there, Amadey, the light."

Estenskar did not turn. He looked ahead, down the long straight street, and said, "Come on, this horse wants to run." The fretting bay, then the brown mare broke into a trot. They were spirited, their riders good horsemen, a handsome sight as they rode from the city towards the first sunrise of the year's fall.

173

By eight o'clock, from the climbing streets of Grasse, Itale could look back and see all Krasnoy lying along its sunlit river, beautiful and smoky in the morning warmth. Then leaving the little town they crossed the crown of the ridge and lost the valley, its river and city, behind them on their way.

Down all day among the hills, a faint warm wind in their faces bearing the smells of earth, hay, woodsmoke; at dusk a village ahead in the next fold of the hills, trees and thatched roofs and chimney smoke, offering rest, firelight after the long day's ride. "There'll be an inn," Itale said. He began to sing "Red are the berries on the autumn bough," and his mare pricked her ears and stepped along towards hay and dinner. Dusk was heavy under old trees as they rode up into the village, and the sign of the Golden Lion creaked in the evening breeze. "What a good place," Itale said, dismounting. There were no other travellers at the inn; they were served good beer before the fire, and a big old hen roasted crisp; they left nothing of her but bones. Then Itale stretched out his legs and, for the ritual and completeness of the thing, lighted the clay pipe provided by the host of the Golden Lion.

"Never saw you smoke before," said his friend.

"Never smoke," said Itale. "How do you keep the damn thing going?"

Estenskar went on watching him, since Itale, extended in profound comfort and puffing hard on the pipe, was oblivious. "I'm glad we're travelling together," he said.

"Of course."

Estenskar smiled, and turned his gaze back to the fire.

"It's good to get out of the city. You must take the mare tomorrow, she has a lovely gait. How long since I rode a horse, let alone a good one? This is a holiday. More than holiday. Escape. . . ." Itale waved the pipe, which had gone out. "I was full up, Amadey. Absolutely full up. Now I'm empty again. At last! Air, sunlight, silence, space. . . ."

Estenskar got up and went to the door of the inn room, which gave directly on the village street without threshold between the hard earth outside and the hard earth of the inn floor. The darkness under the wide-armed oaks was cool and soft. Wind

174

stirred now and then, the sign creaked, in the black foliage a few stars shone fitfully and eclipsed behind the restless leaves.

"Is it so easy?" he said after so long that Itale, befogged with exercise, fresh air, beer, and well-being, was not sure what he was talking about. "You set out . . . you set out to make yourself. To make the world. All the things you must do, and see, and learn, and be, you must go through it all. You leave home, come to the city, travel, miss nothing, experience it all, you make yourself, you fill the world with yourself and your purposes, your ambitions, your desires. Until there's no room left. No room to turn around."

"There is, here," Itale put in. "I told you. I'm as empty as that beer-jug. Air, sunlight, silence, space."

"That won't last."

"It will. It's we who don't last."

Estenskar leaned against the doorway, gazing out into the country darkness.

"Now that I know that I can't choose," he said, "now that I've finally learned that there are no choices, that I can't make my way and never could, that it was all deceit and conceit and waste—now that I've given up trying to make my way, I can't find it; I can't hear the voice. I'm lost. I went too far and there's no way home."

In later years when Itale heard his friend's name spoken what came to him always was this moment, the big dirt-floored room, the candle and beer-jug on an oaken table, the fire, the stir of autumn wind in dark branches, the silence that underlay and surrounded and closed over Estenskar's voice so that the last word, softly spoken, seemed to fail and die away in the immense unheeding quiet.

"But by going back to Esten—" Itale began, and stopped, knowing his words were stupid, but wanting to change Estenskar's mood. He had been happy that day and was sorry to let happiness go.

"That's not my home. It's too late. One road goes east, another west, but there's no destination unless you're given it. Given it! You don't choose it. You only accept it—when it's offered—if it's offered. Why am I going to Esten, then? I don't know." He spoke

175

harshly, glancing around at Itale with a vindictive stare, but Itale had learned long ago that Estenskar's anger was never for him.

"It always makes a difference where you are," he said. "Come back and sit down. We just got free. No point worrying about where we're going, yet."

Estenskar obeyed him; he came back to the table and sat down, putting his elbows on the table and his head between his hands, ruffling up his coarse reddish hair. "All I do is think about myself and talk about myself," he said miserably.

"It's a worthwhile subject. But I wish I . . ."

"If it hadn't been for you, this last year . . ."

They were both embarrassed and there was a short silence between them.

"That dream of yours. Are you chasing it?"

Estenskar shook his head.

"Was Esten a part of it?"

"I don't know. I only know that since it I've known I had to get out of Krasnoy, get away."

"You knew that the first time we talked together. At my place."

"And ate that cheese. Two years ago. And I was still living with Rosalie then—right in the depths of it. God! What a fool!"

Itale investigated the beer-jug again, found what he expected, nothing, and got up, stretching his arms. "I'll be stiff tomorrow morning, I'm out of condition for riding."

"Look here, Itale. While we're talking."

"Aye. While we're talking?" Itale looked down at him, grave.

"What about Luisa Paludeskar?"

"So I ask myself."

"What's gone wrong?"

"I don't know. I don't understand . . . what it is she wants."

"You never will. —What is it you want?"

Itale put his hands against the heavy mantel-piece, looking down into the fire. "To sleep with her."

"Is that what she wants?"

"I thought it was."

"But now she wants more than that?"

"No. —Less." Itale spoke very slowly, trying to say what he

176

did not know how to say. "I don't understand it. We are in love but we . . . we don't get on. We hurt each other a good deal. I don't understand why."

"'I don't understand, I don't understand,' said the straw in the fire. —In love. . . . Love is an invention of the poets, Itale. Believe me, I should know! It is a lie. It is the worst of all the lies. A word without meaning. Not a rock but a whirlpool, the emptiness that sucks down the soul."

"But there must be . . . Oh, well, I don't much want to talk about it. I'm running away, for a while, maybe I'll see things clearer. Afterwards. You wouldn't look back when we left Krasnoy. You were right."

Estenskar nodded; but twenty-four hours later, after their night at the Golden Lion and a day's ride through pleasant, quiet country, when they were lying on a great strawmound in a barn loft, each wrapped in a horse-blanket lent them by the hospitable farmer, all the smells of barn and stable strong in their nostrils and all the stars brilliant outside the great loading-window of the loft, he returned to the subject.

"Luisa is trying to make the world," he said. "The way I did. And she'll destroy it, the way I did. Don't let her pull you off course, Itale."

"I don't know what my course is! I thought I did. . . . I don't know what's right, what I ought to do. I don't like this—she calls it freedom—an affair, a love-affair, secrecy, nothing ever to count on—"

"That is her freedom. She's no fool. If she married you then you'd be free and she'd be the one trapped! Love's the game where there are only losers. Listen, Itale, I won't bring this up again, it's none of my business, I know that. I've known Luisa for years, I might have fallen in love with her if I hadn't met the other one first. She's like me. She tries to take and choose. She sees you and she can't let you be—if she can't own you she will destroy you—you do not know, I hope you never know the envy that eats her, when she looks at you. But I know it. Look out for her, look out for me. We will destroy you if we can, Itale." His tone was cold and playful.

"But you can't," Itale said, slowly, not playfully.

177

"Go alone," Estenskar whispered. "Go alone."

The stars shone splendid in the great square of the window, Vega overhead, the Lion like a mower's sickle left lying in the white wheat, the Swan on the river of stars, and in the southwest Scorpio huge among lesser constellations, cold above the warm earth-night. The horses and cattle in the stalls beneath snorted, shifted, slept their queer waking sleep. A few late crickets trilled, no longer alarmed by human voices. Itale slept, and waking before dawn opened his eyes to colorless gulfs of space where, fading, Orion stood, hunter and warrior of the winter sky.

They came that day to Sorg, a little city on the confluence of the rivers Sorg and Ras, and following the Ras for a few miles in late afternoon left the Frelana province and entered the Polana. As if waiting for them there the east wind rose after sunset, carrying the chill of great spaces crossed, long plains and empty hills. They stayed at a village inn, wakened often from sleep by the bleating of hundreds of sheep penned in fields behind the inn, the clanking of sheep-bells, the carousing of the drovers in the commonroom beneath. The next day was cool; a fine fog was dissolved through the sky so that in the pale glare reflected from horizon to horizon the sun looked small and wan. As they went east and south the wind blew in their faces. The land grew poorer as they rode. Ploughlands yielded to grasslands rolling to an interminable distance. They rode all day alone between earth and sky, with few trees or streams or houses or men to keep them company in the middle space. The road mounted, taking a whole day to rise a thousand feet. As they neared Esten the slopes became steeper, the rare farms poorer, crouched with their sheep-pens under the western side of a hill in the lee of the endless wind. They came to the village of Kolleiy in the late afternoon and pushed on four more miles to Esten, arriving after night had fallen. All Itale saw of the house then was its lights hidden among trees at the foot of a hill whose high, smooth curve blocked out the east wind and the eastern stars. All round were dark hills in starlight, no light to be seen but the stars and the one house, lonely as a ship in midsea. After a brief supper with Estenskar's brother and sister-in-law the travellers went off to bed. Itale was given a room at the southeast corner, high, sparsely furnished, clean as bone; all the house was like that. The house, the room smelled of the country. It was utterly silent.

Waking late, he opened his eyes to a flood of white sunlight. In the yard below his window a stable-boy was singing as he curried a stamping, snorting horse. Itale had never heard the tune, and the dialect was hard for him to follow.

> In Rakava, beneath the high walls,
> I left my love forever,
> I came to live among the barren hills
> Where runs no river. . . .

The archaic turns, the high, harsh, fluent voice pouring over trills and catches as a shallow stream pours over rocks, it was all part of the stirring bright windy morning, and Itale got up ready for whatever came next.

He took breakfast with Amadey in the long dining room; Ladislas Estenskar was "on the fields" as his wife said—at work. She sat with them, though she had got up long before, when her husband did. She was quiet, dark, barely eighteen, she had been married five months. Her manner was more that of a girl at home than a woman head of her household, and she was evidently in awe of her brother-in-law. With Itale she got on at once, and he said to his friend as they climbed the hill above the house, "I like her, your little sister."

"Ladislas is a man of sense."

"And taste. . . . They don't come like that in the city. I knew a girl like her, at Malafrena. . . ."

"What became of her, the girl at Malafrena?"

"They sent her to convent school in Aisnar, married a rich widower— Should never have let her leave the country. Town spoils them. My word, what a view!"

Beneath them now the house and stables huddled at the head of the vale, at the edge of a sparse, straggling wood. All round the barren crest where they stood stretched pale, rounded hills, even in the farthest distance hardly blued by the dry, pure, sunlit air. The grass on them was short as stubble after mowing. Here and there the flocks, ragged grey like patches of dandelion in

179

seed, were scattered on the slopes; sheep-bells made a faint, sparse music over all the great landscape. Northward, beyond the end of the woods, on a scarped and wrinkled summit higher than the other hills, something stood at the edge of sight, a wall or tower.

"What's that, Amadey?"

Estenskar turned. The wind and light made him squint; his hard, thin face looked as if it was made of the same stuff as the high, pale, arid land. "That tower? Radiko, it's called."

"Castle?"

"Blown up in the War of the Three Kings. Not much of it left."

"Which king did they back?"

Estenskar laughed. "The Pretender. People here are never on the winning side. . . ."

. When they came down from the hilltop the cessation of the wind was a relief, as was the presence of things close at hand, walls and trees, giving shelter from the pale distances.

They met Ladislas coming into the yard, and with him went to the stables to look at the two horses Amadey had bought in Krasnoy. Admiring the brown mare, he stroked her neck and said, "You always had an eye for horses, Amadey," and it was plain that he was glad the younger brother had come home, that he loved him, admired him, and was afraid of him. In the afternoon they rode out to show Itale the estate. The elder brother talked farming with him, the younger was mostly silent. Sheep were raised in the Montayna but Itale had had little to do with them and had never seen flocks or pasturage on anything like this scale; he was impressed, fascinated, asked Ladislas endless questions, to which the answers became increasingly technical and complete as Ladislas discovered that he was talking to a man who had worked "on the fields," and began to forget that the guest was a literary fellow from the city. They reined in beside one of the deep, stone-mounted wells, and dismounted to look at it, and remounted but neglected to ride on, discussing intently and with passion the principal problem of farming in the Polana and its principal difference from farming in the Montayna, the lack of surface water. Amadey sat silent, patient on a patient old horse from the stable of the farm, gazing at the hills.

180

As he rode back to the house with Itale he said, "It's queer, coming back. Like coming to a foreign country, utterly foreign, and finding one speaks the language perfectly. . . ."

That night after supper they sat talking by the fire. Ladislas' wife began to gather courage, and when Amadey said something about his book now in press she asked, in her soft voice, "Have you brought it with you?"

"Only my rough copy. Rochoy has it, it'll come out early in '28."

"You're the cause of our meeting, Amadey," his brother said. "Givana wanted to see what Estenskar's brother looked like."

"I'm Estenskar's brother And glad to have been of use. It's the first time I've heard of my reputation doing any good to anyone."

"He is weary of fame," Itale said. "Soon he will get weary of being weary, I hope. He always runs his books down, too, the better they are the more he reviles them; this next one may really be quite fair, going by that indication."

"Is it a novel?" asked Givana. "What will it be called? Can you say what it's about?"

"It's called *Givan Faugen,* and it's about him," Amadey replied, with an evident effort not to intimidate her. "Very gloomy. It didn't really come off."

"See?" said Itale. "No one has seen it, but we've all been told how very poor it is."

"It's not poor," Amadey said. "I wouldn't publish it if it were."

Ladislas grinned; either he liked to see his brother teased a bit, or liked to see him fire up.

"It's merely mediocre," Itale said.

"It's not what it should have been. That's all. It's not as good as Karantay's book. I wish it was."

"The Young Man Liyve?" Givana asked, timorous, her eyes very large and dark, her hands tensely clasped in her lap.

"There's young Liyve, you know, in person," Amadey said, indicating Itale, who at once got hot in his turn: "Oh, rot, Amadey! Givan Karantay was writing that book before he ever met me—besides there's absolutely nothing in common—"

181

"Sorde, too, is weary of fame."

"Sorde's dignity is hurt, and he can't think of anything clever to say," said Itale. "Is that a piano, hidden over there?"

It was a delicate and cranky old harpsichord, and Givana played for them, formal little salon pieces of the last century; her husband stood protectively near her while she played, turning the pages of the music; they sang together, a Scottish love-song so the yellowed book said, a yearning tune in which their voices blended with a reticent clarity. They had sung it before, alone in the lonely house, for their own pleasure. Itale, watching them, thought: But this is how it should be, how have they found it so simply? —and for a minute there in the peaceful room by the fire listening to that music, it seemed to him that life was an infinitely simple thing if only one looked at it clearly, without fear; that if one were thirsty, one need only look to see, close by, however dry the land, the deep well, the well of clear water.

But it wasn't his spring, it wasn't his land.

He stayed a week at Esten. He went about the farm with Ladislas, went shooting with Amadey in the sparse forests, talked with the brothers and Givana in the evenings; he felt half at home because it was the country, a farm, and half strange, a city visitor among these hard-working people, no part of the spare silent current of their life. Amadey was increasingly silent, speaking curtly and sometimes at random out of some inner preoccupation. On his last day there Itale suggested they ride over to the ruined tower, Radiko.

"No," Amadey said.

Then becoming aware of the uncouthness of his refusal he scowled: "Nothing there," he said. "I'd rather—I want to go there alone. I'm sorry." His face was angry, obdurate, suffering. Everything, Itale thought, came hard to him, he could take nothing lightly in life. Even Itale's admiring, undemanding friendship caused him pain. All love hurt him. "The ropes burn my hands," said the ferryman of the icy river in his first book.

"Stay a while longer," he said, late that last night; Ladislas and Givana had gone to bed, leaving them talking by the fire.

"I promised to meet Isaber."

"It's a foul city, Rakava," Amadey said, brooding, gazing into

182

the fire. "You shouldn't go there. Only easterners can understand the east."

"Then come with me. Help me with these articles."

Amadey merely shook his head.

Next day at noon, beside the little, dusty coach that would take Itale to Rakava, he said, "When you see Karantay this winter, tell him . . ." He paused for a long time, shrugged, looked off down the dusty, straggling street of the village. "It doesn't matter," he said. The driver was up on his box, it was time for Itale to mount up beside him. "Don't stay here too long, Amadey, come back to your friends," he said, putting out his hand to touch his friend's arm, to embrace him if Amadey would: Amadey pulled away from him, saying, "All right. Goodbye, have a good trip," and without looking at him turned and went off. Itale stood a moment nonplussed, then swung himself up on the high wheel and took his place; the coach set off with a jangle and commotion of harness and wheels and shouting. Itale looked back through the dust thrown up by the horses' hooves and saw his friend already mounted on the bay horse, riding off on the road to Esten; behind him the mare, her saddle empty, followed quietly.

II

Late that night Amadey lay awake and listened to the wind. It had risen strong and cold, bearing gusts of rain. When it was still a moment there was sighing sound which might be the settling of the house whose wooden walls strained against the blast, but which sounded like breathing, as if the wind itself took breath before its next sweep across the hills into the west. Amadey sat up at last, groped for the tinderbox, and lighted his candle. The room appeared around him, an island of dim light in the night and the storm of wind. On one high wall hung a map of Europe which he recalled from his earliest childhood, the Latin names of realms, the strange indented coastlines, the boundaries of nations all changed by eighty years of history, the decorative

183

monsters sporting in the ocean he had never seen. The east wind in the darkness blew towards that ocean, towards the remote and cold, autumnal sea, over the hills, plains, cities of the inland, the dawn behind it and the sunset ahead; sunrise might catch it on the coasts of France, or it catch up with evening on the Atlantic, near the shores of the western world. A great gust like a stormwave struck the house. Voices cried along the eaves and roof-peaks. The candle flickered, smoky. "I'm through, I'm done," he whispered furiously in the sighing stillness after the gust. "It's gone, all gone, there's nothing left, what do you want of me?"

Silence, wind, darkness, the walls of the room where he had slept as a boy. When he blew out his candle he could see the window as a paler oblong, and as the clouds streamed westward glimpsed Orion fiery in the black gulfs.

In the afternoon he went to the stable to take out the bay horse. The other horse he had bought in Krasnoy, the brown mare, was in the next stall. He heard Itale in the Golden Lion inn saying, "You must take the mare tomorrow, she has a lovely gait," the pleasant, easy voice and the open, easy dialect, the generous heart— Again tears came into Amadey's eyes as they had when he tried to say goodbye to Itale beside the coach, no warm sentimental expansion but a painful and frightening storm of grief like an attack from behind, which he met as best he could, turning to face it with surprise and rage.

He saddled up the mare instead of the bay, and set off alone towards Radiko. In the forest October was setting its somber fires, the birches were beginning to lose their leaves; the wind had blown itself out. The mare's long gait soon took them out of the trees and up the long slopes towards the high place. The hills were empty except for his brother's scattered flocks, the agile, heavy-bodied sheep turning their remote gaze on the rider. The sky was pale blue. Once a hawk circled indolently near the sun, and flew off to the north.

At the top of the hill he dismounted in what had been the courtyard of the keep. A long mound broken by angles of half-buried stone showed where the walls had stood. The wind that never stilled on these summits played in the yellow grass. The

184

body of the castle was gone except for a fragment of the gateway and, overhanging the scarp, some ruins of the outer defense wall. The tower stood scarred and intact, sharing its eminence with two things: the sun now sinking to the west, and, far off in the east, more sensed than seen in the obscure distances of autumn, a violet bulk, the mountains of another land. A ramp led up inside the tower to a first floor of stone. The higher floors had been burned away when the castle was taken, a hundred and eighty years before, leaving only stone beam-supports and a jagged blue circle of sky overhead. Weeds flourished between the stones of floor and walls; in a window fifty feet above the floor a few purple daisies nodded. Amadey went to the south window of the first floor, a narrow bright shaft of view over sunlit hills. An inscription was scratched in the sill, in the hard yellow-grey sandstone:

> Amadeus • Ioannes • Estensis
> anno MDCCCXVIII
> vincam

He had cut the words there two days before he first left Esten for Krasnoy. He had been seventeen years old. He remembered in one intense imponderable vision full of scents and weathers and the light of other sunsets all the times he had stood alone here in Radiko. The first time he had come had been in the days after his mother's death. He had come to the tower on foot, he had climbed up the broken ramp and sat down, worn out, here under the south window, and found himself in a place where death had no power, all here being dead and yet enduring, invulnerable. The sun had gone down, the tower had filled with blue shadows. He had heard his name called on the hills, and at last had answered. His father, Ladis, the servants had been out looking for him, calling; he had been only a boy of ten.

Again the tower filled slowly with shadow, and as it did so grew cold, as if the shadow were clear, still water. He went out and sat on the ruined wall over the cliff in the sun's last warmth, looking out over the vast landscape that as a child he had pretended was his domain, he the prince of the fallen castle, until the shadow had risen to the top of the highest hills. The

185

frightening pang of loss that he had felt parting with Itale, all the bitter restlessness that had followed him from Krasnoy, dropped away from him at last, here, among the largeness of things, the high ruin, wind, evening. When he stood up at last he still lingered, surrendering to those things, acknowledging their absolute, healing indifference and their absolute claim upon him. He stood alone at last in the only place where he could be alone, could be himself, and free. "This is it, the place. This is where I was to come," he thought with triumph. In the same moment he turned again, seeing himself posing and boasting, a fool in the house of grandeur. Why had he refused to come here with Itale? Because he was ashamed. He did not want Itale to see the word scratched on the stone of the tower, *I shall conquer*, and, in his ignorance and magnanimity, believe it. For Itale believed in victory, in the spirit's struggle and triumph. He had not lived in the ruined tower, on the barren land. He had not seen that there was only a single choice, between illusion and hypocrisy, a choice not worth making. What am I doing here? Amadey asked himself jeering, and went to remount; once off the steep heights he put the mare into a run, leaving behind him in the dead place his defeat and his irrecoverable glimpse of peace.

In a bad mood that night, he got into a worse one seeing his brother meet his sullenness with patience, and the "little sister"—Itale's voice again—grow shy and circumspect. But why couldn't they let him alone? He could not manage their interest, their affection, their human needs and offerings; he was not able, he had never been able, to live with people. He should leave them and go. But he did not know where to go.

"I liked your friend very much," Ladis said, days after Itale had left. They were in the stable yard, he had asked Amadey to help him rehang the gate with a new set of hasps from the smithy in Kolleiy. They had just got it mounted and he was testing the iron latch-tongue, his dark face bent down to his work, as it mostly was. "He wasn't what I'd imagined your friends there to be."

Amadey flooded his hands at the pump to get the rust from the old ironwork off them. "Friends," he said. "He's the only person I met in ten years there that I ever think of, here."

"Are you planning to stay here?"

"I think so."

"It's all right," the older brother said, "you know that. Where I'm concerned, and Givana. It's your house. But how old are you, twenty-six or seven, this is no place for a man unless you want to come into the farming with me. There's nothing else here."

"You seem to find enough."

"I'm a farmer. Also I've got a wife. I had to ride sixty miles to court her. You need more than that. What do you want with rye and sheep? That would be to waste your work."

"I have no more work to do. It's done."

Ladislas looked up then from the gate-latch. "What do you mean, your books? You're done writing?"

"It's done with me, is the way I'd put it. Finished. Used up and thrown away."

Ladislas' eyes were extremely direct, a steady gaze. "You can't give up a thing like that," he said, with certainty.

"I tell you, it's given me up."

"Ah!" Ladislas said with disgust. "You haven't changed at all." That brotherly comtempt based upon knowledge and unshakable loyalty, that unanswerable, just, forgiving assessment of character, left Amadey wordless. He felt like a child who has said something very foolish, and he flushed up red as he stood with his arms on the pump-handle, staring at Ladislas.

That night after supper Amadey spoke not at all to his brother, but more than usual to Givana. He made her laugh; he disconcerted her by praising her understanding, and reassured her again by a blunt correction; he began to describe, for the first time since he had come home, the life he had lived in Krasnoy, people he had known, the fashionable, the literary, the actors, the politicals. It was all the Arabian Nights to Givana. She was enchanted, shocked, fascinated, she begged more detail, more circumstance, her eyes were dark and bright and she said, "I don't *believe* it, Amadey. . . ."

That night in his room in bed Amadey heard her, "I don't *believe* it, Amadey!" and saw her round, strong, childish hands clasped across the dark bodice, and cursed himself aloud to get the sound of her voice out of his head, and turned over, and lighted the candle at last. The other one, the older one lay in his bed in the darkness beside her while she slept soundly, and heard her voice, "I don't *believe* it, Amadey!" and clenched his hands in anger, jealousy, and savage self-accusation.

Three more nights passed the same way. After supper Amadey and Givana talked, laughed, played the harpsichord; Givana sang for him, or mocked and admired the bizarre impromptus he played for her. She had become quite at ease with him, and teased him as she never teased Ladislas, ordered him about as if imitating the Krasnoy great ladies he described to her, flirted with him. The idea of the theater fascinated her, she asked endless questions about the stage, the plays, the players, the actresses, women whose lives were in all ways, in all things the opposite of hers: where do they live? how are they paid? what do they do with their money? do they ever have children? on and on, commanding Amadey to answer; and the young man, with his jarring laugh, obeyed her, while Ladislas sat silent beside the hearth.

The fourth night Ladislas left the house after supper and went down to the sheepfolds. He sat a long time with his shepherds by their fire there, as silent and dour as he had sat by his own fire. But when he came back to the house his wife sat alone sewing by the hearth, looking tired and a little scared. "Where's Amadey?" he asked in an unnatural tone.

"In his room."

"No music tonight, eh?" he said, and winced.

"The wind's so bad," she said. They always said that in the Polana. She looked up at him, and put up her hand to him timidly.

"You look tired," he said. "Go to bed." His voice was very gentle. She went upstairs; he stayed by the fire and did not follow her till after midnight. There was light under Amadey's door, the thin rayed fan of gold across the worn hall carpeting: he was awake, alone. The older brother stood outside the closed door in the darkness broken by that fan of light at his feet and fought for the strength to be silent, not to speak. —On the other side of the closed door Amadey sat hunched over the scarred writing-table seeking the word, the gift of speech, in an emotion-less ecstasy. He had got from Givana what he wanted of her, the excitement of nerves, the uneasy impatient tenacious desire blocked at its own inception, which was his poetic mood. As soon as Ladislas left the house he had left her and come up to his room, rancorous with shame and self-contempt; he sat down to write a letter to somebody, anybody in Krasnoy, he had to get out of here and go back to Krasnoy; as he cut his pen to a new point words appeared in his mind, shifted, stabilised, reshifted: "Here at the ruined tower, the end of hope. . . . Here at the house of desolation, Prince. . . . At the tower at the edge of hope. . . ." The words fell apart, the pattern changed, the resonance returned and filled the universe out to its boundaries and he dipped his half-sharpened pen blindly and began to write, scribbling, crossing out, scribbling again, wrestling the angel skilfully, cleverly, a professional fighter out to win.

For four days he stayed mostly shut up in his room; when he appeared he was goodhumored and heedless; he ate whatever was put in front of him, answered questions at random, and went back up to work. On the fourth night he came into his brother's study, a cold shed of a room where Ladislas shut himself up to do his accounting. "Can you spare me a half hour?"

"Come in! I'm sick of this."

"What is it all?"

"Taxes. Three years running I've appealed to Rakava for clarification. They send back the same stupid orders from the administration in Krasnoy. How do they think our peasants can pay this new house tax? Do they want blood? They'll get blood all right, one of these days, if the Estates can't change things!"

"My God, here too! . . ."

"Taxes make revolutions, you didn't have to go to the city to learn that," Ladislas said with irony or self-irony. "What's that?"

"Want to hear it?"

Ladislas sat down at his desk; Amadey, standing, read the long poem aloud in his harsh, clear voice, that scarcely softened even for the most musical lines. It had all the fluent tenderness, the sweetness of sound, that his verse was famous for, none of

189

which was in his voice as he read it, or in the sense of the words, a fantasy or dream-piece on the ruined castle, a flood of somber and precipitous images in darkness ending with darkness, obscure, abrupt.

When he was done there was silence, then Ladislas in a curious gesture held out his empty hands before his chest and looked from one to the other with a smile. "There you are," he said in a whisper.

"No, not I. It, the place, Radiko. Unless I've failed."

Ladislas looked up at him. "Radiko? In nightmare. . . ."

"In reality. In itself." The poet's voice, now, was softened by the release of feeling after reading the work.

"The only road across the hills goes to it, and there is only one road to it—it's like a dream, where you never choose, there are never any choices— It is frightening, Amadey," the older brother said in his grave, diffident voice, and Amadey smiled accepting, for a moment, praise, victory.

"You were always my best reader, Ladis." He sat down and they faced each other, Ladislas dark and watchful, Amadey, dressed as always carefully and formally, his reddish hair well cut and combed; he crossed his legs, tapping his knee with the rolled-up manuscript of the poem. "It was a dream, of course. This isn't the place itself, it's a dream—a vision of it—months ago. Last July. I don't know if I can describe it. I hadn't done anything for weeks, hadn't written anything for months. One night in July I went back. . . . I went back to a house I used to go to, a woman. . . . You know that story. I'd broken with her more than a year ago, I was beginning to respect myself again, working with Sorde and his lot, I was— So I went back to her, and she took me in, of course, it amused her a good deal, she sent away her current lover to make room in the bed for me, I got drunk and cried and she turned me out again finally, it was . . . I went around the city all night, I remember parts of it. . . . Got home in the morning and went to sleep. I got up in the evening. It was hot, July in Krasnoy. I was sick of course, it was . . . it was farther down than I'd been. . . . I sat at my window for a long time. I kept those rooms five years because of that window, looking out over the park, down the mall to the Sinalya. The big

190

chestnut trees under my window, and then the lawns and the mall full of people and carriages in the slanting light on an evening in summer, and behind all that the façade of the palace, long and regular behind the trees, a kind of dreary splendor, a melancholy, the end of something. . . . Well, I sat there where I had sat ten thousand times, with the warm wind blowing in over my table, and the light getting broken up in dusty shafts between the trees, not thinking anything, run out, run dry at last, empty. . . . And then I had this dream, if that's what it was. I wasn't asleep. I don't know what it was. I don't know what it was about, even. . . . In the novel, I tried to write about a man who couldn't get away from his destiny, all he did was part of it even when he thought he was acting freely. The dream was like that. I saw my own life—behind me and ahead of me. As if it were a road, lying along the hills. But I wasn't on it. I could see it, and the hills, I could see places I knew, but had I known them before or did I recognise them because they have always lain ahead of me? And that—that's all, I can't describe it, I can't bring it back." He sat poised, as if listening. "No use," he said, and shrugged. "But then, when I came to write this," and he tapped the paper on his knee, "when I came to the passage about the castle at night, then I realised I was describing one of the the things I had seen in the dream. Radiko at night, in the rain, in the dark, before sunrise. I saw that. I saw it in broad daylight two hundred miles away. Why? How? What does it mean? I don't know, I've given up asking. I have no right to ask. I've forfeited my rights. I lived in my mind, in my emotions, in my vanity, I lived in the world I made, and made the rules for it. I chose to dream. But then when you wake up you have lost your citizenship in daylight. You have forgotten what real things mean. You have forfeited your rights. . . ."

"Had one ever any rights?"

Amadey sat silent. Ladislas stood up, solid and stocky in the sheepskin vest he wore for warmth in the cold room; he walked up and down the room a couple of times. "When I was twelve and you were six we went over to Fonte for the Easter mass. Do you remember that?"

"We did that most years, didn't we, when mother was alive?"

"But we came back by the old road, by Fasten and Radiko, that time, because the bridge over the Garayna was out. It took all night to come back. We passed below Radiko a while before sunrise. I remember it, because you woke us all up, you were wide awake at the window trying to get it open and saying, 'Look at the castle, look at the castle!' And father gave you a cuff and we all settled down again. But I remember waking up suddenly like that and seeing the tower looming up on the sky, with the darkness just lifting behind it. Exactly as in your poem. You are describing that moment."

"I don't remember it at all. Twenty years ago! Queer how the mind works, isn't it?" Amadey said; his hands were shaking uncontrollably. This moment of his childhood which his brother could remember but which he could not, this was no explanation, no answer, but an abyss. From it he turned away in terror. "It's cold in here, Ladis," he said. "Let's go in by the fire."

"Go on," his brother said. "I've got to finish this."

III

Winter settled down over the Polana with cold and rain and the endless east wind blowing. At evening under a ragged iron-grey sky the flocks came in over the hills to the great paddocks of Esten. The fields lay grey and poor, the forest was grey, leafless. Givana and Ladislas followed a steady routine, the girl as methodical in her housework as the man in his farmwork. Amadey lapsed into listlessness, finding nothing that needed his doing. At times he found it impossible to get up, cross the room, and trim a guttering lamp. The ounce of energy was lacking; he sat still. His need to make poetry had been his master; having lost his master, he had lost his freedom. Like a tree grown up on a hillcrest where the wind always blows the same he had grown all in one direction, trunk and branches shaped to the wind, and the wind had ceased to blow. He would stand at the window for an hour at a time, looking out at the rain-lashed garden and

192

yards, staring, not thinking, not wondering even why he had come here and why he stayed here in this winter of boredom, this waste, this prison.

The new year came, and in a burst of energy he wrote all his friends in Krasnoy, Itale, Karantay, Helleskar, Luisa, that he was coming back as soon as the roads were fit to travel. He wrote them long letters full of crazy puns and jokes. He would come back to the city in April or in May, when the lindens would be flowering along the Molsen Boulevard, and the chestnuts in the park, and the pretty women on the mall; he would leave behind him at wind-beleaguered Esten all his cobweb notions, his self-torment, the last, senseless tatters of his adolescence. For that was all the trouble. Given up to his imagination, to the drunkenness of words, he had never taken time yet to become a man. It was time to face the real world.

"What would I be running from?" he said angrily to the night, as if denying a grave, heedless accusation; and the wind went on in its tremendous tides to the west, to the sea, under Orion standing bright above the January hills.

He thought of his boast and promise scratched in the stone of the tower of Radiko: *I shall conquer:* the word now remaining both lie and truth, as enduring as the stone of the tower itself that ignored, in its solitude, all conquerors and all defeat.

When Ladislas and Givana called on their wide-scattered neighbors he went with them, and they had people come in as often as they could, perhaps in an effort to entertain him; he was aware of their shy attempts to offer him work or talk or simply mute companionship, though he was not able to make adequate response. The evenings with other people were easier. The visitors did not really want him to talk. They were daunted by him as a poet, a famous man, a city man, and wanted at best to look at him, then to turn back to one another and discuss sheep, weather, neighbors, politics. The political arguments got hot; he kept out of them, listening with a sense of detachment and disloyalty. Ladislas was a strong reformer and constitutionalist, and was supported by the parish priest of Kolleiy; most of the other *domey* and farmers combatted his opinions, but not out of love for the government. Things were not going well in the

193

country. Taxation fell heavy on those who had no cash to pay it, police investigations and arrests were becoming common even in small towns, and the eastern provinces, where independence and conservatism were so extreme as to deserve the name of anarchism, were in a resentful, stormy temper. So Ladislas and his neighbors argued and grumbled; and Amadey was silent, always with that vague sense that his silence betrayed something or someone; and when there were no other women, kept home by the bitter weather and the foul roads, Givana also was silent, busy with her handwork and with looking after the tea, the supper, and so on. She was pregnant, and beautiful in pregnancy. She had gained in self-possession; she was gentle, reasonable, timid in manner, yet Amadey saw in her now also the unshakable strength, the assurance of her womanhood. She knew her way. She was happy. He watched her, without envy or hope of participation. Ladislas and two neighbors were going at it hammer and tongs; she came over to the harpsichord, near which Amadey was sitting, sat down, and with a smile of mockery began to play very softly. He came to stand beside her. "Oh, they are so boring," she said joyously. "They'll never even hear this, it won't bother." And she played and sang, half under her breath,

> From out my tower window
> I saw the red rose and the may,
> From out my tower window
> I saw the red rose and the thorn.
> Who rides beneath my window
> Before the break of day,
> Who rides beneath my window
>   Before the morn?

"Go on," said Amadey, who knew it from childhood, the ballad of Death who carries the girl away, but Givana smiled and said, "I can't sing, I'm so shortwinded," and went on playing one of her quaint old sonatinas. When she was done she tuned a couple of the wires, which forever needed tuning, and then sitting back on the bench asked him, "Do you still mean to leave in April?"

"I don't know," he said absently, his gaze following the design painted on the front of the harpsichord, a wreath of roses and hawthorn, chipped and faded on the cracked varnish. "I don't want to leave."

"Then why?"

"Because I know it's a mistake, so I do it."

She played a C-scale, one octave up and down, a tiny ripple of clear notes.

"It's foolish to talk that way."

"I know. I'm sorry."

"If you go, will you come back?"

"No. I don't think so. There is no reason to. I came here looking for the reason to come here, but I haven't found it. You see, when I went to Krasnoy, I knew exactly why I was going, what I had to do. To write my books, meet people, make my way, fall in love, all the rest of it. I did all that. I went through all I had to go through. And now it's done. It's all done."

"At twenty-six—"

"Don't think I'm lazy, Givana. You've scarcely seen me work. I worked very hard, when I had work to do. But it's done. So, I can go back to Krasnoy, or anywhere else, and write articles, and earn a living, take up life as most people do, get married, go on from day to day for fifty years if I like— I can see that; but I don't believe it. I don't see my life ahead. I have already lived it. All the rest seems meaningless. Do you know what I mean? You foresee your own life to come, in a way, don't you?"

"I never did until now. Since I've been pregnant. I see things . . . as if the baby saw them dreaming . . . a summer evening out there, under the poplar, the child and I are standing there waiting, for Ladis to ride home I suppose, and it's a lovely summer evening, a little sad . . . because the wind is blowing." She smiled. "And because I'll be older, then."

"Do I ride home with Ladis?"

"That's for you to see."

195

They had forgotten the others; she spoke without the least convention, and he answered, harsh and pleading, "But I can't. I can't see anything ahead. There's no way to see ahead through one's own eyes, it's the child as you say, the future you bear, that's your vision, the truth, but I—I have lost the way— I can't see."

"You worked so hard, you said so yourself; you're tired, you're worn out. You have to wait. It's like winter, everything has to rest and wait." She spoke earnestly, with confidence.

The thaws came early, there was no snow after the last week of January. In February he received the first mail to come through to Kolleiy since Christmas: two letters from Karantay, one dated in early December asking if he had any news from Itale, the other an empty envelope, the seal broken. There was also a packet from the Rochoy publishing house, copies of his new book, *Givan Faugen*. He gave one to his brother. "Read it next winter!" he said, for Ladislas was in the thick of lambing season, at work twenty hours a day, and often not at the house for two or three days at a time. "No, in a week or so now," Ladislas answered seriously. "But give it to Givana. It will please her."

"I will. Where are you off to?"

"South paddocks."

"I'll be along."

"If you like." Ladislas swung up on his little horse, raised a hand in salute, and rode off. Amadey went to find Givana in the garden west of the house. It was a cold day, the wind blowing light and keen; sunlight flashed, dimmed, flashed in rain-pools on the raw black ground. Givana was stooping over a bed of dirt, her figure bright and frail in the restless light. "My crocuses are up," she said proudly. "Two of them, see them?"

"And my book's out—see it?"

She took the book, looked at the title, turned it over, did not know what to say. He showed her the flyleaf, on which he had written with the bad pen and gummy ink of the Kolleiy Post Inn, "For Givana and Ladislas from their loving brother Amadey." She read the inscription and sought for words to say, then suddenly breaking through her own constraint she smiled and

196

said, "Read me some of it!" She sat down on the garden seat, putting up her feet on a paving-stone to keep them from the mud under the bench.

"Now?"

"Now," she said with her little air of command.

Standing there in the uneasy sunlight he opened the book and read the first page aloud; he paused, and shut the book. "It seems years ago, someone else's book. . . ."

"Go on."

"I can't."

"How does it end?"

"You shouldn't know that before you read it."

"I always look at the end before I begin."

He glanced down at her, then opened to the last page of the book, and read aloud in his hard voice: "'Givan made no reply for some minutes, but leaned on the railing of the bridge in mute contemplation of the river, which ran fast beneath, foam-streaked and yellow, swollen by the torrents of Spring. At length, raising his head, he said, "If life is anything more than a brief exile from the kingdoms beyond Death—"'"

He stopped again. He closed the book and laid it down on the bench beside Givana. She looked up at him, helpless. The wind blew, the sun shone out and faded on the high, pale hill above the house. "It's a very gloomy book," the young man said.

"Amadey, you are going back to Krasnoy, aren't you?"

He shook his head.

"But there's nothing for you here—"

"All my kingdom is here. It always was." Hands in his pockets he turned away to the gate, then turned back as if to speak again; he smiled a little as if in apology, shrugged, and went on around the house.

Givana soon followed him, wearied and oppressed by the cold wind. She lay down in her room and dozed uncomfortably. Through halfsleep she heard Amadey's voice down in the yard, the stamping of a horse. Rain began to patter on the roof and window, and she slept.

"Perhaps he went out to shoot in the forest," she said, that

197

night. Ladislas, at his long-delayed supper, nodded and went on eating.

"It's been dark two hours," he said, setting down knife and fork. "There's been some accident with the horse, maybe."

He got up. Givana, watching his exhausted face, said nothing.

He came back from the forest past midnight. "Gil is going on to Kolleiy with the lantern," he said. Givana helped him pull off his mired boots; he sat back on the hearthseat, and almost at once fell asleep, before he had lain down. Wakeful in her pregnancy, Givana sat with him, keeping the fire built up; the old house-keeper brought quilts and they made a bed of the hearthseat. Ladislas slept there until dawn, when he woke suddenly. Givana was asleep, curled up in the armchair by the fire. Ladislas went quietly upstairs to his brother's room to check that no one was there, then put on his boots and went out into the icy white sunrise. The crest of the hill above the house was lipped with gold; stables, yard, house, trees stood pallid and rigid in the dawn light. Ladislas pulled the collar of his coat up around his neck and went to the stables. The stable-boy came clambering down to meet him from the loft room.

"Where's the Rakava bridle," Ladislas said, his voice hoarse with sleep and cold, "did Dom Amadey take it?"

"Aye, for the mare."

"I'm going out towards Fonte, by the old road, tell them in the house."

He set off on his little black horse through the frostbound forest, up the hills now bright along their eastern slopes, riding towards the summit and the tower that stood yellow in the level light. As he came over the last rise before the valley under Radiko he saw the brown mare standing halfway down the steep ascent, her reins dragging. She shied away as he rode close; she ran a little, stumbled on the reins and stopped, turning her dark nervous head to watch Ladislas. He rode up past her and across the fallen wall of the courtyard, dismounted, and went to the foot of the ramp leading up into the tower. Amadey had set the gun, a hunting rifle, against his chest under the heart, and had fallen forward, sprawled out, his head turned to the side. His coat was soaking wet with rain and his hair looked black.

Ladislas touched his hand which lay on the muddy ground, mudstained and as cold as the ground or the rain. The wind kept blowing on the hills, the domain of Radiko, as it always did. Amadey's eyes were open, so that he seemed to be looking westward over the ruined wall and the hills at the sky where, for him, there had been no sunrise, the night continuing.

PART FIVE

Prisons

I

"In Rakava, beneath the high walls . . ." The tune had stuck
with Itale all the way from Esten, jolting in his head as he jolted
over the roads of the Polana on an outside seat of the springless
coach, in the wind, between hills that hid themselves at last in
slow-drifting clouds and veils of autumn rain. It was in the rain
that he first saw the high walls, and from the south. Coming to
Rakava from the north, from the plains, one would see first a
swell of land, a hill rising a thousand feet so gradually that it
could hardly be seen as a whole, and below the long skyline a
patch of something like broken pearls, that as one came closer
would take form, becoming a walled city built of white and
tawny stone, towered and battlemented, remote, magnificent.
But coming up from the south over the crest of the great hill, Itale
first saw Rakava below him, exposed and dingy in the rain of an
October afternoon. The houses had spread out far beyond the
walls; the towers huddled in a maze and jumble of streets,
dominated by the featureless bulk of several buildings that stood
massive at the north edge of the city, the cloth factories. In older
centuries Rakava had been the pearl of the east, the glory and

fortress of the province, the untaken, the unsullied, *Racava intacta*. Now the high walls were breached in fifty places to let in and out the swarms of men and women going to work in the factories, coming back from work in the factories. There was still wealth there; industry was modern and on a scale unmatched in any other city of the land. Wool and silk was the city's wealth; silkworms were raised, baled fleeces stored, yarns spun and dyed, cloth woven and cut, in the huge sheds and buildings along the northern wall; the life of the city was there, and the old towers of feudal defense stood useless, like the rusty iron fingers of a gauntlet thrusting up through the chalk of a barren hill. The coach passed under those towers and Itale looked up at their blind, massive walls uneasily. One, a fort, all but windowless, was the St Lazar Prison, another next to it, higher and elaborately battlemented, housed the provincial Courts of Law; he saw no sign of use or habitation in the others, their dark gates barred. Dusk came fast in the narrow streets. The coach rattled down cobbles slippery with rain. One of the horses slipped, plunged, and went down with a sickening crash, leaving its mate straining to stay afoot in the broken harness and the coach tilted over, so that Itale half jumped and half slid down to the street, where he too slipped, and so greeted the stones of Rakava on hands and knees, his head badly jolted and his palms scraped raw. The horse had broken its knees, a crowd has gathered immediately and pressed in close on the horses, the coach, the passengers. Itale got his valise out of the boot and pushed his way out of the crowd, his head still ringing; he got directions from a woman and set off down the street to the Rosetree Inn, where Isaber was waiting for him.

The ex-student-teacher, nineteen now and an ardent acolyte at *Novesma Verba*, was very glad to see him; he had been alone in Rakava two days and had apparently had a wretched time of it. He talked all the time Itale had his bath, which was the first thing he had ordered, a hot tub in front of a hot fire. Even as he finally got warm he could feel the cold he had taken on the rainy trip settling itself in his throat and nose and eyesockets, moving in, making itself at home. The quantity of hot water brought up had been meager, the fire did not burn well. As he stood on the hearth to towel himself dry he observed two cockroaches the size of his thumb bickering over a greasy spot on the floor. "No rose, this Rosetree," he said.

"The rats run up on the beds at night. It's foul. The whole city's foul."

Itale shivered. "Hand me my shirt there, would you, Agostin? Thanks. Well, is it any worse than the Krasnoy slums?"

"Yes. Because that's all there is. The rest of it is dead. And the people are like rats. They won't even talk to you."

"You're an outsider. You're not one of 'em. All provincials are suspicious. I know, I'm a provincial." He always found himself reassuring Isaber, trying to cheer him up, making light of difficulties; it made him feel much more than five years older than the boy, and roused a sense of hypocrisy in him. "They are probably human, anyhow," he said drily. "Come on, I'm hungry."

"I ordered mutton, there isn't much else," Isaber said, despondent, and they went down to a greasy supper in the gloomy depths of the inn. When Itale got to bed, with his cold, and a sharp ache in his wrist where he had wrenched it landing on the cobblestones, he reflected that his arrival in Rakava had been inauspicious; and indeed that the journey had begun ill; why had Amadey turned away like that without a word, as if he could not wait to see him go? A rat scrabbled in the wall, or under the bed. The air of the room was sour with the smell of the cheap tallow candles just blown out. "What am I doing here?" Itale thought in discouragement, and let the unanswered question magnify his sense of being in a strange room among unfamiliar walls and streets, until his own tired, unrelaxed body felt strange to him. The pain in his wrist and hand increased. He could not find an easy position. As his waking intelligence began to blur, the pressure of the alien and the inimical increased until he felt himself unable to move, lying as still and tense as a hunted man in hiding yet half-asleep and longing for full sleep, and still the stupid question hanging in his mind, "What am I doing here?"

Next morning he had not forgotten that night-mood, and could not shake it off entirely. Only the question had resumed its primary form, waiting for him among the stones of Rakava as it

205

had waited for him in a kindlier disguise among the fountains and gardens of Aisnar, borrowing from them the aspect of desire, or of longing; here it was undisguised and blunt, a mere question, "What am I doing?"

There was no disguise here, no distraction. Here in this city whose existence was a suction of crowds into the factories and rejection of them, suction and rejection, repetitive unvarying activity like that of a powerful machine, work irrelevant to climate, to season, to the land or the hour of sunrise or sunset, or the wits or the wishes of any soul among those crowds, here, Itale thought after he had been in Rakava a few days, he had crossed some boundary towards which he had been tending for a long time; but he did not know where he had come, or why, or if there was any way back home.

He did, of course, what he had come to do: called on factory owners and managers, used Oragon's introductions to meet the political leaders of the city and among the workers, studied the functioning and organisation of the factories; he was profoundly impressed by the men and the city, by the vigor, the tremendous, inorganic energy of the system, which, less than twenty years and only beginning to reach full development, had transformed the lives of a hundred thousand people. After a fortnight he had so much material for a series of articles that he began to write them, calling the series, with an irony perceptible only to himself, "Industry in Rakava." He was industrious enough, his mind worked with speed and concentration, he was tireless; only he had to avoid certain questions in his writing and his thoughts, or they would lead him back round to the one he could not answer. And it seemed to him sometimes that his senses were dulled, here, so that he did not feel keenly nor see clearly; his emotions too were cool, as if insulated off.

Isaber worked hard for him, and stuck close to him. The boy was not the companion Itale would have liked. His loyalty verged too much upon dependence; he demanded that Itale lead and inform him. That Itale should question his own purposes was unthinkable to him. They were working for Freedom and that was all that was needed. Sometimes this trust was a comfort to Itale, sometimes he was moved by it to destructive cynicisms which he did not let himself say aloud. Perhaps he had no right to do what he was doing; certainly he had no right to destroy the whole fabric of Isaber's beliefs and hopes.

The days went by rapidly, evenly. They were well into November and rain or sleet and snow fell every day. Itale put off his plans to leave. He continued to gather material for his articles, his understanding of the subject continued to grow. He wrote to Brelavay that he might stay on till Christmas, if their money held out. Under his steady activity there was a lethargy, an unwillingness to move again, to go on or go back. He was here, he would stay. He kept returning to the factories to watch the rattling grey-black efficiency of the wooden and iron machines out of which came long webs of pure white wool, fragile silks the colors of jewels and flowers, patterned velvets, splendid and delicate products of the looms and racks, the stinking vats of dye and sizing, the crazy dancing spindles, the endless trays of leaves and worms. The big new Ferman Wool factory had two steam-driven looms, the first in the country; he had read Sangiusto's descriptions of such machines in the northern English cities, and went to see them in some intellectual excitement, but was drawn back to them again and again simply to watch them work: the swift endless back-and-forth, the deft, effaced men that served them. He could stand watching them for an hour, all the time with a slightly sick feeling in the pit of his stomach. They were the same motions, it was the same product, as Kounney working at his loom in his rooms in Mallenastrada; it was weaving, there had been weaving done since the dawn of human time, why did the powered looms so fascinate and frighten him? He wrote an article describing them, their structure, their product, and their probable effect on the economy if more came into use. "What a lot you know about all this," Isaber said reading it, admiring as always. "What are you calling the piece?"

"Freeing the Hands," Itale said.

The workman told off to demonstrate the powered loom to Itale was named Fabbre. Itale had quickly discovered the man's politics to be radical, and they had struck up a kind of friendship, very cautious on both sides. Fabbre lived with his wife, his father-in-law, and five children in a four-room house outside the east wall. The Ferman managers had built this row of houses for their skilled workmen: Fabbre was an aristocrat, and treated as such. The houses had floors, and small fenced front yards, though the back doors opened on an alley of mud. The children played in troops in the alley, never in the little bare yards. These houses fascinated Itale as the machinery of the factories did. The slums of Rakava were like the slums of Krasnoy or any other city; that dirt and misery was old, coeval with the cities, the poor you have always with you—but Fabbre and his family were not poor; they were not dirty; if they were miserable it was not by the ancient causes of cold, hunger, and disease. They did not plant flowers in these front plots, or vegetables, which would be stolen, Fabbre's wife said, it was not worth the trouble. Anyway they would likely move soon, there were new houses being built by the East Gate, water piped in to a pump in your own yard, they said. "The Company keeps us well enough," she said factually and yet with a cold irony.

Itale knew the peasant houses of Val Malafrena: more crowded even than this house, darker, and warm. Opposite the hearth would be a partition and visible and audible across it the cow and perhaps a couple of pigs or goats. The enormous bed, usually next to the stall, the clothespress, the table and chairs were of oak. Everything smelled of hay, manure, bedding, onions, woodsmoke. Whatever the housewife owned of pewter, copper, or painted ware stood out on a shelf above the table. One was not asked into those houses, any more than into a badger's earth or a foxes' den. One stood in the doorway speaking to the housewife or the husband, the youngest children staring from the rich darkness. In such places people had lived always, on the land. The houses of privilege, Valtorsa and the Sorde house, were the same house made light and large, and the cattle moved out. But this house, Fabbre's house in the double row, this was something else; it was slave quarters. "The Company keeps us well enough. . . ."

Itale saw them stand in groups on the streets on Saturday nights, knots and clumps of women and men, dark and forceful then, null when they walked alone; he listened to their talk in the soft, nasal dialect, always of the factories and politics; he saw they knew more, wanted more, hoped for more than the peasants, and sensed their violence, the will to justice too long outraged; and he wanted to withdraw from them, to dissociate himself from their impotence and violence, their inchoate lives and the clever, inchoate, slave minds of their spokesmen such as Fabbre. He could not do so. He was one of them. He and they could talk, could understand one another's ideas. He could never be one of or one with the peasants of his home: the difference of experience and knowledge, the difference of privilege there was too wide and nothing could annull it, nothing bridge it, even, except personal affection, personal love. But here among these people who understood what he was working for he began, for the first time, to doubt his own purposes. If this was progress, if this was the future, did he want it—did anyone want it except the rich, the powerful, the owners?

In Krasnoy crowds formed and unformed easily, coalitions and driftings-apart of individuals; here it was the crowd that was the center, not the man, and the mob temper was always uneasy, angry. There was little street oratory in Krasnoy, beyond street-corner debates in the River Quarter; here there seemed always to be a speech going on somewhere in the city, and a crowd around the speaker. The governor of the Polana province had forbidden public meetings, any man seen addressing a crowd was liable to arrest and imprisonment, but it made no difference: they spoke, they met, they lived in unrest, resentment, wakefulness. They had all that Itale had sought first as a student in Solariy: the sense of justice, the spirit of revolt. But then revolt to what end?

He let some of this break out one night talking with Isaber. "Whom are we really working for, I wonder? For whom are we making the way plain? The king—old Duke Matiyas—a restored constitutional monarchy . . . That's a bit flat but perhaps it's the best of a bad lot. Better than working for Emperor Franz and Metternich, by making an armed rebellion which they can crush and use for an excuse to snuff out national independence altogether. Better than working for the Ferman Brothers by telling the poor they can better their lot, they can rise in the world, so long as the Ferman Brothers rise on their necks, of course."

Isaber gaped, scared, for he had never seen Itale bitter. "But as the people become educated—" he stammered.

"Educated!" Itale jeered, but then he looked at Isaber, the fragile enthusiast whom he had educated, for whom he was literally responsible. "Forget it, Agostin. I'm in a bad temper, this place gets on my nerves."

He turned back to the table and got on with his writing. A half hour passed. Isaber was restless, roaming around the room—they had taken a two-room tenement flat, since it was cheaper than staying at an inn—stirring the fire, rearranging papers. Itale knew he wanted reassurance, but he had none to offer. His conscience was heavy. Isaber was a born follower; and he, he had seen himself as a leader, guiding men on towards the light. A leader! Had he outgrown that ambition, or merely fallen short of it? It was hard enough to keep the single candle alight in the depths of one's mutable, vulnerable being, against the indifferent winds of heaven; it was hard to stand up alone, and know where one stood, let alone where one was going.

The next night he was to speak to a meeting of journeymen silkweavers, a strong association despite the government bans on laborers' unions. They wanted a report on the Assembly meetings in Krasnoy, and he could not refuse them. Since his journal was prevented from publishing the news, he was obliged to give it as he could; that was one reason, perhaps the best reason, for his coming to Rakava. Isaber did not go with him this time. His talk went well enough. They asked questions for an hour after, and that was an ordeal, for, lacking a politician's unfailing flow of words, he thought before he answered and while he answered: so he was slow, and his audience grew impatient. They wanted quick answers and definite ones. He got still slower, more cautious. He heard his own voice, dry and hesitant. The blood began to burn in his cheeks, he resented the men, sitting so patient in their worn clothes, the tired, intelligent faces, the minds impatient, destructive, arrogant. "Why don't the Assembly do something about the Bura' o' Censorship then? Why don't they question its pow'rs?'' a thin, persistent man demanded. Itale flung out his hands and laughed, driven out of patience. "Why don't they question the powers of the emperor of Austria? Why don't they question the powers of Light and Darkness? What can the Assembly do, man? If it once directly questions the government's authority, the government will dissolve it by force. Would you defend it then? Do you want armed revolution? That's what you're asking for. Are you ready for it? We've got no arms, and no allies. Yet suppose we rebelled and won out—then what? What next? You know what you don't like, and I don't like it either, but what is it you do like—when there's no censorship what are you going to say?''

He had found his tongue at last, and set them all against him. It was inevitable. They turned on him because he was an outsider and because he was middle-class, and yet they demanded that he offer them hope. He, feeling that to promise them hope was to lie to them and to deny them hope was to betray them, stood answering their questions, fighting back at their attacks, defiant and sore-hearted.

When the meeting broke up, one of the officers of the weavers' association, a man named Klenin, caught up with him in the hall. "Will you come out this way, Mr Sorde," he said, leading him away from the main door where the crowd was going out.

"Are they that angry?" Itale said sarcastically, but began to cool down as he looked at Klenin's face, sensitive as were so many faces among these city workmen; he looked like Itale's neighbor in Krasnoy, Kounney the linen-weaver.

"They don't stop us meeting, since '21," Klenin explained in his soft voice, "but lately they've been taking up some o' the speakers, different places in the city, and questioning 'em. Just bogeying. If they don't see you then you're spared the trouble. You had to answer enough questions tonight, maybe." He smiled.

"I let them down tonight. I'm sorry."

Klenin looked at him. His eyes were blue, a soft blue, intent and serious. "The men always jump Krasnoyers, you know. I respect what you said, Mr Sorde. There's no use pretending it's easy."

They were at the door, and Itale said, "Thanks, Klenin." He wanted to tell this man that he was grateful, he wanted to express the liking he felt for him, his blue eyes and fine, tired face, but all he could do was say "Thank you" and shake his hand, the one human touch, the one meeting with another man, of the whole evening. They parted on a dark street in the rain.

II

He was glad to look up from the dark streets at last and see the light shine from his windows. Isaber, with a Krasnoyer's instinct for good cheer, had put up red curtains which he had got for a few pennies as mill-ends. The candle light shone rosy through them, and Itale felt his heart lighten a little. At least he was not alone here! Isaber was a good fellow, with his loyal heart and his red curtains. He climbed the unlit staircase and turned off at the second landing; a baby was crying, a thin, almost ceaseless wail, on the floor above. As he felt with his key for the lock he thought he heard Isaber call something, "Come in!" or "Don't come in!" As he hesitated, startled, the door was opened abruptly from within. He saw Isaber standing by the table, and other men in the room, one at the door not a foot from him. His first action was to step back and turn. A man stood behind him halfway up the stairs. His conscious reaction was to the fixed, staring look on Isaber's face: this troubled him, and he said, "What's wrong, Agostin?"

The boy did not answer. The man holding the door open said, "Mr Sorde?"

"Who are you?"

"Please come in."

Itale came in, followed by the man who had been on the stairs. The man who had opened the door closed it, carefully, taking the trouble not to be noisy, rather like a butler, Itale thought.

"You are Itale Sorde, employed by the journal *Novesma Verba* of Krasnoy, is that correct?"

"Yes." Isaber was looking down now, still with a stuporous expression. The other men stood wooden-faced, a lot of posts. "Will you sit down, gentlemen?" Itale said in a clear, harsh voice. They all went on standing. None of them looked at his face. "Stand if you like," he said, and sat down in his usual chair by the table.

"Are you the author of these writings, Mr Sorde?"

They were his last dispatch to Krasnoy, two articles and a private letter to Brelavay.

"When I saw them last they were sealed," he said, and leaned back in his chair a little to keep himself sitting down, to keep his rage under control. "Is opening mail your profession or do you do it for pleasure?"

"Did you write them?"

"Who are you?"

"My name is Arassy," the man said with annoyance. He had a tenor voice, an intelligent, inexpressive face.

"And mine's Sorde, as you know, but that gives me no right to ask you questions, I think? Who are you, and am I under arrest or merely being intimidated?"

"You're under arrest, Mr Sorde, and I think the rest of this can wait—all right, Gavral?"

One of the others, a somber man in his twenties, nodded.

"You'll want your coat, Mr Isaber. This room will be sealed until you've stood trial, Mr Sorde. You might want to bring along a change of clothing."

"Let me see your authority."

Arassy produced a warrant signed by Kastusso, commander of the Polana militia.

Isaber still had not moved. Itale went to him. "Come on, Agostin," he said, and then, lower, with irritation, "Don't freeze like a rabbit. Get your coat."

Tears started into the boy's eyes and he whispered, staring at Itale, "Sorde, I'm sorry!"

"Come on, get your coat."

They rode in a closed cab through the dark rainswept streets uphill to the building Itale had seen when he first entered the city, the Courts of Law. Its crenellated tower loomed up through

213

sweeping clouds of half-frozen rain, dizzying in the flare of the cab-lamps. In a warm shabby room without windows Arassy interrogated them briefly before a secretary. "Very good, Mr Sorde," he said, rubbing his hand over his forehead as if he had a headache. "Thanks. You and Mr Isaber will be detained here until trial."

"What are the charges against us?"

Article 15, activities prejudicial to public order. It's a very common charge, Mr Sorde."

He was not bad, this Arassy; polite, tired, matter-of-fact.

"I know. How long is it likely to be before we stand trial?"

"I can't say. Possibly in a few days. Usually within two months."

Arassy bowed. Two militiamen came at his signal and took Itale and Isaber off down a corridor, up three long flights of stone steps, and to a dark room at the end of a last, curving corridor. They entered the room, the soldiers with them. "Gentlemen, please, you carry knives, penknives, any metal instrument?" The accent as usual was foreign, German or Bohemian. Isaber mechanically surrendered his penknife, Itale as mechanically did not; in fact he was surprised to find it in his pocket next morning. "Very good. Good night, gentlemen." The door of the room closed with a loud, peculiar click.

"What do—" Itale began and then backed against the door with a start, seeing a faceless figure rear up from a couch or bench almost under his left hand. It gave a kind of groaning snarl. The only light in the room came from a lamp or candle down the corridor, reflected dimly on the ceiling through a grating high in the door. Everything was high, the ceiling eighteen or twenty feet, the door ten or twelve, a queer effect in the faint wavering light. The shapeless figure on the bench pushed its face out of blankets, though no features were visible, and said, "Cell-mates?" Only at the word did it occur to Itale that this curious room was a prison cell.

"Right," he said, interested; but he had to turn and give his attention to Isaber, who had crouched down onto his heels and was rocking back and forth, back and forth, saying nothing. Itale talked to him but he squatted there silent, swaying. At last Itale hauled him up by the arm, by main force, and said, "Sit down!"—pushing him onto the bench that ran around two walls of the room. "Get hold of yourself!" He was rough, and his voice was very angry. The boy sank his head into his hands and burst into tears.

"How long were they there before I came?" Itale asked him after a while, casting about for some hook of simple fact to draw Isaber out of his formless and grotesque abasement.

"I don't know. An hour." He tried to stop sobbing. "I don't know."

"What did they ask you?"

"I don't know. I tried not to answer. Oh, Jesus, Mary!" He clenched his hands over his face. "I'm sorry, Itale, I'm sorry!"

"Look, Agostin, they are trying to frighten us; don't give them that pleasure."

"I believe you gentlemen are politicals," said the third man, sardonic, still faceless in the shadowy deep room.

"Yes. My name's Sorde." He did not know if giving your name was prison etiquette; he did not introduce Isaber, who was still crying.

"Sorde? From Krasnoy? Yes. What an honor. Not surprised perhaps, but honored." The man gave an edgy, ingratiating snicker. "I'm Givan Forost. I'll be out in a few days, and you gents will have more room."

"Is this St Lazar Prison?" Itale asked, remembering that the two towered buildings, the court and the jail, adjoined.

"St Lazar! Are you joking! This is the Courts tower, this is no jail, look at it, a palace! Blankets, light, window, all the comforts. Thought you political gentlemen knew more about the inside of jails than that. "What's wrong with sonny?" Forost got up, trailing the blankets he had cocooned himself in, and approached them.

"Let him be," Itale said stiffly.

"Needs his mammy," Forost said. "All right. So long as he doesn't keep it up all night. Choose your beds, plenty of room, in Lazar there'd be forty in a room like this. Piss-pot's in the corner. Sleep well, gents." He rolled himself up again in his blankets and was silent. Itale talked a little while softly with Isaber, persuaded

215

him to lie down, and then did the same himself, feeling suddenly dead tired. Forost had not shared his blankets with them, but the bench was covered with a burlap matting and the air, though cold, was still and fresh. Itale stretched out and at once felt comfortable. He closed his eyes, all his thoughts escaped him, and he fell into sound and peaceful sleep.

Forost was with them for a week. He never said what he had been arrested for; he was apparently some kind of clerk, but was vague about that too. He was certain of being released, and was indeed released at the end of the week— "Friends in power," he said with his snicker. He gave them detailed descriptions of the St Lazar Prison, without ever saying if he had been jailed there or visited it or spoke from hearsay: the wards of twenty to a hundred men, sick and well, sane, insane, and imbecile, murderers and petty thieves all together; the rats, fleas, lice, bedbugs; the typhus, typhoid, and smallpox that twice in the last forty years had, in Forost's phrase, "cleaned out the prison"; the solitary cells, and the cells below street level, where the water was a foot deep on the floor in winter. "That's a real prison," Forost said with admiration. "But see, you gents don't fit. Rioters, sure, they get locked up in the wards in Lazar, commoners, workingmen, lock 'em up, who cares? But you gentlemen politicals, they don't want you on their hands. You two aren't going to stand trial yet for a while. They don't want to bring you up and sentence you, see, because they don't know where to put you when you're sentenced. If they get orders from the government, from Krasnoy, give this one a sentence, then they're in for it, they have to do it, but God knows where they stick him. So the longer you wait the safer you are. You'll wait six months, then be released without trial. That's how they like to do it. Cool you off a while here in the tower, then let you out; you run off quick; and they don't have to worry about you any more."

Itale listened with interest but no particular emotion. Six days or six months, there was nothing he could do about it, and probably, as Forost implied, it was just as well that he could not. He thought of his escapade in Solariy and the house arrest that had been his punishment. This was not all that much worse. He lay back on the bench, his shoes for a pillow, looking up at the single window set high in the high wall, and sang under his breath, "All the best Governments, Have replaced Common Sense, With Von Müller, and Haller, and Gentz. . . ."

"Go on," said Forost, who was paring his nails with Itale's penknife. "Give us a concert."

"What would you like?—'Beyond this darkness is the light, O Liberty, of thine eternal day! . . .'" Forost grinned, Isaber looked scared. He was still depressed, brooding miserably most of the time.

"What do they sing where you come from?"

"Not jail songs. What do you sing here?" He began the song he had heard at Esten, "In Rakava, beneath the high walls," knowing only the first line; Forost picked it up in a sweet tenor. "That's no jail song, that's an old song," he said when he had sung it, and he began a monotonous and obscene ballad to which Itale listened, grateful for any entertainment. He liked Forost for never complaining. When Forost was released and left them with a jaunty bow and a "Goodbye, good luck, Robespierre, don't cry for me, Sonny!"—Itale was sorry to see him go. At this point cheerful degradation was worth more to him than noble gloom. He did not hold against Forost his flat refusal to try and smuggle out a message to Itale's friends; Forost had no reason to take risks, no hope of profit from the game Itale was playing.

Still, the isolation worried him, the not being able to write to any one of his friends, his family, "I'm here, I'm all right."

Isaber, sensing his low spirits, fell into one of his fits of apathetic, self-accusing despair.

An hour passed in total silence. Itale fell asleep, and slept an hour or more. When he woke, Isaber was sitting in the same position, brooding. Itale felt a spasm of hatred, of loathing for him, which terrified him by its intensity. He turned away, as well as one could turn away from another person in the featureless room, and began to whistle the tune of a Mozart rondo Luisa had used to play. He stood up. "I have to do something, I have to move," he said. "I need exercise. Can we get up to that window? See if you can stand on my shoulders. Come on!" So the guard bringing their evening soup and bread found Isaber balanced on

Itale's shoulders, clinging to the bars of the window, describing the view. "Stop that! Stop them! Guards!" the soldier, a big Swabian, shouted, startling Isaber so that he fell rather than jumped down. Itale began to laugh. "You cannot escape—you must no do that—it's forbidden!" the guard roared. Isaber too began to laugh.

"Escape? Are we three inches wide?" Itale said. The Swabian, embarrassed, motioned away the other guard that had come at his call. "It's forbidden, gentlemen, I'm sorry, forbidden, no climbing!"

Itale stifled his laughter, Isaber snickered, both of them exhilarated by the physical exertion and by the guard's discomfiture. After that they took turns daily on each other's shoulders to look out at the jumbled view of rooftops and the winter sky. Itale's turns were short, as Isaber could not long support his hundred and fifty pounds. The boy's health was shaky; an orphan, born in the waterfront slums, fed by parish charity and housed by luck, he had not had a good start in life. The flour soup they got gave him colic, and racking headaches kept him wakeful in the night.

One such night, their eighteenth in the cell, both were awake. As the almost jovial serenity, the acceptant mood of the first days wore away, as he began to suffer from the frustration of all physical and mental energies, Itale had become as if in compensation more patient with Isaber's lassitude. Compunction and compassion were strong in him this night, and when he heard Isaber move and sigh, he sat up and asked, "Headache?"

"Yes."

"Do you mind if we talk a minute?"

Isaber propped himself up on his elbow. It was never fully dark in the tower cell, or fully light. Itale saw him only as a dim shape.

"I wanted to say that I'm sorry I got you into this. All of this. I have meddled with your life. I had no right. At first it made this harder for me—realising that I'd pulled you in after me, that it was my fault— But what I wanted to say now is that all the same I'm glad you're here. I don't know how I'd get through this without you. Without your friendship. That is what it comes down to."

"I'd rather be here with you than free if you were here," the boy said, urgently, with relief.

"I'd rather we were both anywhere else. But as it is . . ."

That was all they said. Isaber soon slept. It was cold in the deep room; the first heavy snow had fallen that day on the city outside their narrow window. Itale huddled under the thin blanket, wearing his coat, and when he finally got to sleep he dreamed vividly. Most of his dreams these eighteen nights had been of open places, familiar faces and voices, the mountains. This dream began in horror. He was in the tower cell trying to wash his hands, which were dirty, as were the walls and floor, with a sort of soot or black, charry grease. The wash basin was filled with acid, printer's acid, such as they used in the shop where *Novesma Verba* was printed. "It'll wash it off," Forost said. — "I can't use this," he explained, "this is printer's acid." — "It's not acid," Amadey Estenskar told him with a sneer, "look there, it's not eating away the basin, what are you afraid of?" But from the lip of the basin a fine yellowish smoke was rising; the metal disintegrated, the smoking acid ran out over the table and over his hands, eating tracks in them like worm-tracks in wood, painlessly. Then he was kneeling down staring into a pool of water, into which the disintegrated pieces of the basin had fallen. His arms were bare, plunged up above the elbow in the cold, dark green water which was slowly rising. The dim, clear surface came nearer and nearer his eyes. He looked up with a great effort. The water stretched on, quiet and deep, shining darkly, a lake. Above it and reflected on its surface was one immense shadow of a mountain, the Hunter. The reflection reached close to his eyes. Behind it, in the water and in the air, was nothing: the vast, pale, empty gulf of the sky after sunset.

He woke; he was shivering; the pale light of snow was reflected on the high ceiling.

One of the guards told them that day that they were to stand trial the following day, Isaber in the morning and Itale in the afternoon. Isaber's spirits went up, this time, while Itale's went down. If Forost had known what he was talking about, the later their trial came the better. He kept his misgivings to himself, and sent Isaber off next morning with the guards, trying to believe or at least to act as if he believed that everything would be well.

Isaber returned before noon. "Released!" he shouted before the guard had got the door unlocked. "Released!" A rush of unexpected, overwhelming relief, joy, hope welled up in Itale, he hugged Isaber, his eyes filled up with tears— "You're free, then? you're free?"

"I'm to be out of Rakava tonight and out of the Polana by Wednesday noon. Do they think I'm likely to stay, the fools?" He laughed a long, shaky, triumphant laugh. Itale hugged him again, jubilant, laughing.

"I didn't really hope— Thank God, thank God! But what are you back here for?"

"I asked to come back till you're through. They agreed, they're not as bad as I thought they'd be— Let me tell you about the trial." He did so, excitedly and not very coherently. As they talked Itale's mind began to recover from the shock of hope.

"A defense attorney who's never even talked to us," Isaber said, "it's a farce, what kind of justice is that?"

"Imperial justice," Itale said. "What did he say, Agostin? Anything?"

"Oh, he talked about my youth and inexperience, a lot of rigmarole,—nothing important." He became uneasy, he was suppressing something the attorney had said, probably a plea that Isaber had been led astray by older men. Isaber's mind was quick at apprehension, and he knew that Itale had picked up his omission; after that they were ill at east with each other, pretending confidence. Yet Isaber had been released, set free, his trial a mere formality; it did not matter what the attorneys said or did not say.

When the Swabian came to take Itale to the courtroom Isaber came with them. He was barred from entering the court and they did not even shake hands in the hallway outside the courtroom, as Itale was hurried on by a second guard.

In the courtroom the defense, a tall, sad-eyed lawyer on state pay, consulted with Itale for five minutes. "It's all about these papers, you see. These articles you wrote. We'll admit that you wrote them."

"I signed them. Of course I wrote them."

"Yes. Then you spoke to a workmen's meeting on the seventh, and again—a different group—on the twentieth."

"Yes."

"Yes, well, we'll just admit that, and throw ourselves on the mercy of the court; the charge is activity prejudicial to—"

"I know the charge. What can I expect from the mercy of the court?"

"Don't ask to speak," the lawyer said, looking down at the papers and scratching his lined, ill-shaven cheek. "Believe me, Mr Sorde. Don't try to defend yourself."

Itale knew he was right.

Prosecution and defense took about a quarter of an hour. The three judges conferred and talked with one another most of that time. When the two lawyers had finished reading their case the judge on the left asked something of a clerk, took up a sheet of paper, and read in a loud voice, "On this evidence and the defendant's confessions and on the recommendation of the Chief of the National Police in Krasnoy, under Article 15 of the law of June 18, 1819, this court judges the defendant Itale Sorde guilty of the crime of inciting and participating in activities prejudicial to the public order, peace, and safety, and sentences him to five years imprisonment without labor, the sentence to be effective without delay." He laid the paper down and spoke again to the clerk. Itale sat waiting, he thought the judge was going to speak again, say something else. The lawyer for the defense, sitting beside him, muttered something, shaking his head. There was a scraping of chairs. The judges got up and left, two of them still deep in talk. The guards who had brought Itale into the courtroom reappeared, jerky and wooden like figures that appear across a clock-face at the hour. "Get up, sir," one of them was saying; Itale realised he had said it before. He got up. He looked for the lawyer for the defense to ask him what was happening, but the lawyer was gone, none of the courtroom officials was left

221

but the clerk, still writing, under the judges' long desk. "Come on," the guard said, and in front of one guard and behind the other he left the courtroom, went down a hall, and outside for the first time in three weeks—into a snowy yard, where the frozen wind, the east wind of the Polana, cut his breath off short. His eyes watered in the cold, he looked up in bewilderment. They were between two enormous black buildings, crossing a courtyard with an iron fence. Itale stopped. "Let me see Isaber," he said. He heard his voice thin as a boy's in the wind.

"What's that?"

"My friend, Isaber—he was tried this morning—"

"Not now, sir. Where's he to go, Tomas?"

"Ask Ganey," said the guard behind.

"He's specially recommended," the first guard said doubtfully.

"Yes, specially recommended. Ask Ganey. Here, watch your step!" Itale, turning, had slipped on the ice; the guard's grab at his arm off-balanced him, and once more he went down hard on hands and knees on the stones of Rakava. He scrambled to his feet and the guards led him into St Lazar walking blindly with his head back, very erect. His head rang and there was a taste of blood in his mouth.

When he became clearly aware of the world again he found himself in a small, dark, cold room. Light came in faintly through a grating high up in the door. The ceiling was high. He was standing up; he had been measuring the length and width of the room in paces, he realised. It was four paces by three. There was a sleeping-bench long enough for one person, and under it an earthenware basin covered with a shingle. It was cold, the damp heavy cold of a cave or cellar, but the air was close. Down the corridor outside the door a baby was crying, a thin, angry, ceaseless squall; he kept thinking that it was the baby he had heard crying when he climbed the stairs the night he was arrested. That was stupid, it could not be the same baby. He went to the door and tried to look out, but could see nothing but the wall of the passage opposite. He stood there a long time. He did not want to sit down. If he sat down it would seem that he was going to stay here.

A guard came and unlocked the door, not a soldier but a civilian prison guard, a big old man taller than Itale, with a square grey face. He asked Itale to change clothes.

"I don't want these," Itale said, looking at the heap of grey clothing the guard had put down on the bench.

"Regulations, sir. You can keep your coat."

"I don't want this stuff," Itale repeated. He heard his voice shake. He was ashamed. "I want—" he began to cover his confusion, and stopped.

"They'll keep your things for you, sealed up. It's regulations," the guard said. Like Arassy he had the coercive yet reassuring manner of a good servant, so that Itale obeyed him, beginning to unbutton his shirt, since he was expected to change his clothes.

"I want something to write with," he said.

"What's that, sir?"

"Paper, ink, something to write with."

"Have to request that of the governor of the prison, sir. You're specially recommended." Like the other guards he said these two words in a respectful, portentous tone. His voice was rather loud and flat, he was probably somewhat deaf. Itale noticed this, he identified the grey material of the prison shirt and trousers as the rewoven stuff they called "shoddy" in the mills here, he noticed and thought vividly and quickly but none of it hung together; he did not understand. "That baby, crying," he said, "why is there a baby here?"

"Born here, sir. The mother's in one of these solitaries like your honor, she'll be sent back to the ward soon." The guard gathered up Itale's things, handing him back his waistcoat. "Keep that if you like, sir, for the warmth," he said. He was respectful and kindly, he went out and locked the high door behind him.

The prison clothes were loose and rough, without much warmth; he put on the waistcoat and his plum-colored coat, which was creased and somewhat grimy after the three weeks in the tower cell, but warm; and the silken sleeve-lining touching his hand as he put it on gave him a moment of pure comfort.

He sat down again.

223

He had been in the tower for three weeks, twenty-one days, that was over now. The judge had said something, he had said something about five years, but that did not mean five years in prison. That was impossible. Five years, after all, that was a very long time, he would be thirty at the end of it. Three weeks had gone on and on, three weeks was enough. This was December. Then January; then February— He succeeded in stopping himself from reciting the twelve months. The guard brought soup, the same flour soup, he ate it, the bowl was taken away, after a time the light in the corridor was put out and in the cell it was totally black, for a while, until the eye learned to see the faintest hint of form, the dull stone echo of some distant lamp, and to cling to that. The night passed and did not pass. Sometimes his mind worked fast, excitedly, and sometimes it did not work at all. His heart pounded and pounded, paused, pounded; he tried to count minutes by his heartbeat. He was afraid he was going mad. In this darkness without event swollen with empty time to come the hot sting of the vermin that swarmed in the bench-matting was welcome, it was life.

He was worn out by that night when the day came, and dozed all morning, lying contentedly enough on the bench. In the afternoon a pair of guards came and took him out to a courtyard for exercise. It was a small inner courtyard, forty or fifty feet square. The snow had been trodden into a firm greyish-black floor, holed and stained yellow with urine against the walls. The two guards watched five prisoners, who were not permitted to speak to one another. One of them was taking his exercise methodically, trotting round and round the court, pumping his arms; his legs moved oddly, in short steps. Itale knew that that was the right thing to do but he could not make himself do it; his legs were shaky. He must get control of himself. He must try to keep himself fit. He would plan how to use this time in the open air, and also try to exercise himself in the cell. To plan the time, and measure it out, and use it, that was the thing to do. Right now, even if it was very difficult, he should walk once around this courtyard, and breathe the clean air as deep as he could. He started out. One of the guards stopped him as he came by, a thin, red-faced man. "Was that the fellow stood trial with you that hopped?" His dialect was heavy and he was missing most of his teeth; Itale was not sure he had understood the words.

"Isabey?" the guard said.

"Isaber— What about him?"

"Was he crazy? He had a release, didn't he?"

"What do you mean?"

"What did he want to do that for? Jesus, what a thing to do, eighty feet down, was he crazy?"

"Shut up, Anto," the other guard said with a chopping gesture, and Itale walked away from them. He longed to kneel down and put his hands into the snow, get his hands and wrists cold, ice-cold, but the stuff was hard-crusted and dirty. The guards called the prisoners; he came last, feeling the others looking at him, unable to look at them. He was locked into the cell. He lay there on the bench. He did not think of Isaber, but of Estenskar, of one of the days they had gone shooting in the woods of Esten; he could see how Amadey had looked and hear the tone of his voice so clearly that he said his name aloud, very softly, but the sound of his voice frightened him. He put his head into his folded arms and lay still. The color and smell and feel of his coat was familiar, he held onto the double thickness at the cuff, seeking reassurance.

"Come on. Come on, sir."

"Where now," he said, sitting up sick and angry. "Let me alone."

"Smith's shop, sir," the guard said in his loud toneless voice. "Come on."

When Itale understood he took hold of the bench with both hands as he sat on it, and said with a kind of gasping laugh, "No, no. I won't come on. Not there. I won't—I won't put my own neck in the collar."

"It's regulations, sir. Has to be done."

"No," Itale said.

The deaf guard called two others. Adept, and without much brutality, they pinioned Itale, frogmarched him to the prison smithy, held him while the smith welded the loose ankle fetter

225

onto his leg, brought him back to the little, dark, cold room, fastened a short length of chain between the fetter and hasp set into the wall, and left him. He was trembling and cursing, in tears. "Sorry, sir," the deaf guard said as he left. "You'll get used to it."

III

Under a grey sky Piera Valtorskar left Aisnar on December 19, 1827; under a grey sky the family carriage lumbered southward over the roads of the Western Marches; and as it passed through the village of Vermare, high in the foothills, the grey sky descended softly all at once in flakes, heavy, thick, silent, filling all the air, whitening the fat rumps of the horses, the fur cap of the driver, hiding the way ahead. With a great push Piera got the window down so that she could put out her hand and feel the cold touch of winter. "Oh my dear we'll catch our death, oh do put up the window, oh do put on your gloves!" cried Cousin Betta Berachoy, who had gone all the way to Aisnar in the carriage alone to fetch Piera back, since Count Orlant had come down with a very bad bronchitis a week before he was to set off for her and spend Christmas at the Belleynins', but Cousin Betta was only too glad to go, indeed she was, the idea of that poor child coming all the way alone in the carriage like a pea in a gourd even if old Godin was as trusty as could be— At any rate, Cousin Betta was so upset that Piera raised the window again, only murmuring, "It never snows in Aisnar."

"Oh I believe it does, indeed it does I'm sure. I suppose the Warm Fountain quite melts it, wouldn't that be odd, does it? Oh dear me how very thick it's coming—if we should be snowed in up in the passes— Far from any house!" Cousin Betta's eyes shone. From time to time romances, stronger fare than *The New Heloise*, had been finding their way up to Portacheyka, and Cousin Betta read them, and though the possibility of getting snowbound on the mountain road was neither remote nor pleasant, the phrase "far from any house" sounded so like a novel that it thrilled her. Piera merely said, "The wind mostly keeps the Portacheyka pass clear." Cousin Betta had discovered already that Piera had become a strongminded young woman at the convent; she was always calm, and doubtless never read romances.

The snow made little trouble for their horses. It melted as soon as it touched earth after its fall through the soft windless air. Only as they reached Portacheyka at the end of the afternoon was it holding, icing all the roofs and gables of the steep town as a baker ices a dark plumcake. "Oh but look, look," cried Piera, not calm, "the mountains, look at the snow on the roofs—" and then she fell silent. The golden lighted windows of the little town under the great slopes almost veiled in driving snow and nightfall, the welcome of the lighted windows amongst the strangeness of winter, that was too much for her. All the way down from Portacheyka to the lake she was grateful for the falling snow and darkness that hid from her the orchards, the fields, the mountains, the lake. She did not want to see them. They were not hers to see. Even as the carriage rolled onto the paved court in back of her home, even as she saw her father, bundled up till he looked more like a bolster than a man, coming to her with snow on his shoulders and his arms held out, she was saying in her heart, "Why did I come home, why did I come home!" Then she was in her father's arms, squashed against his rough coat, the snow off his shoulder cold on her ear.

"Are you all right, papa— Are you well?"

"Yes, of course, I'm fine," said Count Orlant hoarsely, while the tears ran down his handsome face. He had been quite ill, and was sixty-two this winter. It had occurred to him that he might die. He was not particularly afraid of dying, but he had been afraid of not seeing Piera again. "Well, well, well, what a commotion," he said, still with his arm around her, and then the others were around them, Eleonora and Laura and Mariya the cook and Miss Elisabeth who lived on at Valtorsa, old Givan and the rest, bandying Piera about and bringing her inside in a flurry of welcoming faces and voices, warmth and light. Guide Sorde

227

had not come outside, and treated the excitement coolly: "Well, contesina, three months away and you see how your value's risen?" It was true she had been gone only three months, but last summer had been her next to last visit home, this was her last. Guide knew the difference as well as any of them. He consistently called her you, now, instead of thou. None of them forgot that she was to be married, that she no longer belonged to them nor they to her, that this was the last time they would see Piera Valtorskar. When she was in her own bed, in her own room, she lay thinking, and her thoughts were as bleak as her body was comfortable. The last time. Itale had been right, of course, you can't come back, there is no coming home. She looked over at her bookshelf. There was the book he had given her, the *Vita Nova*, the New Life, its gold-lettered back winking comfortably in the firelight. But she did not want the New Life. She wanted the old one.

The next night, Christmas eve, all the Valtorsa people but Auntie, with the Sordes and Sorentays and many people of the estates, went in to Portacheyka for the midnight mass. It had snowed again during the day, clearing after sunset. Carriage-lamps and lanterns crossed yellow beams over the snow, snow on the forests of the mountainsides showed faint in starlight. The church of Portacheyka was crowded from wall to wall as always on Christmas, the little boys of the choir sang shrilly, babies squalled, old men sighed long, horselike, devout sighs and scratched their necks under their holiday white shirts, little old women who went to mass daily muttered the service a word or two ahead of the priest; in the hot candle light the cross shone like molten gold above the altar; now and then one got a dry, clean whiff of the pineboughs that decorated the church, through the smell of packed humanity, or shivered in an icy, inexplicable draft of air creeping along the stone floor amongst all the legs in skirts or trousers. It took the crowd half an hour to come out of the church, and everyone stood around in the street waiting for the rest of the party. Children got lost, horses stamped, snow-dust glittered in rays and shafts of lantern-light and lamp-light. While the older people found the friends and relatives they had brought in or wanted to greet in town, Piera and Laura joined the young Sorentays, who were singing the old carol of the Angels.

> We have heard the angels sing
> Sweetly on the mountainsides,
> And the echoing valleys ring
> With the song that well betides:
> Gloria in excelsis Deo!

Alexander Sorentay went flat on the Glorias and his betrothed, Mariya the daughter of Advocate Kseney, cried, "Oh, Saandre! don't sing so loud!" and everybody laughed. On the way home, crammed in the Valtorskar carriage with Count Orlant, Guide, Eleanora, Cousin Betta, Emanuel, Perneta, and the overseer Gavrey, Piera and Laura kept up their carolling until Guide himself joined in his baritone on the Glorias, and Eleonora, looking up into his face as she sat squeezed next to him, said, "Guide, I haven't heard you sing in twenty years!"

"I have," said Laura. "When he shaves, but he always stops in the middle."

"Sing on, then," Guide said, and they all sang; Count Orlant had lost his voice when he was ill, but he thumped time on the windowframe. They all stopped at the Sorde house for the supper and Christmas cake after the mass; the cake, shaped like a log, was twined with holly and ivy; Count Orlant discoursed on hollytrees, standing stones, and druids; nobody went to bed till five. At eleven some of them went to the morning service at St Anthony chapel up the lake-shore. The pines above the chapel sparkled with melting snow in the wintry sunlight. On the north side of each headstone in the little churchyard snow lay white, though the graves themselves were bare. The words of the service were half lost in the sound of the wind in the forests of San Larenz. After the service Piera and Laura walked in the churchyard, waiting for Eleonora. They separated a little as Piera wandered on reading the inscriptions. All the stones were old, the churchyard was not used any longer. Many of them were small, unmarked, the graves of infants dead a hundred years ago. All the names were familiar names. Itale Sorde, 1734–1810. *In te Domine speravi.* — She stood still. She looked at the graveyard dappled with patches of snow and shadows of the pines, at the squat stone chapel, its eaves dripping with thawing snow, at the lake lying calm in the winter noon, at Laura coming towards her, tall and pale in her coat and fur-trimmed cap.

They stood side by side there for a minute.

"I can remember him standing in front of the south windows. I had to reach up to hold his hand. He seemed so tall. . . ."

"He died the year after I was born."

"It's strange, how when Itale and I die, there won't be anyone, anyone in all the world, who ever saw him, ever knew him. Till then he's not really dead. But after that. . . ."

"But there's an afterlife," Piera said timidly.

"Perhaps," Laura said, still looking at the grave.

"You're not sure?"

"No."

They spoke simply and thoughtfully.

"It doesn't matter, does it?" Laura said. *"In te Domine speravi.* . . . Just for it to be all over, all gone; air and earth and sun. Would that be so bad?"

"But—but I was just thinking— Your grandfather, he was young, a young man, seventy years ago. Young, like—like any young man now—like us. And then we get old. And maybe he was in love. Of course he was, with your grandmother, and they got married, and they lived, and had two sons, and they thought, and talked, and wanted things, and there was wind and rain and sunshine on the snow and they saw it, and . . . now . . . It seems so strange. And there were the people before them, and now us, and the people that come after us, and we can't know any of them, because time keeps going on and on. What was my own father like, when he was twenty? Does he even remember himself? — I have to believe in the afterlife, I think. It would be so strange and senseless without it—never to understand—" She looked around the graves streaked with sun and shadow, and her light voice shook a little. "Why were they ever young?"

Gavrey came round the corner of the church. "Your mother

230

was asking for you, Miss Laura," he said, standing cap in hand by the wicket-gate.

Piera walked home with him and Cousin Betta. He had proved a good, reliable manager, and had taken the onus of running the estate from Count Orlant, but he had never spoken to Piera more than civility required him to do. They did not speak now; but Cousin Betta did. Piera escaped from her to Count Orlant's study, where, a bit tired by the long Christmas night, he sat beside his fireplace bedecked with garlands and Cupids and a few stray French horns carved in the same greyish native marble as the headstones in St Anthony churchyard; there was a bright fire on the heart; Piera sat down next to him, and they talked. Count Orlant had discovered, this past summer, that he could talk to his daughter. It was very like talking with his wife, in the old days; after all she had not been much older than Piera was now. They rarely said much, but somehow it was very pleasant. In fact it was the pleasantest thing he knew; especially now, in this winter cold. He had spent some desolate hours the past month when he was ill. He foresaw and accepted his loneliness when Piera should be married and gone. But the comfort of her presence, now, outweighed it all. He was content.

Piera herself was not content, but was happy, as she sat with her father before the fire; happier, at least, than she had ever been last summer. All those weeks at home had been a time of strain, suspense, toneless and colorless. She had been waiting, waiting, for what? It must be for marriage, for love. She was home but not home for good, betrothed but alone, in the middle, suspended, waiting. It had been all wrong. She had written Givan Koste every post, a dull note once a fortnight. Writing them had been a chore, as bad as her compositions for Miss Elisabeth, the Duties of the Young Female. . . . If Given loved her why was he not there? She had left home, gone back to Aisnar, with relief. Had she been happy then this autumn, in Aisnar? Of course, but still it had been waiting; now the waiting was over, now time went fast and she clung to the moments, treasured them. Everything now was for the last time. She would not think either back or ahead.

Twelfth-night came and passed bringing snapping cold, clear weather. The roads were frozen so the horses' hooves rang like bells, the sun was bright in a sky of dark, blazing blue. Laura and Piera rode in to Portacheyka for the mail, and the overseer Gavrey, having business at the mill, went with them, still saying nothing. The girls went on to the Golden Lion leading his horse, as the Lion served as tavern, hotel, coaching station, post office, and livery stable; as they went Piera said, "Of all the close-mouthed men in the Montayna that one's the closest."

"He can talk," Laura said, indifferently.

"I doubt it. He guards his tongue as if it were golden."

"Who does talk, here, but us women? I suppose men jabber all the time, down there?" Laura often teased Piera about the sophisticated ways and customs of Aisnar, it was a game between them, but just now there was a sting in her words. Piera knew she had in some way been tactless, and said no more about Gavrey. They greeted the old hostler of the Lion and gave him the horses, and after his due bit of conversation went on in and greeted the innkeeper's wife in her shining domain of oak and brass; she was ready for them, handing three letters across the bar, one for Piera, two for Laura. "Ah!" said Laura, coming alive. "Thank you, Mrs Karel!"

"Oh aaye, from Dom Itaal, I saw it this mornin first thing in the sack, I know his black writin'," said Mrs Karel with a smugness that declared mere illiteracy no handicap. After her due bit of conversation the girls set off for Emanuel's house. "Come on, Peri," Laura said, "hurry up, I want to read it. What's this other one I wonder, it must be for uncle. And yours is from . . . ?"

"Oh, yes," said Piera.

"Itale's still has the return address in Rakava on it. That's why we haven't heard from him for a month. The mails must be slow in the east. It's such a long way." Walking at twice her usual pace, and studying the cover of the letter, which she would not dishonor by opening on the street, Laura strode down the cobbled streets and steps, Piera in her wake, to Emanuel's house. He was out; Perneta received them, and without wasting any more time she and Laura opened Itale's letter and read it

232

standing, while Piera retired into a chair by the window that looked out northward through the pass, and read her letter from Givan Koste. It was a quiet, fond letter, husbandly. Little Battiste enclosed a note written in a round clear hand: "Dear Countess Piera, the preserved ginger was very good although it was very hot so that I ate a little at a time, but I have eaten it all. I hope you are well. Father is well. I am well. My rabbits are well. They like to eat oat meal as you said. With all good wishes for a happy New Year, I am your loving friend, Battiste Venseslas Koste."

She wanted to show the child's note to Laura, and yet did not do so. It was so queer, that is, it would seem so queer to Laura, that this child was to be Piera's child, her stepson. Here he was, seven years old, eleven years younger than Piera, your loving friend Battiste Venseslas Koste—well, Laura was not used to the idea, as Piera was. No need to embarrass her. "What does Itale have to say?"

"Read it, my dear. Now, Laura, you've read it twice, let Piera have it. What's that? Another letter?"

"Oh, yes, I forgot. Look: 'For Mr Sorde of Val Malafrena, Portacheyka, Mont. Prov.' —now who's it for? Father or uncle?"

"Emanuel will know. I must look after my baking, I'll be back."

Laura perched on the arm of the chair and reread her brother's letter as Piera read it.

"Rakava, 18 November 1827."

"Look at that!" said Laura, "two months to get here! Even in winter and clear across the country, how can it take two months? His first letter from Rakava only took two weeks!"

"Now hush," said Piera, reading.

"My dear family: I'm sorry I missed last week's post, and trust that you have not given me up for lost. I have been busy ever since I arrived here, and my quiet week at Esten seems several centuries in the past. My impression of Rakava remains much the same as when I last wrote: I still dislike the city, and still find it exceptionally interesting. The misery of the poor here is beyond anything I have seen. I am glad not to be alone in a place where it is very easy to become discouraged. Young Agostin has put up a pair of red curtains to cheer up our rooms and save us washing the windows. My contribution to the domestic economy has

233

been a large box of Gossek's Wonderful Powder. I would not myself call it wonderful. The Prussians eat it up enthusiastically, no doubt thinking it a thoughtful gesture on the part of a stranger."

"The Prussians?" said Piera.

"Cockroaches. Eva always calls them Prussians."

"Oh! I thought he meant people. Let me read that over."

"—of a stranger. I wish they would all die in awful agony, but I don't think they will.

"If my letters are delayed, please don't be alarmed. The State mail service has existed for only three years in the Polana—the Polana is historically disinclined to do anything the other nine provinces are doing—and I am assured that it is as slow and as untrustworthy as any censor's heart could desire. Agostin and I will probably take the Krasnoy coach during Christmas week, and when I am back in Mallenastrada you can trust my letters to come regularly again. And what's much more I can look forward to receiving yours. I have not heard from you since the week before I left for Esten (I am not accusing, you know, only lamenting) and feel rather as if I had made my way to the nethermost pole of the Earth."

"We have written him, every post," Laura put in. "I despise that Polana province, why did he have to go there?"

"—the nethermost pole of the Earth. But knowing how faithful your letters are I think with comfortable anticipation of finding a whole bundle of them when I get back to Krasnoy.

"I have not much to tell you beyond what I wrote in my last. Please tell me if the *Bellerofon* is coming. The two boys in charge of circulation by post are very green, and when I left Krasnoy they were in a fine muddle. If it's still not coming regularly and you are interested in it, I shall see to it myself that your copy gets on the Diligence. Karantay is beginning a new story in the December number. He says, and I incline to believe him, that it will not be as good as *The Young Man Liyve*. One can't ask for such a work as that again, so soon, even from such a man. There is no going back, or doing things over, I think.

"My dear mother and father, my dear sister, my heart is with you now as always. My loving duty to uncle and aunt, to Count Orlant, to them all by the lake. If this letter should be the last to

234

reach you before Christmas may it bear my affectionate wishes for the new year and always. Your loving son, Itale Sorde."

As Piera read the last paragraph her eyes began to prickle and burn. She read the words over, the moment passed.

"His hand has changed a little," she said.

"It's probably a bad pen."

"He signs differently. Less of a flourish with the S."

"He doesn't sound very flourishing," Laura said wistfully. "The letter doesn't really say anything at all. Except that he's homesick."

"It doesn't say that," Piera replied, firmly.

"Of course it does. Oh dear! Mama's been worried about him for weeks, and this isn't going to cheer her up, one page and no news. Is it because of the censors, I wonder, or because he's trying not to sound unhappy when he really is?"

Piera bowed her head as if rereading part of the letter. "What did he say," she asked at last, "what did he write, I mean, after he was in Aisnar, last April?"

"Why, I told you, didn't I? He couldn't say much, because you'd asked him not to mention your betrothal—you explained that later. I know I wrote you that he wrote that you looked very tall and very pretty. Is that what you wanted to hear again?"

"No. I was just thinking . . . It shouldn't have been me that got to see him. It should have been you or your mother. Things work out so stupidly! . . ."

"So long as one of us saw him."

"But it was such a stupid conversation. I never told you. We didn't know what to say. And he looked so different, not changed, really, but completely different, a man, you know, and he was just a boy when we were all here. And he said we'd probably never meet again, that if we did it wouldn't mean anything, it would just be like people who don't know anything about each other meeting and parting, and neither of us, he or I, would ever really go home again. And—" But her voice, which had been getting strained and faint, choked off in a sob. "This is so ridiculous!" she gasped, "please don't pay any attention, Laura, I've been doing this ever since I got home—it goes away in a minute—"

Laura, at a loss, stroked her hand; Piera got control of herself

235

very promptly, and stood up to greet Emanuel with a smile as he came in.

Seeing, from Laura's face rather than Piera's, that something was amiss, he went on upstairs at once, after one question: "Anything from Itale?"

"Yes, here, the letter's weeks old, he was still in Rakava."

"I'll read it in a minute."

When he heard his wife talking with the girls he judged Piera's fit was over. What would be wrong with the child? Waiting for marriage, no doubt, this fashion of long betrothals was detestable. He came downstairs. "Where's dinner, women?"

"Ten more minutes, Emanuel."

"Three women, a cook, and no dinner ready. Su! You're nearly as inefficient as we are at the Magistrature. Well, let's see what was new in Rakava six weeks ago."

When he had read Itale's letter, Laura showed him the second one: "Which of you is it for, uncle?"

"Why, for Guide. I'm not of Val Malafrena."

"But then it says Portacheyka."

"They knew the post coach stopped here."

"But why don't you open it. If it is for you, someone would have to ride back with it, and if it's estate business father will consult you about it anyhow."

"Practical woman," Emanuel said. "Very well." And carefully, reluctantly, he opened the cover and began to read.

Piera was watching him, curious about the letter as the others were, but she noticed nothing; it was the wife who said quietly, "What is it, Emanuel?"

He looked at her for a moment, blank-faced. "Let me finish it," my dear," he said as quietly. They waited in silence. He finished reading the letter, folded and unfolded it, sat down in the chair by the window. "It's rather bad news," he said. "Itale. He's all right. It would appear he has been arrested. They don't actually know very much."

"Read the letter," Perneta said, standing still, as did Laura and Piera.

"It is intended for Guide," Emanuel said, and then looking up into their faces opened the letter again and read: "Sir, I must take

236

the liberty of introducing myself as a friend of your son Itale Sorde, in order to ask you to have the very great kindness to write me whether you have received any word from your son since the middle of November last, or to tell me if you have any news which confirms or, God willing, disproves the report we have received here of his arrest, together with the young man who was with him, by the Provincial Government of the Polana, in November. The first such report we received appeared unsubstantial, but we now have heard a more circumstantial report from an apparently reliable person, coming to Krasnoy from Rakava, stating that both men were tried on the charge of inciting activities prejudicial to the public order, convicted, and sentenced to five years' imprisonment. If this is true they are presumably in the St Lazar Prison in Rakava, as State prisoners. We have heard nothing from Mr Sorde since November sixth, but are now aware that mail both in and out of the east is under supervision and liable to be read and stopped, or read and resealed, without notice. To the best of our knowledge the posts in the center and west are not tampered with as a general rule, but this rule may be changed of course at any time. As you know your son has many friends here all of whom earnestly desire to be of use to him and to support him against this monstrous injustice, but at this time and until we are certain of the facts, we are following the advice of a man very familiar with the political situation of the eastern provinces, who counsels us all to wait, since an attempt at direct intervention or personal appeal could at this time do more harm than good. I beg you to write me if you have better, or more certain, news of him, and I pray God to uphold a just and candid man, my friend and your son, in the knowledge of his own integrity and of our steadfast affection and loyalty. I am, Sir, your servant, Tomas Brelavay. Krasnoy, 2 January 1828."

Emanuel folded the letter. His face appeared thoughtful, still a little blank. "This Brelavay sounds like an honest fellow," he said at last. "Itale's mentioned him often, I think."

"They were in Solariy together," Laura said. "He runs the journal's finances." She spoke clamly. It was Perneta who, shaking her clenched fists in front of her breast in a jerky, quickly-repeated, strange motion, said in a loud, high voice, "I never had, I never had any son but him!"

"Come, Perneta!" Emanuel said roughly, and went and stood at the window while Laura comforted his wife. She had never broken down on him before, never once. It was as if something in his own body broke at the sound of her voice crying out, as if the strength went out of his backbone; he could not look at her.

Piera came over to him and took his hand. He looked down at the girl, her pale face and clear eyes. "If we're going out to the lake," she said, "I should go tell Gavrey not to wait for Laura and me."

"That's right."

"He'll still be at the mill. I'll be back in ten minutes."

She left, moving light and fast. In the depths of his confusion and distress Emanuel considered her and Laura with wonder: both of them calm, efficient. Yet he knew what this news was to Laura, and as for Piera she had been weeping about something or other not a quarter of an hour ago. They were all nerves till you came to the test, and then, my God, they were sword-steel. And here were he and Perneta no better than two blocks of wood, wringing their hands, struck dumb. He sat down and reread both letters to give himself the countenance of doing something. But the two girls did and decided everything, until the moment when he was on his own again, alone with his brother in the library of the house by the lake. "Well, what's up, Emanuel?"

"Itale's letter—"

"That's not what brought you out in the middle of the day."

"No. It appears that, a few days after he wrote that letter, he was arrested."

Guide waited. Emanuel cleared his throat. "It's not certain," he said. "Here's all we know." He gave Guide Brelavay's letter, and watched him read it. Guide read it through attentively; his expression did not change. At the end he lifted his head a little and said after a pause, without expression, "What am I to do?"

"Do? —How should I know? No doubt the fellow's right and there's nothing we can do, nothing at all. But is this a time to say

238

I told you so, is your self-righteousness—" He stopped short. Guide was not looking at him.

"Arrested him," Guide said softly, as if trying out the words. "What right have they to judge him—to touch him—" His face contorted into a strange frown. "What have they done to him?" he said aloud.

He turned away and was silent.

Emanuel sat down at the table, rubbing his hand over his forehead. He had misjudged his brother utterly. He had forgotten how ignorant Guide was, how, in this sense, innocent. Guide had been furious with Itale for debasing himself, but it had never entered his head that any human power could debase Itale. Evil to him was personal vice, greed or avarice or cruelty, envy, pride: a man fought such evil within himself and in other men, and with God's help prevailed. That injustice could be institutionalised under the name of law, that inhumanity could embody and perpetuate itself in the form of armed men and locked doors, this he knew but did not believe, had not believed, until now. He did not separate himself from Itale, had never done so, even in his anger. What they did to his son they did to him; this letter was his sentence. He was 58, and this was the first hold that human evil had taken hold on his hard, uncompromising soul; this was the first time he had ever been humiliated. He had held himself apart, kept himself clean, and now, very late, he must pay the cost of cleanness.

"Guide, if this is true, which we do not know—but if it is true, then we have got to look at it squarely. It's very bad but it could be worse. They haven't sent him to jail in Austria, they haven't given him a life sentence. Five years— Five years is—"

Emanuel had been a law student in Solariy. He had visited the provincial prison there several times, in a deliberate self-discipline. It was because he knew what prison was like that he had refused to qualify himself to be a judge, and, when offered the judgeship of the county court, had thrice declined the honor.

"One can wait five years," Guide said.

"Listen, Guide. I have excused myself, since Itale left, for having encouraged him to go— I thought it his right, his choice, I still do, but I was responsible, partly responsible— I have no

239

excuse, I never looked to see what danger, it was my fault much more than his, he was very young!"

"No matter," Guide said. "That's all past. Does Laura know about this?"

"She was there when I read the letter. She got Perneta over the shock of it. And Piera did the same for me. They're with Eleonora now. I left it to them. They're better at this than we are, Guide."

"Aye. This is their world. Their time, not mine. I've known that since he left."

Another silence. Guide sat down across the broad table from his brother.

"I used to wonder if he'd not marry Piera," Guide said. "Forty years ago there'd have been no question. A good match, a good pair. They'd have married. He'd never have run off."

"Our father left, you know. Is it the times or the man?"

"He came back, though."

"So will Itale!"

"He sat there where you're sitting now, when he told me he meant to go. I was angry, I called him a fool and worse."

"For God's sake, Guide, are you going to blame yourself? Of course you were hard on him, do you think you've ever been soft? He's not soft either. He's your son, God knows!"

"I was not blaming myself. Or Itale. The time for all that's long past. I blame the men who dared judge him. I would give my life—" But he did not go on. There was no vengeance to which he could give his life, and no redress. There was nothing at all he could do.

IV

Count Orlant was overwhelmed by Piera's news. She had hoped for comfort from him; instead, to her surprise, she found that she must and could be the one to offer comfort. She knew of course that her father was fond of Itale and had been deeply distressed by what he, too, called his "running off"; she knew that he tried to read *Novesma Verba* and to understand politics, and that it always left him puzzled and depressed. He was unworldly, as Piera had learned, or as he himself put it, he hadn't a head for these things. That had led her to assume that he would not be too much dismayed at her tidings. After all, what did he know about state offenses, trials, accusations, prisons? Less even than she. But his ignorance instead of protecting him left him open to the blow. "In prison? They put him in prison—Guide's son?" he said over and over. "Why, that's absurd. It must be a mistake. What would Itale ever do to make them put him in prison? He's a gentleman, he's a gentleman's son, he's not the sort of fellow they lock up in jails!" Then as he began to believe her and his imagination grasped the event, his protests ceased; he fell silent, and soon said in a humble voice, "I think I'll lie down for a while, my dear. I feel a little tired."

She went upstairs with him and built up the fire in his hearth, for he said he felt the chill. He looked old as he lay there on the leather couch, old, patient, quiet. Why must this, too, hurt him? the girl thought with outrage, kneeling at the hearth. Orlant Valtorskar had never wished harm to any creature, and for all good that had come to him he had been grateful. Now he was old, not well, Piera would leave him soon, after his death his estate would be sold. Everything he knew, everything he had, was slipping away from him. It was as if he had written his name on the wind. Why then must he suffer the ills of other men?

"I suppose they'll let the boy have letters from his people, at least," he said, moving his head restlessly.

"Emanuel thinks the man in Krasnoy is right, they shouldn't do anything at all just at first, not even write. So the people who had him arrested will forget about him."

"You mean they're to behave as if no one cared what became of him? But how will that make him feel?"

"Emanuel thinks they wouldn't let him see the letters anyway."

241

"Not let him see letters from his own people? What harm can it do, when he's locked in jail? I don't understand it. I don't understand any of it."

"Perhaps they will let him get letters. And of course Emanuel plans to make an appeal if he has to. But it's really all so unsure, now; where he is, even."

Count Orlant was silent for a minute. "I can't believe it," he said. "Do you remember when he came over here to say goodbye, in the storm, that night? It seems no time at all since then."

It seemed a long time to Piera since that night, but she said only, gently, "Don't talk as if he was dead, papa. He isn't. He'll come back. Laura says so too."

And Count Orlant accepted, at least for the moment, the weighty judgment of Laura and Piera.

When she left her father Piera put on her coat and went outside into the early dark, the cold and starlight of winter night. She could not stay shut in the warmth indoors. The sky was hard and the stars bright, small, multitudinous. The lake lay black. There was the queer snapping silence of frost, and the air bit throat and lungs as if instead of breathing one were drinking ice-cold water. Piera walked down to the shore and stood there under the pines looking out to the lake and the height of the winter sky. Orion hung there, the belt and sword of stars, the bright dog at heel. Piera stood still, her bare hands thrust deep into the sleeves of her coat, shivering now and then from head to foot, and in that hour she came into her inheritance. She knew the great hour as it passed. She accepted without reservation what it brought her: the passion of her generation; the end of her childhood.

If this was her world, she was strong enough to live in it. She was a woman, not trained for any public act, not trained to defiance, brought up to the woman's part: waiting. So she would wait. For any act done consciously may be defiant, may be independent, may change life utterly.

But one can act thus only if one knows there is no safety. So she thought, that Epiphany night, looking up at Orion and the other stars. One must wait outside. There is no hiding away from storm, waste, injustice, death. There is no shelter, no stopping, only a pretense, a mean, stupid pretense of being safe and letting time and evil pass by outside. But we are all outside, Piera thought, and all defenseless. There is no safe house but death. Nothing of our own building will protect us, not the jails, nor the palaces, nor the comfortable houses. But the grandeur of knowing that, the pride and grandeur of being on one's own at last, alone, under the enormous and indifferent sky, unhoused and unprotected! To be nothing, a girl, confused, grieved, frightened, foolish, shivering in the January frost, all that, yes, but also to learn at last the stature of her spirit: to come into her inheritance.

She went back to the house presently, and sat alone by the fire in the living room. Her thoughts went on, calmer, less exalted, though sourced in that hour's exaltation as a stream in a rising spring. She did not think now about Itale, yet he, the man in prison, the absent one, was the cause and center of this change. She thought of Laura, of Guide and Eleonora, and of her father; and of Aisnar, of Givan Koste, of herself.

"I don't belong there," she thought, and presently, "What I have to do is here, here at home." She could not have explained what it was she had to do. She was not carrying on a dialogue, not questioning and answering, but discovering.

"I don't want to go back to Aisnar. Papa's getting old, he's not well, he needs me. But I wouldn't stay here, if that were all. He wouldn't let me stay here, if that were all. He knows you have to send your children away. But I have no reason to go to Aisnar. I would just be safe and comfortable there. That's Givan's life, not mine. He has work to do there. I don't. I'd keep his house, I'd be a good wife, I'd help bring up Battiste, I could do it. I could do it perfectly well. I'd be in jail. I'd be in prison for all my life. I can't leave Malafrena. I have to do what I have to do, not other people's work, I have to find my way, I have to wait, to wait. . . ."

She thought of Givan Koste, his dark, grave face, the turn of his head. She had not the least sense of disloyalty to him in her thoughts; that would come later, along with self-doubt and shame, when the social human world came back into the balance.

243

At the moment she was still as far as Orion from all that. She was alone with herself trying to find out the truth, and nothing was in the balance but truth and lies. She had lied to Givan Koste, promising him what she could not give.

"Givan!" she said his name aloud.

The house was still; she could hear the cook and a maid talking back in the kitchens, a murmur of voices like a brook far off.

If he would wait for her, until she had done here what she had to do. . . . But what had she to do here, but wait?

There was nothing urgent. No one could not get on without her. No one needed her to stay. No one wanted her, perhaps, so much as Givan did. "But it's me he wants," she said, and now the inward dialogue began, and would go on for a long time. "And who am I? He doesn't know, neither do I. I have to find out by myself, or else I never will. I have to wait. But he won't understand. . . . If he'd come here, I could make him understand, here. I'm not myself in Aisnar, I'm always what other people want me to be, there. Here is the only place I will ever understand. . . ."

Laura would understand her. Laura had understood Itale, when she had not. She had never until this night understood why he had left home; now it was perfectly clear to her. He had felt towards Malafrena as she felt towards Aisnar: it was a shelter, not part of the way. They had all known what to expect of him, here, and all they asked of him he could have done, easily, too easily. He had had to go off and try to find what it was that he and only he could do, what was necessary to him. So, in Aisnar, if she chose, she could avoid ever staking herself. She could do and be all they asked of her, and the reward was sure.

It looked now as if Itale had staked himself, and lost.

Piera thought of the stars she had seen flaring over the lake and mountains outside. In daylight, in summer, if you could see the stars, they would be those, the stars of the midwinter.

What she had at stake, what she had to give and to lose, she thought, did not amount to much. She had no talents at all, no great intellect, and nothing special to undertake. All she had to do was, like all things women had to do, a matter of daily redoing, an endless reaffirmation, nothing ever finished and complete. It would never be done, and it had to be done. It was her life she wanted, the whole of it: not a reward. Such as it was it was hers to live, so long as she would take the risk; so long as, having received her inheritance, she would not let it become a prisonhouse; so long as she set freedom first.

But it was very difficult. No one had ever spoken to her about what freedom is for a woman, what it might consist of and how it is to be won. Or not won, that seemed the wrong word for a woman's freedom; worked at, perhaps.

She heard her father moving about upstairs; he soon came down, and they went in for supper. The overseer Gavrey, just returned from Portacheyka, joined them. When he had reported his negotiations at the mill to Count Orlant, he asked Piera, in his low husky voice, "I hope it wasn't bad news that took you and Miss Sorde home, contesina."

Piera let her father reply: "Aye, it was bad, Gavrey. Young Sorde has been put in prison in the east somewhere."

Gavrey looked taken aback, but said nothing, evidently feeling that he could not with propriety ask what a gentleman had done to get put in prison. Count Orlant stared gloomily at his plate. Piera spoke up: "He didn't steal somebody's watch, you know. He's a political prisoner. I suppose the government doesn't like something he printed in his journal. So they put him in jail for five years."

Gavrey winced. "I didn't know they'd do that," he said. "We're a bit beside the way of all that, up here. It seems very hard." And he added, surprising Piera, "This is hard for Miss Laura, she thinks the world of her brother, I guess."

"She'll think the higher of him for this."

"She'll need to."

She caught what he meant at once: the talk, the gossip around the lake, the speculation and commiseration, the gloating on disaster. "They don't know what it means," she said haughtily.

"I don't know what it means but shame, and waste, and pain, for the lad and his people," her father said.

"Itale did what he believed he ought to do, what he had to do.

He's freer than the men who put him in jail, he's freer than any of us. Even if he died there it wouldn't be wasteful, it wouldn't be shameful!"

"You may be right, daughter. I don't know much about these things; neither do you. It seems a waste to me when a man of twenty-five is thrown away like that, locked up to do nothing. And how can Guide help but feel shame when they say to him where's your son? And how is it for Eleonora who can do nothing for him, maybe not even write to him? All I can see in it is grief and long worry, and praying the good Lord to look after the lad, for he never meant harm to anyone, that's clear."

Gavrey spoke: "Times I think a man's lucky to work out his evils done here, where he did them, and so can go to dying without fear."

She looked curiously at him. What he said was not new to her, it was only a variant on the somber tenet of all her people, but there was in his voice a note of intense, suppressed emotion, echoing obscurely her own inward, dark exaltation. And the last word he spoke stayed with her. The builder of the prisonhouse, the sneakthief, the weakener, the enemy, was fear. There was no way to serve fear and be free.

During the next weeks she saw Laura daily, for most of each day, their companionship of the old years regained, and more than regained. It had used to be onesided, Laura listening to Piera talking, Laura comforting Piera distressed; now Piera could give, and listen, and comfort. It was a joy to her to be of use to Laura; and thus to receive as it were a sign or confirmation of her change from girl to woman, her wealth, which she could give away, spend as she chose.

One afternoon near the end of the month they were together. They had been silent for half an hour; outside, snow was falling again over the snow that whitened hills and fields. It was a hard winter, and this week was the cold heart of it. Guide was out in the cattle barns or the storehouses, Eleonora was lying down upstairs; she had not been very well. Laura and Piera sat sewing by the downstairs fire, looking now and then to the high south windows outside which the snow continued to fall thick and straight. "I have to write a difficult letter," Piera said, a little while after the clock had struck three. Laura looked up, but did not ask to whom; to whom else could Piera consider writing?

"I want to ask him to come here for a little while."

"But you'll be back in Aisnar in a few weeks."

"Well, I don't know. That's it, you see."

Laura rethreaded her needle, leaning forward to catch the tremulous, snow-thickened light of the windows.

"You want to talk to him about it."

Piera nodded.

"May I say something I've been thinking?"

"Indeed not."

"You look like Auntie, you know, sometimes. I wonder if Auntie wasn't very pretty, once."

"Papa says she was quite beautiful, but she never liked any of her suitors. Isn't it strange. . . . Poor Auntie, she hates cold weather. She hasn't said anything but No all week."

"Does she need new yarn? I was thinking she might like this coral color."

"We can try. She hasn't even wound yarn this week. It's the rheumatism, or else she doesn't care any more. Oh, Laura, I hope I die young, sometimes!"

"I know. . . . Well, it was just this. You haven't talked about the wedding, and so on, at all, really. I wondered if you were feeling a . . . sense of duty, that you ought to stay here."

"No. That isn't it. Do you know, I don't think I believe in duty."

"It is an odd idea, when you think of it," Laura said, thinking of it.

"Like Miss Nina Bounnin in Portacheyka. Living and living and living with that awful mother of hers who goes on dying and dying and dying, she's been dying ever since I was born, and poor old Lontse Abbre who was supposed to marry Nina, he must be sixty now, and still running errands for Advocate Ksenay—oh, no, not that kind of duty. That is just cowardice."

"Yes. Very well. But Count Orlant isn't awful."

"No. No, he's not. He is a very, very good man," Piera said soberly.

"Is that it?"

247

"No. Because Givan Koste is a good man, too. I do love him."

"I know you do. Then what is it, Peri? It isn't us, it isn't me, you're thinking of; you're not that foolish."

"No. I'm not that generous, I'm not that useful to you. I'm selfish, Laura. I'm thinking only of myself. But I'm not clever enough to settle my own fate."

"Then let Mr Koste do it for you."

"I can't," Piera said. Then after a rather long pause, "I find I can't, Laura. I don't know why. In Aisnar I could. It's all so simple down there, ready-made. But up here I seem to change. To have changed. I'm not the person who is to be married in Aisnar in March. And that can't be! If I'm to marry I must marry with all my heart. Anything less would be wrong, a lie, an unforgivable lie."

"I believe that. But we may be wrong, Peri. Does love matter as much in marriage as the will to love? I don't know. I keep watching people, trying to find out. —Is it simply that you're away from him, that makes you feel you've changed?"

"No. It's that whenever I am with him or whenever I think of him, I'm indoors. Inside. In the light. And how can I turn my back on all the rest?"

"The rest?"

"The darkness," Piera said, looking up from her work. "Air. Space. The wind, the night. I don't know how to say it, Laura! The things you can't trust, the things that are too big for you, that don't care about you. I am just learning what that is and what I am, and I can't leave it, give it up, not yet!"

"Then you should ask him to wait," Laura said slowly. "I don't know if I understand you. But I think you have that right."

So that night Piera sat down to write the most difficult of all her difficult letters. Her spelling had improved at the Ursulines, but she still hated to write things down: on paper they became remote and trivial, humiliating.

"Valtorsa, Val Malafrena, 24 January 1828.

"Dear Givan:

"We are all well here and I hope you and Miss Koste and Battiste are well. It is still snowing and is the heaviest winter since 1809 the year I was born papa says. All the bays of the lake-shore are frozen and on some of them the ice will bear for skating which is very unusual. But it does not last for long.

"This is difficult to write and I hope you will understand if I ask if there is any possibility that if the roads clear you might come here to Valtorsa for a short visit some time in the next few weeks before I planned to come down to Aisnar. Are you very busy at the Customs? If so I shall certainly understand! It is hard to write and I hoped to talk to you if possible but if not do not worry, I will come as we planned. My father is not quite well yet from the larangytus in December and it is partly that which I want to talk about with you, but I hope we can talk because it is so hard to write. But do not worry if you cannot come, I will come. My love to Battiste. I am as ever your very affectionate friend, Piera Givana Valtorskar."

The letter went down on the Aisnar Post on Monday, and back with the Montayna Diligence the following week came Koste's reply, "I shall arrive on February 8."—"Oh Lord," Piera said to herself, "now I've made him come in the dead of winter, and wait to change coaches at Erreme, and leave his work"—Koste was head of the Secretariat of Customs Inspection and Regulation for the Western Marches—"and I've got to tell papa what I've done. . . ."

"Papa," she said that night after supper, "you know I wrote Mr Koste last week."

"You always do, my dear," Count Orlant said reassuringly. He was comparing astral maps, trying to decide how many Pleiades there were.

She came to the table and looked over his shoulder for a while. "Is that one a Pleiadee?"

"A Pleiad, my dear. One Pleiad, several Pleiades, it's Greek. No, it's a neighbor. D'you see, this map shows seven, it agrees with our peasants, who call the group the Seven Sisters. But most people can see only six. And the book says at least twelve can easily be seen with lenses. But this map shows eight. It's very odd, I wonder if they eclipse from time to time."

"I wanted to tell you about the letter."

"Letter? Oh yes." Count Orlant sat back in his chair and rubbed the bridge of his nose.

249

"I asked him to come here."

"To come here!" said her father, looking scared, and also a little affronted.

"I'm sorry I didn't ask you first, papa. I was so . . . I felt so stupid about it. In case he couldn't come anyway."

"What is wrong, Piera?"

"I need to talk to him."

"But you'll see him next month in Aisnar!"

The count was really shocked, and Piera's heart sank. "I want to talk with him, and with you, about putting off the wedding for a while."

"I see."

"I didn't want to tell you before he answered my letter, in case he couldn't come. Because I didn't want to worry you. And I'm not really sure about anything. But he says he will come. On February eighth. So I wanted you to know," she ended feebly.

"He'll stay here, of course," Count Orlant said, also feebly.

"I expect so."

"Yes, where else." Count Orlant had met Koste only briefly, and was afraid of him. "But is it—are you regretting your engagement?"

"No. But I want to wait." It was the only formula she had, and the only explanation Count Orlant, and later Eleonora, could get out of her. She shook her head, knitted her broad, stubborn forehead, and said, "I have to wait. . . ." Then she would say imploringly, "Don't you think he'll understand?" Count Orlant thought he would, but Eleonora said, "I think he'll agree, dear, since he is a gentleman. But I'm not at all sure he'll understand."

Givan Koste arrived in Portacheyka towards the end of the winter day. Piera and old Godin met him with the open buckboard, since the heavy horses that pulled the family carriage were not sharpshod and the road was icy. He was half-frozen from the coach journey, and almost completely frozen by the time they had driven down through the foothills in the still, bronze-colored, bitter cold mountain twilight to Valtorsa. He was so humanly grateful that even Count Orlant was unable to be afraid of him, and took pleasure in reviving him with food, drink, fires, and early bed. And Piera, alert and silent, watched him. She had known him always in one setting: Aisnar, his

250

house or the Belleynin house, afternoon or evening, among people he knew, dressed as he was dressed, speaking as he spoke. Now she had seen him out of place, on the snowy street of Portacheyka, wearing a fur-lined Russian overcoat, looking cold and tired and anxious; and this man, this stranger, attracted her powerfully.

Next morning she came downstairs in her old red skirt and peasant blouse, and the cook scolded her. "Contesina, what sort of a way to dress is that when there's a gentleman in the house?"

"There's always a gentleman in the house while my father's here, and I dress to please him!" said Piera, and then, because the old woman was huffed, she made up to her again, hugging her and whispering, "O Mariya, Mariya, don't scold me to-day. . . ."

The sun had come out brilliant on the snow; they spent a pleasant day, Count Orlant, Piera, and their visitor, walking down the shore to the Sordes', receiving a visit from Cousin Betta and the Sorentay girls, and riding to St Anthony's. On the second morning Piera and Koste walked down to the lake-shore alone in the bright wind of the thaw, and there came to the point. He spoke rather brusquely: "Piera, I hope that you know I want no explanation. I was very glad to come. It has troubled me sometimes that I had never been here, to meet your people."

"It was partly that. I wanted you to see me here, too. And I wanted to see you here."

"You're no different here, or anywhere. Not to me, Piera."

His gentleness made her flinch. "I am different, here," she said, hearing the cold, stubborn sound of her voice.

"You love this place and these people very deeply. I knew that. But you were right to bring me here." He stopped, and stopped walking, standing to look out over the flashing, windy water to the Hunter, dark under its crown of snow. She said nothing, and presently he went on, "And—forgive me, once again—you're very young. Eighteen years old. And are your father's only daughter and only child. There is time— There is no cause, no reason to rush you. If you wish the engagement between us to end, if you wish to be released, you need only tell me."

She stood beside him, pulling her shawl up round her neck as the cold, bright wind rose, rattling the trees. This was, of course, the one thing she had not expected. She never did expect the right thing. This was so easy, too easy, this cutting of the Gordian knot. You can't go about cutting knots, or things begin to fall apart. . . . He was being kind, ultimately, sacrificially kind to her, as he was bound as a gentleman to be. But it was not kindness she wanted.

"I didn't mean to ask you that, Givan. I only want—I think—to wait. For a while. If we'd married right away, last spring, it would have been all right. But I—I feel I must wait, now. But I don't want to make you unhappy!"

"It would make me very unhappy to know that I had in any way lessened your happiness. Piera, don't perjure your heart in trying to be merciful to me."

He was a gallant man. She turned to him as if in anger, her eyes alight: "But that's what you're doing—not I! I don't know what I want, and you do!"

"I can't ask of you what you cannot freely grant," he answered, stiff.

"There's no chance of our ever living here," she asked at last, childishly, very softly, knowing the answer.

"No," he said, and unable to say more he walked away from her along the shore. She watched his spare, slight figure against the wintry brightness of the lake, on the empty shore between water and sky.

He came back and stood near her. "Isn't it best, " he said, quietly enough, "to break all bonds, Piera, and let time work as it will? I had intended to ask you to wait until you're twenty. Perhaps you had that in mind. But it is scarcely fair to you, and it could be much harder in the end, if there were promises left between us. You know in any case that I won't change. But that's not a promise, only a fact. I can't help it." He smiled and turned away, unable to look at her, waiting for her answer.

"But can't we— But what will you—" She clenched her hands in a kind of rage. "All right, Givan. Let it be so. I wish you'd chosen better, chosen a woman who knew her own mind!"

"I never saw you till now," he said turning back to her, "I never knew you!" He spoke the truth; he was afire, his restraint broken, so that they stood face to face for once. Piera raised her hands open towards him, her eyes on his.

He looked down.

"I'll leave tomorrow on the Post," he said in a contained, dry voice. They started back to the house together in silence. He took her arm to help her over a patch of thawing mud on the path. She looked down at his strong, thin hand on her sleeve. He said nothing and did not look at her.

That night she had to tell her father that the engagement was broken, not extended, and that she had broken it; but inwardly she protested her words. It was he, not she, that had refused. He knew, now, that what he asked of her she would give; and would not ask, denying his own passion, denying her the right to passion.

V

Piera had thought that no one would take much notice of her broken engagement, aside from a flurry of gossip which she did not care about. The only people beside her father whose opinion mattered to her were the Sordes, and the Sordes had troubles of their own. They would sympathise with her and that would be that. But it wasn't that at all. Guide and Eleonora had met Givan Koste; they had accepted him as Piera's bethrothed; when they found the promise broken and him gone overnight, they did not condone. Laura bore the brunt of their disapproval. Neither of them said anything directly to Piera. But Guide did not joke with her any more, or greet her with a smile, or go back to calling her thou. She knew she was out of his good graces and might never, he being the man he was, get back in them.

"If he was too old for her," he said to Laura, "she might have known it a year ago. If there's twenty years between them now, there was twenty years between them then. I don't like it that she gave her word and then took it back."

"A broken engagement's better than a bad marriage," Laura

answered, as dogged as he. "Besides, she didn't jilt him. She wanted to wait. He insisted they break it off."

"Because he saw, no doubt, that she meant to go back on her word, soon or late."

"I just don't understand," said Eleonora, "what it is she wants and why it came up so suddenly. There wasn't a hint of all this till after Epiphany. She says she wants to stay here. But what is there for her here, once Count Orlant is gone? The day's coming, and she knows it, when she'll be alone. And if she stays here she'll be left to run the estate. Is that what she wants? I don't believe it."

"I don't know that she particularly wants it, but if she wants to stay at Valtorsa she knows somebody has to look after it."

"Aye," Guide said, getting up and turning rather heavily to go out. "We must leave our land to women, it would seem, if not to strangers, in the end."

His wife and daughter were silent. He went out, straight and stiff, with his heavy walk.

Eleonora took up her work. Presently she said, in her mild voice which no longer had much lilt or lift in it, "It isn't that I blame the child, you know. But it seems . . . So much goes to waste. . . . I liked the man."

"So did I. So did she! But he was so— So good."

That made Eleonora laugh for a moment.

"All right," she said. "But what is it you want, you two? If the good men are too good—and there are few enough good men up here, goodness knows—and you won't consider a man from down below, because he'll take you from home— Who are you going to marry?"

"I don't know that I want to marry," Laura said placidly. "Where are the sheets that wanted mending? —Piera will marry, I expect. In time. She could run Valtorsa perfectly well by herself, better than Count Orlant, I expect. She takes more interest in running the estate than in the house, really. I begin to wonder whether anybody could win her away. He'll have to come and help her run Valtorsa. . . ."

"They're there in the bottom of the work table, aren't they? Well, all right, but what about you?"

"I wish father would let me help him more."

Laura spoke intensely, and her mother listened, alert.

"I would like very much to be able to help him."

"With the farm work?"

"No—I know there's a lot I can't do— But he isn't doing so much actual work any more, you know, mother, of that kind. But the accounts and the sales, and going in to Portacheyka, and the management, I could learn that. I could help him with it and—help carry the estate over till Itale comes back."

Eleonora did not answer, and presently Laura said in a lower tone, "I know it—I know the idea doesn't suit him."

"He believes very deeply, my dear, that we're each called to play the part we were given as best we can. As woman or man, or master or servant. That we are to do what we were given to do. That to try to do otherwise is idle, or folly, or . . . ruin. . . ." Eleonora's voice died out on the last word.

"Do you believe that, mother?"

But she could not choose between the husband and the son. She shook her head. "I don't know, Laura."

"Would he teach me to help with the accounts—just that? Would it be wrong to ask him?"

"No. Of course not. Ask him," Eleonora said with a little increase of firmness; and added presently, "Talk to Emanuel about it. I think he might agree with you."

Laura shook her head.

"Why not? Have you spoken about it to him already?"

"No. I can't. He feels . . . you know, as if he were to blame, as if father blamed him for . . . He won't interfere for me. I can't ask him."

"I think you can," Eleonora said. "When he comes back."

Emanuel had gone to Krasnoy, late in February, following a second letter from Brelavay. Brelavay wrote very briefly that they had received official confirmation of Itale's conviction and sentence and knew him to be in the St Lazar prison in Rakava. It was a cold, guarded letter. Guide had not replied to the first, and clearly Brelavay had expected some response.

"You should answer this, I think," Eleonora had said.

"What good?"

"To thank him."

"For telling me my son's in jail? What thanks do I owe these men that led him into ruin?"

"Nobody led him," Laura burst out. "He went his own way. It's the government and their police that put him in jail, and if you won't write this man to thank him for trying to help and for sticking by Itale, then I will!"

"You will not," said Guide, and she did not. He did, however; and posted the letter along with a letter of request to the regents of St Lazar prison, composed under Emanuel's guidance. No answer came to the latter; Brelavay answered promptly. There was enough encouragement in his reply that Emanuel decided to go to Krasnoy to meet him and see if the machinery of appeal could be set going, or to try to win permission to visit Itale, or all else failing, permission to write to him.

He came back in March with nothing. Stefan Oragon, with a caution that was the reverse side of his oratorical flamboyance, had felt out the ground and found it impossible to take a step: The men jailed in the eastern provinces in November and December were object-lessons, warnings, their disappearance was precisely their importance to the government; to bring attention to any one of them was to increase his risk. Only if they were allowed to become or to appear unimportant would there be any chance, after some lapse of time, of bringing them back into the light. "Every time you say Sorde's name you put a bar on his window," Oragon said. "I could wish your name were different, sir, so long as you're here in Krasnoy. . . ." And Emanuel, cowed and embittered, had soon left Krasnoy.

"I didn't know," he said to his brother. "I didn't know what it was like. I thought the law— I am a lawyer, I thought I knew the power of the law. I knew nothing about it! God help me, I thought it drew its power from justice!"

In October there was a letter from Rakava: a refusal of Guide's request for permission to visit or write the man in prison.

"Eight months to send me this," Guide said, crushing the paper in his hand, and his hand shook.

Early in 1829, on Oragon's advice, he wrote to the governor of the Polana Province renewing the request. He received no reply.

In March Emanuel, who had kept up correspondence with Brelavay and others, received a hand-delivered note from Givan Karantay: "Lately in the east and north the families of suspects and prisoners have been brought under suspicion and in some cases held by the police for questioning. It is surely best that while this situation lasts you cease writing us; we will try to keep you informed of any news we get, but not through the mails, which are now closely surveyed. . . ."

The year had come in mild, but in April there was a late hard frost for a night and a day when the peach orchards were in full flower. The crop was lost, a crippling blow to those tenant farmers whose livelihood was in the orchards. Guide's own profits came principally from grain and vines, and he could afford to help his tenants through the bad year; but the loss galled him, the waste of those acres of fair, gnarled little trees. That May and June he would go to the orchards and walk down the grass between the trees that bore no fruit. He would return to the house frowning, erect, walking heavily. In July the rejection of his second plea came from Rakava. That night, coming to bed late and without light other than the starlight in the windows, he lay down and lay still, knowing from the quality of her silence that Eleonora was still awake. He spoke in the darkness, not loud, but harshly.

"You must not lie there and think of him."

She did not reply.

"It's no good, Eleonora," he said more softly.

"I know."

They lay side by side, both silent, hearing the crickets trill and trill in the warm furrows and along the roadsides in the summer night.

"Oh my dear, my dear," she said turning to him, putting her arms about him; but even she, his life's stay, his one enduring joy, had no comfort for him.

That night Laura too lay awake, in her room down the hallway, by the window that gave on the fields where the crickets were trilling. She had turned twenty-three in June. It was an age she had long ago picked as a dividing age, a watershed. It had seemed a remote goal, even when she was twenty. When

257

she was twenty-three she would be certain; she would be settled in the course of her life, through with yearnings, turmoils, and reversals: a woman, beginning to be wise.

But here she was unsure, unwise, worse off than ever, and worst of all, alone.

Three weeks ago Piera had come over in the afternoon with a book to read aloud down at their old place by the boat house below the road. They had gone there but had never opened the book. Piera, very lively and pretty in a new flowered cotton, wanted to tell her friend something. "Well?" Laura said at last, lazy and teasing. "I haven't asked the right question yet, I can see that; tell me what to ask, please."

"Oh, nothing. All right, very well. Ask me who proposed marriage to me!" Piera blushed, and blew the seeds off a dandelion clock.

"Oh my! Oh, you trophy-hunter! How many times is Sandre going to try?"

Alexander Sorentay had been jilted dramatically by Advocate Ksenay's daughter Mariya, who ran off two weeks before the wedding-day with an itinerant buttons-and-needles vendor from Vermare and never appeared in Portacheyka again. This event had quite eclipsed the duller gossip-matter of Piera's broken engagement. Alexander had restrained his determination to marry as long as decency demanded but not a day longer, and on that day had laid siege once more on his first love. This time his wooing was overt and all but spectacular; he was past shame, and need not fear damaging her reputation since everybody knew he was having no success. "He coorts and she discoorages," Marta Astolfeya had said, and this became the general summary. "Still coortin?" Emanuel would ask when the Valtorskars came over to sit on the Sordes' terrace above the lake after supper, and Piera would answer, "Oh aye, uncle, and I'm still discooragin!" She had been distressed by Alexander's suit at first, having never lost her guilt concerning that letter written him from Aisnar; but his persistence wore out first her pity and then her patience. She was civil, and skilful at avoiding offense to his family, who favored the match; but she had no intention of accepting the leavings of the lawyer's daughter.

258

"Alexander indeed," she said. "No, no. This was a surprise. A bolt from the blue. Guess! You'll never guess it."

"There isn't anyone," Laura said, reviewing mentally. "The fact is, there are no men here, when you look at them in this light."

"Our overseer. Gavrey."

"What about him?"

"It was him."

"Gavrey," Laura said.

"Yes. Out of the blue. Nothing to prepare me. No warnings. He scarcely speaks to me, as a general rule, except on business, of course. We get on very well working, I will say that. But to turn to me with no preparation at all over the rental account book and, 'Contesina, will you—' No, I won't imitate him. I don't feel like making fun of him, really. In fact I am a little upset, I think."

"But you said no?"

"Of course."

After a little silence Laura said, "Because of the . . . differences between you."

"What do you mean? That he's a farmer's son, and apparently illegitimate? Is that what you think? I was afraid he would think that, but I thought you— All right, of course one would consider that; but if I wanted to marry Berke Gavrey I would do so. In many ways I wish I could. We work together well, as I said. I believe we could make a very good thing of the estate. He knows that, I suppose that's why he brought up marriage. He is a very practical man. And an ambitious one. But he is not a man I wish to marry."

Piera had completely dropped her embarrassed, mocking tone; Laura had seldom heard her speak so seriously, or so bluntly. She made only the most conventional response, and they did not stay much longer there by the boat house. Piera went to rejoin her father, who had been in ill health for some weeks, and Laura went up to her room and got by herself at last. "The coward," she whispered, and it was all she found to say, there in the wreckage of what had been passionate emotion and now was nothing at all. "The coward!"

Two years ago in spring, while Piera had been away in Aisnar,

259

a little while after Itale's letter describing his meeting with Piera at the convent school, there had come a week of sweet April weather; and Laura, long confined to the house with a lingering bronchitis, was released rejoicing into the sunshine. She walked up into the peach orchards, just coming into bloom. The morning sun shone on the trees and the short, fresh, young grass between them. She did not walk far, but put down her rug and sat down. The soft wind blew. All around her were dark, vigorous trunks and branches, twigs knotted and knotted with pale flowerbuds. From the barnyard eastward down the valley came the ring of metal on metal, the hiss of hot iron in water, the creaking of an ancient bellows. Bron's great-grandson, Zeske, would be working the bellows; they were fitting horseshoes, shaping them on the anvil; shoeing, too, perhaps, for she heard the stamping and sharp neigh of a draft-horse, distinct and clear as were all sounds here, yet softened and made miniature by distance and by the vast, southward motion of the air. Then Gavrey had come running down through the trees, and stopped short, seeing her. His gun was on his back, his hound Roshe was with him, panting. He had been up in the forests, in the high places, and the strangeness of the forests was still with him. He stopped not ten feet from Laura. Neither spoke. His gaze, at first simply startled, became the intent look that was characteristic of him. He stood there, from motion to stillness in one instant, gazing.

"Do you know me, Gavrey?" she said, mocking and afraid.

He moved then, took off his cap and ran his hand over his sweaty, dark reddish hair. "Aye, I know you, Miss Laura," he said hoarsely. "You took me by surprise, sitting there."

She patted the hound, which had sat down by her and dropped its head nearly to the ground.

"Here then, Roshe, get away!"

He drew a long breath; he was as winded as the dog.

"Let him be. No game up on San Givan?"

He shook his head. He sat down on the grass, at some distance from her. "Now I've stopped I can't stay up. . . . Went up this morning before light. To get up high. Where they say the she-wolf is."

"Did you find her?"

"Never a sign."

"No one's ever run her, these five years. I wonder if there really is a wolf, if she's only a hunters' dream."

She watched him as he sat there, his loose dark hands on his knees, his chest rising and falling as he got his breath, the sunlight glinting in his hair.

"She's up there, all right. Your Kass saw her last month. But the dog fell on a deer scent. Led me half over the mountain and back, you fool dog. . . . It must be getting on to noon. Ah! the . . ." He shrugged, looking over at Laura, a curious, quick, comradely glance. "I lost my last place, in Altesma, for too much hunting. Once I'm on the mountain I could go a week and never know it, same as this fool dog."

When he had gone, his hound trotting sore-footed at his heels, she could not get him out of her thoughts, that sharp, frank look of recognition, the half-smile on his face that had always been shut and set. She had caught him off guard, seen him himself, the hunter. She could not forget the moment, and when she met him again she saw that he had not forgotten it. He would not look at her, now. He never had spoken much to her, but he had used to look at her, in his intent, calm way, as if he were looking at a picture in a book.

After a time she got used to him again, to his not looking at her. They met only at Valtorsa, in company with her parents, Count Orlant, Cousin Betta, Auntie, Rodenne and the rest. When a vist game was in session she would notice Gavrey's hands, fine-boned, loose, and dark; she knew, without knowing she knew, the angle of his wrist, the position his left hand took half open on the table as he waited for the next card to fall.

In the autumn she spoke to him again alone. She was at St Anthony's, bringing flowers for the chapel for the service of All Saints; old Father Klement had kept her there. She was fond of the kind, ignorant, dirty old priest. She was the woman of his life; he did not know it, but she did. He had no assistant, and she had helped him set out the chrysanthemums, dahlias, and autumn daisies she had brought from her garden, flowers colored like fire and ash, crimson, russet, gold, dun and pale. The colors filled her eyes, the fresh rank smell of them clung to

261

her hands, as she knelt in the dark chapel, hardly listening to the priest's whispering mumble. The few old women who always came for the evening service were there, and Kass, who had been sent to fetch her, and, coming in as the service began, had got stuck with it. He was a young fellow, a bantam, not one to come pray with the old biddies if he could help it. There was another man, and presently she saw from the set of his shoulders and the thick curling hair that it was Gavrey. Had he gone devout? She doubted it, but there was no telling with these silent men. The peasant woman, wrinkled and toothless at forty, who never missed mass, took communion, confessed, boasted of her nephew in the seminary, kissed the priest's hand, she might tell you, if you asked, that she did not believe in God. "But there's the Saints, and the holy water is a great thing," one such woman had said to Laura, rock-sure in her paganism. Then you might come on one of the hard-faced men who called the church a place for priests and women, come on him in pain and glimpse a spiritual intensity, a terrible longing for God. They had a name for these crises. "He's borne down," they said. —"Why's Sorentay's Tomas off at church then?" —"He's borne down hard, these two months. . . ." Suffering, misery, mystery, what was it that bore them down? They could not say, but they recognised the agony; and so did Laura Sorde. She glanced again across the chapel at Gavrey. Was he borne down? Was the hunter caught? It was a strange thought. Sometimes when she saw a man in church she was strangely moved. A man on his knees, his dirty thick bootsoles sticking up behind him and his head bared and bowed, asking for help, used as she was to it it was strange, moving her to a pity very close to shame.

Gavrey came out of the chapel directly after her, and spoke. Young Kass was waiting for her, Father Klement would follow. Well defended, she felt bold, curious, wanting to provoke the man who would not look at her. "What brought you out here tonight? Are you borne down?"

"I came to see you," he answered.

She thought she had stopped, there on the steps, but found herself walking on beside him.

"What for?" she said at last, and winced at her own words and tone, hypocritical, false.

"How do I know? I came to see you. That's all."

"Very well, you've seen me."

He stopped and faced her, by the wicket gate of the church-yard. They were the same height, their eyes met straight. "Did you ever look at me?"

She glanced round at Kass unhitching the horse, at the old women chatting on the path. He had spoken aloud as if they were alone in all the world, in a passionately resentful voice; but self-defense was a strong habit in him, and her movement roused it. He half turned from her and spoke lower. "Why did you ask me was I borne down? What's that to you?"

Laura, with a wolf by the tail, said, "I'm sorry I said that."

"Aye, sorry. Will you leave me alone? Will you leave me alone?" He was gasping for breath as when he had stood above her in the orchard six months ago. He broke away from her, strode off into the dusk along the road under the pines of San Larenz.

As they drove home with Kass, Father Klement asked, "What was Berke Gavrey telling you, then?" The old priest had a piping voice. Laura felt that every ear in Val Malafrena, every beast in the dark woods, could hear him piping, "What was Berke Gavrey telling you?"

"Nothing."

"Eh?"

"Nothing, I said."

"Oh aye? I thought he was telling you something."

Laura kept silent.

"He's a good fellow," the priest said, pipy and sententious. "As good as need be no matter what they say of him."

"I never heard anything against him," Laura said, and at once accused herself of complicity with him.

Father Klement was delighted: new ears for old gossip, irresistible. He never considered what was suitable for a priest to repeat, whether the gossip he relayed was offensive or malicious; to him it was all words, stories, the savor of existence. "Why, now, you never heard what that Val Altesma woman had to say?" And he went on to tell Laura that Gavrey had left Val Altesma because he had got a girl pregnant, a peasant freeholder's daughter at Kulme. "She had nobody but womenfolks and an old granddad, the Altesma woman said, so there was nothing she could do but tell the story, and she did that, and so he got away and went to Raskayna where he was under-steward, and they say he was a terror among the young women there as well."

"That's stupid, a stupid story," Laura said. "If all that was true Count Orlant would never have taken him on."

"Why not?" the old priest asked, puzzled. "It's true enough, but so's it true that he don't make trouble here. He's a good man and a good steward, none ever said different in Val Maalafren." He sought a suitable moral and said at last with satisfaction, "Young men will be wild, before they settle down."

What do you know about it, you fat old capon? thought Laura; and she upbraided the priest for gossiping. Father Klement got flustered and looked beseechingly at the gentle, tall, soft-voiced girl who had suddenly turned on him as stern and hard as her father. "But I did say he's a good man!" he appealed.

"A good man! If he's done what you say, what right have you to call him good? I don't want to talk about it any more."

All the trees of San Larenz were listening, and Gavrey the hunter hidden amongst them listening, understanding.

What was terrible to her was that, with nothing said, with hardly a word and no touch between them, for they had never touched, yet she understood him, and he her. There was no place to hide.

She had believed that only in the spirit is there true understanding: flesh is the darkness that hides the light, the barrier to communion. Now all that unquestioned belief fell away from her. It is the spirit that is alone, she thought with a kind of horror of certainty, and the spirit that dies. Only in the body do we know communion, and hold fast to the present, which is eternal. The shadows will not wither away to leave the child soul bathed in light at last: what will last, what endures, is the darkness, the opacity and weight of shadow-casting body; the breath of life is breath itself. One night in November she was sewing after supper with her mother, and rose to refill the bronze oil-lamp at her elbow. She poured in the oil too fast, overfilling the lamp; the flame on the wick sputtered, flickered, went out, drowned in the fuel that fed it. She watched in fascination. The oil spilled on her fingers, on the table, "Why, look what you're doing, Laura," her mother said, "don't get it on your dress!" The girl stood staring at the lamp, the drowned wick, a little black scrap. The shadows had closed in about her. She turned to her mother, and Eleonora got up, spilling her sewing things about her— "Laura, what is it?"

"Oh, mother, I'm borne down," Laura said, and began to laugh, then cry; then she got control of herself, all within a minute, and would say no more to Eleonora except that she was overtired.

She went to bed and lay awake, trying to exorcise from herself, from her body, by sheer force of will, the presence of the man who obsessed her. She did not pray.

In the end she found her help in the knowledge that had undone her in the first place, the knowledge that he was as helpless as she. His desire, which conquered her, put him at a disadvantage: he was driven by it, but unwillingly, afraid to trust her. When his chance came he missed it. They spoke together, having met by chance, by the lake-shore in a red December dusk.

"I'm leaving Valtorsa," he said, "going away."

The sunset light was on his face, making it ruddy, vivid.

"Going away? Why?"

"For the same reason I left Altesma."

"I thought you were fired, there."

She knew how to hurt him. "Fired? Who told you that? I left of my own will."

She looked scornful and said nothing.

"And to get away from a woman that wouldn't let me alone," he said in his rancor.

"Shall you go back and marry her, then?"

"Not I! Why the devil should I? Do I look the marrying kind?"

"Better than to burn," the girl said, weak with hatred of him, spite, fear, yearning. "No matter what kind you are."

"Oh aye! and no doubt you'd have me, to save me from the fire?"

He flushed up crimson in the red light, and took a step backwards. Trapped and self-destructive, afraid, he said hastily, "I don't know why I said that."

"You torment yourself, Berke," she said, looking at him and speaking with her old natural gentleness. He did not know he was her equal, and she was never going to tell a man who did not know it without being told.

"And you?" he muttered.

"Maybe, but what's that to you?"

And she smiled at him; but he did not answer, standing wordless and helpless. When she saw that she was ashamed of him. "You should stay here," she said calmly. "You'll run out of places to move to. Besides, you owe something to Count Orlant, I should think."

"Aye, that I do," he said. He spoke almost submissively. She longed to be away from him. She pitied him and wished him gone, out of her sight.

"I talk of going, but I'll stay, no doubt," he said.

"I suppose you will," she answered indifferently.

She no longer looked at him, but out over the lake, where the red light was fading into obscure brown-violet dusk. She was desolate. Now he came to her, reached out to touch her, and she allowed him: because he must have it that she allow him, that she permit him, that she be the lady and he the servant, that there not be between them any honesty, but only this game of owner and beggar. He felt her unresponsiveness and let her go, saying, "It's no good—why do you make a fool of me?"

She looked at him then. "You are a fool, Berke," she said. "It's not my doing. If you haven't got the courage to walk this road then you'd better go back to Val Altesma, to the first girl you ran away from." She turned and went down the shore away from him, towards the promontory. He let her go.

That was the end of it, she told herself, and so it was, though he did not leave Valtorsa. When she had to be with him she spoke to him as little as possible, ignoring his cringing, questioning look and her own humiliated, defiant longing for a kind word

266

from him, the touch of his hand. She could not shake him off. He was the first man to waken her. No other took his place. The weeks and months went on, and without knowing it Laura nursed the sterile desire, tried to keep it alive. There was so little in her life, and he was the only man who had ever touched her. She let herself dream of some future reconciliation and understanding, as if there were anything left to reconcile or explain.

Now she had lost even that pretense, the last bit of warmth in the cold. She wondered at first if he had proposed to Piera simply in order to hurt her, Laura. She told herself that that was mere self-flattery. He was afraid of Guide Sorde, and not afraid of Orlant Valtorskar, that was the principal key—perhaps. Perhaps he wanted Piera more than he had wanted her. She told herself she must accept this possibility, but she did not. It was because he did not desire Piera as a woman that he was bolder, able to propose the marriage that he had not dared even envisage with Laura, the hunter caught in his own trap: of this she was certain, and then she called herself a fool for her certainty, for her vanity, for clinging to the love he had never even offered her. And now he had succeeded in dividing her from her friend. She was not jealous of Piera. She was envious, she always had envied Piera, envy was part of the rock their friendship was built upon; that was no harm. But he had spoilt the frankness between them, prevented the unreserved conversation that was the one relief to Laura's essential loneliness. She had never told Piera of the sensual storm she had gone through, never said anything about Gavrey at all; partly through inability, lacking the very words to speak of that middle ground, that obscure country, between the vocabulary of animal sex which she as a farmer's child of course knew but was not, as a lady, to speak, and the vocabulary of love and sentiment; partly also because she had felt no need to speak. Now that she wanted to, in order to clear the air and restore the trust between her and her friend, she could not. She was ashamed to. She was ashamed of the meanness of the story, ashamed of herself for wanting to tell it, even.

And this was the wisdom and strength of her womanhood, of her twenty-three years. . . .

The worst of it was the fear of losing Piera. That she could not bear, and it was not many days before she set her teeth on her humiliation and told her friend as much of the story as she could. She did it awkwardly and unclearly, so that Piera did not understand at first, asking in dismay, "But you mean you love— you loved him, Laura?"

"No," the older girl answered steadily, "I mean I could hardly keep my hands off him. And it was the same with him. For a while."

She saw Piera climbing up over that fence, looking at the strange lands on the other side. She felt herself corrupted, corrupting. But Piera said simply, after a little while, "No wonder you understood about Givan Koste."

Laura was afraid to speak.

"We came at it different ways. You found too much of what I didn't find enough of. . . . But what's wrong with Berke, what was he afraid of?"

"It wasn't his fault."

"You; he was afraid of you," Piera said, brooding. "Not of me. Because I'm not as strong as you; because he's not in love with me. So it's me he proposed to. How stupid he is! How stupid it all is! —I thought of accepting him, Laura. That night. I knew I could get him to ask again. He's a very good overseer. I was afraid he might leave. And I can work with him. I'm beginning to learn what to do and how to do it, how the estate should be run. He's taught me most of that. So—" She smiled rather bleakly.

"Why should you not marry him?"

"Because if I am marrying for practical reasons, Sandre is a much better match."

"Why should you not marry Sandre?" Laura asked in the same tone.

"Why should I marry?"

"I don't know."

They talked now quietly and openly, no shadow between them.

"I don't understand it," Piera said. "I don't really understand what happened between you and Berke. I don't understand what love is, or what it's supposed to be. Why is it supposed to be my whole life?"

268

Laura shook her head. She looked up at the golden slope of grass above the boat house.

"Itale always said the time will come. But we wait, and we wait. What are we waiting for, Laura? Why does he have to be in jail, why do men have to be such fools, why are we wasting our lives? Is love the answer to all that? I don't understand, I don't understand. . . ."

PART SIX

The Necessary Passion

I

The way into the St Lazar Prison was through a twelve-foot gate in an iron fence, across a strip of cobbled yard, through a second gate in a second fence and under a tunnel of naked stone formed by the four-foot-thick walls of the building, and so into a corridor off which a large, vaulted room opened to the right, the warders' room. The air in the corridor and the warders' room was damp, with a sweet, musty odor. Windowless, the room was as silent as a wine-cellar or a cave, yet a queer, disagreeable rumor just beneath the range of hearing suggested that behind the further walls and doors the place was not silent, not empty, but crammed full, jammed, swarming. Luisa Paludeskar kept her head high as she and the official who accompanied her waited in the warders' room for the prison clerk. She held her silk skirts in one hand to keep them from the moist, filthy floor. She had worked for it for twenty-six months.

Two clerks hurried in, wiping their mouths from lunch, and then an immensely tall, fat man in the uniform of a lieutenant of the Polana militia. The official with Luisa opened his mouth to speak but she beat him to it, saying in a clear voice the words that she had earned the right to say: "Lieutenant, Mr Konevin brings you an order from the High Court, signed by the prime minister, countermanding the sentence of the prisoner Itale Sorde." The big man put out his hand for the paper which Luisa's companion offered him. "How do, Mr Konevin," he muttered, staring at Luisa. "Yes, indeed. Your servant, miss."

"Baroness Paludeskar, Lieutenant Glay," Konevin muttered; muttering seemed to be the natural form of speech here. "You'll find it all in order, Glay. Immediate release. See there." They bent their heads over the document and muttered lower. The lieutenant held the paper away from his enormous body as if afraid it would scorch him. "Yes, yes, Larenzay, look up Sorde Itale, entered December '27."

Both clerks raised their heads. On entering the room they had gone one to a table, the other to a desk, and sat down, without speaking and scarcely glancing at Konevin and Luisa. The one at the table had a head that grew straight out of his shoulders, with a warty, grey face. The one at the desk was thin and wiry with long, lank hair and a mouth like a razor-cut. "Sorde?" he said, and the name spoken aloud was startling in this muttering oppressive silence. "Sorde's dead."

"Dead? When?"

"Last week. End of the week."

"I see. We're having the epidemic, you know," the lieutenant informed Konevin and Luisa. "Worse than usual this year. Look up the entry, Larenzay."

"White ledger. Specially recommended prisoner," the neckless clerk mumbled in a deep bass.

"Get the burial list for February, Larenzay. Please to sit down, baroness, please to sit down." The huge lieutenant brought up a chair for her and dusted it with his sleeve. Luisa did not sit down. She feared to move at all. Her ears sang, a shrill hum. The lank-haired clerk argued, the neckless one mumbled, the lieutenant muttered, Konevin put in an exasperated remark. She heard nothing they said, only their grotesque voices, frogs on the marshes of hell.

"Please to sit down, baroness."

"It may take some time, baroness," Konevin said.

She gave in and sat down, letting her silken skirt drag on the floor. Summoning up all her self-control, she said very softly to Konevin, who stood beside her, "Is he dead, then?"

"Apparently not, baroness," Konevin replied. Ears here were tuned to whispers: the lank-haired clerk shouted reproachfully as if the others had all been in the wrong, "On the sick list, not the death list," and the neckless one droned, "Specially recommended." Luisa shuddered all over and put her hands to her cheeks. The blood which had dropped sickeningly from her head was returning in a hot wave, dizzying her. She sat perfectly still until she knew she could trust herself not to faint and then said in an even voice, smiling a little, to Konevin, "I wonder that a man can stay alive two years in this place."

"Much longer than that, baroness," the official answered stiffly. He had made it clear when she met him at the office of the governor that he did not like the business she was on; since entering the prison he had been completely rigid, wearing a fixed look of distaste and exasperation on his round, ruddy face.

"What is the epidemic?"

"Prison fever, I suppose," Konevin answered, and drew a short breath. He was afraid of infection, Luisa realised, and the thought gave her pleasure.

"He has been ill, then? Are they going to release him?"

"Yes, baroness. Look here, Glay, I can't spend the afternoon here. Tell them to get on with it."

"In a minute, Mr Konevin, in a minute," the huge man answered, cringing yet unmoved; this was his domain, not Konevin's, and both knew it. The lank-haired clerk was writing, his pen scraping with a loud, hard sound like his voice. The lieutenant went to the table, shifted papers about, muttered with the neckless clerk. There was no clock. Luisa sat turning a ring on her finger, pressing her right hand hard with her left, staring at the watery gleam that ran on the grey silk of her skirt; she could barely hold still, she could not endure to wait any longer, but still the unmarked minutes went by and went by, and there was no telling if the time was long or short or if it was passing at all. There was a noise out in the corridor and a guard in militia uniform came in with a tall, bald man in his sixties. They stopped just inside the doorway. The bald man stood stooped over, staring vaguely; he was wearing shapeless grey trousers and an old coat too large for him, and was barefoot. Realising that he was a prisoner, Luisa looked hastily away from him.

"Sorde Itale," the lieutenant was saying, and the guard was also saying the name, "Sorde, specially recommended!" Sick with disguest and anger Luisa sat still and said, "This is not the man. Will you act on this order of release, lieutenant, or must I come here with the governor of the prison?"

"Not the man? What ward, Liyvek?"

"Sick ward," the militiaman said. "This is him."

"Extraordinary inefficiency," Konevin said, and the lieutenant, suddenly angry and frightening in his anger swung his great bulk and height towards the militiaman: "Who is this, take him back," he said, while the militiaman repeated stolidly, "This is him." The prisoner stood as if indifferent, his empty gaze crossing Luisa's. He raised his hands to rub his eyes, and with terror she recognised the gesture.

"It is him, it's him," she said in a whisper to Konevin. Again all the others heard her whisper, the lieutenant drew himself up righteous and vindicated, the militiaman stepped back and the clerks muttered. Konevin looked at her coldly. She sat still. It was Konevin who went up to the prisoner, although not close to him, and said, in a stifled and embarrassed tone, "Sorde—Mr Sorde?"

The man stood patiently, unresponding.

"We're here with your release, Mr Sorde. Your sentence is countermanded by the High Court. Do you understand?"

He came back to Luisa. "The man's very sick," he said with nervous distaste. "I have no idea what you can do. An impossible situation. Are you quite certain that you . . ."

"Will you have them finish whatever formalities are necessary, please."

She did not look at the prisoner.

"One of our officials is bringing the prisoner's possessions, baroness," the lieutenant explained, officious and self-confident now, looming over her. "All his belongings when arrest was effected, they've been in confiscation, do you see, baroness, nobody has disturbed them."

276

"Better send for the blacksmith," the lank-haired clerk said, and the neckless one snarled, "Don't need the smith, he's been in the sick wards," and the lieutenant muttered, "Has he a fetter, Liyvek?" and the militiaman answered, "No," while Konevin walked away down the room clicking his tongue in a fit of impatience and disgust. And finally a guard came in with a valise, a string-tied bundle of clothing, and a small parcel wrapped in paper. The lieutenant opened the parcel and spread out its contents on the table with his enormous, white hands: a silver watch and chain, a pair of cufflinks, some copper change, a penknife. "The gentleman's jewelry and all, you see, baroness, nothing has been touched," he said. The valise and the bundle were spotted with a soft, bluish mold. "Can we go now?" Luisa said, but there were still papers to be prepared, the neckless clerk was writing something that must be written before they could go.

"You can't put the man in your cab, baroness," Konevin said to her in a low voice as they stood at the desk. "The . . . state he's in . . ."

"What do you suggest I do instead?" Luisa demanded, and in reaction to Konevin's pusillanimity she brought herself to go up to the man in grey and speak to him. She said his name and did not know what else to say. He did not seem to look directly at her, nor did he answer directly, but after a while he spoke, in a thin, hoarse voice: "May I sit down?"

His body and clothing stank of sweat and sickness. The coat he wore had been red or plum-colored, but was black with dirt. She could not touch him. She pointed to the wooden chair. "Yes, sit down." He did not move. Once he rubbed his hand hard over his face in that gesture terribly familiar to her, and then stood again, patient, blinking his swollen eyes.

"The fever, you know, baroness," the lieutenant was saying as he held out a set of folder papers to her. "Makes 'em dull, no doubt he'll be better soon. This here is the order of release, this is his passport, Mr Konevin will explain, the guard will take his things out for you. An honor to be of service to you, baroness."

The guard who had brought Itale in was gone, and Konevin would not help her; the clerks and the lieutenant were watching, malevolent. She had to take Itale's arm to make him move, to make him come with her, out of the warders' room, under the stone arch; he shuffled, lame and unsteady. When they came out onto the cobbled yard into the clear, cold sunshine of a day of March he stopped and put his hands up over his eyes in pain.

"Come on, come with me," she coaxed him. The guards at the prison entry, the guard at the outer gate, stood watching, curious and without sympathy. What she was doing was wrong, was against what they wanted, what they stood for, what they stood there for keeping the gates locked and the doors shut. What she had imagined and anticipated a thousand times as the moment of triumph was humiliating and grotesque. The driver of the cab that she had kept waiting stared at the shambling man with her and said, "Not inside," and she had to give him ten kruner before he would let Itale ride inside the cab. Then she must climb into that cramped box with him and sit beside him, in uncontrollable aversion from and fear of his misery, his illness, his abjectness. He sat crouching, the hairless head nodding when the cab jolted, the hands lying lax on his thighs very large and dead white, like the hands of the lieutenant in the warders' room.

Konevin, who rode with the driver, proved most serviceable when they reached the hotel. She had planned to spend the night at the hotel and then take Itale on in her carriage to her Sovena estate, fifty miles to the north; the first part of that plan was dropped without discussion. Konevin found her horses and a landaulet, and got the hotel people to make up a bed in Luisa's carriage. When this was done it was late afternoon. Itale in her carriage, and she in the landaulet with her maid, set off one behind the other, down the steep streets of Rakava, out the old north gate, past the factories, onto the long downslope of the highroad north.

Roads were bad after the March rains. The Ras was in flood, and they had to go thirty miles out of their way to Foranoy, to cross at the bridge, and thirty miles back to the north road, so they were three nights and two days getting to their destination. The sick man continued most of the time in the same lassitude and indifference, asleep or in stupor, but when they arrived in

278

the early morning he was feverish and could not walk at all. Luisa's letter to the housekeeper had suffered the usual mail delay, so the house was half ready and half in cold disorder. It was raining. Luisa had the sick man put to bed, and sent for the doctor; but before he arrived she went to bed herself, worn out, and slept for twenty hours.

The doctor, a sour man of the veterinary-barber-physician breed, said the patient was suffering a relapse brought on by the cold and discomfort of the journey. "Cold and discomfort," Luisa repeated sarcastically, thinking of the walls of St Lazar; but she made no explanations to the doctor, having learned already, from the guards at the prison gate, from the cabdriver, from her maid, from her own feelings, not to mention jail. If the doctor knew, or could admit that he knew, where his patient had spent the last two years, he would consider both the man and the woman whose house he was in with contempt. He would take her money of course and provide his services, but he would hold himself superior. Good men do not get put in jail.

Why was it like this, why was all her triumph turned to shame and mere, wretched inconvenience? He lay there sick and stupid day after day. He had never even clearly recognised her, never said her name, he was utterly out of reach, his mind gone. She did not dare ask the doctor if that blank stupor was caused by the disease or not, if it might lessen if the disease were cured, what hope of recovery there was. She looked into the sickroom once a day. She was unwilling to admit to herself that the sight of Itale now frightened and disgusted her, the bald head (shaved for lice, the doctor said), the blank look, the bony, yellowish body restless and yet slack. If she must look at that sick body it would take the place of the remembered lover, the young man in his strength. Those few nights, those few hours that she held to be the chief treasure of her life, the only time she had ever touched another person, would be tainted, degraded, with the prison taint, the smell of sickness and mortality. She would have nothing left at all. She must cling to the past, and to the future, when he would be himself again. But this was the future that she had dreamed of so long: Itale freed, the two of them here in the lonely house in the returning spring.

It went on raining. They could not keep the house warm. The old housekeeper was ill and querulous; the steward of the estate came daily with questions she could not answer intelligently and justifications for loans, purchases, and sales he had made which she knew nothing about. The doctor came and went, silent and sour, with his bottle of fat black leeches. She rode out daily on one of the stiff-kneed old horses; there had been no hunters or riders to keep up the stables for many years. The peasant tenants went about their business, indifferent to the presence or absence of the landowner. She knew no one any longer in the town, six miles away, where her grandfather had laid the foundations of his fortune speculating on wartime food prices, and had been a great man. Bored and wretchedly lonely, Luisa felt as she had when she was a child here: shoved aside, forgotten. Yet it was she who had isolated herself, telling no one her plans, so that she and Itale could be alone for once. . . . She wrote to Enrike, in Vienna, that he must take his leave early and come spend it at the estate. "I must have you here," she wrote. "I am at my wits' end."

Never had the trials and setbacks, the affronts and efforts of her long siege on the Krasnoy government so exhausted and defeated her as she had these two weeks since she went with the order of release to St Lazar. She knew now how much she had enjoyed that siege, the strategies and flatteries, the slow build-ing-up of her influence, the outwitting of the malicious and outpacing of the stupid. She had, always with the single goal, though she might not speak or even think about it for days or weeks, made herself a considerable figure in the politics of the capital. She had done small and great favors for men and women less astute than herself; she had got her brother his diplomatic post in Vienna; she had become a friend of the grand duchess, and a friend of the rabble-rousing deputy Stefan Oragon; Prime Minister Cornelius came to her house on Roches Street for conversation with clever and discreet people; the new minister of finance, Raskayneskar of Val Altesma, had proposed marriage to her as a speculation that would profit them both. The Krasnoy *Intelligencer* was full of gossip about her, but no one had made a slander, personal or political, stick to her name. She had used all her gifts, used them gallantly, and made a complete, recognised conquest of her aim. She had conquered. And the conquest won by that brave career through the rooms and offices of the powerful, was this.

The sight of the sick man, the memory of the sight of him, tormented her. Why must she be punished? Had she not worked to set him free, had she not succeeded? What was freedom, then? This desolation?

The doctor had supplied a woman from town to look after Itale. One night when this nurse was downstairs eating her dinner Luisa went into the sickroom, driven by an angry restlessness. There was no light but that of a bright fire. She thought the sick man was asleep, but as she came near the bed he spoke: "Who's there?"

"I am," she said. "Luisa. Do you know me?" She went up close to him, and spoke aloud, impatient and challenging. She could not see his face.

He answered; his voice was weak but natural, his own voice. "I can't remember," he said. "Where's Amadey?"

She went cold and the breath stuck in her throat.

"He is not here," she whispered at last.

The sick man paid no attention. He turned his head a little. The red firelight shone on the dry curve of his cheek. He lay there gazing straight ahead. Luisa went to a chair at the foot of the bed and sat down; she was shaky now, and soon stood up cautiously to leave the room. As she did so he gave a long sigh and murmured something, then spoke two words clearly: "The snow," and lay silent again.

She hurried out of the room, went to her own room, and stood at the window that looked out over the front garden. Between running clouds the full moon shone and faded. She saw the road, a straight, light streak between dark fields, leading away from the front gate. When she was a child she had seen that road, on which adults, visitors, her parents, came and went, as freedom: to be hers, her way, when the time came. She would be free to go, to come, as she liked, dependent upon no one. She went on that road now as she liked, she had her freedom. The word had lost its meaning, like the word love. Had she not loved

Itale? and he her? But she did not know who he was. She had worked to free a man, and he was not that man who lay sick in the room in this house. What did it mean, that they had been lovers? What had she been to him? He did not know her. He had not said her name. He had asked for a dead man, and he had said, "The snow." The memories, accretions, complexities, affections, anxieties, the trivial and immense world of which she had for a while been one element, she could hear fragments of that if she wanted to listen to his mind wandering in fever, but then where was she? Astray in a strange place, the world as Itale knew it, his world, of which she was not and had never been the center. To accept the limitless richness, the independence, of a being not her own, was to lose herself. She could not do it. She had never been able to do it but those few times, those hours, which she now denied. What was the good of that, of love so-called, of hands and bodies touching and meeting, all that, when this was the truth, this miserable isolation of the dying body—the sick animal?

She dreamed that night that she was wandering in the streets of a town she had never seen, a town amongst the mountains, and the streets were packed snow; she could not find the place where she was to go, where the packhorse was stabled.

The next day late in the afternoon a caller was announced as she came in from a long ride: Mr Sorde. She stared for a moment in pure bewilderment, almost panic, collecting her wits only when she saw the man waiting for her in the drawing room, a middle-aged provincial gentleman in black.

She came forward, on guard. "I am Luisa Paludeskar."

The man bowed. "Emanuel Sorde, baroness."

"Itale's father?"

"Hie uncle. His father's health doesn't permit him to travel at present. I am sorry to intrude myself on you, baroness. May I see Itale?"

She had not written Itale's family, nor had she notified any of his friends in Krasnoy of anything beyond the fact of his release from prison. They had written to the family in the Montayna, and this man had travelled across the country simply on the chance that Itale was here. If he had not been here he would have found him wherever he was. He did not ask why she had not written, he did not care; he was simply resolute, he was going to see Itale. She took him upstairs at once.

She left him in the sickroom and went to her room to change, in a dry, bitter mood. How long would it go on? Instead of love and secrecy, she had got sickness and loneliness. Instead of triumph, shame. Instead of Itale, his uncle for company. . . . It was a bad joke. Had she been wrong to look forward to Itale's release as happiness, for her as well as for him? If she had not been seeking that happiness, how could she have carried on for two years and done all she had done to win his freedom? Where did the fault, the error lie?

The uncle's presence at dinner relieved her at least from the endless brooding over such questions. He was tired, and hungry, and preoccupied entirely with his nephew. His manner was stiff and wary, but essentially indifferent: she was not what interested him. She began to feel at ease with him. When they spoke of Itale's illness she asked Emanuel Sorde a question she had never brought herself to ask the doctor. "Even when his fever is down, he . . . he doesn't seem to notice things. . . ." She did not explain what it was she feared, but Sorde appeared to understand her, replying, "It's the disease, I believe, baroness. It's what the word typhus means. A stupor. It passes. What does your physician say?"

She shook her head. "He won't tell me even whether Itale is worse or better."

"The woman says his fever has been down the last two days."

She had not known that. She sat silent over her scarcely touched plate, while Sorde ate.

"Baroness," he said rather abruptly, "I saw Mr Brelavay as I came through Krasnoy. He told me what your modesty prevented your writing us. We are so deeply in your debt that it is presumption in me to speak of it."

She was taken aback; she answered without forethought. "I am not modest, Mr Sorde. I act in my own interest. Itale was my friend. That friend was taken from me; I acted to get him back. That's all."

Surprising her again, the provincial lawyer simply smiled and raised his glass with a slight, formal bow of the head. He was, she realised, like Itale, formidable.

"All I ask," she said, "is to see Itale as he was."

"That we will not see, baroness."

"But he is recovering—?"

"I hope so— I dare think so, having seen him, changed as he is. But I do not hope ever to see him as he was."

He finished eating, laid down his fork quietly, across the plate, country style. He was hateful in his provincial, middle-aged self-assurance. He did not care for her. He did not care what she lost. He was old, and like all the old did not care for the future, did not believe in it.

But if he was right, if Itale was changed, would not be the same again, what future was she looking for? —Again the figure of the warders' room, pitiful and repulsive, stood between her and the handsome, kindly boy who had been her lover: as if the fever had burnt up all that image like paper, like a bit of paper money in a fire. What was left? The old man, the uncle, was right. They were always right. There was nothing left of Itale but that man upstairs, whom she did not know, whom she did not want to look at, or be near.

II

A bar of morning sunlight slanted across the bed. The cool gold bathed his hands. Outside the window swallows dipped and swooped, building their nests in the eaves above. He could not watch them long, his eyes blurred, dazzled by the light.

Emanuel was in the armchair, with a book open on his knees, but presently engaged in trimming his fingernails, with a pleasurable concentration on the act.

"How's Perneta?"

Emanuel looked up keenly, then returned to his trimming-job as he answered, "Very well indeed. A grandnephew of hers

284

came up from Solariy last year, that's her brother Karel's daughter's son, Karel Kidre he's called, nice young fellow. Gives her a good deal of pleasure to have a relation to spoil. He's in our office, in fact he's supposed to be looking after some of my more onerous recurrent duties while I'm here, those damned property lines in Val Modrone. Nothing like a three-generation-long boundary dispute to keep a lawyer cheerful. But I imagine young Karel's mostly out at Valtorsa, if the weather there's like this."

"Count Orlant?"

"He's fine. Piera is the attraction."

"Piera?"

"You haven't forgotten Piera."

"She's married. Aisnar."

"How did you know that story? That's right, you knew about it before we did—saw her in Aisnar, didn't you? No, she broke the engagement. They were to be married at Christmas and it was put off till spring and then all at once it was off altogether. That must have been a little while after you were arrested. Never did understand the whys and wherefores. At any rate she's still not married. Count Orlant lets her do exactly as she pleases, of course, always has. Lets her manage the property, in fact; I've handled several matters for her the last couple of years. She is a much better manager than her father, I have to admit. But I don't know what's got into these young women. Here's Laura wanting to do the same thing, as if Guide would let her, and she hasn't the head for it at all. What do they want to be stewards for? what's wrong with marriage and a family these days? Handsome women they are, too, both of 'em. Wasteful. . . ."

Emanuel's voice was deliberate, serene, long pauses between sentences. Itale listened, watching the sunlight on the red cover of the eiderdown on the bed: a dark red, somewhat faded; the fine threads caught the light in infinitesimal streaks of silver. The worn satin was very soft under his fingers. Warmth; softness; sunlight; color; these absorbed him; he must relearn them, little by little. Emanuel's presence, his voice, his hands, that was the buoy, the raft. It was Emanuel's touch that had first brought him back from the endless, limitless wanderings of fever: a hand held out, literally drawing him back, holding him in life. And his voice, now, talking easily, meandering among all the names of home.

A week or so later Luisa came up in the evening to sit with them. Itale was propped up a little so that he could watch the fire in the hearth. The lymphatic swellings that had followed the typhus fever were much reduced, and he was comfortable, able to enjoy warmth and rest. Emanuel and Luisa talked a little; he did not pay attention to what they said. She turned to him. "Itale, do you remember the trip from Rakava?"

He thought a while. "No."

"We had to come round by Foranoy because of the floods. None of the ferries could cross."

"No. . . . But when . . . the day I came out. It was bright."

"Yes, it was sunny, between storms. Windy."

"I saw the sun."

"Did you never see the sun in prison?" Emanuel asked, without emphasis, but Itale did not answer.

He never spoke of the twenty-six months in St Lazar, and Emanuel did not press him, saying to Luisa, "It's best he puts it behind him, no doubt."

As he grew stronger he did not talk much more. He asked very few questions even of Emanuel, none of Luisa. She left a copy of *Novesma Verba* on his table, but did not know whether he read it. When he was able to get up, his desire was simply to get outside, to be outside, sitting at first, later able to walk a little in the wild, half-ruined gardens. People of the estate stared at him, tall and unearthly thin still, with his stubble-covered head, a strange figure.

The night before Enrike was to arrive—for he had faithfully answered her plea with a promise to spend part of his leave with her, coming straight, or as straight as possible, from Vienna—she said to Emanuel, "Mr Sorde, I need your advice."

"Not on anything very important," Emanuel said drily, and she took the compliment and smiled. They did not like each other, and had come to respect each other's wit and willpower, and indeed take considerable pleasure in it.

"It is very important."

286

"Itale or estate law?"

"Itale."

"Good."

"Is he strong enough to hear bad news?"

"I don't know, baroness. What is the matter?"

"You know that he was a friend of Estenskar, the poet. They were close friends. Estenskar is dead. He killed himself a month or two after Itale was arrested. He probably never knew about the arrest; he was under surveillance too, we now know, his mail was stopped, they were trying to make a charge against him. After his death his brother was arrested and held for a couple of months, and finally released without any charges. Itale stayed with them just before he went to Rakava. So far as I know, he was never told, he doesn't know that Estenskar is dead. Have you ever mentioned it? has he said anything?"

"No," Emanuel said with a shake of the head. He clasped his hands and looked down at them, grim. "I'll tell him, if you like," he said. "I doubt he's entirely unprepared."

"No; thank you for offering to take the burden, but you should not darken your last days with him. I knew Estenskar. I'll tell him after you're gone. If you think he is . . ."

"Oh, he's hard, baroness," Emanuel said, still speaking grimly. "He can take it. I think he can take almost anything, now. What he cannot do is give. If you can spare him that, if you can shield him from having to make choices and decisions for a bit longer, let him be here away from people, you'll have done more for him than that horse-faced doctor did."

Taking his own advice, Emanuel left that week without ever asking Itale what he intended to do when he left the Sovena. Itale tried to raise the subject himself, the night before Emanuel was to go. "You're sure that father is all right?"

"You read your mother's letter."

"You've both been sparing me."

"No, not really. I believe I told you almost exactly what Dr Charkar told us. His heart is not strong, neither is it actually unsound. He is as active as he ever was, within sensible limits. After all, he is over sixty."

"That is the problem," Itale said; and Emanuel frowned.

287

"Listen, Itale, there is no need for you to decide anything yet, just because I'm off home. Stay here as long as you can, find out where your course lies, don't let yourself be forced into anything."

Itale looked at him and then looked away. "Would I be welcome," he said, so indistinctly and speaking so much aside that Emanuel did not at first understand him, and when he did answered without thinking, shocked, "Of course, don't be foolish," brushing aside the question, which only much later, when he was hours gone and well started on his way back home, returned suddenly into his mind, so clearly now and so painfully that he all but cried out aloud, "My God, Itale, how can you ask that? What have they done to you that you can ask that?"

Enrike Paludeskar had arrived a few days earlier, in a wild rainstorm on the first of May, very much out of sorts. He had loyally come to his sister's call, but that did not prevent him from resenting her expectation that he would coop himself up in the dreary house in the Godforsaken provinces with her and a convicted seditionist fresh from jail. She had no sense, she refused to realise that she was imperilling his position, his career, by making him come here, and indeed by insisting upon keeping Sorde here even while he Enrike was in Vienna or Krasnoy. He impressed this upon her pretty forcibly and at length, but when Itale came into the room he turned, stared, and then put out his hand. His heavy face had gone pale. He tried to say something but could not; he shook Itale's hand, and put his left hand timidly on his shoulder, then awkwardly pulled away. "I hear, I hear you've been ill," he said stammering.

He never succeeded after that in looking Itale in the face or talking naturally with him. Fortunately Itale spoke very little, and Enrike did not have to try to explain his guilt and revulsion to Luisa. He could not make it out. It was the government, the commonplace, decent men he worked with, whom Sorde had been trying to subvert; it was the same government, the same decent men, who had taken Sorde and done this to him. It was incredible, unreasonable. He could not solve the problem, and Itale, by embodying it, made him miserable.

"How do you like your work in Vienna?" Itale asked him once,

conventionally enough, and Enrike gasped and groped— "It's—
interesting, and all that— I don't do anything significant, really—
open letters, you know, and all that—"

"Harry," Luisa put in, drawling, "you mean you censor the
mail?"

"No, no, no, nothing of that sort, for God's sake, Luisa! What
do you think I am? No, official letters, letters to the ambassador—dispatches and that sort of thing!"

He said nothing more to Luisa about sending Sorde away. He
planned to leave himself, however, as soon as he could. Luisa
did not need him, anyhow; she had begun collecting acquain-
tances as she always did, a crazy mixed lot, but she always mixed
her lots.

These were neighbors, some of them neighbors at a distance of
thirty miles, but they thought nothing of riding clear across the
province if a full table and a hot political discussion awaited them
at ride's end. Duke Matiyas Sovenskar, heir to the Orsinian
throne, lived on his enormous estate twenty miles to the north,
and no one forgot his presence though he had not left that estate
for years. The province was thick with retired officers of the
defunct national army, old now but still bitter. Their club, the
Friends of the Constitution, had lately been revived in emulation
of the young liberals in the capital. They sounded out Luisa
cautiously, until they found who the man staying with her was.
In Krasnoy she was considered a woman who had liberal friends
but whose influence lay in conservative circles; in the Sovena,
because Sorde was with her, they took her for a radical patriot.
Enrike protested, accused her of hypocrisy and of meddling with
things she didn't understand, was reminded that she had despite
her lack of understanding meddled him into his diplomatic post,
and left, defeated as always.

Luisa had begun to enjoy herself again. Grey-headed ex-
colonels fought Leipzig over in the echoing salon, while their
sons, landowners of the rich Sovena estates, toasted first Duke
Matiyas—"Sovenskar, the Constitution, the Nation!" and then
their hostess. Baron Agrikol Laravey-Gotheskar, six foot two and
black-mustached, broad-chested, magnificent, drank to her and
smashed his glass into the fireplace. She missed the weight of

such men as Raskayneskar or Johann Cornelius, whose benign manners concealed real political power, yet she liked these noisy, quarrelsome Northerners. Their power was only personal, but it was immediate. She wanted to laugh whenever Laravey-Gotheskar smashed another wine glass, and yet she was stirred, her eyes met his fiery gaze. "Baron, your flattery has cost me three pieces of my grandmother's crystal," she told him, and he, furious as she expected, "Flattery! You misjudge me, baroness!" —and stalked off frowning tremendously to sulk, until the nearby discussions turned the course of his passions and he threw himself into the fray shouting, "But Vienna will hear no voice, gentlemen, but the voice of blood and iron!"

They were all, even Laravey-Gotheskar, very gentle with Itale. He took no part in their discussions, and generally excused himself early from the company. There was no need to explain or excuse his silence and withdrawal; the reason was all too visible, though he had been gaining a little weight and color as spring turned to the clear, bright northern summer. He still spent all day outdoors if he could. He could walk and ride a little; he talked with people on the estate; there was no reason, Luisa thought, why he could not talk with these men, his equals in education and like him in background and opinions. What kept him silent, then?

"There is a chance Laravey-Gotheskar might get the vacant seat for the Sovena. You could tell him so much he needs to know about the Assembly, Itale. He is extraordinarily naive."

"I'm not the one to tell him."

"Why not? Who knows more about it than you? The mistakes you could save him from making—"

"But I don't know about it. I'm out of date. I didn't even know till recently that Amiktiya had been suppressed. I can't seem to take things in." He looked at her for a moment, diffident. "And Estenskar," he said, very low, as if apologetic.

It was three weeks since she had told him of Estenskar's death. He had taken the news quietly and spoken of it quietly, asked questions, and then let it drop. She was disturbed by his mentioning Estenskar now, inappropriately.

"I wish you would help Laravey-Gotheskar. He's very young,

very naive, but not stupid. I should think he is exactly the kind of man young people want in the Assembly."

"He is."

"He reminds me sometimes of you. When you were fresh down from your mountains."

Itale smiled a little forcedly, and she realised that she had hurt him by the comparison.

But everything hurt him, it seemed, and he was afraid of everything. He dodged away, evaded, withdrew; he would not commit himself, would not participate. The only person he had sought out for himself was the Lutheran pastor of the village, an amateur mathematician, an uncouth elderly misogynist. He and Itale would sit out in the garden with a book or two, the pastor explaining, Itale listening, a lesson in gibberish—calculus, binomials, God knows what. When Luisa's impatience expressed itself in mild sarcasm, Itale explained stiffly that he had tried to occupy his mind with mathematics "before he was ill," and finding he knew very little had wanted very much to learn more. "I can do that now," he said. She had to let him and his pastor be. But he could not sit forever in the garden pretending to be a schoolboy again, evading all the problems about which he had been so passionate, the cause for which he had suffered, avoiding her.

There was a houseful of guests; in the evening, when once again Itale escaped again as early as he could, she felt some resentment or humiliation, and said to Laravey-Gotheskar, "If only I could interest him in all the things that meant so much to him!" The young baron, deaf to her self-pity and tolerating no criticism of the her, frowned. "We talk, we talk, why should he listen? He has lived what we talk about!" Luisa was pleased. Itale had used to scold her that way, but no longer; Laravey-Gotheskar was the first man in years to give her a moral rebuke. "I'm afraid it was my disappointment speaking," she answered meekly, "I miss him when he hides himself away." —"Of course," said the young man, and brooded, sunk in an awful tangle of enthusiasm, admiration, and jealousy, exactly where Luisa wanted him.

It was the trouble with him. For all his unpredictable pride, she could put him where she wanted him. There were only two men whom she had never been able to bend to her whim, though one had twice asked her in marriage and would ask her again if he thought it any use, and the other had been her lover: George Helleskar and Itale. Helleskar had taught her all she had ever known of fidelity; Itale had given her, a few times, for a little while, fulfilment. He had freed her, then, as she had freed him.

Why was that not enough, to be free and set free, to unlock the doors?

When her guests had left, and she must face again the long days of silence, a seeming intimacy that was increasing estrangement, she found herself angry with Itale, impatient; it was time he pulled himself together. "Why will you not talk to them?" she demanded. "They believe all you used to believe—do you hold yourself above them?"

He looked at her with an incredulity that shamed her for a moment.

"What can I say to them?" he asked, in the diffident tone she disliked in him.

"Have you lost your faith in the power of words, then? Or in the Constitution, and impartial law, and all the rest of it, all you went to jail for—has that become unimportant to you, like everything else?"

"Like everything else?"

"You are indifferent to them, to me, to everything."

He had no answer.

"You won't even speak. How am I to know anything of you, or you of me, after this—this time—"

"What can I say?" he repeated, rigid, obdurate, and she realised with horror that he was holding nothing back from her: that he was in fact unable to speak. He was hard, Emanuel Sorde had said, but it was the hardness of rock, without resilience, mere ultimate coherence like a rock that is itself until it is broken. She could break him. He had no defense. He could do no more than resist her, withstand her, who had freed him and was now his jailer.

On St John's Eve the wide horizon of the night flared with scattered bonfires. Every village, every outlying farm had its fire.

292

Bagpipes droned by the crackling, lurid stacks of heath and straw, the young men and women danced, the old men drank; the night was full of voices, noises, half-lit, running figures. Luisa stood with her maid in the zone between darkness and firelight, and watched the girls of the village tuck up their skirts and leap across the coals, in the rite as old as the fields they worked, the leap across the fire from barrenness to fertility. The older women watching laughed and shouted obscene encouragement. Men were quarreling already over by the big fire, working up to the fight that always followed drinking. Luisa watched, repelled, excited, envious, contemptuous, until Agata, who found it all frightening, made her come away. When she was back at the house she felt stifled indoors, and went out again at once to walk in the garden, watching the distant glare and dying of the fires.

"Luisa."

She stopped short. He stood not far from her, on a path by an overgrown hedge which made a mass of blackness in the cloudy moonlight; she could not see his face.

"I didn't want to startle you."

"You didn't," she said, though he had. "Who could be afraid on a night like this? Were you out to see the fires?"

He came towards her and stopped again. He was bareheaded in the warm night. He stood there tall and patient, and again she saw the grotesque and pitiful figure of the warders' room. Why must he look like that, why must he stand like that?

"They were dancing at the bonfire in the village, it was exciting to see. The peasants here are pagans, underneath all their sour Lutheran twaddle. They're not civilised at all."

"May I talk to you a moment, Luisa?"

"Nothing would please me more!"

"I think I should leave soon."

"I see. Well, that would certainly prevent any further conversation. . . ." She could not control her irritation, more than irritation, a blind anger with him.

"You know that I am grateful," he said very low.

"For God's sake, Itale! It's not your gratitude I want. If you want to stay, stay, if you want to go, go. You're free, you don't seem to realise it. All I want is for you to realise it, to behave like it."

They walked on to the end of the path side by side. The moon, some nights past full, stood over the low black lands eastward. To the south four fires reddened the smoky darkness.

"Your wanting to go implies, I gather, that you've decided we are no longer to be lovers."

He stopped and faced her. "I have decided? Luisa—" His voice shook. He took a breath, and with painfully evident effort said, "It has been decided for us."

"Nothing is decided for me. I make my own choices!"

"Can you choose to want to touch me?"

"What do you mean," she said, terrified.

He stood still, and she knew that he could say no more, and that it was the simplest thing in the world to prove him wrong: all she had to do was take his hand, touch his cheek, touch him. Or let him touch her.

She took a step back from him.

"It isn't fair," she said in a whisper. "It isn't fair!"

After a while he said, "I don't know very well what's fair any longer. I don't want to cause you pain, Luisa. I never wanted to. And never did much else."

"Why must it be so stupid!" She looked at herself in the dim light, her shawl and the heavy skirt and flaring sleeves of her dress, her hands. "Why am I like this, why am I trapped in this? Why can't I be free, free of it? Why can't we do what we like?"

"O my dear," he said in shame and pain, and he held out his hands to her.

"I wish I was dead," she said, and turned, and walked away from him.

In the morning when they met she was calm and polite. "Well, what shall we do, Itale?" she said. "Shall we effect a joint triumphal entry into the capital, or shall we go back one by one? How soon do you want to go?"

"I don't know."

"Are you well enough to ride, do you think?"

He nodded.

"I think I must stay for Laravey-Gotheskar's party. He invited

294

Duke Matiyas, I should love to see that old man. . . . Do you want to stay for that? it's in two weeks. If not I don't know why you shouldn't go when you choose. Take old Sheikh, I suppose he's the likeliest one of the old nags to last all the way to Krasnoy."

His gaze was on her, unhappy, the blue eyes.

"Then I'll follow in mid-July. Enrike goes back to Vienna then, I may go with him. I've learned not to stay in Krasnoy in the summer. It's dead. Dead center of a defeated country. I hate defeat."

She looked at him as she spoke, and he looked down.

"When shall you go, then?"

"Tomorrow," he said.

"Very well."

"I haven't much to take," he said, getting up. "And all of it your gift. You know that, Luisa. The horse, the . . . the shirt, the life. . . ."

But she would accept no comfort; not from him.

He left in the early morning. She bade him farewell in the house, downstairs; he went out to the stables, she up to her room. She stood at the window and watched him ride out the gate and straight away down the straight road between the level fields. He looked back once, half turning in the saddle. She did not lift her hand.

III

Itale rode down from Grasse in late evening of the last day of June. Tired, on a tired horse, he rode through the drab fields of burdock, shards, shacks, tramps, sour earth, and into the long streets of the Trasfiuve, and crossed Old Bridge under the statue of St Christopher of the Wayfarers, remembering the morning of the autumn equinox three years ago. He put up at a small inn just off Molsen Boulevard, ordered dinner, and went to bed very soon after he had eaten. He would look up his friends, take up

295

his life, tomorrow; tonight he wanted only to sleep. The room was small and with the curtains drawn very dark. He got up again at once and drew back the curtains, opened both the windows wide to the warm, noisy city night. He had almost fallen asleep when the bell of the cathedral, a few streets away, struck ten. After that he lay wide awake in the darkness suffering all the memories and presences of his time in Krasnoy from the moment when he had first heard that bell strike, the two years in which so much life had been compressed that they seemed to lie like a fiery bar of sunlight between the remote, long, quiet years in the shadow of the mountains and the unimaginable but immediate past, the twenty-seven months of darkness.

As he breakfasted in the hot morning at a street cafe in the River Quarter he debated going back to the inn, lying low for another day. He had not got much rest; he mistrusted himself, his energy, his strength. What would he have to face, here? Riding from the Sovena he had been very nervous at first, avoiding every town entry and possible check-point that he could avoid, dreading the request to show his papers. That dread had lessened as he was, at one point and then another, checked cursorily and passed. But what was the situation here? He did not really know, and was apprehensive. However, he had to take Luisa's horse to the Paludeskar stables in Roches Street; and he was going to have to get some money. He could not afford another night at the inn. Emanuel had loaned him fifty kruner, of which he had sixteen left in his pocket; less than he had arrived with the first time, five years ago. Less all round, he thought, coming back down from Old Quarter to the river and walking up the boulevard under the trees by the bright water. Less cash, less strength, less time to live; less of a man to stand up against the storming of the human world and the universe at his mind and body, the storm of light and wind and sensation and passion that never ceased, never rested, until death; for the walls of a building, a prison, were dust in that storm. He felt peculiarly slight, light, insubstantial as he walked up the wide street by the river, a flickering thing, exposed, uncertain. This mote, this speck between the sun in its gulfs of light and the earth with its long shadow, this was himself, Itale Sorde, and he was supposed to withstand the entire universe in order to remain himself; not only that, to do his job; to be a part of it. It was a strange business to be a man walking in the sunlight, stranger than to be a stone, or a river, or a tree holding up its branches in the July heat. They all knew what they were doing. He did not.

He passed two little girls hurrying with their hard-breathing nurse towards the far mirage of a sherbet-vendor's cart. He saw their pigtails bob on their thin shoulders. How long since he had seen a child? He had reached the office of *Novesma Verba*. He turned to the parapet and leaned his hands on it, watching the bright Molsen go towards the sea. So far to go from this inland country, *my shoreless kingdom* Amadey had called it in the Ode, so far to go for a bitter end, and nameless. . . . Come on, he said to himself, come on, Itale, and straightened up, turned, crossed the street, went up the stairs to the journal's office. In his determination, and out of old habit, he did not knock but went straight in. A young fellow stepped out in front of him from behind the table: "What d'you want?"

"Who's here?" Itale said stammering, unnerved; he did not know whether he had forgotten this man, or never known him.

"Mr Belavay is busy with a visitor. I'm Vernoy."

He was young, twenty at most, and shone with self-confidence. Itale, vulnerable to every impression, was impressed by that youthfulness, and casting about for something to say asked, "Are you from Amiktiya?" Then he remembered that the student society had been put under ban and several of its leaders at the University in Krasnoy arrested, a few months before his release. It was a very stupid question, and the boy rapped out, "Who are you?"

"Sorde, Itale Sorde. Sorry. I wanted—"

"You're Sorde?" Itale said yes, he was. Vernoy fell to pieces like wet paper, waved his hands, ran for Brelavay. Brelavay came, carrying his dark face like a long, ironical signboard on top of his long body, exactly the same, unchanged, so that Itale laughed with pure joy at the sight of him; but his friend, embracing him, sobbed and would not let him go.

"Here, come on, Tomas. . . ."

They could not look at each other.

"Come on. Wait, here it is." Brelavay found his handkerchief and blew his nose. "Almighty Christ, Itale," he said tenderly. "What did you have?"

"Have?"

"What were you ill with?"

"Typhus."

"No joke, eh?"

"Not a very good one."

"Here, come along, why are we standing around my handkerchief like a scene from Othello? Sangiusto's in here, remember him, Itale? Almighty Christ! to say your name again! —Where are you staying? I didn't try to write you in the Sovena, your baroness said better not to when she wrote, has to watch her reputation, political of course. She kept you hidden there long enough. I expect you needed it." He had his arm around Itale's shoulders and was steering him into the composing-room, where, considerably shaken by his own feelings and Brelavay's, Itale found himself returning a handshake and looking into a face that completed his confusion by bringing around him the moonlight, the sound of fountains, Luisa's voice, Piera's voice, the carriages on Fontarmana Street. When all that subsided he was sitting down feeling a little sick, and the others were around him looking concerned. "Sorry, I'm still shaky—how are you, Sangiusto?"

"Very well, Sorde."

"You're staying in Krasnoy?"

"Yes, since two weeks. I'm tired of England, I come here," said the Italian. He spoke mostly in the present tense; his voice was calm, his manner relaxed, and in his smile there was a hint of complicity. Itale felt at ease with him at once. "But it's not the same mood here as in '27, even in Aisnar. It's agitated . . . bad-tempered. But who knows? I come from England. Everyone on the Continent is agitated and emotional, neh?"

"What about Paris?" Brelavay asked.

"Oh, well, Paris. The Ultras, Royer-Collard, Article Fourteen, lovers, chestnut trees, old men catching little fishes in the Seine, Paris is always the same and who can predict of her?" They laughed, and again Sangiusto shot a quick accomplice's glance at

Itale. With some sense of playing a role, Itale asked the questions Brelavay had a right to expect him to ask: about recent events, political trends and changes. "If there's any change," Brelavay said, "it's a change of mood, as Sangiusto said. Underneath—in people, in the people. On top, nothing. The ministry's the same except for Raskayneskar replacing Tarven, the Assembly mumbles on, the grand duchess is ill—maybe—not ill—maybe; all rumor."

"But three years ago there were no rumors," said Sangiusto.

Taxes were heavier, Brelavay went on, political arrests increasingly common, "administrative sentences" without trial or term had been introduced, the student society and several other groups had been put under ban, censorship was massive and all mail likely to be read, there had been two bad harvests and unemployment in the cities of the east and center was high. "Some cause for bad temper," Itale said.

"They blame it all on the Assembly. Even the bad harvests."

"Your Assembly is the expiatory—what do you call it, the scapegoat for Austria; the prime minister sees to that."

"How's Oragon been doing?" Itale asked.

"Damn Oragon," Brelavay said. "He's not our Danton, Itale. He's our Talleyrand. A demagogic one—the shit's in a wooden shoe instead of a silk stocking— The nation be hanged, if Stefan Oragon can climb a little higher on the gallows!"

"Luisa said that my pardon was largely due to him."

"It was. He needs our good press, and you were the price he had to pay for it."

"Well. How . . . How is Frenin?"

"Fine. He's in Solariy."

"For the paper?"

"Living there."

"In Solariy? What's going on there?"

"What always did. Students, cattle fairs, everybody asleep by nine. He's a grain shipper. Doing well, I hear. He left Krasnoy a few weeks after we heard you'd been arrested." Itale still looked blank. "He got cold feet," Brelavay said gently.

Brelavay, Frenin, Itale had been friends long before they thought of coming to the capital, and it had been Frenin who

299

brought them, Frenin who said, how long ago, in the park by the blue Molsen in the sunlight, "I'm thinking of Krasnoy. . . ."

It was an old bitterness to Brelavay, to Itale a blow; he could not escape the conviction that to have suffered, to have submitted to evil, though he had had no way at all to refuse it, had made him a cause of evil. It was because of him that Frenin had given up. In the conscious and painful acceptance of this responsibility, he sat silent for a minute; he weighed a broken inkstand that was on the table in his hand, and said finally, "Tomas, did you . . . do you know anything about Isaber?"

"Absolutely no trace. Nothing. They denied consistently, from the beginning, that he was in St Lazar; claimed he'd been released with an order to get out of the province. Beyond that, nothing."

He had lived with the boy's death for two years in prison; he had not known till the hope was taken from him how much hope he had kept, hidden, that when he came out he would find it had been a mistake, a cruel hoax, a nightmare of his own, and Isaber was alive.

This also, this inescapably, was his responsibility; he was answerable for this death.

Brelavay asked him nothing, seeing that he was distressed and assuming that he knew even less than they about what had become of the boy. Sangiusto stood up, stretching, and said in English, *"To fresh fields and pastures new. . . .* I have eaten nothing."

"Come on, I told Givan I'd meet him at the Illyrica at one," Brelavay said, relieved to get away from the unlucky subject.

Givan Karantay had not changed; he was dark and warm as a banked fire. They sat two hours over their coffee-cups, talking. Two or three young men came up and asked if they might be introduced to Mr Sorde. Itale shook their hands and was short with them; they went humbly away.

"You're their hero, their Valtura, dear fellow," said Karantay.

"God forbid!"

"God forbid indeed," Brelavay said. "Valtura's dead. Died in the Spielberg in '28."

"Where Silvio Pellico, who knew Byron, is now," said Sangiusto in his calm voice. "There must be good company in the Spielberg prison." Now Itale knew why Sangiusto looked at him as if there were a tacit bond between them. There was. Sangiusto had spent three years in the Piombi in Venice as a political prisoner. Brelavay, Karantay, the young men wanted to hear and dared not ask about his jail term. Sangiusto did not want to hear, did not need to ask. Foreigner, exile, he was Itale's compatriot.

Arguments concerning Stefan Oragon surfaced occasionally, and in the course of one of them Sangiusto put in, "But he is a professional, isn't he? and you are amateurs, myself too. The coups d'état are made by professionals. They succeed. The revolutions are made by amateurs."

"And fail?" Brelavay inquired.

"Of course!"

"But listen, Sangiusto," Karantay said, "the words are good, it was amateurs that made '89, all right. The crowds, the people that walked to Versailles and took the Bastille. And the Assembly, the Girondins, the Jacobins, they were lawyers, provincial men of letters, not politicians. But as they learned their trade, as they became professional, the Revolution began to fail, to lead inevitably towards the coup d'état that betrayed it."

"They did never learn their trade," the Italian said. "Robespierre is always an amateur. The professional is Napoleon. The question is really this, what is failure, what is success? The Revolution failed, yes, and Napoleon is a very successful man, a conqueror, an emperor, but it was the failure, not the success, that gives hope to our life."

"*Vivre libre, ou mourir*," Itale said, and laughed.

"Exactly, Vergniaud. A professional lawyer, very successful in his profession. A nice lazy fellow, an amateur deputy, unsuccessful. Sklk!" Sangiusto cut his throat with the side of his hand. "A fine career cut short. But first he told us to live free or die. Why did you laugh, Sorde?"

"Found I'd rather stay alive even if not free."

"Of course. For two years, three years. Or longer. But here we are now, alive and free."

"Alive," Itale said.

His money problem had been promptly solved, as Brelavay

told him peremptorily that he had twenty-eight months' wages waiting at *Novesma Verba*. "It's been very useful, the most cash we ever kept on hand, I don't know how many loans we've made from it to get people over a thin time. But they always repaid because it was your money, if it was my money or our money they'd have embezzled freely. . . ." Karantay had asked him to come share his rooms; he hesitated. "A friend was keeping my old rooms for me when I went to Rakava. I should go see whether he's there."

Karantay went with him into the River Quarter, past St Stephen's and the Street of Hangman's Feast, the swarming courts and alleys under toppling houses in the shadow of the Hill of the University. "No change here," Itale remarked. "Not for five hundred years," said Karantay. At 9 Mallenastrada, Mrs Rosa, cat-beleaguered, greeted her long-lost tenant without warmth. "Your things are here, Mr Sorde. I'll be glad to have 'em out of my way."

"Is Mr Brunoy here?"

She looked him up and down. "No."

She knew him to be a jailbird. But his voice and clothing said gentleman. She wanted him to be a gentleman, she had had enough of jailbirds in her life, but she could not trust him; he had let her down, and her voice was vindictive as she said, "He died here, two years ago. Kounney's got the rooms."

"I see," Itale said. After a moment he asked submissively if Kounney was in. Mrs Rosa stood aside, and he and Karantay climbed the dark rickety stairs. Kounney came from behind his loom: "We was very sorry to hear, Mr Sorde," he said. "It's good to see you." Itale shook his hand, and stopped to play with the baby, not born when he left and now a solemn two-year-old. The delicate face, the dark eyes gazed into Itale's. "What's her name, Kounney?"

"It's a him, he's on the small side, makes him look like a girl. We called him Liyve. There's a couple of things I kept for you here." Kounney rummaged in the other room and returned with a small packet of papers which he gave to Itale: several letters written from Malafrena in the autumn of 1827, and a scrap of

paper, one downhill scrawl of barely readable writing on it—
"Prometheus no chains eternal."

"Mr Brunoy wrote that for you a day or two before he died,"
Kounney said.

Itale gave it to Karantay and walked away to the window.

"Did you know him, Givan?" he asked.

"Not well. He used to come to the office for word of you."

Itale stood with his back turned. "He was an upright man."

"That he was," said the weaver. "And a good death. He
couldn't talk when he wrote you that, but at the end he spoke; he
raised up and said, 'I'm ready,'—like a bridegroom going to his
wedding. I looked to see who he was talking to. And he lay back
quiet and content, and his breath caught like, and he died. I
wished the priest had stayed. I never saw a better death."

"Aye," Itale said. "It was what he knew how to do."

He took the slip of paper back from Karantay and slipped it
folded into the back of his watch.

"How does it go, Kounney?"

"I've kept working." He looked up at Itale. "We're in your
rooms now, there being six of us we spread out a bit, but if you
want—"

"No, I won't be coming back, Kounney. Did she raise the rent
on you?"

"No, and she didn't ask rent of Mr Brunoy at the end, so that
the little he had put by for it and the books and his watch paid to
bury him. She's all right. Knows when times are hard."

Kneeling, Itale put out his hand to the frail, solemn little boy in
his sexless, shapeless, worn dress. "Goodbye, Liyve," he said.
The contrast in size of their hands was too much; he touched the
child's cheek. He stood up, shook hands with Kounney, bidding
him goodbye.

They went on to Karantay's rooms south of the Eleynaprade.
Karantay had kept a letter for Itale from Amadey Estenskar,
dated February 6, 1828. Itale began to read it, laid it down, and
put his head in his hands. "I can't read any more letters from the
dead," he said.

Karantay had the top floor of a house, a set of big rooms,

sparsely furnished, with high, large windows. Itale paced down the uncarpeted floor and back, and sat down again, wearily.

"They all died today," he said.

"They haven't been very good years, these last two or three," Karantay said gently.

"What's wrong—what is it that's wrong, Givan?"

"I don't know. Speaking for myself, nothing. I go on writing, it's all I care about, you know, really. I make a living by it; I'm going to get married in September."

"Married! —To Karela?"

Karantay nodded. He had been in love a long time, and had never been willing to talk about it; Itale could not tell even now whether his reticence expressed coolness of feeling, or suppressed a happiness he felt egoistical and unseemly.

"So as I say, I have all I have ever asked for, for myself. But for us all together, they haven't been good years. You in jail, Amadey dead, Frenin giving up. . . . Who can blame him? We knew all along we were pounding our heads on a stone wall trying to knock it down. But one's head gets sore. And addled. . . . Then there've been so many searches. And summonses—Tomas has been called up three times now. And these damnable administrative sentences, they frighten us all. And the censorship so heavy I wonder why anybody still bothers to read *Verba*, sometimes. . . . But they do read it. Our subscription list has doubled in the last year and a half. And there are young men coming up, and men like Sangiusto—there are more of us than there used to be. It's only that the waiting's long, and we've never known for certain what it is we're waiting for. No change there. But we're a couple of years older."

Itale smiled. The kind sobriety of Karantay's temper refreshed him now as always. "Waiting . . ." he said. "That's not true of you, Givan. You have your work. But I have never worked. I've only made ready."

"The time will come, Itale."

"Will it? Is there any time but now?"

Karantay did not answer.

"I don't know, Givan. I have lost—I have no right to speak of this."

"You have earned the right to speak of anything."

"No. That's exactly it. I have earned nothing—nothing. You don't earn, you don't gain, where I was, Givan. You lose. You lose the right to talk to people who have—who believe in the powers of light— What I learned there was that I have no rights, and infinite responsibility."

"That would be infinite injustice. It's false, Itale."

"I would rather trust you than myself," Itale said. "I wish I could. I was—I was a better man, before—" He cut himself off, standing up abruptly. "I'm very tired, maybe I should lie down for a while."

He went off to the spare room. At eight Karantay looked in to go out to supper with him. He was sound asleep, and Karantay hesitated to waken him. He looked down at Itale's face, worn and sleep-submerged, and then out the uncurtained, open window westward over roofs and gables and chimneystacks, the high view smoky and shadowed in long evening light. It was hot; there was no wind. Karantay stood there beside the friend he had not hoped to see again, wishing that there would be a wind off the river, darkness, rain. But the weather was steady, it would not change. On the bureau a silver watch lay open. It said two-thirty. Karantay tapped it, but it did not run. He spoke to Itale at last, rousing him, and they went down to the inn where Karantay took his meals.

July passed, a long, hot July, and August came in hot. Itale was still with Karantay. The novelist had pressed him to stay, and he had yielded easily, lacking any real wish to go out and find himself a room. The impermanence of the arrangement, Karantay's affectionate, reserved companionship, suited him. Companionship, friendship, he wanted very much, but he could not take hold here, he could not recommit himself to anything but his friends. He waited, irresolute, drifting, and increasingly tense, though his health continued to improve; taking comfort in being with Karantay, Brelavay, Sangiusto, and the others; waiting for alternate Mondays when the mail from the Montayna Diligence came in; waiting to decide where he was going to stay

305

in Krasnoy and whether he was going to stay in Krasnoy; waiting, he did not know for what.

George Helleskar was travelling in Germany, not due back for a few weeks. Itale had gone to pay his respects to the old count and had been received with emotion that was painful to him. The tough old man was over eighty now, and his invitation was pleading: "You could stay here, you know, I've lost count of the rooms standing empty. . . ." He asked about Luisa, and even mentioned Estenskar, whom he had never liked. "A bit of the real fireworks, that lad. One fine burst and it was over. He had the sense to know it, and not go sputtering on for fifty years, boring the cosmos. . . ."

"I wonder if most of us don't bore the cosmos," Itale said to Karantay as they strolled back through the Eleynaprade in the fag end of the warm evening.

"It's my profession," said the novelist. "Anyhow, I'd rather bore it than be bored by it."

A man in what had been a respectable coat came up to them begging; Itale talked with him a while. "That's a new trade for him," he said when the man had gone off with their small joint contribution. "How many out of work now? One of every three or four, I should think."

"Vernoy says the river-docks are working less than half the men this summer."

"So's the Assembly," Itale said with a glance at the Sinalya Palace looming pale and somber behind the splendid chestnut alleys.

"I wonder why the grand duchess has shut herself up in the Roukh."

"Afraid of demonstrations, Oragon says."

"The Sinalya is more vulnerable. I wonder what it is she really fears."

"Damned Austrian cow in the throne room of Egen the Great. She needs to be taught her place."

Karantay laughed. "You're fierce, lately."

"So's everyone else. It's hot. We're tired. My God! we're tired. Will it ever change? I came here five years ago. All that time—all my life, all our lives, Givan—since we were born, the net's been drawing tighter, the air's been getting staler, there's been less and less room to move. Europe is like a pond in drought, drying up. . . ."

"And the Austrian cattle drinking the last of the water," said Karantay. They walked on. An owl flew across the path in front of them from one oak to another, hunting, soft as a tossed ball of dark wool in the dusk.

Brelavay, who had taken over Itale's editorship of *Novesma Verba*, wanted to give it back to him, but Itale had temporised, and most of the others agreed with him that they had to be cautious: he was, after all, a convicted seditionist, and any public act put both himself and his collaborators at risk. He had drawn enough to live on out of the fund that Brelavay insisted was his back wages, but was not currently on the staff. He served, however, as an unpaid employe, along with Sangiusto, who was working as a very slightly paid reporter at the Assembly. Their reportership was more than anything else a test, to find if they could with impunity reconnect themselves with the journal. So the two of them sat in the gallery of the Assembly Room in the hot afternoons listening to the order of the day dragging on, in Latin, below them among the scanty ranks of the Eastern General. No other reporters ever bothered to attend; the *Courier-Mercury* got its list of motions direct from the president. Sangiusto and Itale allayed their boredom one afternoon by inventing the debates in the Egyptian National Dynastic Assembly of Both Kingdoms on August 11, 1830 B.C. —"*The President:* I recognise Mr Aphasis, the Deputy from Karnak. *Mr Aphasis:* My lords, gentlemen! Are we to credit the unsupported allegation of the honorable deputy from Ptu-upon-Nile that two wagonloads of perishable produce such as pullet-eggs and radishes and a small cart containing mummified cats were detained for sixty-two hours for examination at the West Gate of His Divine Highness' capital city? Is it positively known, can it be subject to material proof, that the pullet-eggs and radishes were rendered unfit for consumption and that the mummified cats deteriorated in quality due to the alleged detention for examination? . . ." Brelavay slipped their farce into *Novesma Verba*, signing it "Cheops," and the Censor passed it. It was the journal's last report of debates in the Assembly.

At the opening next day, Prime Minister Cornelius appeared on the rostrum to request adjournment of the Assembly until October, on the part of the Grand Duchess Mariya, whose indisposition, aggravated by the inclement weather, forbade her the study and exercise of judgment required for the sanction or veto of decrees voted by the Assembly convened by her gracious favor. The president, a rightwing noble, closed debate and adjourned the session, and as protest began from the left a concerted exit by the right took enough deputies out that the protesters lacked the quorum of seventy. It all took six or eight minutes. Itale and Sangiusto had to compare notes to be sure they knew what had occurred. They went off at once to the Cafe Illyrica with the news, but it had preceded them; men out of work wanted nothing better than a subject of talk, a subject of indignation. The closure of the parliament to which nobody had paid any attention drew the attention of the whole city. Itale and Sangiusto, themselves out of work again, wandered the hot, restless streets watching and listening. The park was full of people, as if it were some festival day. The City Watch had been posted at the gates of the Sinalya Palace, empty now at the end of its long chestnut-shaded mall. The Palace Guard were on duty at the Roukh, which stood tawny and dour over its square, baking in the August sun. Shops along Palazay Street between the two palaces were mostly closed and shuttered as if for holiday. Molsen Boulevard lay long and empty above the empty river; one barge came down, black in the blinding sun-glare, as Itale and Sangiusto strolled to the journal's office. Oragon was there, fresh from Court. All doors there, he said, were locked, all mouths shut. Only one rumor was afloat, that a courier had arrived last night from Vienna. But couriers were always arriving.

"The emperor's dead," said young Vernoy.

"Almighty Christ!" said Brelavay, "it's Metternich that's dead!"

"Impossible," said Sangiusto. "Metternich lives forever. Is the grand duchess perhaps really sick?"

Oragon, sitting sideways on the long composing-table, his coat off and his stock loosened, shook his big, rough head. "No sicker than yesterday. She was at mass this morning in Roukh Chapel. Cancer she may have. But that won't explain today's move." His voice with its slurring eastern accent dominated all others, and though he looked hot and baffled he was enjoying his power to dominate, to give answers, to force the respect of these selfwilled journalists who had lost confidence in him. He turned now as he always, instinctively, turned to the man in whom he sensed authority or symbolic value for the group, and spoke to him as deep unto deep. "What's the mood in the streets now, Sorde?"

"Do I know?" Oragon's knowingness jarred on Itale. "The same as the mood in here, I suppose. We're all in the same boat."

"It's the unemployed mobs they're afraid of," said young Vernoy with his sententious and irresistible self-assurance. "They've closed the Assembly because it's a potential rallying-center."

"Rallying about what?" said Brelavay. "Why the huggermuggering in the Roukh? Why have all the Ostriches put their heads in the sand?"

"Well, Vernoy must be right," Karantay said, "but why so abruptly? They've created the disturbance they were trying to avoid. It's not like Cornelius. His reasons must be pressing."

The discussion went round and round, moved on to the Illyrica, went on, got nowhere. Words and men came and went. It was nine o'clock. Itale's head ached; he sat gazing at his glass of beer, the drift of foam at the rim. He picked it up and drank it off, and as he set it down saw Oragon making his way among the tables to him. The deputy bent down and said in a low voice, "Come out of here a moment, Sorde."

"What's up?"

"I want a word with you."

He took Itale's arm and led him off across Tiypontiy Street, but he could not wait till they had got across the street into the park to speak. In the midst of passing traffic, in the dusty darkness broken by cab-lanterns, he said aloud, his face close to Itale's, "There's been a revolution in France. King Charles is dethroned. He went too far, violated the Charter—the city wouldn't take it, they fought in the streets— The Duke of Bordeaux will be made constitutional king."

They stood still amongst the horses, the rolling wheels.

"Is that it, then?"

"That's it. Charles tried to dissolve the Chamber of Deputies. Overshot his authority. He abdicated on the thirtieth of July. The fighting must have been over for twelve days now. The new king will be sworn to fealty to the Constitution. It's the end of absolute monarchy in France."

"The end," Itale repeated. The flashing darkness and noise of the traffic, the smell of dust and horse-sweat and hot stone, it was familiar, he knew these words, this moment.

"And the beginning—"

"Where did you find out?"

"Friend in Vienna, through a friend in Aisnar. You and I are among the dozen or so people in the whole country that know it." Itale was struck by Oragon's evident satisfaction as he said this, mixed with a kind of urgent confusion. Still gripping Itale's arm, the deputy went on, "What do we do with it—what do we do with it? It's a bombshell. Cornelius knows that. What do we do with it, Sorde?"

"Throw it. Let everybody know. That's what they're afraid of, isn't it? You announce it at the Illyrica. I'll get some fellows to print up something for the provinces." Itale laughed as he spoke. He felt that the moment was much too large for him, that the noise of hooves and wheels on cobblestones was the only convincing part of it; he and the rest of them were suddenly playing a role in history, and for this reason he felt artificial, like any private man up on a stage. At the same time it was, at last, easy to make decisions. The time had come. All one had to do at such a moment, when the walls fell down, was go ahead in the direction one had always tried to go.

Oragon was flustered and two-minded only because he had never had any one direction to his actions, any fidelity. Enormously ambitious, energetic, emotional, he lacked the necessary passion. But he was very quick. He caught Itale's meaning at once and wanted no more from him, having received his impetus. "All right, good. Here's the note from Vienna, with the details. Go to the press as fast as you can before they close it on us. I'll let the city know."

As Itale, Karantay, and Sangiusto left the Illyrica together they heard Oragon, up on one of the sidewalk tables, telling the news in his big slurring voice. "The French Revolution is accomplished. They've got the freedom they fought for forty years ago. The last Bastille is fallen! And their chance is ours. The same choice, the same chance! Is this France's victory and glory, or Europe's, ours? Will we sit quiet and let Metternich send more troops here to keep us quiet and suck us dry? I say recall the National Assembly, and Sovenskar to the throne of the free kingdom!" The traffic seemed to have halted, cab-lamps and cafe lanterns shining on many faces upturned to the orator: all things moveless, as things seen in a flash of lightning. The three men slipped away, hurried down dark streets towards the river.

IV

The short, warm, summer night went by full of the thump and rattle of the presses, shouting, laughter, orating. They printed up a news-sheet over the journal's name headed, in 72-point type, REVOLUTION. The shop was snowed under with it, it was all over the streets, men and horses were found to carry it to the provinces. It announced what they knew about the Paris revolution, and stated that the National Assembly was remaining in session to consider the urgent questions of relations with the new government of France, tax control, and succession to the throne of the kingdom. "Lots of fuses to that bomb," Brelavay said when he read it. He and Oragon had been about the city all night, going from one deputy's house to another to inform them that the Assembly would meet as usual at nine tomorrow. Leaving the printer's shop Itale went with him and Sangiusto to Cathedral Square, which had been the center of agitation during the night. In the cool of August dawn, under a high, cloud-brindled, colorless sky, the square looked immense and empty.

311

The cathedral stood indifferent as a mountain, intent only on holding up its ponderous, delicate towers and ranks of stone saints and kings. They went on to the Eleynaprade. Down the mall, one behind the other, stood the cavalry of the palace guard, the men sallow and sleepy on tall horses. Behind them on the lawns under the trees swarmed an aimless crowd, thousands of people drifting, dispersing, regathering. The constant movement and the low but immense sound of the voices of the crowd was improbable, bewildering, in the austere and indrawn hour of dawn.

Itale had meant to go on to Karantay's flat for a few hours' sleep, but stayed with the others in the crowd. Brelavay went to buy bread and cheese, since they were hungry. He went off and came back at a run, fearing something momentous would happen while he was gone ten minutes. The sky grew lighter, higher. Sunlight touched the crowns of the chestnuts. Nothing momentous had occurred but sunrise. It became a warm August morning. The crowd, grown enormous, now covered all the lawns beneath the grave, ignorant old trees. Itale and the other two had slowly pushed their way along the front of the crowd to the fence surrounding the gravelled area before the palace, and could see and hear the deputies of the left, gathered on the mall in front of the gates, arguing with officers of the guard. Itale was not paying much attention, as he was distracted by the increasing pressure and aimless turbulence of the crowd, and also was extremely sleepy.

"There's Livenne," Brelavay said. "Leftwing Noble from the Sovena."

"They talked about him there. He hasn't attended all month," Itale said, and yawned till his eyes watered and he could not see the big, fair, young man who was saying, "Herr Colonel, you have no authority to keep the gates locked. The Assembly Room belongs to the Assembly."

"Distinguished Sir, there has been no change in our orders," the colonel of militia said for the tenth time.

"You had best send to the Roukh Palace requesting a change in your orders, Herr Colonel," Livenne said loudly, and the crowd

312

pressed against the fence a few feet from him shouted in support.

Sangiusto nudged Itale: "Look, they catch two crows." Two clerical deputies who had come up the mall out of curiosity were trying to depart and found the crowd closed across their way and jeering. They hesitated and came back to join the forty or fifty liberal deputies waiting in front of the iron gates. More jeers and insults rang up and down the edges of the mall, now continuously walled with men; the guardsmen's horses shifted feet, one tossed its head up and down until controlled. There was a sudden outbreak of shouts and cheers, hats and caps flew up into the sunlight, a gig came rolling up the gravel of the mall between the tall horses and the crowd-walls. "Who is the little old man?" Sangiusto asked as the cheering broke out all around them.

"Prince Mogeskar. Matiyas Sovenskar's cousin. Nobilissimus. Took some courage to come here. —Long live Mogeskar!" Itale shouted, swept up by the crowd's enthusiasm. "Long live Mogeskar!" The prince got out of his gig, a pinched, brusque, neat, very old man, and said to Oragon and Livenne, "Good morning, gentlemen. Why are the palace gates shut in our faces?"—himself caught by the affronted, restless, lively temper of the crowd. But they waited. Ten o'clock struck on the deep bell of the cathedral. Eighty deputies stood on the sun-white gravel before the gates. Prince Mogeskar had invited an elderly priest to sit in his gig: "Hot work, this, for old men," he said, and sat on, stiff and speckless in the blazing light. Stefan Oragon was always near the gig, even held the horse made nervous by the crowd. He was heliotropic, drawn to power as if his own power of winning men was less a gift than a deficiency: he could not stand alone. Yet he knew far better than Mogeskar, or Livenne, or the colonel of the militia, what power was; he knew himself to be the focus of the crowd, the soul of this immense, conglomerate, temporary entity. When he chose to act, they would act.

Itale, bored, thirsty, and half-asleep, shifted from one foot to the other because both hurt. He was staring at the mansards of

313

the palace against the hazy sky, counting windows, when abruptly he felt himself lifted off his feet, picked up, and cried out, "What is it?" in a surge of excitement. He pushed and was pushed, they were no longer standing still, no longer waiting; he heard a guardsman bawling an order in German about the relief of every second man, and the men around him shouting, "What is it? They're going to fire!" Oragon was up above them all, up on one of the cannon that flanked the iron gates, shouting, pointing to the palace. The noise was unbelievable, he could not believe that mere men could make such a noise, yet through it he heard clearly a different sound: tat, tat, a remote, cross, spinsterish voice, and then the scream of a panicked horse. They were pushing, forcing, ground and sucked step by step out of sunlight, into booming corridors, marble underfoot, garlands of roses on the ceilings overhead. Then all at once the ceiling rose up very high, and there was air and room to breathe; they were in the Assembly Room. Itale found he was close armlinked with Sangiusto, and began to comprehend that he with the crowd had forced their way into the palace. Oragon was there, up on the platform shouting orders, trying to gather the deputies out of the mob. Itale rubbed his arms which were sore, rubbed sweat off his forehead, stared around him. "Let's get out of this, up to the gallery," he said, and found himself hoarse, as if he had been shouting for a long time; perhaps he had, he did not know. They tried to get to the side door that led to the reporters' gallery, but were stopped at once by a group coming in, men carrying heavy sacks. The sacks were put down beside the rostrum. The noise of voices in the huge room sank down steadily like waters at ebb. The rostrum was the center of the hush. With all the rest, Itale and Sangiusto came past, and saw that the sacks were dead men. The face of one of them had been shot off. His hands stuck out from his cuffs, stiff and posed, and his cracked shoes stuck up the same way. The ear was visible, normal, intact, a man's ear, just below the bright red porridge of the face. The other man, middle-aged, did not look dead, but lay there startled, with open eyes. Above that, at the rostrum, they saw a blond, young, strong face, Livenne's. He was speaking in a clear voice. "These two and the others killed paid a debt not owing. No more! We

314

are not buying our country but claiming it as our inheritance, ours by right. Remember that! There is no need for violence, no need for sacrifice. We are the creditors, not the debtors!" Tears ran down Itale's face as he stood there, then stopped as suddenly as they had started. He and the Italian began again to try to make their way to the side door and the gallery, but they never got there.

For six hours they stood side by side against the back wall of the Assembly Room while the Assembly, a hundred and thirty deputies among thousands of others, held session. They voted to speak their own language in debate, voted this and all decrees subject to validation by the king alone, voted congratulations in the nation's name to the new king of France, though they did not yet know who he was, the Duke of Bordeaux or Louis-Philippe of Orleans, and rumors now claimed Lafayette as the president of a new French republic. "They'll pick Louis-Philippe," Sangiusto said. "For a whole generation the old mushroom has been waiting, waiting. All things come to him who waits." Itale nodded, not listening. He listened with strained attention to each speaker but found it difficult to understand or remember what they said. Prince Mogeskar now had the floor. His brusque, precise voice trembled with effort and age. "I will give my allegiance to the House of the Sovenskars, as did my ancestors, and yours. I will do so with joy, when the time comes. But the time has not come. We can call Matiyas Sovenskar king but can we crown him? Can we defend him? Metternich will hear our requests, for he needs peace, but he will not listen to our defiance. We have not the strength to defy that power! For the king's own sake I beg you to wait in determination, not to act rashly!" And all this seemed clear and true to Itale, until Oragon and others replied and proved with equal clarity that the only hope lay in rapid action, the installation of Matiyas Sovenskar on the throne before Austria could intervene. Fait accompli, bloodless revolution, fatal procrastination, Austrian troops, uprising of all Europe, the words spun round, and all the time the point of all the words was incomprehensible, was missing. It was five o'clock. Itale startled himself awake from a momentary standing doze and said, "Let's get out of here, Francesco." Again they did not get where they were headed. A deputation from the Roukh Palace had just come in: a dozen palace guards, Raskayneskar the minister of finance, and the prime minister. Cornelius went towards the rostrum, spoke to Livenne and Oragon, smiled his pleasant, bland smile. "Gentlemen, thank you for permitting me to interrupt your debate. I bear a message to you from the sovereign. Her Grace regrets the disappointment caused by the adjournment of session of the National Assembly and, attentive to the wishes of her people, will tomorrow request the reconvocation of the Assembly on Monday next. She has asked me to notify the present gathering that fraternal greetings have been sent to King Louis-Philippe of France, and to thank them for their share in maintaining law and order in the city during the day, trusting that such order will continue without incident, and that the—"

"Without incident? What about the men shot down this morning?"

The interruption from the floor set off a roar of voices, a surge towards the platform, checked by Oragon shouting out, "This is not a gathering, this is the Assembly of the Nation! Tell the duchess that until King Matiyas reaches Krasnoy the sovereign is here, in this hall! Tell her that peace and order depend on her submission to us, the government of the kingdom!"

Cornelius looked at him, looked around, and shrugged. "This is simply folly," he said. He turned to go, and because he was decisive and the crowd was more intent upon the speaker, he got out, with the chalk-faced Raskayneskar and the dozen guardsmen. "The die is cast!" Oragon was roaring; the hall seethed fantastically in turmoil, frenzy. "Come along, come along," Sangiusto said, and this time they got out, and stood dazed outside the palace in the still, clear evening air.

At midnight Itale was standing in the darkness on Ebroiy Street a block from Roukh Square, sucking one of his fingerjoints that had been scraped raw in handling cobblestones, and carefully studying the torchlit barrier that had been raised across the street where it debouched into the square. Two men near him were arguing in a dreary, savage monotone; he could not distinguish one voice from the other: "Three thousand militia three miles down river at Basre— We've got the Roukh cut off— Count on the militia joining us— Who says they will, they've got the guns— The guns—" Still nearer him two women sat on the curbstone, one suckling a baby, and they spoke now and then: "So then I told him, I forgot the eggs, I told him . . ." — "Oh aye, mother of God, what can you do at a time like this?" One sighed, one laughed, "Save up and wait, I told him! . . ." Men ran by up the street, followed by a queer hollow roaring sound. A group of thirty or more came pulling and pushing a black thing up the street towards the barricade, a cannon. The iron wheels made a gobbling roar on the stones, torches flared around making the shadows lurch and fly. Itale looked down in the torchlight. The baby was very young; its head, lying on the mother's bare arm, was unbelievably small. After the cannon had gone by he could hear the small smacking noises the baby made in sucking, the women's dry easy voices, "So I says Oh don't tell me, you old sow, I didn't hatch out last week," and the men arguing, "The streets— The guns—" He went on up the street to the barricade and rejoined Sangiusto there.

It took a long place to get the cannon in place and the barrier rebuilt around it. Men kept coming to see it, to give advice on loading and firing it, to touch it. Of all the men behind the Ebroiy Street barricade one in twenty-five or thirty had a gun. Most of the *Novesma Verba* men were there, but not Karantay; some said he was still with the Assembly, others that he was on the Gulhelm Street barricade. Itale clambered up to the slanting top of the barrier over the cannon and looked down on Roukh Square. In the uneasy dimness of torches, stars, windowlight from the palace, the big cobbled square sloped slightly downward from the iron palisades of the palace, empty. It was empty all night.

Several men pulled up a couple of the mattresses laid as shot-stoppers on the barricade till they could lie down on them. Sangiusto and Itale lay side by side, their chins on their arms, watching the palace. It was about forty hours since they had had any sleep. At long intervals they spoke to each other.

"What's that?"

On the next barricade north, Palazay Street, there was something going on, something was being set up or put in place.

"Got another cannon."

"No, it sticks up into the air."

They could not make out what it was in the uncertain torchlight. Itale put his head down on his arms. He dreamed and waked in starts and waking did not know what he had dreamed; it was like being in a small boat on quiet water, trailing a hand over the edge so that sometimes the waves touch it sometimes not, one does not know if one is touching air or water. Vernoy climbed up beside them. He shook Itale gently, offered him something, bending down his tired, pleasant young face. He had come by a hatful of apples down in the Ghetto. They all sat up and munched apples, were cheered by eating, talked a little.

"What d'you think they'll do come daylight, Sorde?"

"Wait."

"I think they'll try to blow us up."

"The whole city? They'll do better to wait for the militia. Apple, Francesco?"

But Sangiusto had gone back to sleep.

"Not long till light, now," Itale said softly, and then they were all silent for a long time. Northwest over the roofs a pink glow flickered, faded, flickered again, a fire that had got out of hand; there had been a lot of burning in the Old Quarter and other districts. The pink glow faded. The few lighted windows of the Roukh looked wan. Itale looked up: the sky was grey, it was dawn. He woke wide awake, turned over and sat up on the steep-set mattress, looking eastward over Ebroiy Street that dropped away sharply downhill and over the Ghetto lying many-roofed, jumbled, shadowy, between the barricade and the river. To the left rose the Hill of the University, on the far side of which he had used to live. There on the highest point in the city, the cross on the spire of the university chapel, light struck, trembled, steadied; gold crept down the spire, down chimneystacks and roofs of houses crowded rank above rank on the hill. He turned again and saw the battlements of the palace tawny red, alive

318

against the dead blue-grey of the western sky. It was a fine summer morning. He was no longer tired, only very hungry, and though he was excited his thoughts no longer rushed but came simple, detached, concrete: thoughts of what the men in the besieged palace were probably planning, thoughts of people out in the suburbs going about their business and wondering what was going on inside the city, thoughts of what it would be like to be shot down in the street, the stones against his hands and face. He loved Krasnoy, he loved the steep shadowy roofs beneath which people still lay asleep, the sunlit hill, the old palace fierce red in the sunlight, the streets and the stones of the streets. It was his city; his people; his day. "I wish I could shave," he said aloud, and Sangiusto nodded and yawned. They stood up, stretching, and balanced on the crown of the barricade between the fortress and the risen sun. With the act of standing up the simplification, the clarification of thought and feeling was perfected. Itale was completely happy, standing there empty-handed beside his friend in the indifferent calm of the morning. He had nothing left in the world but the day's light, no weapon, no shelter, no future. It was for this he had lived and waited. Almost tenderly he thought of the soldiers sweating inside their stone walls there; what was there to worry about? It was the break of day, and standing up there he could have crowed like a cock at daybreak, in pure joy, in celebration of the light.

He glanced at his friend and said, with his hands in his pockets, smiling irrepressibly, "Do you believe in God, Francesco?"

"Of course. Don't you?"

"No. Thank God!"

Sangiusto shook his head. He was exhilarated but not exultant, being busy with a premonition amounting to certainty that he was going to get killed today. Freedom was freedom, and often enough he had honestly wished for the privilege of such a death, and yet now it came to the point he was bitter that he could not die for his own country, on his own ground; he was homesick.

"The light shineth in the darkness," Itale sang aloud, "and the darkness comprehendeth it not!" Sangiusto laughed at the words

319

and the cockcrow tune. Brelavay climbed up beside them, looked around, sat down and took off his shoe. "Had a rock in here all night," he explained. "Look at that hole in my stocking."

"You ought to marry. Get your stockings darned."

"Not till I can marry a countess, like young Liyve," Brelavay said, cocking his sharp, dark face up at Itale. "Or a baroness at least."

"She won't darn your stockings. Look there!"

On the Palazay Street barricade a long pole had been set up, and on it hung, almost unmoving in the quiet air, a red and blue flag. All the men looked at the flag. None of them had seen it raised for eighteen years. Most were too young to remember ever having seen it.

"I'm going round to see if Karantay's at Gulhelm Street," Brelavay said. Itale stopped him as he started to climb down: "Listen, if you find Givan tell him we should all try to meet tonight— At the *Verba* office, I suppose."

"That's no good if things go badly."

"At Helleskar's, then. All right?"

"That should do. See you in half an hour. Don't wait breakfast for me!" Brelavay went off, the others stood talking, waiting. A third of Roukh Square now was sunlit.

Since he could not cross the square Brelavay had to make a long semicircle to get round to Gulhelm Street; coming up it, two blocks from the square, he ran into a crowd: civilians surrounding men in uniform. Brelavay could see the white and gold of militia uniforms, but could not make out how many soldiers there were. Evidently a detachment had been sent from the garrison at Basre to make contact with the Roukh guards. A lieutenant and a captain argued with the chiefs of the barricade; the men around Brelavay were pushy and restless, crowding in thicker every moment, itching to get their hands on the soldiers' guns. They shouted at their spokesmen and at the officers. There was an effort to clear a passage down the street, away from the palace, and Brelavay heard one of the barricade chiefs, a workingman in his forties, telling the captain with exasperation and despair, "Get your men out now, get them out!" The captain took offense. "We shall march on to the palace," he said in his

German accent, and turned to give the order. Brelavay was knocked right off his feet and carried forward some way, suffocated by the pressure of the mob, kicking out like a horse and grabbing for any support. What he had hold of when the pressure lessened was a militiaman's shoulder strap. He and the soldier stared at each other, their frightened faces six inches apart, while a tremendous continuous noise and the rocking, swaing pressure they were caught in confused them both. "They're firing," the soldier said, staring at Brelavay. He tried to break away, and as he did Brelavay wrenched the musket out of his hands. Using the gunstock as a ram to clear his way, he got out of the thick of the crowd. "I've got a gun, by God!" he yelled in triumph. He saw nobody to shoot at, and presently it occurred to him that he had no powder and shot. There was no more firing, the mob was scattering. What had happened, what had become of the troop of soldiers, Brelavay did not understand. He saw men lying on the street, a dozen or more of them; there were white uniforms. There was the captain's gold braid on a body crushed together like a crumpled rag, beaten to death and trampled. Brelavay stood staring at that terrible body. The crowd was streaming on up Gulhelm Street towards the barricade. They would have ammunition. He ran after them in a state of wild excitement, shouting, as several others were shouting, "Wait!"

On the Ebroiy Street barricade, they had heard from the left the small dry sound of shots and then a dull roar like flooding water heard far off; then they saw a confused dark tide come boiling up over the Gulhelm Street barrier and into Roukh Square, now white with sunlight. As the crowd spread into the square it thinned and looked sparse, aimless, like grasshoppers jumping in stubble, Itale thought, but it was hard not to join them, as other barricades began to spill over and feed running men back into the square. At the same time he was yelling, "Keep back! Keep back!" to the men who after waiting all night in the streets had heard gunfire and noise and pressed forward trying to see or get onto the square. "Keep back, keep the line!" His teeth jarred together and he thought he was falling. "What was that?" he said to Sangiusto and then realised that the cannon, almost under his feet, had been fired. "Too much powder," Sangiusto was growling in the smoke. Young Vernoy pushed between them, leapt down from the barricade, and vanished into the mob that now swarmed black across the square and against the iron fence around the palace. Another man tried to do the same but Itale blocked his way and pushed him back and down with all his strength. "Keep back, damn you, hold the barricade!" he shouted in fury, turning constantly to see what was happening in the square. The mob at the iron fence seethed, scaling it, swarming over it, smashing the gates, jamming at the palace doors. "They're in!" men shouted, and now Itale crouched ready to jump down, to join, he could not hold himself back any longer. But as he paused there the whole scene seemed to pause. Little puffs of smoke which had appeared a moment ago at the windowslits of the palace were evaporating quickly in the sunlit air. The enormous steady crowd-roar continued the same, but there was some change in the crowd's motion, a swaying and scattering, men still pouring in from the barricades but also a counter-movement, a press back towards the barricades, heavy and disordered, under the white puffs of smoke. Then there was a noise that seemed to stop everything so that Itale crouched motionless, paralysed: the cannons of the Roukh. Nothing now but clambering men around him, men running, and the monstrous, endless sound. Then it ceased and he heard human voices again and saw the square emptied out. The crowds had shrunk away into separate swarms at each barricade; at the iron fence and on the sloping cobblestones men were lying down here and there as if waiting for something. Around the heads of some of these were streaks and blotches of bright red, and a man that came clambering up the barricade at Itale had a great smear of the same red stuff, like paint, over half his face and in his hair. "Leave your guns here at the barricade," Sangiusto was saying, quiet as a butler taking coats, and several of the fugitives who had muskets handed them obediently to him. "Here, here, take it," he was telling Itale, and Itale took the gun and shotbag. Red coats, of that same bright paint color, now appeared filing rapidly out of the doors of the palace, which hung open like a black mouth. Sangiusto lay down on their mattress and loaded his gun, aimed it, and fired it; reloaded, aimed, fired. Itale

322

imitated him, but had trouble with his gun, an Austrian army musket; he had never shot anything but a hunting-piece. Presently he lowered the loaded gun, got up, and said, "Come on, Francesco."

"Why?"

"They've gone over the Palazay Street barricade, they'll be coming around behind us. Let's head down toward the river."

They started down Ebroiy Street.

Brelavay had lost his gun and been knocked down twice getting out of Roukh Square. He was now on a rooftop overlooking Palazay Street midway between the Roukh and the Sinalya, along with six other men and a heap of paving-blocks and furniture. The throng below were all civilians, angry after panic but aimless in their anger; the palace guard had turned east and south to isolate the barricades and join up with the militia. Brelavay scanned the crowd constantly, looking for a short dark man and two tall ones, Karantay, Sorde, Sangiusto. They could be anywhere. They could be lying dead on Roukh Square. He was sore, sick, and wrathful. A dozen times he thought he saw one of their faces, then lost it or saw it was a stranger's. A spatter of gunfire from the south; he listened and watched. If he believed those three were dead he would give up, run, run home. He looked about the quiet rooftops in the morning sunshine, hating the impassioned, hysterical city, the crowds below him. If Sorde and Karantay were dead he would as soon throw himself over with the paving-blocks they had carried up here to dump on the soldiers when they came by. It was not hope that kept him there, in control of himself and of his little rooftop mob; it was the thought of his friends. He had a hopeful spirit, but deeper in him than any conviction lay loyalty, and on that bedrock, obstinate and ironic, he waited.

Hooves were clattering by on Ebroiy Street, while Itale and Sangiusto stood in the darkness inside an arched doorway in the courtyard of a tenement block. The squad passed by, going up the street towards the Roukh. As Sangiusto and then Itale came out of hiding a stooped young woman appeared in the court, two little children huddling close to her. She stood still, looking at them.

323

"Can you give us water?" Itale said.

She nodded, returned in silence with the children to a dark staircase, and came back with a dipper so that the two men could drink from the covered well in the courtyard. She stood watching them, her face quiet, and when Itale thanked her she said, "Go to Mendel's, the butcher's, the men have gone there." So they went, and found in the yard behind a kosher butcher shop, under silent shuttered tenements and the blank back wall of a synagogue, a couple of dozen Jews planning the Ghetto's part in the insurrection. They were calm and methodical. One, a man in his thirties with beautiful weary eyes, dominated the discussion by natural authority and because he had a good supply of powder and shot for their empty guns. Itale heard him called Moyshe, and called him so, never learning his last name. Under his direction they occupied a block of rooftops on Ebroiy Street. Presently a file of the red-coated guards appeared coming down from the Roukh, on shining restive horses. The men on the roofs opened fire, a dry clatter of cracks and bangs, foolish and exciting to hear as firecrackers. There was shouting, horses galloped, others with empty saddles neighed, ran down the street, stopped with their reins dragging and looking nervously, peaceably around. In the pause that followed Itale said to Moyshe beside him, "Where did you come by all this ammunition?"

"Last night, when we burned the old armory on Gelde Street."

"What are you in this for, Moyshe?"

"Because where we stand any change is for the better," the Jew said, tapping his flask to loosen the packed powder. He glanced aside at Itale. "I could ask, what are you in this for?"

"I like the open air."

"It's a game to you."

"No. It's not a game."

"Eight," Sangiusto said, counting the men they had killed in the firecracker burst. His mouth was tense and he squinted a little, so that he did not look like himself.

Far up at the head of the street where the mounted troop had retreated, on the broken barricade, several small figures had appeared. One raised a megaphone and they heard a thin, bawling voice: "Lay down all the weapons and proceed to your houses . . . four hours . . . proceed to your . . . general amnesty is granted for four hours . . ." Shots were fired from a rooftop, the small figures vanished.

During the morning the Ghetto was not cut off, and men came through constantly with news of fighting on Palazay Street and around the Eleynaprade. For a long time after noon nothing moved on the streets below Moyshe's group, no one came from north or south. They waited, and their isolation became more and more certain and unbearable, driving them to reconnoiter recklessly, to try to provoke attack. Roukh Square was now full of militiamen from the garrison downriver, and evidently was supplying troops to the northern part of the city. Moyshe's group at last worked their way back to the rooftops over the barricade and began shooting. The troops got below them and fired the houses on the north side of Ebroiy Street. The wooden tene- ments burned like haystacks. Women, the women who had been in hiding all day in the courts and rooms, ran out into the street, threw their belongings from windows; as they ran down the plank stairways, the insurgents passed children huddled waiting on the landings, and Moyshe paused to call some urgent question to an old man, who for answer only shook his fist at them and cursed them with impotent hatred. They ran on, out of the buildings, across the sun-bright, crowded street, full of men and women, scared horses, broken bedsteads, falling beams of fire. Moyshe led them in and out of the warren of the Ghetto, coming back always to one place or another on Ebroiy Street, now deserted, scoured by troops of the mounted guards, where they could hold up for a while at the windows of deserted rooms and shoot; but their shot was running out. There were always fewer of them at each run for cover, and in the last they scattered; only Itale and Sangiusto kept together, following Moyshe, and ran straight into a squad of militia, face to face, before any of them had time to lift a gun and fire. They clubbed their muskets, fought through, ran under fire, dodged into a house, through a courtyard, ending up in the butcher's shop from behind which they had started that morning. They were not pursued. They waited there in hiding. Sounds from the street grew fewer, quieter. An hour went by. Itale got up from his

325

crouching half-doze and went to the door of the shop. It was evening. The sky was clear greenish-blue at the upper end of the street, where he could see the squat north tower of the Roukh. Gutted façades of houses across the way stared calmly at nothing. The air was smoky, warm, and sweet. At his feet lay a bundle of clothing and an old shoe, dropped by a family fleeing the fire.

"It looks like it's over," he said.

Sangiusto, then Moyshe, came out beside him. In the last encounter a soldier had brought a riflebutt down on Sangiusto's hand, and the Italian sat down now on the curbstone holding the injured hand against his thigh with a soft groaning curse. Moyshe went off to look at the body of an insurgent lying down the street near a dead soldier; he turned the head gently so that he could see the face, shrugged, came back.

"Now what," said Itale. "Now where."

"To the devil," Sangiusto said in Italian. His hand, already badly swollen, hurt increasingly, he was sick at heart, he had not been shot down and killed but had to go on, go through it all over again, the long exile. "Oh what a bitch of a life!" he growled, this time in Piedmontese, and with his left hand whacked the butt of his empty gun on the stones of the street.

"Home," Moyshe said with his shrug. "And you?"

Itale stood silent.

"You're welcome to come with me," the Jew said coldly, ready for the rebuff.

"Thank you," Itale said, turning to look at him. After this day he knew this man's face and voice and fine stern eyes as if he had known them all his life, better than he might ever know any other face, but there was nothing between them but trust—everything, nothing. There was nothing left for them to say. "We have to try to find our group," Itale said. They parted with constrained words of farewell.

Itale and Sangiusto set off for Helleskar's house, around the Hill of the University, through River Quarter, past the cathedral and across its square, a dream walk, very long, through the red sunset, the dusk. They went tentatively at first, later they walked

326

boldly. They were not halted even by the militia posted in Cathedral Square. Troops of mounted guards passed clattering, foot patrols of the city guard were posted here and there, but not in very much greater number than usual; the streets were emptier than usual, but not empty, there were other men in ones and twos walking, silent and not loitering. No women. A city without women. Itale and Sangiusto talked as they went, sometimes quite coherently, discussing probable causes of the apparent amnesty, trying to construct some idea of what had gone on during the two days of insurrection, what might have happened in the Eleynaprade while they were in the Ghetto, what condition the Assembly was now in. Itale was talkative, made jokes to cheer Sangiusto up, and once remarked, "Well, work's certain and reward's seldom . . ." In Sorden Street he asked what day it was, and as they crossed Roches Street he asked it again. "The fourteenth," Sangiusto repeated.

"I asked you that before, didn't I?"

"Yes."

"How's your hand?"

"Like a fire."

"It's not far now. We could . . ." He stopped himself. He had been about to say that perhaps they could stop a minute and rest, and that was foolish, with only two blocks left to walk. He stumbled. "We can stop," Sangiusto said, his face drawn askew again. "No, it's just up the street," Itale said, "with any luck Tomas will be there already." He thought he had said that before too, and gave up talking. They came to the big, stately house, went under the portal with its coats of arms and caryatids, knocked, and were admitted by the liveried servant. They were crossing the salon to the library, where the lonely old man rose eager and alarmed to meet them, when Itale reached out for his companion's arm, stumbled again, and pitched down in a faint. Sangiusto, not in much better condition himself, was utterly dismayed, alone among strangers; he fell on his knees beside Itale and tried to wake him, whispering in despair, "Listen, my dear, my friend, listen to me . . ."

V

The next afternoon Sangiusto came into Itale's room with a special edition of the *Courier-Mercury*, a single sheet printed— since the government presses had been burned on the night of the thirteenth—on some commandeered press, perhaps *Novesma Verba*'s. The paper contained no news from Paris, nothing about suspension or reconvocation of the Assembly, nothing directly about any event of August thirteenth and fourteenth; only a bulletin, dated the twelfth, of the grand duchess' request to the Estates General, and a police notice to certain individuals considered illegal residents of the capital, who were hereby ordered to depart the Molsen Province by noon of the 16th August 1830, after which time if found in the City or Province they would be liable to arrest and imprisonment as conspirators against the Government of the Grand Duchy. There followed in smudged, badly set print a list of sixty-three names. Sangiusto read them out, hesitating and squinting, his foreign accent very noticeable. "Breve, Givan Alexis. Rasenne, Luke. Yagove, Pier Mariye. Brelavay, Tomas Alexis. Fabbre, Raul. Frenin, Givan—"

"They're out of date," Itale remarked.

Sangiusto went on, twenty or more names Itale knew as acquaintances and some he did not know at all, then, "Oragon, Stefan Mariye."

"Oragon! And the first deputy. Is Livenne on the list?"

"Count Helleskar has heard that Livenne was killed on Palazay Street."

"Go on."

"Palley, Tedor. Palley, Salvate. Vernoy, Roch. Sorde, Itale. Eklesay, Matiyas Mark. Chorin-Falleskar, George Andre."

"Another deputy."

Sangiusto finished reading the list. There was a pause.

"Karantay is not on it," he said.

"No."

The old count had kept his servants out collecting what news they could and bringing it to him and his two refugees. Karantay was said to have been seriously hurt in the fighting on Palazay Street; there was no report at all of Brelavay or young Vernoy.

"Even Oragon under ban," Itale said. "That's a blow." He spoke rather unnaturally. He was sitting up in bed, one of the mighty beds of the Helleskar house, with great goosefeather coverlets and curtains like the stage curtain of the Opera. He looked haggard and meager, as if he had lost weight again and even height.

"You should get out of Krasnoy at once," Sangiusto said. "There will be no pardons henceforth."

"If only I could get some word of Brelavay."

"He will be in hiding or in jail. You can't wait to hear of him. You have only twenty-four hours."

"Will you come with me?"

"I'm not on this list."

"You may be on another."

"Almost certainly I am." Sangiusto spoke with composure. "I'll wait a little," he said, "until all is quieter, and then go back to France."

"I'm going home. Come with me. For a while at least."

"Thank you my friend. At a better time, when hospitality is not dangerous to the hosts, I shall come with great pleasure."

"As a favor to me. You can't try to cross the border now. You can get to France later when things have quieted down. Of course you'll want to go there, it's all over here, there's nothing for you to stay here for, but it's not safe to try to leave the country now. You can lie low in the mountains a while. We came out of this together. If I can keep you from getting arrested it's one thing I can do, there's nothing else. Let me—"

"Very well, I will come with you," Sangiusto broke in on the accelerating rush of words. Itale stopped, drew in his breath, and said, "Good."

They were silent a while. Sangiusto was profoundly relieved, but could not express his relief.

"If the stages are running as usual, the Southwestern Post leaves every second Friday, and the Aisnar Post the next Saturday. This is what, the fifteenth? It would be the Post this

329

week. Three days to wait, then, and I don't think we can wait here."

Sangiusto shook his head.

"We can walk."

"How far is it?"

"Not much over a hundred miles."

"But we must start at once, to be outside this province tomorrow."

Sangiusto's injured hand had been bound up, and the arm put in a light sling to help immobilise it.

"You can't walk a hundred miles with that," Itale said in self-disgust, looking at the sling.

"Oh, I think so. But you, I think you're not well enough, Itale."

"The count will lend us horses to Fontanasfaray. Ten miles or so. It's in the Perana. We can walk from there, or wait there for the coach."

"Good. Have you any money?"

They stared at each other.

"I have some change, I think."

"In my room at the inn I have a few kruner, but I don't want to go there, it is a risk."

"No, don't go there. The count will lend us enough to get home with. My God! what a fool I am." Itale rubbed his hands over his face and his still short, rough hair with a laugh. The danger, the absurdity, and the hopelessness of his situation were, at this moment, both clear and meaningless to him. The important thing, just now, was that he not lose this friend, this brave amiable man, along with all the rest and the others lost: that Sangiusto not be arrested. This was as far as his mind would go. He could consider his own risk only in terms of Sangiusto's, incapable of directly facing the possibility of himself being rearrested, reimprisoned.

He had no hesitation at all asking Count Helleskar for the loan of horses and money, and he joked with the old man, who was reluctant to let his refugees go. Old Helleskar longed to defy the entire Austro-Hungarian Empire to trouble the guests of his house. He argued that neither of them was fit to travel, and that the police would never look for them "here under an old soldier's roof." —"Discretion is the entire extent of my valor, count," Itale said. "We'll run while the running's good. Tell George, when he comes home, I think he'll applaud my variety of valor." Itale had got up in the late afternoon and dressed in the worn clothes, the old blue coat, that were now his sole possessions. He held himself very straight, to convince Helleskar and himself of his fitness. From time to time he wondered at how he managed to stand up and walk, when he felt so deathly tired, how he arrived at decisions when he could not keep two ideas in order in his head, how he talked and laughed when all the time there was in the back of his throat the tightness of unpermitted tears. From moment to moment he expected this specious vigor to run out, in which case he would no doubt fall flat on his face as he had done last night; and he wished earnestly that he could give up, cast it from him as one tosses away a pebble, and lie down, and rest. There was no more use in it; no point; no direction. But it made no difference. His thoughts and acts stayed chained to that rock of identity, of single unmoved unreasoning will, the will to remain himself.

Once their course was decided he and Sangiusto had agreed that promptness would best serve both their own interest and their host's; so he rode, with Sangiusto and a couple of Helleskar grooms, down Tiypontiy Street, past the trees of the park and the silent Sinalya Palace, past the coachyard at West Gate, past the hotel where he had met Luisa, past the tenements and through the northwestern suburb, out onto the plain that lay dun and gold in the light of summer evening, and on towards the hills. From the road above Kolonnarmana they looked back at the city on the curve of the river, a faint scattering of points of light in the wide grey twilight, so delicate it seemed one could take it up in the hand like a piece of silver gauze. They rode on, upward. Remote in the sky over bare hilltops the crescent moon hung for a while. It had set when they reached Fontanasfaray. The air here, a thousand feet above the river valley, was cool. Gulhelm Street was lit softly with colored lanterns, fantastic among tree-shadows. A few strollers passed, open carriages rolled by. They put up at the first inn they came to. "It looks

331

expensive," Itale said, but Sangiusto said, "We will find one cheaper tomorrow," and he did not argue. He had noticed as he rode that his horse's ears seemed at times far off, yards away, and at other times very near; the same was true of the stars, which now drew off together in a clump in the enormous, barren sky, and now came up so close that he felt the cold prickle of their fire under the skin of his forehead and cheeks, a troubling sensation.

They were given a room under the eaves, the only room he had free, said the innkeeper; the resort was full of vacationers escaping the heat of the city. "Yes, it is quite warm in Krasnoy," Sangiusto said.

As soon as the man left, Itale lay down and closed his eyes. Sangiusto, in intense discomfort from his injured hand, swore a little; he asked some question, but Itale did not answer. He was not asleep yet, and wanted to speak to Sangiusto, but could not speak. He was nearly asleep, and comfortable enough now that he could lie down; only very deep within him, at the depth below dream, the depth where he had lived for two years of solitary confinement, something remained stone-hard, mute, in anguish. Everything was over, finished, gone; only nothing was finished, nothing was done, and he must go on—go back, go home, into exile. He lay still and saw before him in the darkness of his closed eyes the great, quiet slopes of the mountains above the reflecting lake.

PART SEVEN

Malafrena

I

When the Aisnar Post was on time, which it sometimes was, it came into Erreme, a junction point, at about four in the morning, some twenty hours out of Krasnoy. Passengers for Aisnar need only be roused by the changing of horses and then went on as before, briskly, over level roads; passengers for the Montayna had to get out in the cold darkness or colder dawn and change to the waiting Montayna Diligence. If they were new to the journey they looked at the outlandish vehicle and asked with misgiving, "Is this the Portacheyka coach?" If they had previously travelled in the southwest they merely sighed and made ready to endure. Four shaggy horses, short in the barrel and powerful of shoulder, were in the traces; a boy of nine or ten with a shapeless hat and a contemptuous eye mounted the wheeler; a tall dark man whose mouth seemed to have rusted shut, letting out only monosyllables in a flat unanswerable voice, got onto the box and said not "Get up!" but "Hoy!" to the horses, and off the Montayna Diligence would go, jouncing and jolting on a rutted road, its back to the sunrise, towards the mountains that rose blue and forbidding from the retreating night.

335

On the morning of August twentieth, four passengers made the change, stumbling through the half-light from the big coach to the smaller one amongst horses being led about, mailbags being transferred, and other obscure hurlyburly. "Is this the Portacheyka coach?" one of the four, a young woman, asked the driver with misgiving. "Aye," he said flatly. Sangiusto handed her in and soon they were off, with a snarl from the coachman's horn, a shout of "Hoy!" and a groaning protest from every joint of the vehicle, soon to be echoed silently in every joint of three of the passengers. The fourth one was under two years old, and light enough to find the jolts and lurches entertaining. The young mother and Sangiusto promptly went to sleep again; Itale and the baby waked. The baby played with the bundles piled round him and with bits of straw from the floor that had got within his reach; he gazed about him often with a thoughtful and unhappy air, but made no complaint. The air was misty grey and very cold. Itale sat huddled, his collar up round his ears and his hands in his pockets. Ever since St Lazar, where he had suffered from cold more than from any other misery, he felt cold easily, and dreaded it, but had no resistance to it. So he sat now huddled up trying to keep his teeth from chattering. To keep his mind off his discomfort he watched steadily out the narrow slit of front window, through which he could see the wheelboy's hat and the sky and, when the road turned that way, a glimpse of peaks ahead. Day came fast. Now the round hills to either hand brightened with the morning sun, the clear light of a harvest day in the high country. The hay was long since in, the grain coming in; the fields far off on the hillsides Itale would see a line of mowers, the tiny glint of lifted sickles. When they passed through villages or past estates, small freeholds with the house set near the road, white and red hens cackled away from the wheels, dogs ran out and barked till the coach was out of earshot. Over the hills in the sun sometimes a hawk circled, lazy in the dry blue air. Ahead, seen only at the crests of the long climbs, the mountains rose up from behind the yellow hills.

Itale remembered how, years ago now, he had pulled out his watch to check the hour that he first lost sight of those mountains; nine-twenty of a September morning it had been, he

336

recalled the hour though not the date. He had been on his way to Solariy. And from Solariy, in time, to Krasnoy. And to Aisnar, and to Esten, and to Rakava; to the dark cold room where he had been chained to the wall; to Roukh Square at dawn, and Ebroiy Street in the smoky evening. And now he was come round full circle and even so did not know where he was going, or where was any place he could with a clear heart call home. He felt for his watch, but did not have it; he thought he had lost it, then remembered that since it no longer ran he had left it in his room at Karantay's flat. The police probably had it again by now. Let them have it, he thought.

Sangiusto sighed in his sleep. Though a farrier in Fontanasfaray had set and splinted his hand it continued to give him a great deal of pain, and he slept when he could. Propped up in the corner across from him the young mother also slept, her childish, round face curiously stern. Her child beside her had slid down uncomfortably among the bundles and was looking unhappier. Itale looked away from the child guiltily. It was going to cry, and it would be up to him, being awake, to do something about it. Sure enough the baby gave a series of gasps, preliminary to the howl. He looked very sad and helpless. He stared straight at Itale and gasped more loudly. Itale returned his look, uneasily, and said in a low tone, "Don't do that. You'll wake up your mother." The eyes filled immediately with tears, the small face went all into folds, and the baby gave a piteous wail. "Damn!" Itale said, and reached across, picked the baby out of the nest of bundles, and set him on his knees. He was startled at the lightness and fragility of the burden. Really there was not much to a baby.

The baby gasped a couple of times, then settled down with a sigh like a tiny echo of Sangiusto's, put his thumb in his mouth, and fell to playing with a button of Itale's coat. What did the mother call him? Stasio. "Stasio's father died," she had said to someone in the Aisnar coach last night, "in June, the consumption it was." Itale felt a touch on his hand, the faint brush of the child's hand. Not the young man's name nor "my husband," but "Stasio's father"; all the dead man's life was that now, his fatherhood. Stasio discovered the top button of Itale's waistcoat and fingered it delicately as a miser with a jewel; he sucked his thumb and slowly, with many starts and little movements, dropped his head down against Itale's coat and fell asleep. He had been cold, Itale thought, he was warmer now, in the shelter of Itale's arm, and could sleep. Itale no longer gazed ahead at the hills but down at his little, transitory charge. The child's hair was brown, very fine. Itale touched it very lightly, thinking of his friend Egen Brunoy; Brunoy's hair had been brown like this but coarse and dry. Itale tried to recall Brunoy's face, but could not. He could rouse no reality of memory, only a dull regret and a dull shame. He thought of Isaber, and his mind as always flinched away. He thought of Frenin, of Karantay who was hurt or dead or jailed; but from that too his mind flinched away, to Brelavay, but the thought of Brelavay in the dark cold room, chained, was unendurable—his hands clenched, and he had to control his sudden tension lest he waken the sleeping child. But the list would be finished. Amadey, dead. And then last, and unexpected for he had never thought of her as a friend among his friends, Luisa: unkind, unforgiving and un-self-forgiving, loyal: and like the others, self-betrayed. And betrayed, like the others, by him. By his desires and her own, and their hope; by their love. Where he had most passionately set his heart and mind he had done injury; and the worst injury, the worst betrayal, was the knowledge of it. His arm grew cramped but he did not move lest he wake the child. At last he too dozed off.

In midmorning the coach stopped in a tiny village. Itale handed Stasio over to his mother with relief and, rubbing his numbed arm, climbed out of the coach with Sangiusto.

"Bara already?"

"Aye," said the rusty coachman, not uncivilly, for his passenger had said the name of the village with the broad Montayna accent.

"We're on the border," Itale said, coming over to the roadside where his friend stood stretching and yawning. "Walk over to where that pig's rooting and you'll be in the Montayna."

They walked in the bright sunlight down the rutted streets of Bara, and patted a dog that came up hungry and fawning. Neither had anything to say. They turned back to take some breakfast at the hovel that called itself, in faded letters and obscure picture on a signboard, the Traveller's Rest. While the peasant girl left in charge of the place was fetching bread and cheese, Itale looked about the room, at its dirt floor, dirty walls, benches, table, and out the door onto the bright, desolate street where the mangy dog sunned himself and nothing else stirred. The child who brought them sour wine—she had only gaped when they asked for coffee—had a neck thickened by incipient goitre and a dull way of staring. He had forgotten that dull look, that country look.

He sat down at the table to drink his wine, and picked up a couple of printed sheets lying on it, left by travellers; one was the broadsheet of a song such as mountain peddlers sold or gave with their wares, the other a handbill which he started to read without recognition. "REVOLUTION," it was headed. "On the twenty-seventh of July the citizens of Paris rose in the name of the French People to protest . . ." He read no further, though his eyes found the line at the foot of the sheet, "August 13, 1830. From the office of *Novesma Verba*." Sangiusto had wandered over, chewing on a hunk of bread. Itale left the handbill lying, got up and went out. He stood there in the sunlight and looked at the hut opposite, with its clumsy door and oilpaper window, at the pig rooting in the street by a pump where the dust had turned to mud, at the white dog cringing, at the poor, short length of the village where the coach loomed on its high wheels taller than the huts beside it. Behind the huts and before them the street became again the highroad, the road he must follow, that had brought him, so far, here.

"The horses are in, I suppose we leave soon," said Sangiusto, coming out beside him.

Itale turned away and set his hands against the wall of the Traveller's Rest, hard, as if to push the sorry little house down. He felt the hot dry clay under his palms, the heat of the sun on his shoulders. Here I come to ground, he thought. I thought I must succeed, because my hopes were so high, and I have failed. I thought I must win, because my cause was just, and I have been defeated. It was all air, words, talk, lies: and the steel chain that brings you up short two steps from the wall.

For five years he had been sick for home, and now, forced to it as a fugitive, he must come to it knowing that he had no home.

Slowly and steadily the little horses pulled, the coach jolted on towards the mountains that now dominated all the lower sky. After the midday stop at Vermare they still had to climb two thousand feet up and some twelve miles on, winding now more south than west. The air grew yet more clear and dry, the mountains darker blue, the cricket-chant on the slopes deeper and more long drawn out; and the boy riding the wheel horse pulled his cap down over his eyes and sang half-dozing the song that seemed as monotonous and timeless as the cricket song,

> Grey will fall the autumn rain,
> Sleep, my love, and sleep thee well,
> My heart has broken and will break again,
> Sleep till thou wilt waken. . . .

"Don't pester the gentleman, Stasio!"

"That's all right."

"It's too good of you, sir. You come here now, Stasio."

"He's all right here." Itale let the baby investigate his waistcoat, grateful for the distraction, seeing always the mountains rise around him in reproach.

The road wound in and out; the young mother looked down the plunge of a ravine to the right and shut her eyes.

"We'll be out of this in a couple of miles. Then there's a straight pull to the pass."

They were going at less than a footpace now, the tough little horses straining, the wheelboy wide awake, the driver's whip crackling lightly over the horses' necks.

"What mountains are those, if you don't mind, sir?"

"The mountains above Lake Malafrena."

"Hoy there! get on, get on!"

"Now we tip over?" Sangiusto inquired placidly of Fate.

The coach righted itself and settled back into the ruts, the little horses pulled sturdily. Declining, the sun shone to their right, and the long shadow of Sinviya Mountain stretched up the forested slope of San Givan like a barrier before them dividing the mountain valley from the open, golden weather of the hills.

"This is like my own country," Sangiusto said. His voice was soft. "Yet there is no one thing the same." After a while he said, "So I come here with you after all."

Itale nodded, dodging the memory of Easter in Aisnar; but it would not be dodged, and he said at last, "I wish I'd thrown it over then. Gone home. Before I went too far to be able to come back."

Sangiusto glanced at him calmly and keenly. After a time he said, "Five or six months is not long enough. One comes back, Itale."

"But what does one . . . bring . . . ?"

"I don't know."

"I was a fool before I—before that. Now I'm wise, now I know what a fool I was, right? But what use is wisdom, what good is it, when the price of it is hope?"

"I don't know," Sangiusto replied again, very quietly, and with humility.

Itale caught himself, was ashamed, and was silent. He would not talk again. The habit of protest was strong, well-nourished; but it was time to go back to the older habit, silence.

Stasio had wakened whimpering among his bundles again, and Itale picked him up, set him on his knee, let him play with the endlessly wondrous waistcoat buttons, while sunlit and shadowed slopes closed in on the road and the horses quickened their pace. The road levelled out, Portacheyka lay before them in the pass, greeted by the wheelboy's long whistle, Portacheyka, peaked roofs, streets of slate stairs twining between crowded houses, the monastery of Sinviya frowning over it white on the dark mountain shoulder, the Golden Lion where as a child Itale had watched the high coaches roll in, dusty, come from remote and unimaginable lands.

"Where to now?" asked Sangiusto when they were standing on the cobbled street, since Itale, looking bewildered, made no move.

"I don't know. I hadn't thought—"

The innkeeper's wife was coming out, peering curiously at them.

341

"Come on, this way," Itale said, and set off abruptly, leading Sangiusto down a long slate stair, across a little street, through a back alley, and up another set of stairs to a garden gate. There he stopped.

"Itale," said Sangiusto, who had also been making decisions, "this is your family, and you are unexpected. I shall put up at the inn, and meet you when it's convenient."

Itale looked at him with the same angry bewilderment; then he laughed. "You can't," he said, "we haven't got a krune left. Come on." He pushed open the gate, and Sangiusto reluctantly followed him up the path between phlox and pansies to the door; to the little servant girl who went rigid with dismay at the sight of strangers, the stiff, neat, high-windowed parlor, the grey-haired woman who came in looking puzzled, and then looked frightened, and putting her hands to her throat whispered, "Itale— Oh mercy of heaven, Itale!"

"I'm sorry, I'm sorry," Itale said as she embraced him. "There was no way to let you know. I'm sorry—"

"You're so thin," she whispered, and then releasing him, "It's all right, my dear, I was startled but I don't faint, you know," and already she was turning to Sangiusto to welcome him with the fine courtesy and profound distrustfulness of the Montayna; taking his hand and repeating his name as Itale introduced them; inviting them both to sit down; ascertaining that they were tired, hungry, dirty, and looking after their needs. Not a word came from her that could distress Itale, after the first cry. Only she asked in her blunt way, when he had given a sketchy explanation of why he had arrived so suddenly, "Then how long will you stay?"

"I don't know." His tone cut her off and she asked nothing more about his plans; nor did Emanuel, at first, when he came home to find the little maid in a flurry, his wife preternaturally calm and ironical, and his bedroom, bath, razors and clean shirts sacrificed to the unknown foreigner and unexpected nephew. "When did you leave Krasnoy?" was his first question.

"Tuesday."

"What's going on? The Post didn't come last week, still no papers on the Diligence—"

"They weren't printed."

"Why not?" Emanuel exploded, and a summary of the days of the insurrection only enraged him— "You mean that never a word of all this reached us until you came here? Good God! We might have been a kingdom for a week and never known it!"

"But we're only a grand-duchy," Itale said, "so it doesn't matter. Look here, uncle, I want to ask you— I want to go on to the house, to see mother. But I can't— I don't know what my status is, I've been proscribed from Krasnoy but it may go farther— I don't want—"

Emanuel interrupted him. "What difference will that make to them?"

"I don't know."

"What are you talking about?"

"I'm talking about my father."

"Yes—you're right, he ought to be prepared a bit for this."

"I came here because I had nowhere else to go," Itale said, going dead white, "but if there are going to be any conditions, any accusations, I'll go on, now, across the border."

Sangiusto, coming in from the other room, stopped in the doorway, a towel around his bare neck. "Oimè!" he said to himself, and withdrew. The uncle and nephew stood face to face. "You damned, arrogant fool," Emanuel said, "who said anything about conditions and accusations? What I'm talking about is that Guide is ill and needs a bit of protection from shocks."

"Ill?"

"Since November. Why did you think it was I that came to the Sovena, not he or Eleonora?"

"But you said, then—"

"He told me to say as little as possible about it to you. I obeyed him. I've always done what Guide says. Maybe I was wrong, I don't know. He was ill again about a month ago. I wanted to write you. They both said not to."

"I could have come—"

"What good would that do?"

Itale sat down on the bed. He was still very white, and there was a forced rigidity in the way he held his shoulders and arms that made Emanuel realise at last that he was very near breakingpoint. "None," he said.

"He's all right, Itale. No worse than he was, now. It's the same

343

heart trouble, it can go along for years like this, you know. I didn't mean to alarm you. But you cannot walk in on him in anger—"

Itale shook his head.

"Emanuel," said Perneta outside the bedroom door, "if you'll ride on out to the lake and tell Guide and Eleonora we're coming, I'll give Itale and his friend a little supper and put Allegra in the gig and we'll come along in an hour or so."

"Right," Emanuel said. He turned back to Itale, wanting to say something more, to reassure him; but he did not know what to say. The relation between Guide and Itale, the bond of absolute loyalty strained impossibly by competitive pride, the understanding and hostility, the vulnerability of each to the other, all that was beyond Emanuel now as always. Whenever he came close to that passionate and essential relationship in either the son or the father he burned his fingers in the fire of it, fumbled, lost his temper, guessed wrong. And yet it was always he who had to bring the news to Guide, he thought as he saddled his horse and set off through lengthening shadows towards the lake; always he who was the intermediary. Thirty months ago he had been driven down here to tell Guide that the boy had been arrested and jailed, and had gone about it all wrong, jabbed his clumsy fingers into the wound. This time he had as badly misunderstood Itale, when all the young man was doing was clinging desperately to the last fragments of pride. It was always pride with these two; their strength and patience, their violence and vulnerability, all came down to pride, to the resistance of the will to the insults and indifference of time. Resistance, never acceptance. They gave with open hands, but they had never learned to receive. Guide's somber temper had turned ardent in the son, but the root of it still was pride and pain. The world is a hard place for the strong, Emanuel thought; it gives no quarter; no man ever defied evil and got off lightly.

He hoped to find Guide alone, but saw him with Laura in the garden behind the house. To judge by their gestures they were discussing replantings, and they did not see him coming down the road till he was at the fence. Then Laura looked round and came alive. "There's uncle! Was there a letter?"

"Oh aye," he said, smiling. It would have been so easy to tell Laura his news, why was it so hard to tell Guide? "Perneta's coming along behind me. Will you give us dinner?"

"Of course, but where's the letter?"

"I haven't got it, niece."

Laura looked at him, alert and silent.

"It's a message rather than a letter. Itale wants to know if he can come here, Guide."

"Where is he?"

"In Portacheyka. At the house. Came in on the Diligence this afternoon. With another man."

Guide stood still. Laura did not speak.

"What brought him here?"

"He has nowhere else to go. He came with the clothes on his back. There was a revolution in Krasnoy, the Assembly's been dissolved, there was fighting for two days, he's under ban and doesn't know how far it extends— You must let him come without questioning him, without conditions, Guide, he's lost everything he was working for—"

"Conditions?" Guide said. "Tell your mother," he said to Laura. "I'll go to Portacheyka." He was out of the gate and coming round past Emanuel to the stables as he spoke.

"They're probably on the way already," Emanuel said, and seeing there was no stopping Guide, "Here, then, take the horse, he's fresh." He dismounted, Guide swung up and was off. Laura, looking after her father, trembled all over and laughed.

"How strange it is. You riding up there while we were standing here talking about the hollies. And the house, and the road. As if it had happened before. I was standing here and you rode up to tell us he was coming. As if there was only one moment, and this was it."

"Where's your mother, lass?"

"Indoors." They walked, she on this side of the picket fence and he on that, back to the gate. Laura went lightly, hurrying, but before going in she looked back once at the garden in the clear light, the roses, the empty paths.

When they came, she was confused. She had forgotten Emanuel had said there was a stranger with Itale. She could not

345

tell which was her brother as the gig came out from under the oaks in the late dusk. She went forward with her mother and uncle; she felt herself moving over the short grass, in the warm twilight air. A tall man jumped down from the gig and came to them, that was his blue coat, it was Itale, when she held him in her arms he was as thin as a child, but his face was a man's face now; was this her brother? Who was the other man, with his hand tied up in a bandage, holding back from them? "Welcome home," she said to him, and after a moment he smiled, someone else laughed. All at once she was happy, caught the moment passing never to return, was herself and the waiting was over, they were home. "Come in, come into the house," she urged them, the father, brother, stranger.

II

Late in a September afternoon, coming past the orchards of Valtorsa, where the golden light shone broken by transparent walls of shadow that stretched eastward from each row of trees, Itale saw his sister come towards him on the road. "Letter," she called, "Uncle brought it," and then, when they met, "Are the grapes ready to pick?"

"We'll pick the Oriya vines tomorrow." As they walked side by side he opened the letter and read it, frowning against the level sunlight. It was dated from Solariy.

"Dear Itale: The old count writes that you are home. So am I. I was released on the 20th, got as far as Kolonnarmana, then sent back with an escort; released again after three interrogations, got across the street, was brought back and interrogated twice more. Have been home a week now but can't say I count on it. K's fiancée wrote; he had a severe concussion of the brain but is recovering well, and they are to be married in October. I expect you know that young V was not so lucky. Or in the end he may prove to have been luckier, who knows. I have called upon GF.

He wears a corset, satin waistcoat, gold watch-chain, married, infant son, did not invite me to return. Do you have any word of Carlo? No one has heard from him since the party and he is on my mind. I am going to go on and study for the Bar examinations since journalism, I find, does not pay. Let me hear from you. Believe me yours in constant affection, Tomas."

"It's from Mr Brelavay, isn't it?"

"Yes. You know his writing?"

"He wrote us several times when you were in prison. It was he that wrote us you had been arrested. It must have been hard for him, he never had good news for us; but he sounded so kind."

"Here, read it." He had to explain the initials to her. "K, that's Karantay, you know, the novelist. He was hurt in Palazay Street when they fought the guards. V is Vernoy. A student. He was killed. Givan Frenin, he was our college friend. He went home three years ago, he's a merchant in Solariy now. They proscribed him anyhow. Poor Brelavay! he must feel lonely there!"

"Who is Carlo?"

"Oh, Sangiusto. His English letters to the paper were signed Carlo Franceschi. Must be a middle name."

"You've known him quite a long time."

"Well, I met him in Aisnar in '27. But I got to know him in July."

"He was with you in . . . the fighting."

He nodded. He glanced at her fine, rather pale face, her brown hair pulled back in a loose knot. She walked along stride for stride with him. In the four weeks he had been home he had taken great comfort from her presence, yet he had seldom spoken much with her about any but immediate concerns, Guide's health, farm matters and accounts. She had learned to keep the books for her father, but when Itale had complimented her on the order and clarity of the accounts she had sighed and said, "I hate them. I do it because it's all he'll let me do. I keep them neat because I get lost at once if they're not. I hate figures. I'd rather clean the stables, if I could." Then she had laughed and made light of the matter. The great candor of her girlhood had become, in the woman, infinite reserve. Walking now beside her,

347

brother and sister, Itale realised that he knew nothing of her life.

"I try to imagine," she said, "what you did, down there—what your life was. The revolution—"

"The insurrection," he said gently.

"The insurrection. You say of the student, 'He was killed.' I know how Mr Sangiusto's hand was hurt, by a soldier with a gun, hitting him. You spoke once about the fire. I know, in a way, what you did before that, before the prison; I read your paper. But I have never been able to understand, to imagine your life there. As if I lived in another world."

"The real one."

"Why do you say that?"

"Because there is nothing left of that life. It's finished—gone, scattered. Overnight. There never was anything to it."

She walked on beside him.

"Dreams of youth," he said.

"All that has given my life any meaning for five years has been my belief that you were free—that you were working for freedom, doing what I couldn't do, for me—even when you were in jail—then most of all, Itale!"

He stopped, staggered by the passionate and unexpected reproach; their eyes met for a moment. He saw that she knew what he could not say directly, that he had failed, that he was utterly defeated: that she knew it and yet it was not of overwhelming importance to her, she did not see him as a failure or a fool. If she had she would not have reproached him.

"But you must not trust me, Laura!" he said desperately, all pretense of irony abandoned. "When I used to talk about freedom, I didn't know what prison was. I talked about the good but I—I didn't know evil— I am responsible for all the evil I saw, for the— For the deaths— There is nothing I can do about it. All I can do is be silent, not to say what I'm saying now. Let me be silent, I don't want to do more harm!"

"Life's the harm," Laura said quietly, drily.

They walked on, coming in sight of the orchards above the Sorde house, the forested slopes above those.

"If they lifted the ban," Laura said, "would you go back to Krasnoy?"

"I don't know. It's not likely any time soon. In any case, I'm more use here, while father's ill."

"Yes," she said. "Of course. But he . . . Some day he would fall ill; someday he will die; that was always true."

"But I didn't believe it, then," he said very low.

"I know," she said, and he saw to his wonder that she was smiling. "What I wanted to say was that you should not worry about that—about the estate. When the time comes to go. I'm nothing like Piera, but at least I can keep it going. I wanted you to be able to count on that."

"I just got home," he said, "for God's sake, are you trying to send me away again?"

"I am trying to make you see that no matter what the stupid police say you are a free man," she said, fierce. "Am I not allowed to work for freedom? You are my freedom, Itale."

He could make no answer.

When they came into the house Guide called him into the library to discuss the grape harvest with him. Since the recurrence of his ailment Guide had grudgingly admitted that everybody else including the doctor had been right and he must go easy if he wanted to go on. Methodically, then, he rested at certain times, gave up certain labors and pursuits. He was visibly changed, his hair entirely grey, his hands and face less tanned, his spare figure looking both taller and frailer. Itale, entering the study, was struck by his resemblance to Laura, even in the tone of his voice.

Laconic and amicable, they discussed the condition of the vines and the probable pace and order of the grape harvest if the temperate weather continued.

"If it gets hot," Guide said, bringing into their mutual view the frantic and relentless labor entailed by hot weather during grape harvest, and Itale's relative inexperience, perhaps also his not yet fully recovered health "There's Bron, though."

"Aye. Thank God. And Sangiusto."

"He's all right with orchards. You listen to Bron."

Itale smiled. He had been waiting for his father to admit that he approved of Sangiusto. "He's all right with orchards" was the admission.

349

"Have you got the Sorentay wagons?"

"Tomorrow morning."

"Who's going?"

"Karel."

Guide nodded.

"He's a steady man," Itale said. "He needs training."

"What for?"

"It's time we had an overseer."

He spoke with an indifferent bluntness that was new in him, though not in Guide.

Guide was much offended by the proposal, but he was caught. He could not pretend that he was able to carry on the work alone any longer if Itale left, nor could he admit that the idea of Itale's going, implied in the suggestion, frightened him. He sat there on his couch under the windows, trying to think of an argument to defeat Itale's suggestion; he scowled; but little by little, and with singular conviction, he understood that there was no argument. If he had had power of veto he would not even have sought an argument. He was not in control. Some time in these past few weeks he had, without even noticing it, abdicated; and his son, as unknowingly, had come into his inheritance.

"Very well," he said. "You think Karel's the man?"

Turning from the bookshelves to look at him Itale caught in his face a shadow of pleasure, and did not understand. He had expected a battle on this subject. It alarmed him that Guide should give in easily and, giving in, smile. "Maybe I'm thinking ahead too far—"

"Maybe," Guide said. "There's Payssy. Might do better than Karel. Go on, now, I'm supposed to lie here till suppertime."

Itale bowed and went out, and Guide lay back on the couch, obeying doctor's orders. He felt a little empty, lightened; the way a woman might feel after childbirth, he thought: light, quiet, tired. A queer thing to be comparing himself to a woman, and a woman after childbirth. But there was Eleonora's face, the morning of Itale's birth: her smile then, the center of his life. Nothing of his own.

There was a great red sunset over the lake, the weather was turning; the next day was hot, the next hotter.

Itale was up at four, at the vineyards and the winery all day till dark. He saw nothing at all in the world beyond the vines, the grapes, the boxes, baskets, carts and wagons loaded with the grapes, the pressing tubs in a stone courtyard stained and reeking with must, the brief dark coolness of the storage cellars dug into the hillside, the swing of the sun across the hot September sky. Then that work was done; and other harvests from the fields and orchards were coming in. Silent and absorbed, irascible when pushed past the limit of his strength, otherwise patient, Itale got on with the work and never raised his eyes from it to look back or ahead. Most of his waking hours were spent outdoors, in the fields and orchards, and more of his time in the farm-buildings than in the house itself; he came in only to eat and sleep. When the work let up he went hunting several times with Bron's grandson Payssy and Berke Gavrey, with whom he had struck up a taciturn kind of friendship, or with Sangiusto. He went in to Portacheyka as seldom as possible, and paid no calls. When Rodenne or the Sorentays or other neighbors came to call he often stood in for Guide, receiving them with stiff courtesy, seeing to it that hospitality was prompt and unlimited, and then sitting silent, unparticipating, while they talked.

His mother watched him, and said nothing. So she had watched Guide for thirty years. Often at her housework or at night, lying awake in autumn darkness, she thought of the merry child, the awkward, gallant boy, and the man she had seen him—barely seen him—becoming. It had not been this man; this somber, restless, silent man, this second Guide—yet not like Guide as she had first known him, for Guide as a young man had rejoiced in his work, and had suffered no defeat. In Eleonora's heart those October nights was the same bitter resentment against the world that offers so vast a chance to the young spirit and, when it comes to the point, gives so narrow a lot; the same scorn and resentment that her daughter had felt, that Piera had felt, and that she recognised in them, but with little hope for them and none for herself.

Sangiusto worked along with Itale, made himself useful and pleasant in the house, went sailing in Falkone. Karantay's fiancée had sent a necessarily cryptic warning: the government had Sangiusto's name and description and were watching for him at the borders as a professional revolutionary. At this Sangiusto, as if accepting a challenge, announced that he would walk out, over the mountains, past Val Altesma, where there were no border stations. "What for?" Itale said. "Where to?"

"To France."

"Don't leave me in the lurch now."

"I'll go when we have the pears done."

"You can't cross the mountains in winter."

"Next spring," Sangiusto said. And he stayed; so easy, steady, and cheerful a man that Itale, in his present mood, took him quite for granted, never questioning the character of their congeniality, scarcely remembering its origins. He forgot even that before their meeting lay a life of which he knew nothing. One day in late October, the first day of rain, he came by the pear orchards to pick up Sangiusto and could not find him. He tethered his horse and the one he had led, and hunted the orchard aisles for twenty minutes before he came on his friend standing with a peculiar expression under a tree. Off down an alley a garnet-red skirt and white blouse twinkled, vanished. The rain pattered softly, multitudinously, on leaf and grass. "I've been calling," he accused, wet and annoyed.

"Yes. I heard." Sangiusto blinked, pushed off from the tree, came along beside him.

"Was that Marta's Annina?"

"Yes."

Itale strode along through the wet grass for a while. "She's barely fifteen."

"I know."

They mounted their horses, rode in silence. Suddenly Sangiusto began to laugh, and Itale flushed red.

"I know, I know. But someone must talk to pretty girls, look at them, neh? What are they pretty for?"

"I feel—"

"Responsible, of course. I will not make her pregnant."

"I know that."

"Then why are you so angry?" Sangiusto said in a slightly

different tone. "Angry with me? What do you want of me? You want dignity, abstinence, romantic passion? I have had all that. I would rather kiss pretty girls in an orchard. I am ten years older than you, sad to say. I have had the romantic passion. I was in love, betrothed to a young lady. That was in 1819. Oh, God, I was in love, I wrote poetry, I got thin, So also I got sent to prison and got still more thin, and she married, in Milan, she married an Austrian officer. I learnt it when I came out of prison. So. So there I am. Austria has taken my children from me before they were ever born. . . . So I cross the mountains and become nobody, always in exile. But I have nothing more to do with that, ever again, with love, with young ladies. But if I meet Annina and she smiles? Gesumaria, Itale, what do you want?"

Itale stammered, "Sorry, Francesco," and was red, and silent. But as his shame began to cool he wondered a little at the strength, the circumstantiality, of Sangiusto's disclaimer.

The Italian meantime, placid as ever, made his young horse prance, lifted his face to the rain falling from the ragged, drifting clouds, and hummed; he burst out in a strong tenor, "*Un soave non so che*. . . . Ha! that pig Rossini! You know he wrote an oratorio for Metternich, *The Holy Alliance*? Musicians are idiots, blessed idiots, God has exempted them from reason. Look there, your count has already picked his pippin apples. Maybe we start? That little countess is very wise with her orchards."

Itale made no answer. They trotted along through the rain, towards the house on the shore.

Before he saw the Valtorskars on his second night home he had been nervous, but as soon as he saw them his apprehension and excitement had vanished. He had greeted Count Orlant with affection, grieved to see how the robust man had aged. Beside him was Piera, hardly changed, he thought, though she must be twenty-one or twenty-two now: still small, a round girlish face, a timid girlish manner, a smile and a few polite words. The vividness and vitality of her childhood were gone, leached away no doubt by this lonely life, replaced by no richer being, no opulence of womanhood. She was sterile, faded before flower. He saw this with a kind of luxuriation in the bitterness of being once again confirmed in the conviction that had come upon him first clearly in the wayside inn at Bara: the conviction that all he had worked for, that his whole understanding of freedom, had been delusion—moonshine, verbiage. Estenskar had seen it. This girl, in her way, had seen it. The Jew Moyshe knew it; and the girl in Bara, the girl with dull eyes and thick, chapped, dirty hands, knew nothing but her own wants which would never be filled and knew it better than them all: There is no freedom.

Laura was in the garden behind the house, in a tentlike cape and shapeless hat, pruning the roses her grandfather had planted. The year's last flowering was over, and the leaves looked rusty on the gnarled, rainwet stocks. She looked round as the two horsemen came down the road, and held up her pruning-shears in salute.

"Ah, there—" said Sangiusto unexpectedly, made a sweeping gesture, and said nothing else.

Laura came to the garden fence. "Drowned rats," she said.

"You prune back your roses too early!"

"I'm just taking off dead wood and canes."

Itale consciously held back his horse and watched them, the tall woman smiling, her fine, thin hands wet with rain, and the man handsome and vigorous on his horse, asking her something about mandevilia suaveolens.

"Yes, by the front walk," she said. "The only one in the valley. Grandfather planted it."

"Here, I take the horse around and come back."

"I'll take him," Itale said. Sangiusto gave Itale the reins, vaulted the fence, and went off with Laura through the wet autumnal garden.

"Nothing more to do with that ever again, eh?" thought Itale, leading the grey horse to the stables, and his heart was confused between tenderness and rancor.

October ended full of rain and mist, with a few last golden evenings; November came in cold; in midmonth Itale waking one morning saw from his window the Hunter whitened with snow against a dark grey sky. Work slackened, the farm was settling into its winter patience. Though the roads were foul there was much calling and visiting among the farms and households of Val Malafrena, every afternoon there were people in the front room, women's voices, Eva trotting past with a tray of cakes and strawberry wine and cherry brandy, or else Kass was bringing out the gig to drive Eleonora and Laura to the Pannes' or the Sorentays'. In the cold weather Guide seldom went out. He worked at small jobs, the kind of harness-mending, tool-sharpening, furniture-repairing that he had used to leave to servants or get done in a half hour before breakfast; he took his rest on the couch in the library dutifully, and then came to the front room, if there were no visitors, to sit down and work his way slowly and thoughtfully, with long pauses, through Virgil. His copy of the *Aeneid* had been his own in school, then Itale's, and was full of schoolboy glosses. He held it off on his knees to read, being very farsighted. It was strange to Itale, who had never seen him read, to see him sit there perfectly still, the book a yard from his eyes, so that it appeared that he did not so much read as absorb by long silent watching the story in the scarred and scribbled book, the tenderness, heroism, and pain. If visitors came he greeted them but often returned to his solitude in the library; if it was Eleonora, Laura, Piera, he stayed with them. And Itale too, when he came in at dusk and took off his sheepskin coat, was content to be in the company of his family; then, not before. He was at the mercy of a driving restlessness, the same strained, unreasoning energy that had taken him back from the Sovena to Krasnoy, through the sixty hours of the August insurrection, on out of Krasnoy, to Bara, to Malafrena, through the vintage, through the autumn. Now that it was winter and there was less to do he made work, or walked, or hunted. Only when he was physically worn out could he turn home and be content to sit down by the fire, talk with Guide about the work, with Sangiusto about events in Greece and Belgium; with the women he found little to say.

He came in one night early in December. Rain had followed snow, the ground was boggy, the air heavy with a soft, chill mist. Despite his tireless activity he had found that he still got cold easily and suffered a good deal from it: as if he carried St Lazar with him in the marrow of his bones. He was very cold this evening, and headed for the hearth directly. It was a Saturday; Emanuel and Perneta were there, Count Orlant and Piera; even

355

Auntie, now one hundred years old, was ensconced in a straight chair with a ball of red wool in her lap. Talking, they had let the night come in. It was dark except for the firelight. Sangiusto had been telling them something about his years in England—he was as good as any storybook to this audience—and Count Orlant summed up the subject: "A fine, enterprising race, the English. They've done wonders in astronomy."

Guide looked up as his son came by his chair in the firelit dusk of the room. "You're here too, Itale?" he said.

The dark room, four candles, the room where death was, and his father's voice.

"I'm here." He sat down on the hearthseat near Guide's chair, and put out his hands to the fire, repressing a tremor, feeling he would never get warm.

"Itale dear," said his mother in serene greeting. "Are you starved? Eva's having trouble with the chicken. Old George. He's taking hours and all he's fit for is soup in the first place. And the mutton's drying up. But there really is no use even trying to argue with Eva any longer, after all she's run that kitchen thirty years, we must all just get old and cross together. Although it's rather hard on you young ones. But your teeth are better. . . ."

"Is it still raining?" Count Orlant asked.

"Aye. Harder."

The conversation sprang up again, he and Guide sitting silent.

Piera too was silent, across the hearth from him. She spoke little when the families were together. Itale had seen her and Laura talking away a whole afternoon here by the hearth or down on the slope by the boat house, but she seemed to talk only to Laura. He glanced at her, thinking how Sangiusto had more than once remarked on her beauty. Sangiusto was rather given to finding women beautiful, but did he himself in this case, for some reason, merely persuade himself that she was plain? Her features certainly were good, her figure unexceptionable. But she was plain. No wonder, with her life spent between Malafrena and Portacheyka, two years in a convent school in Aisnar, a broken engagement to a widower in his forties, an aging household, filling up her time by trying to run the estate—no wonder she was dry and colorless, a withered branch. Life had defeated her before she had got fairly started. She was weak, and had been given no weapons with which to delay the inevitable, to fight back a while before she lost the hopeless struggle. It was not her fault.

The hot, bright fire had begun to sting his face pleasantly and he felt the heat of it through his shirt. She had put up a hand to screen her face from it. She looked at him above that delicate, red-lit hand. "We haven't seen you for several days," he said, wanting to be kind.

"No," she said, "the weather's been so bad. I have a book for you, I finally remembered to bring it along."

"A book?"

"Yes. It's yours, and I haven't any more use for it."

Itale stared at her.

"You've probably forgotten. It was a long time ago you lent it to me, five years ago. It's called *The New Life*."

"I didn't lend it to you. I gave it to you."

"I'm giving it back," said Piera.

Emanuel was watching the two of them, profiled against the fire. Itale looked floored. Evidently Piera had got tired of being overlooked. She would know how to make herself felt, once she put her mind to it; she had become formidable in her competence. Berke Gavrey, her obedient lieutenant, had told Emanuel that she had doubled the cash income of Valtorsa in two years, and was laying out the profit on improvements. Emanuel had seen her at estate business in Portacheyka, and had acted as her lawyer or legal adviser several times; he had found her both prudent and decisive, an excellent client, though he would have been happier with her qualities if they belonged to a young man. "She's extremely strong-willed," he had said to Perneta, who had replied, "And you would prefer her to be weak-minded?" — unfairly, he thought. But if she could shake Itale out of his silence, more power to her. To do that would require strength, and wits. It was easy to floor Itale, he was never on guard; but it was not easy to touch, or hold, or change him.

"Piera," Itale said, across the hearth, "I—"

"I'll write something in it, if you like, to make it more of a present."

"No—"

"Here ends the new life. With affection, from Piera Valtorskar. Would that do? It's right over there in my sewing bag on the chest."

"Piera, listen, it was—it was a long time ago, but—"

"Times change."

"I won't take it back. Burn it if you like!" Itale got up, strode off to the south windows, and stood there with his back to them all.

Piera sat by the fire; her face half in shadow, half lit red by the flames, had turned to watch Itale. She did not move. Her hands lay clasped together in her lap.

Dinner was announced at last. As Itale went in to the dining room with Perneta he watched his sister and Sangiusto, ahead of him. Laura and Francesco!—sonnets to fair ladies, it was too much. He had been a fool to bring the Italian here, and Sangiusto, a homeless, aimless man, should know better than to play at Petrarch while hiding from the Imperial police. What did he or Laura think could come of it? They were sleep-walking, play-acting. Yesterday Sangiusto had said to him, "I wish all my money was not bound up in our land, in the Piedmont, I think I could be a good farmer here,—fifty acres of orchard like that one—" Then he had laughed, and let his lively horse out, and cantered on ahead of Itale, singing, "*Un soave non so che . . .*"

At table, serious now, he said across the mutton, "Itale, your sister has explained Karantay's letter, perhaps."

A second letter from Karantay had come that week, containing some news of mutual friends and recent events, and, towards the end, in the midst of a sentence about something else, a curious clause: "Now that I am no longer a writer of fiction." They had discussed it at some length, as all letters, all outside news, always get discussed in winter in the Montayna, and had speculated on the implications of that clause, arriving at no explanation.

358

"I wondered," Laura said, "if he means that he hasn't recovered from his injury—that he's not well enough to write. It seems his marriage has been put off. And you said, when his first letter came, how much his handwriting had changed."

"What happened to him?" Perneta inquired.

"A sabre cut, in the charge on Palazay Street. A head wound."

"Poor chap," Count Orlant said.

"I thought he meant—" Itale began, and stopped. Laura's theory was sickeningly plausible. "It can't be that," he said.

"He can get better," Sangiusto said, calm as always, hopeful as always, but revealing for once, unknowing, perhaps to Itale's eyes only, the foundation of his hopefulness and calmness, the intense unchanging sadness that was the condition of his life.

"I enjoyed his book a good deal, in places," Perneta said.

"I loved it," Eleonora said. "I wish you'd give it back, Perneta, you've had it three years, and I've been wanting to see it; when I got near the end it was so upsetting."

"You mean you never finished it, Lele?" Emanuel inquired, grinning.

"I didn't want to. I was afraid he was going to die. I know it's silly to cry over books, but I always used to cry over the *New Heloise*, and there's a great deal more to cry over in this one."

"It has a happy ending, mama," Laura said, with her broad, sweet smile.

"I kept thinking that the young man, what's his name," Perneta said, "—Liyve, was like Itale."

"Of course, that's what made me cry," Eleonora said.

"Karantay had the book planned out before he ever knew me," Itale said with covert violence.

"None the less it can be true to life," Sangiusto remarked. "He writes about his generation."

"But it's not true to life. It's a great book but it's in some ways a false one—Karantay himself is absolutely levelheaded and honest, but the book's all heights and depths and exaggerations; people don't behave like that."

"Why write a romance about unromantic people?" Emanuel inquired.

359

"It's a great book, of course, it's the best we have, but he could have done—he could do much greater things!"

"And will," Sangiusto said, raising his wine glass as if in a private toast. "God willing."

The conversation drifted on, the good, heavy food came and was eaten, the plain, familial faces in the candle light brightened with conviviality. Itale, doubly shaken, avoided looking at Piera at all, and tried to avoid the thought of Karantay; he drank more wine than usual, but his unhappy self-consciousness continued. They were there, around him, his own people, but he was not one of them. They were at home, all of them but him. What have I done? he thought. Why have I no home?

"You wrote about some man once, down there," Guide said to him without preliminary, "that knew my father. Who was he?"

Startled from his brooding, he tried to describe Count Helleskar. His description sounded inevitably like one of the characters in Karantay's novel, and fascinated his hearers; they asked questions, leading him on to explain how he had met old Helleskar through his son, and to mention the Paludeskars, Enrike and Luisa.

"Countess Luisa," said Perneta. "She's in the book!"

"They're not alike."

"The one in the book is very beautiful," Laura said, not innocently.

"So is the one in flesh and blood," Emanuel said, soberly, almost with reproof.

"Yes," Piera said, "she is. I think the most beautiful woman I ever saw."

"Where did you see her?" Itale demanded, shocked into speech by the idea, incredible to him, of Luisa and Piera in the same room.

"In Aisnar; at my fiancé's house."

"I knew she was good," Eleonora said, speaking soberly as Emanuel had done, "I'm glad she's beautiful too." She looked at Itale with a faint anxiety or query.

"She's to be married," Laura said. "It's in Mr Karantay's letter."

"To George Helleskar. This spring," Itale said.

"I drink to her happiness," said Emanuel; and they raised their glasses, and drank to her, and talked of other things.

III

The next day the weather was so foul that only Laura had the determination to set off for church. As she was waiting at the stable for Kass to hitch up the horse—the horse sidling ill-temperedly, trying to get his tail to the wind, and Kass swearing as he struggled with the harness—her brother appeared. "I'll drive you over," he said.

"Don't trouble, Itale."

Unheeding, he brought the horse around with a slap, hitched him, gave Laura a hand up; and they set off along the lake-shore road to San Larenz through the dripping, wind-twisted woods. To the left, between bare trees, the lake lay grey and flat.

"When did you stop going to church?"

"I'm going now," he said.

The horse plodded on through mud, branches dripped, now and then sleet cut and stung in a light shower.

"In jail," Laura said. "When you were in jail—"

After a little while he answered, "I couldn't think about much. My mind wouldn't hold. It was always dark. The closest I could get to God was mathematics. . . . It wasn't much good. Do you know what worked? Not very often, but the only thing that ever did. I wouldn't think of God's love. I would think about the water inside the boat house in afternoon in summer, when the light comes from underneath. Or the plates—the dinner plates, the ones we used last night. If I could see them I was all right. So much for the things of the spirit. . . ."

"Except the Lord build the house," Laura said, almost in a whisper, but with a smile.

He did not know what she meant. Though it had been a relief to speak of St Lazar it had been a great effort also, and he drove on in silence.

Several people of the Valtorsa household had come to St Anthony's: Piera, Berke Gavrey, Mariya and a couple of maids, Godin the coachman. The little chapel was bitter cold, full to the roof with cold grey light. Itale sat, stood, knelt with the rest of them through the Mass. Only when Father Klement began, "Credo in unoom Deoom!" he wanted to laugh, but with sudden pleasure. He saw what Laura had meant. He saw why she had been able to say to him, "You are my freedom," knowing what he had not known, that she was his freedom; that you cannot leave home unless there is a home to leave. Who builds the house, and for whom is it built, for whom kept?

Father Klement, as usual, wanted to speak to Laura after the service. Itale waited for her in the porch of the chapel. Old Mariya and the Valtorsa maids were there, waiting for Godin and Gavrey to bring the buckboard around; Piera came out, retying her kerchief. She glanced at Itale, said hello in her polite way, and went on down the steps, into wind and rain. But there was nowhere to go. She stood down at the churchyard gate at the edge of a sea of mud, small and erect, her back turned.

He followed her. "Why don't you wait in the porch?"

She did not answer or turn round.

"Go back out of the rain. I'll stay down here," he said, softly, half teasing.

She looked up at him with her clear eyes. She was in tears, or the wind had made her eyes water. "If you like," she said, and went back up the steps. Gavrey drove up, the Valtorsa people climbed into the buckboard and rolled off under the pines.

He turned back and stood with his hands on the gate, looking out at the lake and the dark mountains on the other side. The wind was in his eyes. A sky of grey clouds ran overhead, ceaseless, in rapid, silent tumult. He remembered the sky over the courtyard of St Lazar; so the clouds had run there all winter long, three winters long, indifferent, unattainable, beautiful. There was nothing to keep. Life ran like the clouds. One voyaged and the other stayed, yet they met on the way; and in their meeting was all the goal of voyaging, and all the substance of fidelity. The shape and motion of a cloud.

A few yards from him across the gate of the churchyard lay the grave marked with his grandfather's name, his name. He thought of the moment last night, the earliest and most terrible memory roused when his father had said, "You're here too, Itale?" But it was no longer terrible. "I'm here," he said into the wind.

His sister was out in the chapel porch now, and he went round to bring up the trap. As they drove back, the wind was weaker and a fine, wintry, drifting rain whispered on the road and passed in dim masses over the forest and the lake. The mountains were full of the sound of the rain.

The winter was endlessly wet but there was not much snow, and spring came early. By mid-March then the north wind cleared the sky the forest rippled paler green, showing new growth at the tips of the dark branches, and the same light, clear green broke in the waves of the lake on windy mornings. Since it rained hard on the morning of the solstice, Laura and Itale put off the trip they had planned to Evalde until the next fair day. It rained almost daily well into April, and by that time Laura, without consulting her brother, had invited everybody else to come along, and Sangiusto and the Valtorskars had accepted. Itale was annoyed. He had anticipated the trip as he had in his boyhood, a solitary course, at dawn, in the little boat, the ceremony with which spring began. He had thought Laura understood that and felt the same way. This would be a mere pleasure-trip, a picnic over at the caverns, meaningless. And there would be all the constraint of being in Piera's company. Ever since he had seen her drive off under the pines of San Larenz that winter day he had felt he must speak to her, but he was not certain, when it came to the point, what he wanted to say; and in any case he was unable to, since she was unwilling to say anything to him at all.

Falkone could not carry five, and they were planning to go in Mazeppa. That was the last straw. He would not sail across in that cow of a boat. He wanted his own boat under his own hand, and he said, autocratic, "I want to take Falkone." So there he was on a morning of early April, his boat skimming over the water a quarter mile ahead of the other, with Piera sitting in the stern to steer.

They went a mile before anything was said, except Itale's orders concerning steering as he tried to catch the fresh, fitful wind. At last they were sailing steadily, the house on its peninsula grown small behind them under the great slope of San Givan. The sound of the cascade came faint and clear over the water in the silence of the midlake. Piera sat with her hand on the tiller, her dark head turned away from him. "I wish there was more wind," she said, "and we could sail clear to Kiassafonte."

"Takes a good wind and all day," Itale said.

She watched him as he stood up, coatless, long-legged, to recoil a rope from the gear box. The sunlight of April poured down on his head, his back, his hands, the lake beyond him, the mountains above the lake. The wind blew his brown hair, grown out long again, across his eyes; he brushed it away with a gesture she remembered.

"Has anybody ever sailed down the Kiassa?"

"Pier Sorentay took a rowboat down once on a dare. Broke up on a rock just past the village."

"Hoy! Hoy there!"

"There's papa dancing about."

"Shall we turn?"

"No," said Piera.

They went on. The hails from Mazeppa ceased.

"I don't suppose they're sinking," Piera said doubtfully, looking back.

"No. Envious," said Itale, whose heart was growing lighter as they sailed on through the wind and sun. But their wind was beginning to fail them, and the lake lay glassy.

"Are we going to have to row?"

"Probably when we come under the lee of the Hunter."

"It's so still; it's like sailing in air. . . ."

Their wind lasted until they entered the gulf of Evalde in the shadow of the overhanging mountain. There the air was hot and still in the fire of noon, the clear brown water utterly motionless. Itale rowed. Before them loomed the dark cliffs and basalt columns of the shore; they heard but could not see the cascade, hidden from them by the cleft it had cut itself in the jutting cliffs.

"Like rowing in oil," he said, whispering, in the strange hush of the gulf that had no sound in it but the dull vibration of the river plunging to the lake.

They came to the landing place, a gravel beach a few yards long, to the right of the Hermit's Rock. Itale raised the oars and got his breath a minute before landing the boat. "Winded," he said, with reference to the general direction of Piera.

She did not say anything, but took the little dipper from under the stern seat, dipped it up full of the transparent lake water, and offered it to him. He took it from her and drank.

He ran the boat up on the beach with one great push of the oars and a flying leap, when it touched gravel, to pull it up so that Piera could step out dryshod: his timing was perfect, elegant, and he was smiling with pleasure as he handed Piera out of the boat.

Mazeppa was just at the entrance of the gulf, a black blot on the bright water.

"Are they rowing yet?"

Farsighted like Guide, he looked and said, "Yes."

"No lunch for a while, then."

The cascade thundered across the water, muted, tremendous.

"Let's go up to the top of the falls."

A path of sorts wound up past the Hermit's Rock to the top of the cliffs. Piera set off at once, very quick in her dark red skirt, unhesitating even when the way was nothing but a jump from one boulder to another, or when the black broken rock of the cliffside slid and rattled underfoot. Long after her, Itale came out at the top of the climb, in open sunlight, at the head of the falls where the river escaped from the cavern to plunge down its vertical cleft to the lake. They watched it till they were dizzy and deafened, and still went on watching it; at last they went to sit on the stone-broken grass under a low wall-like cliff, the outer wall of the caverns. The dark rock was full of a vibration like distant thunder: the roar of the imprisoned river.

"Will they know we're up here?"

365

"Laura will bring them. We always came up here."

Piera got up again, trying to see the other boat through the pines below the clearing. The sunlit air was warm about them. Restless, nervous, she wandered down the wild slope among the rocks, near the edge of the falls.

"Piera."

"Yes?"

"What is this?"

She came over slowly, listening for the voices of their people through the dull roar of the river. Itale held out to her a spray of small rock plant. She took it, and sat down with a small sigh.

"I don't know. It's pretty; like a fern with flowers."

"It only grows here."

Piera sat twirling the flowered spray, gazing at the contorted rocks, the pines that grew tall among them, the bright lake out beyond the gulf. The sun, straight overhead in the dark blue sky, poured down heat and light till the clearing brimmed like a cup.

"Piera, I need to ask you. . . . Is Laura in love?"

"Of course," she said without turning.

"Francesco spoke to me last night. He said if I decided he should not, he won't speak to father. I don't know what I should do."

She was watching him now; not with the reproach or irony he had feared.

"Of course it's up to Laura. But it will upset father badly. Not without reason. Francesco is a homeless man, dependent on his sister's sending him enough to live on. Austria will hound him all his life, I suppose. He could go to France or England, but what would Laura do there? She never wanted to leave Malafrena. . . . I brought him here. It is my responsibility. I don't know what to say."

"Why shouldn't she leave Malafrena? It was me that wanted to stay. She has always wanted to go, to see things. Where he is would be her home."

Itale was silent for a bit. "He can't leave now. They'll arrest him at the border."

366

"Perhaps not with a wife and a false name," Piera suggested, mildly, but startling Itale.

"You and Laura have talked about this?"

"Not about that. . . . We haven't really ever said much at all. About that. I know she loves him. Why can't they stay here? As long as they want to, I mean. Nobody's using the old Dowerhouse. I thought of having it fitted up. He certainly is a very useful man on a farm."

"Yes, he is," Itale said, bemused.

"You could take him into partnership."

"Into partnership."

"Then if one of you wanted to go back down there, there would be one of you running the estate."

"Yes."

"And since no one is using the Dowerhouse, they could live there. I'd like to have it looked after."

"Wait a minute," he said. Then presently, "It all seems practicable. You must—you must have thought about this a good deal?"

"Of course I have."

Her voice trembled as she spoke. He looked at her again intently, wonderingly; his face was grave and still.

"There was something I wanted to say to you, too," she said; her voice, over-controlled, sounded thin. He nodded, acceptant; she paused for a long time.

"There are so many reasons. Habit. And the land adjoining at so many places. And so on. And I suppose they talked about it when we were children, people always do. I'm sorry I was unpleasant to you, that night, last winter. That was stupid. I was just trying to say what I want to say now. That people will think we will—we are likely to get married, but they're mistaken; and that keeps us from being friends." The small, strained voice trembled continually, like the trembling of water, but remained clear. "I should like to be your friend."

"You are," he said almost inaudibly; but his heart said, you are my house, my home; the journey and the journey's end; my care, and sleep after care.

367

"All right," she said, this time with a great sigh; and they were silent for a while, there on the grass in the great heat and light of noon.

"You will go back, down there, some day, won't you?"

"When I can."

"Good," she said, and smiled suddenly. "I wasn't sure. . . ."

"Then will you keep the *Vita Nova*?"

"I said I was sorry," she said angrily.

"Up this way, Count Orlant!" called Laura's voice down among the pines.

"You have to keep it," he said with intensity. "I didn't know why I left till I came back—I have to come back to find that I have to go again. I haven't even begun the new life yet. I am always beginning it. I will die beginning it. Will you keep it for me, Piera?"

"There they are!" Sangiusto proclaimed from the top of the path.

Piera looked at Itale directly for one instant, then scrambled to her feet and went to greet the others. "Well, well, well," said Count Orlant surmounting the last steps of the way heavily, "what a pull. Hello, daughter."

"Did you have to row? You took so long."

"Indeed we did. Laura and I pulled two strokes to Mr Sangiusto's one, and still we went in circles."

"I thought you two would be keeping cool in the caverns," said Laura. "It's as hot as summer here!"

"Have an apple, your face is purple," said Sangiusto, proffering the hamper.

"What a lovely thing of you to say! Yes, I will. Do we want lunch now?"

"Yes," Itale said. "All of it."

"No, I want to see the caverns," Sangiusto announced, stretching his strong arms and looking about him blissfully.

"Then give me an apple, *fratello mio*."

"Stay him with flagons," Count Orlant said, "comfort him with apples. Are you all going, then?"

"Won't you come, count?"

"No, I want to sit down right here. Caverns and torrents and all that are for the young. Leave me with the lunch. Go on! You don't think I'll eat it all?"

"All right, we'll be back in half an hour."

"Wear your hat if you're sitting out in the sun, papa."

"Leave us some bones and peelings, count!"

"Go on, go on."